THE MOON INTO BLOOD

Lake Maggiore

Laveno

Lake Orta

Varese

Arona

Lake Varese

Lake Comabbio

Sesta Callende

Castelletto

PIEDMONT
(KINGDOM OF SARDINIA)

L

River Ticino

Naviglio Grande Canal

TURIN

Novara

Mage

GARIBALDI AT COMO
MAY–JUNE 1859

Also by same author

The Devil in Harbour
The House of War

The Second Empire Novels:

The Fortress (Finland 1855)
The Cactus and the Crown (Mexico 1866)
Madeleine (France 1870)

and available in Coronet Books

The Moon into Blood

Catherine Gavin

CORONET BOOKS
Hodder Paperbacks Ltd., London

Copyright © 1966 by Catherine Gavin
First printed 1966 by Hodder & Stoughton Ltd
Coronet Edition 1968
Second impression 1970
Third impression 1972

Printed in Great Britain
for Coronet Books, Hodder Paperbacks Ltd.,
St Paul's House, Warwick Lane, London, E.C.4,
by Richard Clay (The Chaucer Press), Ltd.,
Bungay, Suffolk

ISBN 0 340 04354 7

To Daisy Bruce

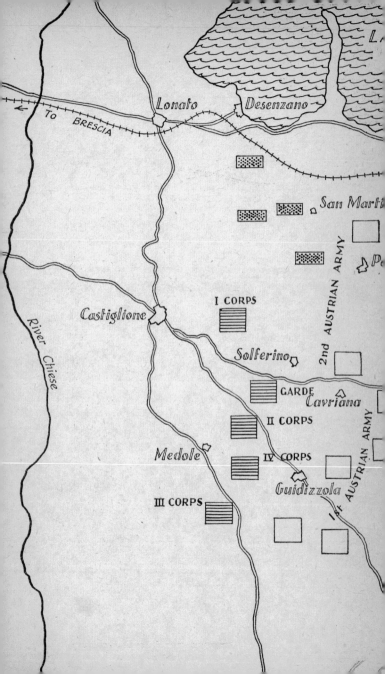

RDA

Peschiera

To VEN.

engo

Villafranca

Volta

River Mincio

THE BATTLE OF SOLFERINO
24th. JUNE 1859

FRENCH	
AUSTRIANS	
SARDINIANS	
Railway	+++++++++

0   5

Miles

CONTENTS

PART ONE

For Italy: Orsini

PART TWO

Enchanter's Country

PART THREE

For Italy: Garibaldi

PART ONE

FOR ITALY: ORSINI

One

THE EXECUTIONERS

ORSINI'S eyes opened on a row of bars, and a dull red glow from the stone passage outside the dungeon. He knew at once that he was in the power of the Austrians, and back in his prison cell at Mantua.

He struck his forehead with his clenched hands and caught his breath. There was no clank of manacles, no groan of protest from the filthy captives to whom he must be chained. The only sound was the ringing of the blood in his own ears as he rolled cautiously over on his back, and felt beneath him the yielding softness of a feather-bed. He was safe in his rented room in Paris, and the red coals had shifted only slightly in the small barred grate.

Orsini dragged himself upright. The clock on the black marble mantel indicated that barely half an hour had passed since he and Gomez had come back, chilled, to the Rue du Mont Thabor. He remembered telling Gomez to prepare a jug of mulled wine. He remembered everything.

It was strange that with this awful clarity should come such lassitude, so clouded a perception of the simple things around him. His eyes wandered vaguely from the clock to the commode by the fourposter, from the unlit bedside candle to the buttoned rep headboard, down to the pillow which held the imprint of his own head. Across it lay a huge splash of blood. Only the clenched hands, this time sealing his lips, stifled Orsini's cry. At

15

the knife-point of horror he recognised his own red cotton handkerchief, crumpled on the linen in the same way as a ripple of slow blood might trail across the sawdust when an assassin's head fell beneath the guillotine.

He jerked the red bed-curtains close with a rattle of wooden rings and collapsed on the pillow, frantic to lose himself again in the dreams of glory which had brought Felice Orsini, after thirty-eight years of fighting and frustration, to the night when he meant to assassinate the Emperor of the French.

He wanted to hear applause again—the kind of applause which, only last winter, English audiences had thundered out when he described the horrors of the Austrian dungeons in Italy. He wanted more of the adulation he had received in London from warm-hearted girls and enthusiastic, rich young men. Above all, he wanted the homage of the leaders of Italian independence—of Mazzini, who had rejected him; of Cavour, who had ignored him; of Garibaldi, once his leader, and now a mangy old lion licking his scars in the sunshine of Caprera.

In the red twilight of the fourposter, Felice Orsini wove a fantasy of summer, and the Rome of nine years ago, when he was a Deputy of the short-lived Republic, and a follower of Garibaldi. He was in St. Peter's Square, and it was the last day, and Garibaldi on horseback, with his Anita by his side, was giving that last grim promise to his defeated troops.

'You who go through the gates of Rome with me, remember——' How did it go? 'I have nothing to offer you but wounds, hardship, bitterness...'

But not murder. Writhing, Orsini knew that the great Defender of the Roman Republic would never stoop to the stiletto, to the bombs flung in the dark.

Then a light which was not the light of self-revelation,

16

but the soft glow of an oil-lamp, brightened his darkness, and the voice of his landlady said apologetically:

'Excuse me for disturbing you, Mr. Allsop! The gentlemen are here.'

Orsini swung his feet to the floor and stood up. Madame Morand was closing the wooden shutters, drawing the curtains; the winter night had fallen over Paris.

'The room is very cold, monsieur. Shall I bring you a shovel of hot coals and build the fire up high?'

'No—no thank you, madame. I like the room kept cool.'

Perplexed: 'I know you do. I brought you a jugful of hot water, at least!'

'Thank you. Will you tell my friends I shall be ready to leave in ten minutes?'

The Frenchwoman stood fingering her apron. She said diffidently:

'Mr. Allsop, I know it's none of my business, but let me beg you to stay indoors tonight. It's such bitter January weather, and I can see you're feverish—you're not yourself. Let me send the other gentlemen away for once, and prepare a nice little supper for you here. Your valet could serve it on a tray in bed.'

Orsini smiled. Few women had been able to resist the flash of white teeth in his dark face, and Madame Morand smiled too, as he patted her shoulder and turned her gently towards the door.

'It isn't possible, madame. I have a pressing engagement in the town tonight. But I'm grateful to you for your concern.'

That's the kindest woman in Paris, he thought, as he stripped off his waistcoat and cravat. And the biggest fool, if she believes four Italians like us are really the foreign tourists we pretend to be. Or does she see us at all, Felice? Does she see anything beyond your smile?

17

In the mirror above the washstand, he saw the glint of the medal his mother had hung round his neck in his old home in the Romagna, long before the hunted years began. He touched it now for luck, and felt the blood throbbing at the base of his throat. Was that where the knife would enter? Or was a man flung on the board face downwards when he was strapped and bound beneath the guillotine?

'*E per l'Italia!*' He spoke the words aloud. *For Italy*— it was his prayer, his faith, his apology; it was what gave him strength to button his shirt with steady fingers and pass a comb through his black hair. His face, he saw, was very pale, and there were faint bruises beneath his eyes, but he seemed calm and resolute enough to impress the men waiting in the next room. As he pulled on his black surtout, he indulged in one more tremendous fantasy: that the three who waited were Cavour, Mazzini and Garibaldi. They waited now for Orsini's word, Orsini's hand, Orsini's leadership...

He flung open the door and was confronted by the scum of Soho.

Red-headed Gomez, the pretended valet, in his London life a waiter at the Café Chantant in Leicester Square, greeted Orsini with a sarcastic bow. Young di Rudio, known as a beggar and a brawler in the shady taverns off the Haymarket, stopped munching a cake to stare at his leader with the eyes of a hunted hare. Fifty-year-old Pieri, with a glass of hot mulled wine already in his hand, grumbled out:

'You kept us waiting, comrade. Are you all right?'

'Certainly. I slept for half an hour, and feel refreshed.'

'I wish I had your nerve,' said di Rudio.

'You'll not fail tonight, Carlino. You didn't flinch on the Gianicolo, did you, when we were fighting our way to the House of the Four Winds? You didn't fail Manin, when the Austrians were bombarding Venice? Gomez, fill the glasses, we have a toast to drink. And standing, if you please! To Italy and liberty! To the fall of a tyrant!'

'*Per l'Italia e Vittorio Emmanuele*,' di Rudio said.

'To a good job well done,' said Gomez.

'Ah,' said Pieri, draining his glass, 'and when the job's done, well or ill, what do *we* do, chief?'

'I told you before: we scatter. Don't come here, don't go back to your hotels. I must come back to get my horse; the rest of you clear out of Paris. You've been given money. Get on the midnight train to Brussels, but not all together. Pieri, remember, don't go near your wife!'

'Is it likely? Toil all the way to Hell Barrier for another sight of the old girl? She'd turn me in to the police, and grab the reward, as fast as look at me.'

'Keep out of her sight, then, and theirs too. Have you all got your pistols?' They nodded assent. Orsini, pouring out the last of the wine, told them to follow him to the bedroom.

When the plot to kill the French Emperor was laid in London, the chosen executioners were all informed that a bomb would be the instrument of death. They knew that steel shells had been made in Birmingham to the order of an Englishman, Thomas Allsop, whose name Orsini had taken as his alias. All three had heard from Dr. Bernard, the French exile who was an accomplice in the plot and had procured their false passports, that the shells would be filled with fulminate of mercury. Orsini alone had borne the responsibility of carrying the deadly charge to France, and keeping the sandy crystals damp in his cool bedroom until the hour when, earlier that afternoon, he had tamped the explosive hard into the lower halves of each shell, clamping the two halves together and screwing home the inward-pointing nipples. Now five bombs of unequal size lay waiting the hour appointed by Felice Orsini to bring death to Napoleon III, Emperor of the French.

It had not occurred to Orsini, who had lived with the idea of the crime for so long, that the sight of the bombs, revealed when he opened a locked cupboard door, would so powerfully affect his confederates. Pieri's brutal face flushed crimson, while Gomez whistled, and di Rudio's diseased lungs expelled a choking gasp of breath when Orsini picked up one of the bombs and tossed it lightly in his hand.

'For God's sake, Felice!'

'It's safe enough, Carlo. These things don't explode at a touch.'

He showed them how the upper half of each bomb had been segmented to shatter into more than a hundred pieces.

'I take two, and each of you takes one. Pieri throws first, then Gomez, then Carlo, then myself, at thirty-second intervals. Pieri, remember to let the first coach pass, the one with the Court flunkeys. When the Emperor's berline draws up in front of the Opera, we throw the bombs hard and low at the cobbles underneath the wheels. Not through the windows—at the ground.'

'What if there's an escort?' asked Pieri.

'He doesn't take an escort to the theatre. The police will be out in strength, but not mounted.'

'Even so, there's sure to be a mob round the coach, and the street packed——'

Orsini shrugged.

Gomez said suddenly: 'Felice, let me have a try with the pistol. Eh? I'm a dead shot, you know. I won the marksmanship medal two years running in Algiers.'

'So you say.'

'It's the truth,' Pieri growled, for Gomez and he had

both served in the Foreign Legion. 'Give the kid a chance, with me to cover, and I'll guarantee we'll pick the Emperor off without a wholesale massacre.'

'So Pianori thought, in April '55. So Tebaldi thought, only a few months ago, and they were Mazzini's crack gunmen. He told them it would be easy to pick Napoleon off, and where are they now? I tell you this is the only sure way. Bombing the carriage—not one pistol-shot, or two, but all of us aiming at the same target, certain to kill!'

The quick violent words silenced Gomez and Pieri. But di Rudio's uncertain fingers were pulling at his lower lip.

'Then the Empress will die with him,' he said.

'So?'

'Felice, do you remember when you and Dr. Bernard talked to me in London? I fought in the War of Independence. I told you Austria was the enemy, the tyrant in Italy, and it should be Austrians alone we pledged ourselves to kill. You two explained then why Napoleon must be the one to die. He joined the Carbonari, but he recanted his vows to Young Italy. He sent French troops to fight us when you and I were in Rome with Garibaldi. But he wasn't Emperor then, and he wasn't married! Eugénie has had nothing to do with the martyrdom of Italy. Why should she die by his side tonight?'

'Has she persuaded him to withdraw the French garrison from Rome?' demanded Orsini. 'Has the Papacy a more ardent supporter than the Empress Eugénie? Let her die with the dog she married; she deserves no pity from Italian patriots!'

On the January night in 1858 when Orsini intended him to die, Louis Napoleon Bonaparte, the Emperor Napoleon III, regarded himself as the saviour of society.

He had, as he stated often and publicly, delivered France from the chaos of party government. He had achieved this, six years earlier, by means of a bloody *coup d'état*, and since he occupied the throne most of those who had opposed him were either dead, in exile or in prison. He had recently fought a victorious war in the Crimea. He was married to a supremely beautiful woman who had given him a son and heir. With unerring showmanship, he added to his triumphs in war and diplomacy by offering the people of Paris a series of brilliant spectacles, making the visit of any foreign personage an excuse for State drives through the city, a profusion of flags and a gala night at the Comédie Française or the Opera. Such a gala had been planned for January 14, 1858, in honour of Duke Ernest of Saxe-Coburg, and it was outside the Opera on the Rue Le Peletier that Orsini planned to throw his bombs.

Coming up the Rue du Mont Thabor behind his accomplices, Orsini was seized again by his hallucination of the lighted passage behind the prison bars of Mantua. Once more, the dark and the light burst across his brain in stripes as fierce as the weals raised by his Austrian jailers in the floggings he had borne for Italy. But this time, the bars were the magnificent colonnades, the lights the elaborate gas lamps of the Rue de Castiglione, and he was a free man carrying death to a tyrant.

He followed his men up the Boulevard des Italiens. People were turning to stare at di Rudio who, with long hair hanging to his shoulders and a battered top-hat put on askew, looked like a ghost returning from the barricades of 1830. Orsini swore under his breath. He had saddled himself with a too-conspicuous accomplice in di Rudio, and he was aware now that he had made a mistake in recruiting Pieri, already well known to the Paris police. He saw them merge one by one with the crowd in the Rue Le Peletier and drift to their stations opposite the lighted theatre before he pressed forward through the crowd round the doors of the Opera.

'Programme, monsieur? Names of the stars, titles of the songs, names and addresses of the corps de ballet?'

A boy of ten in the pink tights of a street acrobat brandished a printed playbill beneath Orsini's nose. The Italian, in terror of being conspicuous, tossed a coin to the child and held the broadsheet up to his face. In the great blaze of gaslight from the lamps above the entrance to the theatre, he read the celebrated names of Ristori and Massol.

Orsini's smile flashed out in spite of himself as he scanned the programme. An act from *William Tell*— down with Gessler, down with the Austrians! that was a good omen. An act from *La Muette de Portici,* which had sparked the Belgian fight for independence. A number from *Un Ballo in Maschera,* the story of a king's assassination. It was a pity Napoleon III would miss such a fine revolutionary performance.

The man was late, of course. The Rue Le Peletier was crowded with spectators now, but still there was no sound of silver bugles sweeping up the boulevard, and with every minute's delay Orsini felt the fever mounting in his veins as he prowled between the darkness and the light. Once he dared to go so near the entrance of the Opera that he saw the Duke of Saxe-Coburg, bored and glum, leaning against a marble pillar in the foyer. Beside him the directors of the Opera waited, holding lighted candles, to conduct Their Imperial Majesties to their box.

It was then that Orsini felt his sleeve pulled, and turned sharply on the grotesque figure of Carlo di Rudio.

'Felice!'

'Get away from here, you infernal fool!' Orsini dragged the boy into the darkness. 'I told you to keep away from me!'

'It's Pieri,' said the youngest executioner urgently. 'I lost sight of him outside Broggi's café, and now I've seen him go by with another man holding his arm. What do you think, Felice?'

Each read in the other's face the words *police* and *betrayal*.

'Where's Gomez?' asked Orsini hoarsely.

'Where you posted him, this side of the Petit Riche.'

'Tell him to move down beside you, outside number 21. If you don't see Pieri when the first coach comes up, we drop him from the order and Gomez throws first. You understand?'

'Still counting thirty, chief?'

'Yes.'

The hare's eyes, staring into his, were bright but steady. Di Rudio bounded away, crossing the street between two of the last cabs to be setting down late arrivals outside the Opera. At the same time, welling up from the direction of the Seine, came the first distant sound of drums and trumpets.

Orsini was carried forward by the crowd, spreading his fingers protectively round the bombs in his pockets as the *sergents-de-ville*, having closed the street to all other traffic, began to clear a space for the arrival of the Emperor. The child in the salmon-pink suit unrolled a strip of tattered carpet and began turning handsprings under the very nose of the police.

'Oh, mamma, look at that little boy, isn't he wonderful? Do give him some money—please!'

Orsini, and many another man in the crowd, appraised the young girl who had spoken. In English—although it was not an English voice, and the dark hair and eyes might have belonged to an Italian girl. But that laughing face, enchantingly framed in a high, white swansdown collar, had never known the sorrows of Italy; Orsini saw and envied it as the bright face of freedom.

A hand in a white kid glove threw a few coins to the little acrobat, which he snatched up, laughing and blowing kisses, as a policeman cuffed him off the carriageway, and another voice exclaimed: 'Jenny Cameron, will you come inside the theatre directly! We'll catch our death of cold out here.'

Orsini recognised the accent now. He had known Americans in London, and these women were Americans, rich and idle, throwing a few *sous* to the street tumblers of Paris as they would throw coins, by and by, to the child beggars of Venice and Rome. He felt the easy rage beating in his temples as the girl turned her head, and he saw the gleam of pearl ear-rings beneath her camellia wreath.

'Mamma, it isn't cold! Please let us wait until the very last minute, and see the Emperor and Empress arriving! Oh, isn't it thrilling? I can't believe I'm actually in Paris!'

She was so unselfconscious, so much in tune with the music of the overture now faintly heard from inside the theatre, so much a part of the light and gaiety of the scene, that the tight band of his obsession loosened round Orsini's head, and he saw the Rue Le Peletier with Jenny Cameron's eyes. The people leaning from the windows of the tall old houses, the crowds on the pavement, the little acrobat in pink and the *sergents-de-ville* adjusting their hats and swords were no longer faceless sacrifices to be offered up for Italy, but members of the human society from which he was about to outlaw himself for ever. Then the girl's words, *let us wait until the very last minute,* came home to him in all their horror, and as the first coach of the Imperial procession swept into the Rue Le Peletier he realised that the last minute had come.

His orders were to let the first coach pass, and count thirty seconds after. But behind the first coach, with pennants waving and silver breastplates gleaming, there came unexpectedly a Lancer escort, fourteen strong, preceding the Imperial berline with its mounted bodyguard. Cheering rose in crescendo from the housetops and the street.

Orsini freed his right arm and held his breath. Would Gomez have the wits to let the escort pass and wait until the berline came to a halt? He saw the American girl take a step forward, her face lifted admiringly to the Lancers. He thought he called out to her, 'Run, signorina, for your life!' There was no sound from his dry throat.

Gomez, confused, flung his bomb thirty seconds after the first coach went by. It exploded among the Lancers with a force which tore away the gas lamps above the entrance to the Opera. Among the screams of men and the neighing of mangled horses Orsini, desperate, heard a cry from the American girl. But di Rudio's bomb came in low and blew the Imperial coachman to bloody shreds: the reeking darkness was filled with shrieks of pain. By the light from the foyer, Orsini could distinguish three figures inside the berline. An aide-de-camp with blood pouring down his face was sprawled in one corner, the Emperor, clay-white, was cringing in another. The Empress, glorious in her diadem and coronal of chestnut hair, had flung herself across her husband's body. Then Orsini, with a groan, drew back his arm and flung his first bomb, and with it all his hate and his pain and his murderous love for Italy.

26

Two

'SET MY COUNTRY FREE!'

JENNY CAMERON was tired of her mother's drawing-room. During her weeks in bed it had seemed to be a cheerful place, from which after dark came the sound of voices and the clink of glasses, and sometimes the smell of a rich cigar. Now that she was well enough to lie on a sofa in the window, she was bored with her surroundings, bored with the view across the Champs Elysées, bored on this dull February afternoon with the expressionless voice of Madame Lamotte, reading from the works of Chateaubriand. Jenny sighed.

'Are you quite comfortable, Miss Cameron? Do you feel chilly?' The elderly Frenchwoman placed a silk bookmark between the pages of *Atala* and went quietly to Jenny's side. The room was warm. The girl had everything in the world to please a convalescent on a table by her sofa: novels, newspapers, grapes, flowers and chocolates. Madame Lamotte observed without compassion that Jenny's face was white and drawn.

'You did remind Michel to get the evening papers?' the girl asked.

'Yes, certainly, mademoiselle. But I doubt if the papers are on sale yet.'

'I thought I heard the newsboys shouting "Orsini!" in the street, while you were reading.'

'You must try not to distress yourself, mademoiselle.' Madame Lamotte's genteel mask revealed none of the resentment she felt at having been employed as a finishing governess to a young lady straight from school, who had the bad taste to become almost immediately one of the victims of the bomb outrage at the Opera. Only the edge in her voice betrayed her dislike of her situation in the too-luxurious, rented apartment on the Champs Elysées, and all that had happened there since Jenny Cameron was carried home, bleeding and unconscious, from the paving-stones of the Rue Le Peletier.

'Is that Michel now?'

'It is madame,' said the Frenchwoman briefly. Jenny turned on her pillow to watch her mother trail a violet taffeta crinoline gracefully across the carpet, and lifted her face shyly for a kiss.

'Mamma! I thought you were driving in the Bois.'

'I came in about an hour ago, but I didn't want to disturb your reading. Madame Lamotte, you must be tired; would you care to rest in your own room for a while?'

'Thank you, madame.' The governess, with an experienced eye, noted the pallor of Mrs. Cameron's powdered face and the compression of her lips. Another storm brewing—and she was a magnificent creature in a temper, with her Spanish beauty incandescent, and her shining black hair electric with vitality. For a woman nearly forty, she was truly remarkable! The child had the same looks, with softer eyes and a fair complexion; she would be much admired when she was well. Madame Lamotte bowed and withdrew.

'Jenny,' Mrs. Cameron began at once, 'there's another man here from the police.'

'The police again!'

'I told him two policemen had been here already, the day after that awful night, when I told them everything I knew. But that was six weeks ago, and now this fellow has specially asked to speak to you.'

'It's not one of the men who came before?'

'No. This is Maître Raynaud—from the office of the Public Prosecutor.'

'But then he's a lawyer, mamma, not a policeman. Why should a lawyer want to talk to me, unless for some reason connected with the trial?'

'Oh, my God, that trial!' Mrs. Cameron bit her lower lip savagely. 'I wish those four villains were guillotined and in their graves.'

'I think you'll very likely get your wish.' Jenny pulled herself upright on the sofa and felt for a stick half-hidden by the folds of her dress. 'Should we ask Maître Raynaud to come in?'

'I hate getting mixed up with the law,' said Mrs. Cameron. 'Oh, Jenny, why didn't you go inside that theatre when I told you to? Just five minutes, and we'd have been safe in the box, and all this spared.' She jerked the bell-rope.

Maître Raynaud, ushered in by the butler, was a tall, heavily-built man with a leather case beneath his arm. He bowed to Jenny when Mrs. Cameron murmured an introduction, and began:

'My respects mademoiselle, and my apologies for this intrusion.' Jenny said quickly:

'Maître Raynaud! Is Orsini's trial over? Is the verdict out?'

'You knew the trial began today?'

'How could I not know? The newspapers have talked of nothing else. The verdict, sir?'

'Can hardly be expected yet.'

Mrs. Cameron held a taper to the fish-tail gas burners in their pink globes, one on each side of the fireplace, and at once the darkness seemed to deepen in the street outside.

'The Public Prosecutor desired me to present his compliments to you, mademoiselle, and also to express his deep regret that a young American lady should have been among the victims of the atrocious crime of the fourteenth of January.'

'Thank you, sir.'

'You suffered a compound fracture of the tibia, I believe, and other injuries to the foot and ankle caused by shell splinters?'

'Yes.'

'Can you walk now?'

'I have been walking for the last few days. Just from my bedroom into this room, and back.'

'Forgive me—I should very much like to see you walk to the fireside, if you will.'

Jenny looked at her mother. Mrs. Cameron had taken up a fan and was counting the ivory sticks. The girl stood up. The clinging folds of her grey dress revealed heavy bandaging of the left leg. The left foot, also bandaged, was in a loose felt slipper, the right in a flat satin sandal. She leaned her weight on her stick, balanced with a hand on the head of the sofa and started slowly towards the fire.

'One!' said Maître Raynaud, following her, 'Two! Three! Very good!'

'Be careful, Jenny!' Mrs. Cameron cried.

'Four, five, six, seven!' Jenny, with a laugh of triumph, reached the safety of an armchair.

'Bravo, mademoiselle. The cane is most effective. Has your doctor suggested the use of crutches?'

'No, thank heaven!'

'Crutches would be better still.'

Jenny frowned. A few weeks back she had been a schoolgirl in an alpaca apron, submissive to authority, but she had her own young dignity, and the lawyer's tone and manner did not please her. He had taken up a position on the hearthrug as if he were the master of the house.

'Would you be seated, monsieur?' she said. 'It makes me uncomfortable to look up at you.'

He assented at once, and pulled up a chair between the two women.

'You arrived in Paris only four days before the outrage, mademoiselle?'

'I landed at St. Nazaire on the tenth of January.'

'From the United States, where you lived under your mother's care, I presume?'

'I was in boarding-school at New York until the end of last year.'

'Considering all I told the police a month ago, and all the forms your hotel-keepers make visitors fill out, I guess you know I've been living in Paris since June,' said Mrs. Cameron. 'I was at the Hotel Meurice until my daughter came to join me.'

'A valued guest, I am sure.' Maître Raynaud appraised the grand piano, the oil-paintings in gilt frames and the Parian marble statuettes which, as he well knew, the John Arthur Agency rented to only the very highest class of foreign clients.

'Mademoiselle!' He turned to Jenny. 'Your awareness that the trial of the Italians has opened makes it easier for me to explain my mission. Up to the time when I left the Assize Court, today's proceedings were purely formal. The accused have been identified, fragments of the bombs produced, and so on. You understand all this, I hope?'

Jenny nodded.

'Tomorrow, the prosecution wishes to introduce evidence of another nature. To present, in court, some of the survivors of Orsini's crime. It is considered highly desirable that you should be among them.'

'Jenny appear in court? You're mad!' raged Mrs. Cameron. 'Haven't those devils made her suffer enough already?'

Jenny spoke reflectively. 'So that was why you thought I'd look better on crutches? The Prosecutor must be very much afraid of Maître Favre for the defence.'

'Maître Favre's eloquence will not affect the verdict.'

'Guilty?'

'Certainly.'

'Then, if it's certain, why should any of the—the victims have to appear in public?'

'In this case we have to think beyond the punishment of the criminals. The trial of Orsini and his accomplices will be closely followed in other foreign countries——'

'Particularly in England. You want to make sure, don't you, that Dr. Bernard is found guilty when *he* stands trial in London for his share in the plot?'

'I hope a British jury will show more sense than the House of Commons, when it takes up the question of plots against France being hatched on English soil.'

'Yes, it didn't take the Commons long to throw out the Conspiracy to Murder Bill, did it? If the British jury acquits Dr. Bernard too, will the Emperor Napoleon go to war with England?'

'My dear young lady, what an extraordinary idea!'

Maître Raynaud studied the girl half-lying in the big armchair. In the soft dress without hoops or trimmings, with her rich dark hair tied back by a plain blue ribbon, she looked childish and frail enough. The experienced lawyer saw the resolution in Jenny's brown eyes, considered the power of reasoning in all she had said, and admitted that she was not at all as he had pictured Kate Cameron's daughter. The Emperor's secret police had provided him with a brief but interesting report on Mrs.

Katharine Cameron, born Maria de las Dolores Catalina Villaverde y Mendoza, her friendship with the Emperor's rejected mistress, Madame di Castiglione, and her share in the gay life of the Second Empire. He wondered if the good lady expected a daughter like this girl to follow in her own footsteps?

'I'm going to send for Dr. Hugo right away,' said Mrs. Cameron. 'He'll tell you to your face that Jenny hasn't even been allowed out for a drive yet.'

'I have already spoken to the doctor, madame. He considers that, with all the proper precautions, mademoiselle could make a short appearance in the Assize Court tomorrow.'

'There's only one reason why I would go,' said Jenny. She still spoke reflectively, thinking aloud, and with her eyes on the sticks of the fan twisting in her mother's fingers. 'I would like to see Orsini—see him as he really is.'

'You didn't see him on the fatal night?'

'Oh, no! I've been told that he must have been standing quite close beside me outside the Opera. But I was watching for Their Majesties, and you know it was the very first bomb that,' she swallowed, 'that hurt me. And I've thought so much and read so much about him, since, that perhaps if I really saw him—in the court—I might understand what drove him to do such a dreadful thing ... and plan it all so badly. Pieri talked, as soon as the police inspector picked him up on the Rue Le Peletier. The other two were easily taken. And Orsini went straight back to his lodgings—went to *bed*; the police found him there with blood all over his pillow, as if he *wanted* to be arrested, wanted to die! Maître Raynaud, that's what I don't understand!'

'No young lady ought to worry her charming head about such sordid matters——'

'But I'm not any young lady,' said Jenny. 'I'm one of his victims. And you want something of me; that's why you came. Why, monsieur? Orsini is not on trial for maiming me and a hundred and fifty others, and killing eight people and blinding three. He's charged with an attempt to assassinate the Emperor of the French, who got away with a cut finger. Why don't you put the Emperor on oath and make *him* testify?'

'The Emperor might well have been the principal victim,' said Maître Raynaud, evading the question. 'His life was saved by two accidents—that the Grand Chamberlain ordered out the Lancer escort without his knowledge, and that the explosive had been packed too tightly in the shells.'

'So the Emperor was saved by destiny,' said Jenny. 'Do you believe in his Star, Maître Raynaud?'

'All France must believe in the Star of the Emperor,' the man said devoutly.

'It must have shone that night,' the girl agreed. 'He sat through the whole performance at the Opera, and then went for a drive through Paris, without an escort, to show how brave he was, and be applauded ... while the poor victims were dying in the wards at Lariboisière.'

'You have been greatly concerned for your fellow victims, mademoiselle?'

'Greatly.'

'Then surely you understand that the appearance in court of a young lady like yourself, an American citizen, will help to bring their present plight to public notice? As matters stand, only the policemen's widows will receive a pension. But after the trial, with your help, it may be possible to open a fund for all the others.'

'We've helped the survivors already,' said Mrs. Cameron. 'I sent one hundred gold napoleons to the sick folk at Lariboisière Hospital, in Jenny's name.'

'Most generous,' Raynaud agreed. 'You are known to be very charitable—and extremely rich, madame! You inherited the great Catalina mine from your late husband, I believe. Was he one of the original Forty-niners?'

'We were in Sacramento in '49,' said the widow shortly. 'Mr. Cameron made his big strike early in '52.'

'And died a violent death next year at a mining camp called Rough and Ready?'

Jenny, with a thrill of dismay, saw her mother's olive skin pale, and a fine line of sweat break out upon her brow. She spoke quickly:

'What has my father's murder to do with the trial of Orsini, sir?'

'Mademoiselle, the point I wish to make is that a lady who has lived through such a tragic experience in California must surely wish to forward the course of justice in France?'

The ivory sticks broke in Kate Cameron's fingers. A drop of blood stained the palm of her hand.

'You are distressing my mother to no purpose,' Jenny said. Her own hands were shaking, as the lawyer saw, but she held on to her self-possession. 'Please do not prolong this scene, Maître Raynaud. If it will really help the bomb victims, then I will do as you ask. I'll appear in the Law Courts tomorrow.'

'Jenny, I say no!'

'I think I ought to be there, mamma.'

'Then go, you stubborn little fool!' Mrs. Cameron sprang up with such a threat of violence in her look that Maître Raynaud instinctively rose to his feet. 'You want to see a man condemned to death, do you? It's not a pretty sight. I saw it happen one night at Rough and Ready, and I saw the man taken out and hanged at dawn. That's how we forward the course of justice in California, monsieur. We lynch our murderers!'

The little anteroom was very cold. It was one of a warren of old rooms in the heart of the Paris Law Courts, smelling of candle-grease and parchments, and heavy with the anxiety of hundreds of litigants and witnesses. Jenny had been carried there by two porters from a discreet side entrance to the Palais de Justice; alone with Madame Lamotte, she was aware of the murmuring crowds in the boulevard outside, the boys and men clinging like apes to the gates and railings, the whole weight of Paris lying on this one building where an Italian patriot was on trial for his life.

Madame Lamotte was silent, sour with the recollection of an angry scene with Mrs. Cameron before they left the apartment with Jenny's doctor as their escort. Jenny was silent too. In the dismal waiting-room, laden with the authority of a thousand years of French justice, her mind had travelled inevitably to the miners' court at Rough and Ready, where her father's murderer had been condemned to die. She knew the court had sat in his own saloon, on the very spot where Big Jim Cameron had been shot down, and she had known all the men who were judge, jury and executioners. But four quiet and happy years at school had so far blurred her memories of that time that she best remembered an October day in San Francisco, when she had been for only six weeks a pupil of the Good Sisters in the Mission. She remembered Reverend Mother's pitying face, and the gentle words which told Jenny that her father had been shot and killed in a quarrel over cards; and after frantic weeping her own challenge to the nun:

'Was it Flash Frank? That bastard's been gunning for Dad for a long time——'

'Jenny, you've been forbidden to use such language here.'

'But was it?' A stamp of the foot as yet unaccustomed to a high-buttoned shoe. 'Go on, tell me! Did Frank Carter kill my Dad?'

Reluctantly: 'It was a Mexican, a newcomer to the camp. His name was Valdez, I believe.'

'Valdez! I never heard of him. What did the boys do? Did they lynch him right away?'

'He has paid the penalty required by human justice. And you must pray for the repose of your father's soul, my child.'

'Dad didn't believe in prayers for the dead. He said you weren't to pross—proselytise me.'

'Then pray for your mother, Jenny. She needs your prayers.'

... 'What a little savage I was,' said Jenny aloud, and Madame Lamotte stared.

'Are you quite comfortable, Miss Cameron?' It was the old monotonous question, and Jenny tried to smile. She was not comfortable; the jolting in the fiacre over cobbled streets had tired her weakened body, and a jagged pain, sharp as the steel splinters extracted weeks ago, had begun to quiver in her injured foot. She was thankful to see Dr. Hugo, who came in with Maître Raynaud at his back.

'Mademoiselle, this is very good of you,' the lawyer said, with a bow to Madame Lamotte. 'Madame Cameron decided not to accompany you? That's understandable. Do you feel equal to going before the court?'

'Now?' Jenny shrank back. 'But I thought—where are the other witnesses?'

'In another waiting-room,' the doctor said. 'Most of them have come straight from Lariboisière, and I refuse to expose you to the risk of hospital fever.' He slid his fingers professionally round her wrist. 'Has Madame Lamotte brought the smelling salts?'

'I don't need smelling salts. Is it far to the court-room?'

'The porters are waiting outside to carry you there.'

'But they mustn't carry me into court, like a cripple! People will stare.'

'I want you to walk to the witnes stand,' said Maître Raynaud.

'I don't think mademoiselle is equal to it,' the governess objected.

'It'll be over within twenty minutes,' Maître Raynaud reassured her. 'The big scene comes on at six o'clock.'

Outside the Assize Court of the Seine, all the young barristers, all the solicitors' clerks and many of the police of Paris seemed to have gathered in a crowd which parted with murmurs of interest as Jenny's chair was set down before the great doors.

'Take mademoiselle's cloak,' said the lawyer, in his brusque way. 'There is a child witness on the stand at present, and we are next but one. Ah! Here they come!'

'Why, it's the little acrobat!' cried Jenny. 'The boy who was doing tumbling tricks before the carriages drove up. Come here to me, darling. Were you badly hurt?'

The child who had been so lively in his bright pink costume was sobbing now, with his black curls pressed against the shoulder of the hospital attendant who had carried him into court. An empty sleeve pinned to his hospital smock showed the toll the little acrobat had paid to the bombs of Orsini.

'Oh, the poor little fellow,' mourned Jenny. 'Madame Lamotte, we *must* do something to help him. Can't you find out who his parents are, and where he lives?'

But Maître Raynaud's bulky figure, more imposing than ever in a black robe with the stole over one shoulder, came between the governess and the child.

'Time for that later,' he said authoritatively. 'Take Dr.

Hugo's arm, mademoiselle. You have your stick—good. The ushers will seat you first inside the door.'

After the dimly lighted anteroom and the twilit corridors, Jenny was startled by the brilliance of the vaulted court. The gas lamps of the Second Empire shone here as brightly as at the palace of the Tuileries: the odour which accompanied the hissing of the jets was mixed with the heavier odours of unwashed humanity. The people of Paris were crowded thigh to thigh on the public benches, shoulder to shoulder in rows five or six deep in the small area where standing was permitted. The vanguard of the milling crowds outside, they had fought their way into the court when the doors opened in the morning, and had been there ever since, hard-breathing, restless, refreshing themselves occasionally with gulps of wine and mouthfuls of garlic sausage and new bread. Their faces in the crude gas light wore the same avid, famished looks as had grinned seventy years earlier across the courtrooms of Revolutionary France. They were ready to shout *'Vive l'Empereur!'* but their straining eyes held the image of a phantom guillotine.

Jenny took her seat with her eyes lowered. When she dared to look up, she found herself looking straight across the court at the Italian prisoners.

All four were dressed in black. Pieri, who had sold his accomplices to the police almost as soon as he was challenged, sat a little apart from the others. Gomez, red-haired, pale-faced, was biting his nails and darting glances around the courtroom from underneath his brows. Di Rudio, with his gaudy cravat, his long hair and wild young face looked like the frontispiece to Jenny's old school copy of *Barnaby Rudge*. His eyes were fixed on a shabbily dressed girl who sat at a little distance from the dock, oblivious of her surroundings, convulsed by sobs.

'His poor little English wife,' Dr. Hugo whispered.

'I wonder who brought her here?' Jenny murmured in reply. She was watching every movement made by Felice Orsini.

He was trying to be impassive, with his arms folded on his breast, but the convulsive trembling which now and again shook his shoulders, the jumping of a muscle in his jaw, showed that the prisoner was in the grip of strong emotion. His beard had been shaved off in jail, and the pallor of his hollow cheeks made him look younger and more vulnerable. Now and again he glanced at Eliza di Rudio, and murmured a word, perhaps of encouragement, to her young husband. Always his look went back with shame and regret to the witness now before the court—a *sergent-de-ville* whose police uniform, carefully mended, showed where the bomb splinters had torn open his shoulder and smashed their way across his ribs.

'Which is the Public Prosecutor?' said Jenny softly.

'The tall man in the red robe.'

'And is that Jules Favre in front of the prisoners?'

'Yes, in black.'

'They don't interrogate?'

'The presiding judge interrogates. Are you ready to go next?'

An usher was stooping over them with a paper in his hand. Jenny edged painfully into the aisle and allowed Dr. Hugo to draw her arm through his as they moved slowly into the centre of the court. It was impossible to walk without limping and leaning heavily on her stick.

Under the gas jets the crowd leaned forward, greedy for every detail. It was known that two Americans had been among the bomb victims, and that one, a man, had died on the way to hospital. Here was the other, a lamed girl, nervous and beautiful, whom the members of the diplomatic corps and the Legislative Body, occupying the best seats, to a man pronounced *ravissante*. Their wives, with raised opera glasses, were ready with a scornful *'pas jolie du tout!'* but the women knew very well that Jenny's plain black dress, with bands of sable at the wrists, was evidence of riches and good taste. Her mother's maid, Fifine, had urged the girl to wear something striking: proposing a lace fichu, a sable muff with a posy of parma violets, at the very least the gold watch set in pearls which Kate Cameron had bought for Jenny on the girl's first day in Paris. But Jenny had quietly refused. The little cap of sable fur was her only adornment. Orsini recognised the altered face beneath it, and for the first time since the trial opened buried his head in his hands.

The three judges in their red robes looked down at her from the bench. Maître Favre looked up, and played with his pen; the Public Prosecutor, red-faced and choleric, stood waiting while Jenny answered the simple questions. Her name was Jane Ann Cameron, aged eighteen. Born in Yerba Buena in Alta California, then a Mexican possession; now a citizen of the United States of America. Had not seen any of the accused in the Rue Le Peletier. Had been told that Orsini was standing near her at the door of the Opera but had no recollection of seeing him there. Believed she was injured and thrown to the ground when the first bomb exploded. Became unconscious and could give no clear account of what had taken place.

The presiding judge took up the tale. This beautiful and innocent young lady ... a guest in our country ... the only child of a widowed mother ... stricken down in her youth ... very likely to be maimed for life ... the rich phrases flowed on over Jenny's head. She was aware that the reporters were scribbling furiously, while two newspaper artists took her picture on their sketching-blocks.

She seemed to be the target of many thousand eyes.

She was aware that the judge was thanking her for coming forward, that Dr. Hugo's gentle pressure on her arm meant that they might go. She gripped the stick in her right hand as if it were her wavering courage and spoke up.

'Monsieur le juge!' The clear voice and the schoolgirl French took the courtroom aback. 'May I say something before I go? I know these men had no intention of hurting me. And I—I'm not angry with any of them because of—my own injuries. They meant to kill the Emperor. He should be here.'

There was a gasp and a long rustle of excitement through the crowded court. The ushers shouted 'Silence!' and moved closer to the mob on the public benches. And Maître Raynaud, waiting for Jenny near the door, was smiling a peculiar smile.

'Bravo, mademoiselle!' he said. 'A spice of temper to liven up the proceedings—excellent! The men are waiting outside with your chair.'

But Jenny dropped into her old place, catching her breath in pain. 'Your big scene starts at six o'clock,' she said scornfully. 'Surely you don't want me to miss that?'

She felt great pain in her injured leg, worse than for three weeks past. While Maître Raynaud scowled and muttered, Madame Lamotte edged her lean form on to the bench beside Jenny and held her smelling salts under the girl's nose.

'You are unwell, Miss Cameron,' she said anxiously. 'I can't take the responsibility of allowing you to stay longer.'

'It's my own responsibility.' Jenny braced her arms against the back of the bench in front and inhaled the sharp ammonia of the smelling bottle. The dizziness of the pain cleared away slowly. She had missed nearly all the testimony of the next and last witness, and heard only the murmur of sympathy as he left the courtroom. It was an old man with a white beard, who had been totally blinded by the bombs of Orsini, and when the great doors closed upon him there was some relaxation of the tension in the court. Several journalists went out to hand their reports to the waiting messengers. The Prosecutor, Monsieur Chaix d'Est Ange, sat down: the red-robed judges conferred with one another. Even the prisoners murmured and shifted in their seats, and the spectators in the public area burrowed in their coat pockets for more refreshments. The Assize Court of the Seine took on the appearance of a theatre in which the audience prepares for the pity and terror of a final act.

Jenny, in a moment of illumination, realised that she had been playing a small part in a consummately skilful theatrical performance. She knew, too, who had staged the performance and displayed the victims best calculated to appeal to public sentiment. A mutilated child, an injured policeman, a young American girl, a blinded old man—the appearance of these and others could only stir up fury against the Italian prisoners. But she, Jenny Cameron, had been egregiously wrong when she blurted out 'The Emperor should be here!' He was there, the invisible showman; the drama of the Law Courts was being directed from the palace of the Tuileries—but to what end?

All this time, as the whispering ceased and the journalists returned to their seats, and the judges and the prisoners sat at attention as if waiting for the three blows before the curtain rose, the counsel for the defence had been the quietest person in the room. Maître Jules Favre sat writing, with his papers in a neat pile before him; even when Pieri, who had been scribbling, flung a crumpled note accurately on the learned counsel's table,

Maître Favre read it and folded it up without any expression on his calm face. He had accepted his brief with some reluctance, well publicised; in fact, the task of defending men accused of an attempt to kill the Emperor was not uncongenial to Jules Favre. He had been the Emperor's sworn antagonist long before Louis Napoleon Bonaparte brought off his *coup d'état*, and now that the Second Empire had stifled every breath of criticism Favre's was almost the only republican voice which continued to be heard in France. Gravely, while the audience leaned forward with a sigh of anticipation, he bowed to the President of the court and began his speech.

He started quietly—quiet in language, and with his slow, heavy voice pitched so low that Jenny, on her bench near the door, could hardly hear or understand him. Gradually, she fell under the spell of that haunting voice, those powerful understatements: she saw that the red-robed judges were intent upon the pleader, that the crowd hung silent on his words.

It was on Orsini, and on him alone, that Maître Favre chose to base his plea. He described the life of an Italian patriot in a land where Austria held the preponderant power: hunted from Italian state to Italian state, imprisoned, battling for the Roman Republic, exiled, and why? Favre paused impressively. 'Because Felice Orsini is a man who tried to do for Italy what others have done for France!'

The audacious allusion to Napoleon III, the equation of the assassin with his chosen victim, brought a roar from the courtroom—but it was not a roar of execration. It was the shout of a fickle mob prepared for one brief moment to destroy its own phantom guillotine, and carry a condemned man shoulder high. Maître Favre seized his opportunity and proclaimed:

'My client, Felice Orsini, wishes it to be known that he refuses the clemency of this court. He will not humble himself before the man who destroyed the dawning freedom of his own country.'

And they allow this, marvelled Jenny. The judges and the Prosecutor make no attempt to stop him! Through a wave of pain which blurred her vision, she saw Maître Favre unfold a paper.

'I have here a letter,' he said, 'written by Orsini in his prison cell. I am going to read it in open court—by the gracious permission of him to whom it was addressed.' He paused for dramatic effect. '"To Napoleon III, Emperor of the French."'

The wonderful voice rose and fell in the hushed courtroom.

'"I adjure Your Majesty to give back to Italians the freedom they lost by the deeds of the French themselves in 1849 ...

'"Remember that so long as Italy is not independent, the peace of Europe and of Your Majesty is but an empty dream ...

'"May Your Majesty not reject the words of a patriot on the steps of the scaffold! Set my country free, and the blessings of twenty-five million people will follow you everywhere and for ever."'

Three

SIGNOR BENSO

LONG after French justice had taken its expected course,
after Orsini and Pieri had died by the guillotine and di
Rudio and Gomez had gone to life imprisonment on
Devil's Island, the Emperor of the French left Paris to
take the cure at Plombières.

It was a charming spa in the forests of the Vosges,
where the baths and fountains had been famous since the
days of the Romans. The philosopher Montaigne had
been cured there of the stone. The Bourbon princes had
gone to Plombières in search of health, and an exiled
King of Poland, Stanislas, had built a miniature palace
there for the sojourns of his grand-daughters, the princesses of France. The Empress Josephine went to the spa
for treatment, hoping to bear a child to Napoleon
Bonaparte, and Hortense, Queen of Holland, had spent
more than one summer season there. Now Hortense's son,
Napoleon III, had taken Plombières under his special
protection. He was financing a new hotel and bath-
house; he was turning the little church into a cathedral;
and in 1858 his visit, for the second year in succession,
meant that wealthy and ambitious people from all over
France had followed their ruler to the Vosges.

It was regrettable, of course, that he had come alone,
but even without the attraction of the Empress Eugénie
the town was full. The old hotels were crowded out, and
the ever-increasing wealth of the Second Empire was ex-

pressing itself in the new villas spreading uphill from the valley of the Augronne in a blaze of geraniums and fresh paint. Sickness and depression were never allowed to intrude at Plombières. When the morning baths were taken and the waters drunk, visitors gave themselves up to enjoyment: concerts and plays, evening balls and parties were considered as important as the cure. In the late afternoons, the narrow streets were gay with parasols and crinolines as the ladies drifted from one bright boutique to another, buying local laces and embroideries, fruit bon-bons and liqueurs made of plums, pears and raspberries from Alsace and Lorraine.

The only gloomy spot in this lively little town was the Pavillon des Princes, the holiday home of the Emperor Napoleon III. It was an ugly two-storey building with a mansard roof and no garden, more like a village school or a country police station than an imperial residence, but the Emperor could reach the National Bath by a private stairway, and being accessible only by stone steps from two different levels of the town, the Pavillon was easy to guard.

About three o'clock in the afternoon of July 21, a visitor left the Pavillon des Princes, nodded to the sentries in the gravel yard, and started down the steep steps leading to the street. He was a tall young man, wearing a snuff-coloured frock-coat and carrying a top hat of the same colour in his hand, and he made a good deal of noise as he ran down the stone stair. When he passed the Cent-Gardes on duty at the foot, he began to whistle.

A man lounging near the locked door of the National Bath stopped him quietly and waited while the young man, with an annoyed laugh, produced a folded paper.

'You checked my orders half an hour ago,' he said. 'Forgotten who I am already?'

'Allez, passez, monsieur.'

The plain-clothes policeman touched a finger to the brim of his greasy beaver hat. The tall man, with a brief salute, walked rapidly off up the Rue Stanislas. It was the hour of the siesta, and no human being was to be seen except a little girl, carrying a bundle of clean linen into the Roman Bath, and a young lady, seated outside the hotel once patronised by the philosopher Montaigne. She had been sketching the eighteenth-century façade of the house built by King Stanislas, but she laid down her sketching block and pencil to look at the young man as he came up the street.

'It can't be Steven Blake!'

He took off his hat with a polite bow, and the girl said joyfully:

'Don't you know me, Steven? Don't you remember Jenny?'

'Jenny!' he said. 'Not little Jenny Cameron from Rough and Ready? Jenny grown up?'

Giving him her hand: 'Of course! Steven, it's been five years! What in the world are you doing in France? We thought you were working in Chicago.'

'I was.' There was a look of heaviness and bewilderment on his face, very different from the girl's sparkling recognition. 'Yes, I was in Chicago for a while. But you—I thought you lived in Saratoga. Is your mother here?'

'Not right now, she's gone to Luxeuil with her friends, Colonel and Mrs. Loder. But this is our hotel, and—Steven, we can't talk on the sidewalk! Come and sit in the garden!'

He followed her into the lobby, with a quick shake of his head like a dog climbing out of a pond. A maid in a smart frilled cap and apron, who had been gossiping with the porter, came forward at once and curtsied.

'Mademoiselle?'

'Steven, have you had luncheon? Well, at least you must have a cup of coffee! Ask them to bring coffee to the rose arbour, Fifine.'

'Certainly, mademoiselle. Shall I ask Madame Vernet to come downstairs?'

'Oh no, don't disturb her; I'm sure she's fast asleep.'

The maid held open the garden door and looked up appraisingly, invitingly, as Steven Blake went by. He barely glanced at her; he knew her sort all right. But her intervention had given him just the minute's grace he needed to pull his wits together for Jenny Cameron.

The thick walls of the ancient inn and its outbuildings had kept the garden cool and fresh through the noon hours. There was a rustic seat and a table inside the arbour, covered with pink climbing roses and banked by blue hydrangeas in tubs. The maid and a hotel servant followed them out with the coffee service and a silver basket of little cakes.

'Please take my sketching things back to my room, Fifine,' said Jenny, and with another look at Steven the girl obeyed.

'Is she your own maid, Jenny?'

'Mamma's maid, but she looks after my dresses too. She came with us from Paris, when we left there at the end of June.'

'You've been living in Paris?'

'Mamma took a furnished apartment there for six months.'

'And who's Madame Vernet?'

'My governess.'

'What does a big girl like you need with a governess?'

'Oh—she keeps me company, and we read Montaigne's essays and Racine. I like her better than my governess in Paris, but she sleeps a lot. Taking baths and lying down, that's all I get to do in Plombières.'

'What brings you and Kate to a sleepy place like this?'

'We're taking the cure too.'

'The cure! You don't look as if you'd had a day's illness in your life.'

Jenny laughed. There was a lovely colour in her cheeks and her dark hair, softly curled, had the burnish of perfect health. Steven Blake studied the extravagantly simple dress of pale pink silk, the lace scarf and all the style and finish of this new Jenny, who had met her old friend with such unselfconscious charm. There was no poetry in Steven's nature, but he thought she looked 'like a rose herself', and he had to touch her cheek just once, even if it offended her.

'You've turned into a beauty, Jenny, do you know that?'

'Oh Steve, I've thought of you so often, and our old days at Rough and Ready! And even earlier, at Sacramento——'

'Your folks were mighty good to me at Sacramento, when my dad was sick.'

'That was the hard winter, 1850, just after the gold rush started.'

'You were only a little kid then, with your hair in two black braids like an Injun.'

'I was eleven.' Old enough to remember the thin red-haired chore boy, sweeping out Jim Cameron's saloon in the winter mornings, carrying away a tin pail of hot food for his ailing father. More than old enough, a few years later, to remember him at the mining camp in the High Sierra.

'Eleven, were you? That makes you nineteen now, and me twenty-five, I reckon.'

'I was nineteen on the second of July. Don't you remember, I was fourteen two days before the Fourth of

July dance at Poverty Flat, when you bought me the blue satin slippers?'

'It was your first dance, I know that.'

'You swam the North Fork to get there in time, with my slippers tied up in your jacket, on your head ... And just a few weeks later I was sent away to school, and father—died. Oh Steve, if only he had given up the saloon, and the drink, and the cards, when he made the big strike at the Catalina!'

'I wish to God he had.'

'You went East, soon after it happened?'

'Worked my way to St. Joe with a wagon train.'

'My mother said you'd struck pay dirt.'

'Pay dirt, did she? You could call it that,' said Steven grimly. 'I did get a bit of a stake just then, but I wanted to hold on to it to get myself some schooling. My father was a schoolmaster back in Ohio, before the two of us went sashaying off to look for the Mother Lode.'

'Remember how you used to help me work my arithmetic examples?'

'Did I?' His laugh was embarrassed. 'I always hankered after railroading, and when I went on to Chicago I got a job in the shops—the Chicago and Rock Island shops, that is, and went to night school in the city. Then I moved on to the Illinois Central and worked on the foot-plate for a year. Fireman first, then engineer—I had a pretty fair experience of locomotives before I went to England and into the shops again.'

'Where in England?'

'Bristol. That's where I met my present boss, when he was looking over the Great Western Railway track,' he concluded. 'A few months later he offered me a job in Sardinian Railroads.'

'I didn't know there *was* a railroad in Sardinia.'

'Not in the island, yet; but Piedmont is the tail that

wags the dog in the Kingdom of Sardinia. Our head-quarters are at Turin.'

'And you really like that, Steven? You preferred staying in Europe to going back to the West?'

'Back to California? It'll be a long while before they lay a track across the Rockies, Jenny. Even the Pony Express only got as far as Sacramento last year! Besides, the job I'm on right now is the biggest job of its kind in the world,' Steven said with pride. 'I'm working up at Bardonnechia on the new Mont Cenis Tunnel.'

'You're a long way from the Mont Cenis here,' said Jenny dryly. 'What brought you to Plombières?'

'I'm on tour with my boss, that's what. We've been travelling for the past two weeks, inspecting the road bed from Culoz to Aix and the header at Fourneaux—that sort of thing. Tomorrow we'll be starting back to Turin.'

'What's his name, this boss of yours?'

'Benso. Signor Giuseppe Benso.'

'A Sardinian?'

'A Piedmontese. First and foremost, an Italian.'

'He must be a very important Italian, Steve. I saw where you were coming from just now.'

'Where I was——'

'From the Pavillon des Princes, wasn't it? You, or your chief, had business with the Emperor of the French.'

Steven Blake lifted a warning hand. They were in a reasonably private place, with nothing behind the arbour but a high brick wall espaliered with fruit trees, but the garden was not large, and some of the hotel windows were sure to be open behind shutters closed for the siesta. There might be listeners in the bedrooms. He lowered his voice.

'I was sent for to take a memorandum to Signor Benso,' he said. 'Some figures he gave me to work out this morning. The railroad through the Mont Cenis Tunnel will join France and Piedmont, Jenny, it's a huge inter-national undertaking. Quite naturally the—the man at the Pavillon wanted to discuss some of the details with Signor Benso. But his visit here is strictly private. I'm not supposed to talk about it.'

'It sounds very mysterious. But then the Emperor loves mysteries!'

'Have you been presented to him, Jenny?'

'No. He has only given one reception, and we weren't on the list.'

'I bet you Kate was mad.'

'Yes, I think she'd counted on it. But otherwise she's having an amusing time at Plombières. She goes to Luxeuil quite often too.'

'What's the attraction at Luxeuil?'

'A game of chance called the *Petits chevaux*.'

'I thought gambling was illegal in France?'

'That makes the *petits chevaux* even more attractive.'

Steven laughed and looked more at his ease.

'Look, Jenny,' he said, 'Signor Benso said he wouldn't need me again until seven o'clock. Can we spend the rest of the afternoon together?'

'But you were hurrying off somewhere, weren't you?'

'Only to have a look at the river. Did you know Robert Fulton carried out some of his first experiments on the steamboat here? Say, Jenny, why don't you walk along there with me? Then we could really talk in peace.'

'But the river's covered over in the town beneath the Baths, and it's too far to walk to the Promenade des Dames.'

'Too far? Why, it can't be a mile there and back! You used to walk ten in the mountains, any day, and never turn a hair.'

'I can't walk half a mile now,' said poor Jenny. 'I was

hurt—I was lamed, the night Orsini tried to kill the Emperor.'

'But are you going to be—will you always have difficulty in walking?'

It was the first thing Steven Blake could find to say when he had heard the whole of Jenny's story. They were sitting in a basket carriage, brought by the hotel porter from a nearby livery stable, and the carriage was drawn up beneath the tall trees of the Promenade des Dames. In the quiet afternoon, the ripple of the Augronne could be clearly heard, but Steve had lost all interest in the experiments Robert Fulton had conducted there in 1802. His eyes and thoughts were only for the beautiful troubled girl beside him.

'Jenny, you *will* get better?'

'Oh yes, of course! I'm better already, and the doctors say I'll be able to do much more after I've taken the cure at Aix-les-Bains. It was going out too soon, going to the trial at the Law Courts, that did the damage. After that I couldn't walk a step until the end of April.'

'God!' he said, deeply moved. 'I had no idea—I knew an American was killed; I never knew about you.'

'They always spell foreign names wrong in the French newspapers.'

'Then I was up at the Tunnel when Orsini's trial came on, and we seldom see the papers there. In January I was in Turin. I remembered my chief in a fury when the news came in from Paris. "This means ruin for Italy!" he said. "The Emperor will do nothing for us now."'

'Signor Benso must be a keen politician,' said Jenny.

'How about your mother? Was she hurt at all?'

'Her gloves were torn, and her cloak was—spoiled.'

'Trust Kate Cameron to save her skin.'

'Don't, Steve, it's been so disappointing for her. All the

55

plans she made for me were ruined.'

'Disappointing for *her*! I guess it's been disappointing, if that's the right word, for you too.'

'Well, yes.' She had told him her story quietly so far, now there was a catch in Jenny's voice. 'I'd looked forward so much to Paris. I thought it would all be moonlight and violins, and dancing with handsome officers. And then to be living with mamma at last——'

'But haven't you been living with her, all this time?'

'Never, since we left California.'

'I thought you were both at Saratoga.'

'Mamma had a house there, but I was in boarding school at New York. She said Saratoga was no place for young girls.'

'She didn't have to show you off at the race-track,' said Steven grimly. 'Well, what about this school? Was it another convent?'

'Miss Lippincott's Academy? Oh, no, it was strictly Presbyterian.'

'So Kate had that much respect for your father's memory. He was very much against the convent, I remember.'

'Why do you speak so unkindly about my mother? Why shouldn't she respect my father's memory?'

They were coming nearer, inevitably, to the moment Steven Blake had dreaded since Jenny rose up in her pink dress to greet him, like a beautiful reminder of the ugly past.

'I only meant,' he said, 'that she cleared out of the High Sierra so damned fast—out of the State of California for that matter—as if all the years with Jim hadn't meant very much to her.'

'You've no right to say that! She did not clear out fast! She stopped over in Sacramento long enough for all the law business—Dad's will and selling the Catalina mine to Dermot Callaghan, and then she went on to San Francisco to get me.'

He braced himself for the dangerous words, the urgent question.

'But you already knew about Big Jim's death?'

'Yes. Reverend Mother told me what had happened.'

'You never read—any of the newspaper stories?'

'We weren't allowed to read the newspapers. Anyway, mamma told me everything when she came.'

The candid brown eyes looked into his, seeking and wondering. Jenny whispered, 'She told me you were there.'

'Yes.'

'How was that?'

'Franchette was off sick, and I was helping out behind the bar. Jenny, don't look at me like that! It was all over before I had time to draw.'

'It was quick then? Dad didn't suffer?'

The livery horse was munching at the grass verge, the reins were tied to the whip socket. It was easy for Steve to put his arm round Jenny, and cover her trembling hands with his free hand.

'No, darling, it was very quick.'

'Steven, who was this man Valdez?'

'Look, Jenny, it's over now, it happened years ago, and you've got your own life all before you. Don't go on worrying and fretting about the past——'

'But that's what mamma said!' she cried, trying to pull away from him. 'In San Francisco, and all the way on the ship till we got to New York! She kept saying not to think about it, and never, never to *talk* about it after she put me in school, because the girls would be mean to me if they knew my father had been killed in a saloon brawl in California. Never to talk about it to anyone! And I promised her, and I've kept my promise; but just lately,

57

just since that awful day in the Law Courts, I haven't been able to get it out of my mind!'

'You poor baby,' said Steven, tightening his clasp. 'You've had it pretty rough.'

Jenny leaned against him for a moment, drawing a long breath. Then she sat up and put her bonnet straight.

'People are looking at us,' she said, unsteadily.

There were only two old ladies to be seen, peering at the basket carriage from under fringed parasols, and a nurse girl restraining a small boy who wanted to throw stones into the river, but Steven untied the reins and started the livery horse along the avenue. He felt a temporary relief, as if he had rounded a dangerous corner; and Jenny helped him by keeping silent, rearranging her lace scarf and touching a handkerchief quickly to her eyes.

'Where shall we go?' he said, gratefully. 'Have you a favourite drive?'

'I don't know the main roads very well. But if we go through the forest, eastwards, I don't think we'll lose our way.'

'Fine.' Steven took the reins again, and they drove along the wide Promenade Des Dames into the forest which surrounded Plombières. The road ran eastward to the distant Rhine, uphill, out of the valley of the Augronne, and a breeze came blowing out of Alsace, scented with pine.

Jenny looked thoughtfully at Steven. He looked better now, as if some burden had been lifted from his mind, and she studied the changes which five years had made in her old friend. He sat taller in the driver's seat, and had broader shoulders, set off to advantage by his well-cut coat. The freckles of his boyhood had disappeared beneath an even tan, and his red hair had darkened considerably; his hands, though better tended, were still the same, calloused and strong. As the reins slipped between his fingers, she remembered the last time she had sat beside him while he drove, on the box of the coach taking her along the first stages to school in San Francisco. He had given her a rough kiss, for luck, when they said goodbye.

Not that this wooded track, into which they had turned, had anything in common with that headlong descent in the Sierra. It meandered between fine copper beeches, the boughs drooping over banks where the wild roses of July flowered among bracken fern, and between the trees there were glimpses of steel-blue lakes and rhododendron thickets in full bloom.

'Isn't the air wonderful?' exulted Jenny. 'It's been so hot and heavy in Plombières.'

'Ah, but you're a mountain girl, and Plombières is a stuffy little place. You'll like Savoy better than this part of France, I think. When do you go to Aix?'

'About the middle of August.'

'And Mrs. What's-her-name, your sleepy governess, does she go too?'

'No, she's going back to her home at Nancy. I'm to have an Italian teacher at Aix, because of spending the winter in Turin.'

'You're going to be in Turin!'

Jenny laughed. 'I nearly told you before, Steven, when you were explaining about Sardinia and Piedmont, and your headquarters at Turin. It's true, we're going in October. We may expect to see you there, I hope?'

The young man gave her the same downcast, unforthcoming look of their talk in the rose arbour.

'I hope so, too, of course,' he said. 'I don't expect to get away from Bardonnechia much this fall. Do you think it's wise for you to go to Turin, Jenny?'

'Why shouldn't I?'

'Well,' said Steven carefully. 'I'm thinking of that horrible experience you had in Paris. In Turin you'll hear Orsini praised as a patriot and a martyr. How would you feel about that?'

'He was a madman, not a martyr,' said Jenny, calmly. 'But it was suffering that drove him crazy in the end. I sent to London for the book he wrote, about the Austrian dungeons in Italy and his imprisonment. Poor man, no wonder he was driven to murder.'

'You're very generous, Jenny. What if you saw his picture, as you very well might, displayed in half a dozen shop windows in the Via Po?'

'He was very handsome,' Jenny said. 'Do you know the Emperor had his head destroyed by sulphuric acid after he was guillotined, in case any sympathiser took a death-mask of his face?'

'Good God!' Steven's hands, closing on the reins, checked the horse to a walk. Jenny leaned out and plucked a trail of honeysuckle from the hedge. He watched her put it to her pretty nose, unconcerned, as if the horrible image of destruction, which she had shown him in a single sentence, were something to which she had become accustomed.

'I gather you're not an admirer of the French Emperor,' he said.

'I don't understand him,' Jenny said. 'After that farce he put us all through at Orsini's trial, showing off the bomb victims in court and allowing Orsini's appeal for Italy to be read aloud and even printed, I thought he meant to spare the prisoners' lives and be praised for his own generosity. But nothing came of that—nothing except more death and misery! Next it was the threat of war. Everyone thought he would invade England after the London jury acquitted Dr. Bernard of complicity in the assassination plot. That passed over too. He takes the baths at Plombières, and talks about the Mont Cenis Tunnel to Signor Benso, and everything seems peaceful and calm. And yet he must be planning something—I'm sure of it!'

Steven Blake looked at Jenny with new respect. She wasn't a child playing at being a grown-up lady, nor yet the pathetic victim of a madman's folly. There was fire here, and quick intelligence; and something he could not define, as delicate and fresh as the honeysuckle spray.

'I'd like to know how you feel about all that, after you've spent a few weeks in Turin,' he said. 'Where are you and Kate going to stay—at the Hotel de l'Europe?'

'We've been invited to stay with a lady my mother knew very well last year in Paris. She has a villa just outside Turin.'

'Really? Who is she?'

'The Contessa di Castiglione.'

'Good heavens, Jenny! Not the Queen of Hearts!'

'What's the matter?'

'I tell you, Kate must be out of her mind! She can't compromise you by taking you to live in that woman's house!'

'*Halte-là!*'

The unexpected challenge shocked them both. Absorbed in one another, they had failed to see the troopers among the trees. Now a double file of mounted Lancers emerged from the forest, and while one seized the livery horse's bridle a young lieutenant sketched a salute to Jenny.

'I regret,' he said, 'access to the highway is temporarily closed.'

'For how long?' said Steve. 'I've got to get this lady back to Plombières.'

'You are a foreigner, monsieur? And madame?'

'Mademoiselle and I are American citizens.'

'Your passports, if you please.'

'Will this do?' Steven handed up the folded sheet of paper which had admitted him to the Pavillon des Princes. The officer read it and saluted again.

'*Parfait!*' he said. 'Then I am at liberty to inform you, sir, that His Imperial Majesty has ordered the highway to be picketed until six o'clock tonight. However, we expect his carriage to pass in ten minutes, and you will then be free to return to Plombières. As a pure formality, are you armed?'

'Yes.' Steven hesitated on the word. The lieutenant looked towards the highway, as if calculating the range of a pistol shot, and said, 'Give me the weapon, if you please.' Steven unbuttoned his frock-coat and drew a Colt from its holster.

The lieutenant weighed the gun in his hand, and looked at Steven. There was no sound in the forest but the jingling of bridles and the muted July song of the birds.

'Are you carrying a gun for Signor Benso, Steve?' asked Jenny, very low. There was no answer.

'Here they come,' the young officer said to his sergeant. There was a sound of wheels, and along the Remiremont road came a stylish phaeton, drawn by two American trotters, lifting their hooves high with a beautiful rhythmic action. Napoleon III, a cigar clamped between his lips, was holding the reins.

The gentleman by his side looked sharply down the road through the woods where the patrol waited. He was blond, bullet-headed, spectacled; tightly buttoned into his frock-coat, he might have passed for some Teutonic professor of natural history come to botanise in the forests of Lorraine. But Jenny had seen those plain features sketched in too many journals not to recognise the man sitting beside the Emperor of the French.

'So that's your Signor Benso!' she said to Steve. 'The prime minister of Sardinia, Count Cavour!'

'Camillo Benso di Cavour,' said Steven obstinately. 'He has a perfect right to his incognito.'

'But Napoleon isn't as careful of it as you were. I wonder how many people saw them driving through the town today? I wonder what sort of schemes they're hatching out together?'

'You're free to go, monsieur,' the Lancer said to Steven. 'But I advise you to wait until the dust settles in the highway.'

The dust settled on the white road and the banks of bracken fern. The Emperor and Cavour, with one groom following out of earshot, drove on endlessly talking, until the sun began to set over the rolling uplands of the Vosges. Then the security patrols rode out of the forest byways, back to stables and barracks, and from there scattered among the wineshops and cabarets of Plombières. They were the advance guard of the tremendous armies one day to be committed to battle as the result of what Cavour had urged through the long hours, what Orsini's last appeal had moved Napoleon III to promise for Italy. Six hundred thousand men, scattered over Europe and Africa, sat down to supper, went to rest, unaware of the fate prepared for them. Croats in the forest lands between the Drave and the Save, Hungarians and Czechs, Viennese preparing for an evening's gaiety in the Prater, welcomed the coming of the dusk. French conscripts in their first year with the colours, Légionnaires in the Maison-Mère at Sidi-Bel-Abbès, answered the bugles as the flags were lowered. Men condemned to die for a free Italy, that great dream, pulled up their stools to rough wooden tables in the mountain villages around Lake Como, or called for wine in the fishermen's taverns by the harbours of Genoa and Nice. Darkness, falling on a Europe still at peace, moved westward from the Danube to the Seine, and mercifully covered all. Finally, in the sinister little house at Plombières, the secretaries put their candles out at last, and the Emperor slept.

But Jenny Cameron, in her white nightdress, sat alone before her mirror, and touched her cheek softly as she whispered to her reflection:

' "You've turned into a beauty, Jenny, do you know that?" '

Four

THE TUNNEL

'I HOPE this fellow's brakes are all right,' gasped Mrs. Cameron, with an arm thrust through the window strap. 'Are you sure we haven't gone off the road?'

Jenny, clinging to the strap on her own side of the coupé, peered through the dusty window at a wilderness of boulders and scrub pines. The diligence, with six passengers in the section at their back, was making the long descent from the Mont Cenis plateau to the valley where a new railroad ran direct to Turin.

'It isn't much of a road, mamma, but we're still on it,' she said, 'and we can't be very far from Bardonnechia.'

'If I'd known it would be this bad, I never would have gone out of my way to visit Steven Blake. I should have asked him to come down to Turin, once we were settled in.'

'But it'll be so interesting to see the Tunnel, too,' said Jenny diplomatically. It was only a week since, at Aix-les-Bains, her mother had told her that a letter had come from Steve, and that they might stop and see him on their way into Piedmont. Jenny had known instinctively that any show of enthusiasm would make her mother change her mind. She had not quite believed in the trip to Bardonnechia until they had actually reached the railhead in Savoy and begun the long, horse-drawn climb over the Mont Cenis pass.

'Look at those shanties!' said Mrs. Cameron, 'we must

be getting near the place.'

'Look at the mud,' said Jenny.

'I'm not going to walk through that, and neither are you, Jenny. Why, they've torn the whole place up, just like——'

Like a California mining camp. Very like some of the places they had both known, and never mentioned, as the two horses splashed across the level ground churned up by the activity of two years, into the crude township of tents and turf huts which had grown up on the scarred mountainside.

'I can see Steve!' Jenny was wrestling with the window. 'And some men with him, waiting on a kind of platform——'

'There you are!' Steven, wearing high boots, plunged into the mud before the coach drew up. 'Jenny, let me lift you down. How are you, Kate? It was very good of you to come.'

'I'd have gone right down to Susa, if I'd known what the road was like,' was Mrs. Cameron's amiable greeting, but she emerged from the coupé gracefully enough with the help of Steven's arm, and that of a young man whom he introduced as 'Peter Easton, one of our surveyors.'

'Mayn't I carry that for you, ma'am?' said Peter Easton, possessing himself of Mrs. Cameron's morocco jewel case. 'This is the worst part, walking on the duck-boards, but it's not bad once we're in the village. And we've tried to make our cabin fit for ladies—the first ladies who ever honoured us with a visit.'

'But where's the Tunnel?' Jenny cried.

'You can't see the header from here,' said Steve. 'Those fellows who crossed the pass with you are going right up to it now. They're French engineers from the Fourneaux side.'

'They're nice. We all dined together at the post-house.'

She was talking at random, excited and happy, and Steven took her arm. There was just room for two to walk abreast on the wooden duckboard, with Jenny's free hand controlling her wide skirt.

'Do you think you can make it as far as the cabin?' asked Steve, anxiously. 'Pretty rough going on these planks.'

'Oh, but I can walk perfectly well now,' she told him. 'I can do everything but dance!'

'And where's Fifine and the Italian teacher?'

'Both sent packing!' She laughed. 'Mamma and I have been looking after each other for the past few weeks.'

'So things are better than they were last summer?'

'Much, much better. Is this what you call the village?'

Bardonnechia had been a pretty mountain hamlet two or three years before, a refuge for shepherds and woodsmen in a fold of the Cottian Alps. Now all that remained was a few chalets, to some of which the original inhabitants obstinately clung while the Tunnel works grew up around their doors, and the Tunnel picks and shovels rang.

'There used to be an inn, but it's a dormitory for the section bosses now,' said Steve. 'Peter and I share that cabin between the two pines.'

The little chalet, built of logs, was more solid than others which stood near, hastily thrown together to house the ever-growing army of Tunnel foremen and construction supervisors. It was raised on a stone foundation beneath which firewood was stored, and entered by a short flight of steps and a door in a small balcony. From the balcony there was a view of the snow-capped Aiguille de Scolette, beneath which the Mont Cenis Tunnel was to run.

There were only two rooms in the cabin. One, which contained two bunks with turkey-red blankets, had been prepared for the guests with fresh water, clean towels and a pincushion. In the living-room were straw-bottomed chairs, a little cooking stove, a cuckoo clock, a cupboard with assorted crockery and a stone fireplace piled with blazing logs.

'A fire, thank heaven!' said Kate Cameron. 'We nearly perished at the post-house last night. I thought it would be warmer as we came down the mountain.'

'We're still four thousand feet up, you know,' said Peter Easton pleasantly. 'Can I make you some hot tea or coffee, ma'am? We have wine and sandwiches for you, and some fruit, if you care for that?'

'It looks delicious,' said Jenny. The table, not a large one, had been placed against a wall and covered with a coarse white cloth. Cream cheese and thinly-sliced *prosciutto* were spread on slices of buttered bread, and there were grapes, pears and figs in a straw basket.

'I'll have a glass of wine,' said Mrs. Cameron. Steve was opening the slim bottles of Soave; he handed her a brimming glass with a bow. They had hardly spoken to one another since their first exchange of greetings.

'Blake makes the best coffee but I make better tea,' said Easton, perseveringly conversational.

'You're English, aren't you?' said Kate.

'My people have a farm in Sussex, near the coast.'

'And do you two boys make your own tea and coffee, and cook for yourselves every day? Don't you have some woman coming in to clean the place?'

'One of the Irish girls comes in to do the laundry, once a week, and she scrubs the floors. But engineers learn to look after themselves up here.'

'Engineers!' said Kate. 'You look more like a couple of trappers to me!' and Jenny laughed. Both young men wore high laced boots and breeches, and thick frieze jackets over flannel shirts. 'They look like miners,' she said. 'I like it.'

'You've changed a good deal in five years, Steven,' said Kate Cameron. Her voice was lazy and caressing.

'You haven't changed at all, Kate. You look magnificent,' said Steve. He stood by the window, staring at her. She was sitting in the morning sunlight of a clear October day, which gave warmth to her olive skin, and in the close-fitting travelling dress her waist was as slender as a girl's. Her black eyes moved quickly from one man to the other.

'Mr. Easton, don't you want to take my daughter to see the Tunnel?' she said. 'I know she's very interested in it all, and I'm too comfortable to leave the fireside.'

'Delighted, ma'am,' said Peter Easton, and Steven flung out: 'Not very much to see, as yet. But I'd like to take Jenny up to the portal myself before you go.'

'Will there be time?' said Jenny uncertainly. 'I know the diligence leaves here at noon.'

Steve looked at his watch. 'It connects with the 2 p.m. at Susa, the best up-train of the day, arriving Turin at 3.45,' he said. 'We'll see that you don't miss it.'

'Run along, Jenny,' said her mother impatiently. 'Steve and I will follow you very soon.'

When the door closed, Kate moved to join the young man at the window, and stood watching. Jenny looked round once and waved. They heard the two voices receding, and then there was silence in the chalet. Kate shivered.

'I thought this was a hell of a noisy place when we drove up,' she said. 'Now it's like a ghost town. Where are all the men?'

'At work, of course. We took a couple of hours off to meet you. Another glass of wine?'

She let him fill her glass and drank it down, with an indefinable change in her manner which matched her

69

freer speech. Steve had often seen her standing thus, lithe and alluring, at the bar of the old saloon in Sacramento.

'What do you think of Jenny, Steven? Is she pretty? Is she sweet?'

He answered deliberately: 'Thank you for bringing her to Bardonnechia.'

At that, the artificial formality which had constrained them both broke down beneath Kate's gust of anger.

'I didn't bring her here to please you, and you know it! I came because of the insolent letter you sent to Aix! How dare you order me to keep Jenny away from the Contessa di Castiglione?'

'Because the Contessa is a whore, that's why.' He heard her catch her breath, saw the Spanish features sharpen and seized his advantage. 'The whole world knows—even Jenny must know—that she was the French Emperor's mistress until he threw her out of France. Before that, she had an affair with King Victor Emmanuel—and a long liaison with Ambrogio Doria, and a dozen others in Turin. Her husband has left her, the house she lives in is notorious——'

'She is a very ill-used woman,' Kate interrupted. 'And she went to Paris as the unofficial envoy of her cousin, Count Cavour.'

Steven shrugged. 'There's a relationship by marriage, but it's not that close. And Cavour, too, has rejected her since she went back to Turin.'

'Her parents haven't rejected her. She's with them at La Spezia now.'

'I know she is, and long may she remain there.'

'You know a great deal about Turin society, don't you? You've risen in the world since the days when you were old Kelly's stable-boy, over at Poverty Flat. Have you forgotten who gave you your start in life?'

'Myself,' said Steve. And over Kate's derisive laughter:

'Yes, I know what you did for me, Kate, and I'm not proud of it. But I could have gambled that money away in one night, or drunk it in seven, if I'd cared that much for cards or booze.'

He wondered if the woman understood him. She said impatiently: 'But what's your motive in all this? What do you care where Jenny and I go, or whom we meet? You went out of our lives five years ago; why should you trouble about us now?'

'Because when I saw Jenny in France last July ... so lovely ... and young, I felt a responsibility to her ... because of what had been. I guessed at the sort of life you'd planned for her, if your plans hadn't been stopped by Orsini's bombs. You were going to use her youth and freshness as a bait to get rich fools to your card table. And then you hoped to sell her to the highest bidder who offered a wedding ring ... and get back to the world you know best, the race-tracks and the gambling hells!'

She struck him at that, across the jaw, and Steve swore, catching her wrist so furiously that she cried out:

'What do you know about me? What kind of woman do you think I am?'

'I know what you *were*, Kate—the best faro dealer in the Sacramento Valley.'

He relaxed his grip, and Kate Cameron put the breadth of the cabin between them as she retreated to the fire.

'You're wrong, *hombre*, you're cruelly, wickedly wrong in what you've said about my plans for Jenny. Haven't I given her the very best schooling New York had to offer? Every advantage—music masters, dancing classes, riding lessons; and when she graduated, finishing governesses to fit her for the best society in Europe. Does that sound as if I'd been raising her to be—as you so kindly reminded me—a *faro dealer* like myself?'

71

'No, but——'

'Do you think I don't want a better chance for Jenny than I ever had? Have you any idea of what my life was before Jim Cameron came to Monterey, second mate in a Boston brig trading in hides along the coast of California? My father was one of the *corregidores* in the *alcalde*'s office: a beggarly half-pay clerk, but as proud of his name and blood as if he had been King of Spain. There were nine of us at home, all hungry, but that didn't matter as long as Don Ramón Villaverde could strut in the plaza of Monterey wearing white silk breeches and kid slippers, and raise his sombrero like a *hidalgo* when the Governor went by. If I had been as low a creature as you think me,' and here Kate's voice became soft and cajoling, 'could I have remained an honest woman? There were girls like me, close to me, in Monterey, who became prostitutes to the Mexican garrison. Don't you realise that could have been my fate too?'

'You could have been an actress, Kate.' The hard young face, stern beneath the tumbled dark red hair, showed nothing but an invincible dislike of her.

'You think I'm acting, do you?'

'It's not as good a performance as you gave the night Big Jim was murdered,' Steven said. 'But it'll pass.'

When Jenny and Peter Easton returned along the duckboard to the plank platform, the diligence was still standing there, with the horses out of the shafts and busy with their nosebags, and the driver standing guard over the baggage with a loaded carbine.

'Good heavens!' said Jenny. 'Is an armed guard really necessary?'

'They're a pretty wild lot up here, Miss Cameron. There are a lot of Irish labourers working on the header and the canal, and all they care about is whisky and—er—fighting, with thieving as a pastime. We have to mount a guard over the storehouses as well as over any coach in transit.'

'Their living quarters don't look very comfortable. Could we walk up among the tents and huts and have a look?'

'Well, not very far. Some of the women are real viragoes; you might find it an unpleasant experience.'

'Ah,' said Jenny gaily, 'but didn't you know I was brought up in a mining camp? Most of the men I knew were derelicts and drifters; your labourers, at least, are working for a wage. I don't think I'll see or hear anything at Bardonnechia to offend me.'

'Was the camp that place with the wonderful name, where Blake was a stage-coach driver? Rough and Tumble?'

Laughing: 'Rough and Ready. He drove the stage to Poker Gulch and back, twenty-four miles, with an hour's stop-over at the Flat, Mondays, Wednesdays, Fridays and Saturdays without fail. Sometimes he took me along, and you should have heard the passengers' language when he let me drive!'

The Englishman studied Jenny's laughing face, whipped to bright colour by the October wind. 'You've had an adventurous life, haven't you?' he said. 'The High Sierra, and then a passage round Cape Horn——'

'Seasick nearly all the time!'

'My sisters would envy you. They were mad for adventure last summer, when the Volunteer Corps was formed in England to resist the threat of a French invasion. They had a tremendous time embroidering banners and pennants for our local company, and watching the drills, but they lost interest after my brother Harry distinguished himself by fainting on parade in the presence of royalty.'

Jenny drew her cloak around her. The autumn wind blew strongly down the pass, and a vulture was hovering in the October blue.

'I can hardly realise that we've actually crossed the Mont Cenis,' she said. The peaks of the Cottian Alps, dominated by Mont Cenis and Mont Genèvre, sloped down to the tree line in a series of cols and chimneys, harmonious as organ pipes and lightly powdered with the first snow.

'I spent more than a year clambering about up there,' said Easton. 'Before we could set out the centre line of the tunnel, the surveyors had to calculate the geometrical link-up between the two portals. Do you know what I mean by the link-up?'

'I think so,' said Jenny doubtfully. 'I got into plane geometry at school. The portal—is that the entrance to a tunnel?'

'Yes. We began to take our bearings on the other side of the mountain, up the valley of the Maurienne, across the pass and down to Bardonnechia—about forty miles in all.'

'How long is the tunnel going to be?'

'Nearly nine.'

'And how many years will it take to finish?'

'It should be open for traffic by 1870.'

'It's a tremendous undertaking.' They walked a little way among the tents, in silence, and the sluttish women, some with infants in their arms, came out to look and scowl.

'And is this what Steve's been working on, the geometrical link-up?' asked Jenny.

'Blake? Oh no, Miss Cameron, he isn't a surveyor. He works on general communications. The canal and the post road to Susa, and the line between the railhead at

Susa and Genoa via Turin—all that. Of course, he's an exceptionally able fellow. He can handle this mixed mob of foreign labourers far better than the Italian foremen; and last winter it was Blake who kept the supply wagons going when we were pretty well snowed in up here.'

Glowing: 'They must think highly of him, then, in Sardinian Railroads?'

'Cavour thinks highly of him, and Cavour is the power behind Sardinian Railroads. Down in Turin, they call him "Cavour's American", one of the young men who are going to do great things for Italy. He's very close to the inner circle—the men who think Italy can be united by a good steamer service and a railway track.'

'Steven has a very generous friend in you, Mr. Easton,' said Jenny, and then they saw him coming, the red head and the brown frieze coat a vivid point of colour against the dingy walls of the tent city.

'But where's mamma?' said Jenny, as Steve came near.

'She wants to rest in the cabin until time for the coach to start. Says she has a headache.'

'I must go back to her.'

'No, let me,' said Peter Easton. 'You haven't seen the portal yet. And maybe a cup of tea would do Mrs. Cameron good.'

He left them with a wave of the hand and, without waiting for Jenny's protests, Steven laughed. 'Poor Kate!' he said. 'I reckon she's condemned to drink Pete's tea after all.'

'Do you think you ought to call my mother Kate?'

'That's what everybody used to call her.'

'No, you called her *la señora*,' said Jenny gravely. 'Steve, have you and mamma had a quarrel?'

'We certainly had an argument. And maybe I've done more harm than good.'

'But what about?'

'You know I don't want you mixed up with the Queen of Hearts,' he said in his dogged way.

'But she's at La Spezia! We've taken rooms at the Hotel de l'Europe for at least a month! And when Madame di Castiglione does come back, I can't very well refuse to call on her, if mamma insists.'

'Oh God,' said Steve, 'I worry about you, Jenny. You're just as stubborn and just as headstrong as you used to be at Rough and Ready.' He took her by the shoulders and drew her close to him. They were hidden from the tent-dwellers by a spur of rock. 'Jenny, does this place remind you of—back there?'

She nodded without speaking, her eyes on his. Ever since they arrived in Bardonnechia she had been reminded of the mining townships of the High Sierra. The distant sounds of pick and shovel mingling with the cascade and the wind in the evergreens, the cold peaks towering above the fierce human activity on their slopes —yes, it was all familiar, but Jenny would not speak one word in agreement. She had said 'Do you remember?' all too often at Plombières; it was her pleasure to hear him say it now.

'If I can't come to see you in Turin very soon, dear— perhaps not for a long while, you won't think the worse of me, will you?' His lips were close to hers.

'But Steve!'

A sound like twenty factory whistles blew across their heads, echoed by the mountain walls, and Jenny started.

'It's only the hooter for changing the shift,' said Steve. 'Half-past eleven. Watch out, though, Jenny, this place will be overrun in a couple of minutes.'

He pulled her further back behind the protection of the rock. From all the tents and huts, men came hurrying out; men who had been asleep on plank beds, men who had been eating and drinking or fondling their slovenly mates: men putting on their jackets, tightening their belts. As they streamed up the mountain, another river of men came stumbling downhill through the mud and gravel, men who were about to eat their dinners at the favourite hour of half-past eleven; Piedmontese thirsty for wine and polenta; Irishmen for the whisky they called 'white beer'. Some of their Italian foremen walked beside them with black stubble on their cheeks, and weary eyes. Not all observed Steve and Jenny in their sheltered spot. Those who did smacked their lips at Jenny and called out compliments: *bella piccola! bella bambola!* She waited, faintly smiling, until the crowds had passed.

'The new shift is on now,' said Steve, relaxing his hold on her arm. 'We'll go right up to the portal, there's no time left to look at the canal. A couple of hundred men are working on the cut.'

'Why must you dig a canal to build a tunnel?' She was hurrying by his side up the steep track, watching the ground and walking with great care.

'To carry water to the compressing machinery. Next year we're going to use five Sommeiller rock drills, operated by compressed air. They're on order at Genoa, and we get delivery in June.'

'Then?'

'Then we'll cut through the mountain twice as fast as we're doing now. See there!'

She saw a gigantic scar, the beginning of a hole, scraped out of the mountain side. It was roughly the shape of a horseshoe, oval at the top and flat at the base, where rock and soil had been blasted and levelled in all directions. Upon this level space men swarmed, men with no eyes for a new woman, no time to whistle flattery, but clambering over the great outline of a cavern which they were tearing from the living rock. Halfway up the oval, wooden struts held up the brick arch which was to

77

support the roof of the Mont Cenis Tunnel.

'This is what they call the header,' Steve explained. 'We're just starting on the second stage of the enlargement. Next year we begin excavation below the arch with the Sommeiller drill. As the drillers go forward the lower half will be lined with stone and the drainage gutter will go up above the finished arch.'

'And all this will take twelve *years*?'

'Counting the time for laying the rails from portal to portal, on to Modane on the west side and down to Susa on this.'

'And do you mean to work on this project until you're nearly forty, Steve?'

'I can't think of any more worth-while job for a man to do.'

She looked up at his face, more resolute, more at peace than she had seen it yet, and tried to say something which the clang of the picks and shovels drowned. Two hundred men, and a great hole in the mountain, and a purpose, a passion which she could not understand.

'Come out of this hellish din,' said Steve, leading her away. 'You won't get a real idea of what it's all about by looking at the header. But I wanted you to see it, because some day trains will run through that portal, through the Alps, just as trains run already through the Apennines at Giovi. Now look down the High Valley. You're looking at the Alta Valle di Susa. You'll take the train to Turin from Susa this afternoon. But you could go on from Turin via Milan to Venice, or via Alessandria to Genoa. So when the Mont Cenis Tunnel is opened, all Italy will be linked with Paris and London. It's Cavour's great hope that when we lay a track to Brindisi and the Suez Canal is cut, Italy will be the bridge across Europe to Egypt and India.'

'Italy?' said Jenny. 'Or the Kingdom of Sardinia?'

'A united Italy, of course.'

'But then the Austrians will have to be driven from Milan and Venice first, and that means war.'

'I'm a railroad engineer, Jenny. I leave politics to the politicians.'

'But you're Cavour's American, aren't you—in the inner circle? Oh, Steve,' cried Jenny. 'I'm so proud of all you've done, and the way you've made those powerful men respect you. But don't, please don't let them use you —as they once used me.'

Five

THE QUEEN OF HEARTS

TURIN, in October 1858, was an exciting city. Jenny Cameron caught the infection of that excitement, which floated, visible as the motes of dust in the golden afternoon sunshine, in the streets through which she was driven from the station to the hotel. There was excitement in the cafés filled with passionately declaiming, gesticulating men, in the baroque splendour of the piazza where the great Duke of Savoy, *'l Caval' d' brons'*, bestrode his charger, immortalised in statuary; even in the halls and creaking corridors of the Hotel de l'Europe. Kate Cameron had kept her veil down in the train, complaining of her headache. She complained more bitterly of the 'old-fashioned' suite of rooms assigned to them, which was indeed chilly and austere, but when log fires were lighted in the ancient grates and warming-pans placed in the beds she was better pleased, and even admired the reflection on the firelight in the wood-panelled walls which dated from the seventeenth century.

The neighbourhood was quiet enough when they retired for the night, but almost before the frosty daybreak a busy hum of life began. The hotel, for all its high reputation, was surrounded by tenements where enormous families displayed most of their joys and sorrows, like their washing, on the balcony. Many a drama of love and jealousy was enacted, to Jenny's amusement, against a background of underwear, pot plants and climbing greenery, and as the Italian voices rose so did the song of the caged canaries hanging at every open window. The Camerons drank their coffee in a crescendo of birdsong and shouts.

But Jenny welcomed the din, in contrast to the hushed and muffled life she had left behind her, and the hours spent in dutiful perusal of Chateaubriand, Montaigne and *I Promessi Sposi*. She was no longer a looker-on; this lovely and exciting city was hers to explore on foot if she pleased, alone if she dared, with only the hotel chambermaid for chaperone. Mrs. Cameron did not intend to engage a personal maid in Turin, and seemed quite satisfied with the attentions of Isabella, the elderly woman who looked after their rooms.

Nor did Kate set up her own carriage, as she had done in Paris. A hired *vettura* took the American ladies on their first drives in Turin, through the lovely linked vistas of streets and squares built of honey-coloured stone, to the Corso and the long river bank of the Po. They went further afield, to the outskirts of the city where textile mills and other manufactories had been encouraged to open by Cavour, and once, coming back by the Genoa station, they saw a crowd of workmen with blackened hands and faces, like the labourers at Bardonnechia, streaming out of the locomotive sheds. It was on one wall of those sheds that Jenny for the first time saw a crude picture of Orsini, burning-eyed, black-bearded, with the emblems of Piedmont and Savoy crossed above his head, and underneath the legend 'Hero—Martyr— *Per l'Italia*—Orsini.'

On the third afternoon, about an hour before the usual time for their drive, Isabella entered the panelled parlour and, with her grave bow, presented three visiting-cards on a tray to Mrs. Cameron. Jenny looked over her mother's shoulder at the names of the Marchese Carlo di

Alfieri, of the Marchesà, and of Maggiore Giorgio Lascaris, 1st Regiment of Bersaglieri.

'Who on earth are all these people, Mamma?'

'The Alfieris are related to the prime minister,' Kate said carelessly. 'Steven Blake said he would ask them to call on us. Ask them all to come in, Isabella.'

'Signora, only the signor maggiore has called in person. He respectfully hopes the ladies will receive him.'

'Come to look us over,' whispered Kate, as Major George Lascaris bent his plumed head to enter the old-world room. Spectacular in his Bersaglieri uniform, he was revealed, when his feathered hat was borne reverently away by Isabella, as belonging to a type less rare in Piedmont than in the south, the blond Italian. He was very handsome, with his cool grey-green eyes and straight fair hair, as he bade the American ladies welcome to Turin in the name if the Marchesà de Alfieri.

'My cousin and her husband hope to give themselves the pleasure of calling in person as soon as you are settled. Madame di Alfieri, as you probably know, is the niece and official hostess of our prime minister. In his absence she read the telegram in which Mr. Steven Blake was good enough to inform us of your arrival in Turin.'

'Count Cavour is not in town at present?' said Jenny.

'He is visiting his estate at Leri, and reckoning up his profits on the harvest, like any good Italian farmer. Now do tell me your impressions of Turin. Are you comfortable here in the Hotel de l'Europe?'

Drawing-room conversation was not likely to languish in the presence of Major Lascaris. He smiled a great deal, looking from Jenny to her mother, giving his full attention to each in turn, and answering readily the questions Mrs. Cameron put to himself.

'No, madame,' he said. 'I'm not permanently stationed in Turin. I've been seconded for duty in the Alpine manoeuvres which begin next week, and then I shall spend three months here on the staff of General La Marmora. After that, back to Monaco.'

'Where's that?' said Kate.

'Monaco, madame, is a principality on the Ligurian Riviera, between Nice and Mentone. It is nominally independent, but actually protected and garrisoned by Sardinia. It's a quaint old place which used to live by lemon trees and sardine fishing and is now best known for its new casino.'

'What do they play?' asked Kate.

The grey-green eyes narrowed. 'Roulette and trente-et-quarante.' He turned to Jenny. 'It's very agreeable to be stationed at Monaco. I have a house not far from there, called the Casa Lumone, at the Capo Martino, where my sister lives.'

'She is older than you are, Major Lascaris?' Jenny hazarded.

'Ten years younger. She is not quite eighteen.'

'Don't tell me she lives alone!' said Kate.

Major Lascaris smiled ruefully. 'Alas, yes. Our parents died in a shipwreck, long ago, and although Claire has faithful servants to look after her, I must admit that she has no lady to preside over the household——'

'No finishing governess,' said Jenny.

'I should pity the governess! Claire decided to leave the schoolroom at the age of sixteen, but she is never idle. She cultivates flowers for the Rimmel perfumery at Monaco, and keeps our olive groves in a highly productive state.'

'She must be a fascinating girl,' said Jenny.

'I hope she may make your acquaintance soon, Miss Cameron. She is coming here to spend Christmas with me. I should explain the relationship with the Cavours—the Marchese, the head of the house and a widower, was married to Adèle de Lascaris, of the Vintimillia branch of our family. He and his younger brother, the prime minister, graciously allow us to regard the Palazzo Cavour as our home in Turin.'

The fifteen minutes prescribed by etiquette for a first call had elapsed, and Major Lascaris rose to take his leave.

'You have come to Piedmont at a great moment in our history,' he said. 'You will live with us through the Risorgimento, when the defeats of ten years ago will be avenged, and the Austrian usurper driven by force from Lombardy and Venetia.'

He took his departure as ceremoniously as he had come, and Kate Cameron went to the window to watch him go.

'He's a handsome brute,' she said. 'See, Jenny, he came on horseback, with a groom.'

'How affected! The Cavour house is only two blocks away.' But Jenny joined her mother at the window, glad of the heavy brocade curtains which concealed them both. The flat-dwellers across the way were less reticent. They stopped the eternal quarrelling, love-making, nursing, spanking, to hang over their balconies and cheer the handsome Bersaglieri officer as he rode away.

'I'm glad they speak French here, but some of his was too fast for me,' Kate confessed. 'What's this Risorgi-something he kept talking about?'

'The Risorgimento, mamma. The resurrection of Italy.'

'It seems a kind of sacrilege to use a word like that.'

If there were sacrilege, it had been committed ten years earlier, when *Il Risorgimento* was chosen as the name of a newspaper founded by Camillo Cavour on the eve of the War of Independence. Now the Resurrection was a faith, a way of life and death to Italians, even those living beyond the bounds of Savoy, Piedmont and Sardinia. In Turin, Italy crucified on the Austrian cross, Italy rising from the dead, were themes discussed everywhere from the great salons to the Caffè San Carlo and the Caffè Fiorio where the Neapolitan refugees plotted their own revolt against their Bourbon king. The daily ride through the city of Victor Emmanuel II was marked by outbursts of cheering, for the king, *Il Re Galant'uomo,* had sworn to avenge the defeat of Novara and his father's death in exile. Count Cavour, too, was applauded as he walked the short distance to the meetings of the Sub-alpine Parliament in the Palazzo Carignano, or of the Senate in the Madama palace. His secret visit to Plombières was no secret now. Every café lounger in Turin knew that something had been arranged there, some bargain struck. The incredible had happened. The appeal of Orsini had not fallen on deaf ears. The diplomacy of Cavour had done the rest, and Napoleon III, returning good for evil, would one day, slowly, in his own time, help Orsini's unhappy land to independence. *Viva Papa Cavour!* The smiling prime minister acknowledged the applause by waving his broad-brimmed hat.

Jenny did not think the prime minister very warlike when she met him in his niece's salon. The whole family lived together in the Palazzo Cavour, which Kate Cameron was disappointed to find was not a palace but a solid mansion containing a regular warren of rooms. The statesman, a bachelor, had an apartment of his own in the palazzo, but attended the family meals presided over by his elder brother, whose authority he good-humouredly recognised inside the house. Usually, after a meeting of the Senate, he made an appearance in his niece's salon, to sip a glass of his favourite vermouth and exchange a few cryptic words with his close friends.

Jenny was rather shy of him, but not of Madame di

Alfieri, who was intelligent and unaffectedly kind. With her as their sponsor Kate and Jenny were launched at once into Turin society. They had been laughed at a little on their first appearance in the Alfieri salon, where Kate's amber velvet and diamonds and Jenny's primrose tulle crinoline were considered too elaborate for the occasion, but soon the American ladies became the fashion in Turin. Sir James Hudson, the British Minister, declared himself charmed by Jenny; the Spanish envoy expressed stately pleasure at speaking his own language with Mrs. Cameron. It was understood that they were extremely rich. The mother, alas, was never seen in any place of worship and the daughter, apparently, was a Protestant, attending the little Vaudois church near the Public Gardens; but Cavour himself had insisted on 'a free church in a free state', and unlike Papal Rome there was no Black society in Turin. Cards of invitation poured in to the Hotel de l'Europe.

In this atmosphere Jenny glowed. She went with Madame di Alfieri to museums and art galleries, joined parties to hear opera at the Carignano theatre or watch the marionettes at the Fantocchini, and revelled in the ardently expressed homage of a dozen young admirers. When the Bersaglieri manoeuvres in the Val d'Aosta came to an end, Major George Lascaris was more often seen in attendance on the beautiful Miss Cameron than on General La Marmora. He seemed happy to stand for an hour at a time beside the sofa she shared with Kate, or to bring them vermouth and *amaretti* in the intervals of a musical programme. Sometimes, when the conversation was general, he would pull up a chair next to Jenny and talk to her earnestly about himself. His family, famous centuries ago in Greece, had lost their lands and castles through the years, and all that remained was the ancient Palazzo Lascaris in Nice, where he kept a pied-à-terre for old times' sake. He had been a boy soldier at Novara. He had been with the Bersaglieri in the Crimean War. He had fought there at the Tchernaya—that Sardinian victory which had allowed Cavour to take his place with the statesmen of Europe, and pose the Italian Question at the peace conference which followed. He talked well, in a deep voice full of the melody of Italian speech, and Jenny listened fascinated.

'They never get sick of it, do they?' Mrs. Cameron observed one night, as she was taking off her gold bracelets and preparing to retire.

'Of what, Mamma?'

'Their everlasting Risorgimento.'

'I thought the talk was very interesting tonight, about the unrest among the workers of Massa and Carrara.'

Kate yawned. 'Talk! A good card game would be a better way to spend an evening than all this talk about the great things they're going to do some day ... You know, when I was your age, the men could talk about nothing but Santa Anna and Sam Houston, and the Yankees taking over California. Then it was John C. Frémont and Stockton. Everybody argued about them, even at Rough and Ready, but I never found it made a mite of difference to *me*. Now it's what Mazzini said in '48, and what Manin did in Venice in '49, and what Cavour said in Parliament yesterday, and who cares? I'll bet there are plenty folks in Turin who're doing well enough without talking politics, and having a good time into the bargain!'

'I'm sure you'll find them if you look around,' said Jenny.

Afterwards she thought of that brief talk as marking a point in her relationship with her mother. In Turin they had been closer to each other than ever before; the new scenes and the new people had given them much to talk about, and they had talked more freely without the presence of the governess and the personal maid. But Kate Cameron was too restless to be satisfied for long with sweet vermouth and the Risorgimento. She soon found, as Jenny predicted, more congenial entertainment in the handsome villas on the way out to Rivoli where the new rich of Turin were installed. Here were the railway magnates, the silk manufacturers, the coach-builders, gambling in stocks and shares while Cavour gambled with the lives of men, and in their over-heated, over-furnished salons Kate Cameron felt at home. She settled down happily to a game of poker, with a glass of champagne at her elbow, while the over-dressed, over-fed wives of the moneymen praised her Paris dresses and her daughter's fresh young beauty. Major Lascaris seemed eager to follow them to those salons too.

It was not until the beginning of December that the Contessa di Castiglione returned to her villa outside Turin. Very little had been heard of her during her absence. Jenny had caught some veiled references to 'the Queen of Hearts' among the younger set, and had seen a few letters, addressed to her mother, with the La Spezia postmark, but Kate never alluded to her friend of Paris days. Madame di Castiglione was one of the banned subjects, like Steven Blake and the murder of Big Jim Cameron. At last, Kate announced casually that 'Nini' had returned, and had invited them both to dine at the Villa Gloria. 'But I shan't take you, Jenny,' she said. 'Nini doesn't care for unmarried girls, they bore her. You spend a quiet evening by the fire, and rest your foot.'

'My foot is perfectly all right,' said Jenny resentfully; she hated any reminder of the time when she was lame. She spent three quiet evenings by the fire while her mother dined at the Villa Gloria, wondering if Steven's scruples were worth much, and if there was any real harm in the Contessa di Castiglione. She had heard nothing of Steven since the day at Bardonnechia, and inevitably his image was growing dimmer in her mind. The excitement at seeing him again, which had sustained her for weeks after their meeting at Plombières, had begun to die out now. Even the little cabin between the pine trees, near the great hole in the virgin mountain where the labourers swarmed—the cabin around which she had woven some innocent fantasies—had ceased to charm in recollection. When, a few days later, her mother offered to take her to the Villa Gloria, she agreed at once.

There was nothing glorious about Madame di Castiglione's villa, in the hills on the right bank of the river Po. Only the lamps of their hired carriage guided Kate and Jenny through a dingy garden buried in dead leaves. The stone-flagged entrance hall was feebly lighted, and an anteroom where a manservant took their cloaks was shabby and poorly furnished. All the illumination of the Villa Gloria was concentrated in the salon, where candles in silver sconces were burning in different parts of the room. Two tall candelabra had been placed at the head and foot of the yellow satin couch on which reclined, in the pose made famous by Madame Récamier, the former mistress of the Emperor of the French.

Virginia di Castiglione, as a young girl, had been famous for her beauty. What remained to her, at twenty-one, was the beauty of a burned-out libertine. Her heart-shaped face, in which a small sulky mouth was redeemed by enormous dark eyes, was heavily powdered and weighed down by a mass of black hair, back-combed into the shape of an eighteenth-century wig. Instead of a crinoline, she wore a robe of heavy silk, bordered with the Greek key pattern, which clung to her limbs like the draperies of an antique statue. Jenny curtseyed, resisting a strong desire to laugh.

'This is my little daughter,' said Kate, and Jenny's cool hand was taken by rapacious fingers emerging from the folds of the antique robe.

'Charming,' said the Contessa di Castiglione. 'Quite, quite charming. Signorina, I am glad to see you here. Do you know Prince and Princess Joseph Poniatowski, and Prince Charles, who are good enough to cheer my solitude?'

Jenny curtsied again. She had already met the Poniatowskis, and had heard that Madame de Castiglione was counting on the Polish princes to reconcile her with Napoleon III.

The manservant announced that dinner was ready. It was a satisfying if not a delicate meal. Ravioli, tagliatelli, fettucine, lasagne, one dish of *pasta* followed another, with grated cheese, tomato sauce and a purée of artichoke hearts in side dishes, then came a pudding of chestnut purée and whipped cream decorated with crystallised violets. Nini's tiny mouth opened wide enough to swallow heaped forkfuls and gulps of rich Barolo wine. Between mouthfuls she spoke tirelessly about herself and the magic period, from the New Year of 1856 to the autumn of 1857, when she had been 'the most admired woman in Paris' and 'the unofficial ambassadress of Italy'.

When coffee and liqueurs were put on the table and the shuffling manservant had left the room Madame di Castiglione turned her huge dark eyes on Jenny.

'How old are you, signorina?' she asked abruptly.

'Nineteen, contessa.'

'I was only eighteen when my little boy was born.' She held out her left hand to the girl. On the third finger blazed a magnificent emerald, set in gold.

'Did you ever see a stone like that, signorina?'

'Never one so large and beautiful.'

'It is worth one hundred thousand francs,' said the Queen of Hearts, and laughed a strange throaty laugh as she rubbed the great green jewel against her cheek. 'It was a gift to me from the French Emperor. It is all I have to show for the love he bore me, and all my services to Italy!'

A reverent silence fell upon the table.

'Nineteen,' she mused. 'How free you are! My mother was a fool to marry me off at sixteen. She should have taken me to France instead. Before the Emperor himself was married! Then an Italian, not a Spaniard, might have queened it at the Tuileries.'

'An Italian does, darling,' suggested the Polish lady, and Nini scowled. She detested any reference to the lovely Florentine wife of Count Walewski, who was the reigning mistress of the French Emperor.

'But Cavour was worse than my mother,' she said passionately. 'It is because of him that my great rôle ended before my life began. *He* sent me to Paris to persuade the Emperor to fight for Italy. I have his letter still. "Succeed, my dear cousin, succeed by any means, but win!" I did as he bade me. I gave myself, my youth, my beauty to the Emperor. And in a year his agents asked me to leave France ... Now Count Cavour would cut me dead if we met in the streets of Turin tomorrow. *"E per l'Italia!"* that's all he says, if he thinks about my fate at all. Another soul destroyed—for Italy.'

Jenny furtively watched the clock. It seemed an age until they rose from table and returned to the salon, where a few young men were waiting. One was a minor attaché from the French Embassy, to whom the Queen of Hearts showed especial favour, the others from the rich industrial society of Turin, and while the Frenchman sat down on a low stool by the Queen's sofa, everybody else took their places at card tables in the adjoining room. It was separated from the salon by an archway draped with gold satin, and near the arch, beneath a girandole of candles, Jenny was installed at a round table covered with albums, keepsakes and books of prints.

She opened the top album, stifling a yawn. An autographed sun-picture of Napoleon III filled the whole of the first page. The other pictures were all of Virginia di Castiglione, who had been painted, drawn or photographed regularly since she was three years old. Her whole career in Paris was commemorated on the thick carton pages—the beauty in crinolines by Worth or dresses specially designed for garden fêtes and fancy balls. Jenny was staring fascinated at one photograph in which Nini's dress was inserted with a number of openwork hearts, and trying to decide if it was the lady's flesh or a layer of gauze which showed beneath them, when a man's hand took the album gently from her lap, and Prince Charles Poniatowski said,

'That's the dress our hostess wore at a Tuileries ball as the Queen of Hearts. Do you know what the Empress said when they met face to face?' He flipped a finger at one of the heart-shaped insertions, placed between the wearer's thighs. 'She said, "I fear you wear your heart too low, madame!"'

Blushing crimson: 'For shame, Prince Charles!'

'Come now, you pretty creature, don't be a prude. Where do you wear *your* heart, signorina—on your sleeve?'

... 'You didn't enjoy yourself!' accused Kate Cameron, when they returned to the Hotel de L'Europe at midnight.

'Not very much, mamma.'

'Well, what can you expect if you sit moping in a

corner all evening?'

'There wasn't much else to do,' said Jenny. 'You had your whist, and Madame di Castiglione had her young Frenchman to amuse her——'

'She was quite impressed by you. She said you could be a sensation if you chose——'

'She being an authority on sensation, I imagine.'

'It wasn't intellectual enough for your ladyship, eh? Not enough Risorgimento? Do you know that the King has actually offered Nini a suite of rooms in the Royal Palace? That shows *he* knows how to value the work she's done for Italy!'

'He having the entrée to the bedroom, I suppose? Oh mamma, how can you let her fool you! How could that silly posing creature influence any ruler, even the Emperor Napoleon, to change his whole policy, to go to war, to do anything whatever for a country not his own?'

'You heard her,' said Kate. 'She gave herself—you know what that means, Jenny—her body, her honour, everything, for Italy; what more could any woman do?'

'She might have tried throwing a few bombs.'

Inevitably, Jenny went back to the Villa Gloria. The contessa's were the only invitations Kate Cameron now cared to accept, although she gave two parties at the Hotel de l'Europe at the beginning of December. These began very sedately, being honoured by the Marchesà di Alfieri and other political hostesses, and ended in a roar of conviviality some hours after these ladies had withdrawn. The manager of the hotel and all his staff were a great deal more free and easy in their manner towards the American ladies after the two evening parties, and after an extensive bill for breakages had been paid.

There was never any noise or broken glass at the Villa

Gloria. That was the odd thing about the court of the Queen of Hearts: it was as quiet as the court of the Sleeping Beauty, and the utmost impropriety Jenny ever saw in its mistress was that she sometimes permitted one of her admirers to fondle her hands and admire the Emperor's emerald. She was a living example that the wages of sin were not death but boredom.

It was only after two or three of the monotonous evenings that the girl was able to probe beneath the smooth surface of the Villa Gloria. A suggestive remark here, a salacious innuendo there; a hot male hand suddenly placed on her own bare shoulder, a cloud of cigar-smoke blown unconcernedly into a woman's face—all these were keys to the courtiers of the Queen of Hearts. The trembling anxiety to please of Madame di Castiglione's poor little boy, who sometimes crawled about her skirts like a lap-dog, was another key to the woman's character. The books of prints and drawings scattered about the salon turned out to be pornographic; the songs sung by the actresses brought out from Turin by some of the wealthy gamblers would have raised blushes on the boulevards of Paris. There was a creeping corruption about the place which made Jenny thankful for the frequent presence of George Lascaris, as willing to follow his American friends to the hills beyond the Po as to the villas on the road to Rivoli.

He sat beside Jenny in the archway between the card-room and the salon, and told her how much she was missed at the Palazzo Cavour, where his sister Claire would soon be arriving for Christmas; and about the house on the Riviera which, he said, Claire would invite her to visit in the spring. Sometimes he spoke of war, the war that never came and the two wars he had already fought, and then he made all wars romantic, with his grey-green eyes burning, and the grand equation of war and love apparent in every tender tone of the voice he used for Jenny. Mrs. Cameron, not always a vigilant chaperone, never allowed these *tête-à-têtes* to last long. She would look round, and call George to take her cards, or a place at her own table, and laugh at Jenny for a silly baby who had scruples about playing cards for money. She was very fond of George Lascaris.

On their fourth visit Jenny gave in and took a hand at whist. She had a clear mind and a good card sense, but she was dismayed to find that it was as possible, and indeed normal in that circle, to bet on the points of a rubber of whist as on a game of faro. Kate gave her a roll of lire, wrapped in a lace handkerchief, to put inside her evening bag for the stakes. Jenny and her partner did not often lose.

Kate lost, noisily and expensively, from the middle of December onwards. Poker was Kate's game at the Villa Gloria, and as the poker sessions grew later and later Kate's Mexican beauty became blurred and haggard; only the kindly candlelight smoothed out the lines which leapt into prominence between her nostrils and the corners of her mouth. She was drinking no more than she had ever drunk in Paris, five or six glasses of champagne in the course of a long evening, but now the champagne was laced with brandy, and the lacing grew steadily more liberal. Once or twice the Queen of Hearts herself deigned to rise from her throne in the salon and trail her Greek draperies into the cardroom, there to stand behind Kate's chair and lay her jewelled hands, with a warning pressure, upon Kate's shoulders. Mrs. Cameron always responded with a grateful look. Jenny saw that her mother's affection for Nini di Castiglione was perfectly genuine, as if the older woman, rich and still beautiful herself, was hypnotised by the miserable beauty who had been a King's passing fancy and the mistress of an

Emperor.

One night—it was December 20—Jenny left the card-room about nine o'clock and wandered through the golden archway into the salon. The Queen of Hearts, for once in ordinary evening dress (the lace bertha not very clean) was sitting by the fire, with Mrs. Cameron for her only company.

'Am I disturbing you, contessa?' asked Jenny politely.

'Of course not, *carina*. Are you tired of whist already?'

'Signor Pellegrini wants to play,' Jenny explained. 'So I've cut out of the next rubber.'

'I expect you're missing George,' said the Queen of Hearts roguishly. 'But he'll be here tonight; he promised me.'

'That will be very pleasant, contessa.'

'Butter wouldn't melt in your mouth, would it, my pet? Tell me something. Your mamma and I were talking about dear George while you were playing cards. Let me hear your opinion: don't you think he ought to resume his title?'

'Prince di Làscari? He thinks it means nothing since the family estates were lost. And I respect him for it,' declared the American girl.

'You wouldn't like to be the Princìpessa di Làscari, one of these days?'

Jenny blushed and was silent.

'Because some good American dollars would restore the Lascaris fortunes quicker than anything else,' said the Queen of Hearts, with a malicious look from Jenny to her mother. Mrs. Cameron knitted her black brows and stared at the fire.

'Just let me give you one piece of advice, *carina*. Don't allow that sister of his to live with you, after you two are married.'

'Don't be ridiculous, contessa. I'm not engaged to

George Lascaris.'

'But he's your slave, my dear! And you'll accept him, when he makes the offer.'

'If you please, I'd rather not discuss the matter.' Standing at a little distance from the two older women with one hand resting on a marble table as if poised for flight, the girl in her pale blue dress looked irritatingly cool and distant. Nini felt it, and her tiny mouth sulked to a pout. Kate Cameron felt it, and her temper cracked.

'George Lascaris is only amusing himself with Jenny,' she said. 'She isn't smart enough to hold a man of the world like him. Didn't you know, Virginia, that Jenny's still hankering after a stage-coach driver we knew back in California?'

'A stage-coach driver!' The Queen of Hearts laughed her throaty laugh. 'How very original! I never would have thought of a stage-coach driver, though I've known some very satisfactory grooms in my time. Was he handsome, Jenny?'

'He *is* extremely handsome,' Jenny said. 'My mother forgets to tell you that the stage-coach driver is now a very successful engineer.'

'I'm not likely to forget anything about that young man,' said Kate viciously. 'If he's in a good job today, he owes it all to me. It was my money, not his talent, that got Steven Blake a start in life.'

'*Your* money?' Jenny gasped.

'Certainly, the money I gave him, before he started east.'

'You said he struck pay dirt at Rough and Ready.'

'In the gold from the Catalina mine.'

'But why—why should you give Steven money? Money that he hadn't earned?'

'Don't you worry about that,' said Mrs. Cameron. 'He earned it all right. I got full value for every cent.'

Six

A SEAFARING MAN

It was not difficult for Jenny to leave the Villa Gloria without being seen. With enough self-command to make a little ironical curtsey to her mother and Madame di Castiglione, and to spend ten minutes in the cardroom, pretending to watch the play, she slipped quietly into the shadows beyond the circles of lamplight which fell on the green baize tables, and from there into the empty anteroom. The hardworked manservant was at supper in the kitchen.

Jenny took the gauze scarf from her shoulders and tied it round her head. Her gloves and fan were left behind in the salon, a fact which was of no importance; she had plenty of money in her netted evening purse. Gently she opened the front door and let herself out to the frozen garden.

The moon was full that night, but hidden behind clouds, and the road back to Turin was only faintly lit as the wind drove the clouds across the sky. There had been heavy rains to swell the Po, and the rush of the river could be heard from far away, but the rain had ceased and there was a rime of frost over the bare hillside. In the distance, across the roofs and campaniles of the city, Jenny could see, when the moon shone out, the majestic snow peaks of the Alps.

She stood with the garden gate closed at her back, drawing in long breaths of the bitter air. It tasted of snow and freedom. It blew away the fumes of the Villa Gloria, the covert carnality, the sly innuendos—the last heard, vilest of them all.

'*He earned it all right. I got full value for every cent.*' The control she had imposed on herself since her mother's taunt was beginning to break as Jenny hurried down the road she had never travelled on foot before, and angry tears came to her eyes. If Steve had been her mother's lover—Kate Cameron's fancy boy, well paid for services rendered—that accounted for his embarrassment when they met in Plombières, and for his failure to come near them in Turin. It accounted for her mother's initial willingness to go to Bardonnechia, and the headache and black silence which had followed. She must have wanted to start over again, and he wouldn't, thought Jenny sorely. And then he took me up to the Tunnel and made that speech about United Italy! There came again to her mind an image of the great hole torn in the mountain and the degraded women waiting in the turf huts for the return of their brutal men.

Jenny had gone about half a mile downhill, walking and running, with no destination, no purpose except to escape from the subtle assaults of the Villa Gloria, when she saw the lamps of a cab coming slowly upwards and heard the wheels. She left the road at once and plunged into a thicket. Bare twigs whipped her hair and her cloak caught on a branch which tore the cloth and even a blue gauze ruffle off her evening dress, but Jenny was aware only of the need to hide. It might be George Lascaris in that cab, heading for the Villa Gloria; it might be some less presentable courtier of the Queen of Hearts; either way, Jenny had no desire to be seen and questioned. She let the *vettura* pass and scrambled back to the road; too late, she realised she had been standing in a ditch. Her bronze kid slippers were cut and soaking, and she stumbled over a boulder in the dark. The thought of damage to her weak left foot slowed up Jenny's rush downhill and she checked her pace, thankful for every flying gleam of moonlight, until she came in sight of the church of the Gran Madre di Dio. It was so near to the city that two or three *vetturini* were usually to be found by the portico, waiting for fares from the hillside villas. Tonight the cold and the snow which had begun to fall had kept all vehicles plying for hire inside the city, but as Jenny came up a little band of youths jumped out from the shadow of the Gran Madre with a shout of *'Bellissima ragazza!'* which made her start, and stifle a scream, and hurry off in the direction of the Bridge of the Po. The young idlers kept pace with her, begging her not to be proud, and asking for a sight of her pretty face, while Jenny with her purse tightly grasped inside her cloak was estimating the length of the bridge, and the distance beyond it to the lights and safety of the town.

'Leave the lady alone, you rascals! Be off with you!'

A man well wrapped against the cold, who was crossing the river, had seen Jenny's plight. Bulky and slow, he was not a formidable figure, and the young ruffians met him with whistles and jeers. But the face they saw through the snow was the most famous face in all Piedmont, and without another word Jenny's tormentors turned and ran back to their lair behind the Gran Madre de Dio. Jenny herself, with a gasp of gratitude, said,

'Thank you, Count Cavour.'

The familiar broad-brimmed hat was pulled off, and the prime minister said,

'My dear Miss Cameron! What are you doing alone here at this time of night?'

'Is it so late?'

'Nearly ten o'clock. Time for a young lady to be safe at

home, or enjoying herself at some gay party.'

'I've been at a party,' said Jenny. 'At the Contessa di Castiglione's. I—I left early.'

'But you are breathless and distressed. Did those wretched fellows frighten you?'

'No—oh no! But I had to walk, and I was hurrying——'

'You ran away,' Cavour said quickly. 'So someone at the Villa Gloria did or said something to offend you. Was it the Contessa?'

'I had rather not say, Your Excellency.' Jenny put her cloak straight, though with trembling hands.

'Does your mother know where you are? No? She will soon be very anxious. Perhaps I should take you straight to your hotel, but—I think you ought not to be left alone. Will you let me take you home to Giuseppina? I know she will be happy to look after you, and we can send a messenger up to the Villa Gloria, to let Mrs. Cameron know where you are. Now dry your eyes, and let us go and find a cab.'

Jenny took the proffered linen handkerchief and passed it over her wet face while struggling to control the breaths on the point of turning into sobs. A man and two women were coming across the bridge, heavily muffled, but with eyes alert for the couple who stood together against the stonework; Cavour turned his bulky body slightly to hide both Jenny's and his own face from their gaze. The light snow had almost stopped falling. Cavour studied the girl by the light of the struggling moon, and saw what Orsini had seen in the Rue Le Peletier—something Italian, and therefore appealing to himself, in the black hair under the blue gauze veil, and the sensuous mouth of the girl from California.

'You're very good to me, sir,' said Jenny, meeting his kind eyes.

'I'm very glad I thought of crossing the Po Bridge tonight. Usually I walk along the town side of the river. Shall we go?'

'Do you walk here every night?' Jenny ventured, taking the prime minister's arm.

'Nearly every night. You see, the people count on seeing me at noon, strolling and smiling on the Via Po. They watch to make sure I'm in a happy mood. He cracked a joke with the shoeshine boy, they say, or the old man selling newspapers, and so all's well in the Kingdom of Sardinia. Sometimes I wear my smile as I wear my spectacles, to get me through the business of each day. In the darkness I'm no longer on show. I can walk where I please, think heavy thoughts and wear a sad face if I must.'

'Do you think heavy thoughts of Italy?'

The man stopped and looked at her.

'Why should I not?' he said. 'You speak the name of Italy gravely, and you are right, but—there is the tragedy—it is only a word. There is no such place as Italy tonight! There is a peninsula with seas around it; there are mountains, rivers, cities, citizens ... above all, there are frontiers. There is the kingdom of Savoy, Piedmont, and Sardinia, the true cradle of liberty. Lombardy and Venetia lie in the power of Austria. The Duchies of Parma, Modena, Tuscany are the vassals of Austria. In the Two Sicilies a Bourbon tyrant keeps the jails of Naples filled. If there is ever to be a real Italy, an Italy united from the Alps to the Gulf of Taranto, these frontiers must all go down, these states become one state. And that can only be done by sacrifices: from the Kingdom of Sardinia, from the royal house of Savoy, and—from me.'

'Madame di Castiglione thinks of herself as a sacrifice,' said Jenny.

'Madame di Castiglione was—expendable. How can I explain it to a child like you?' said Cavour impatiently. 'Sometimes a great cause is shaped by a dirty tool.'

'I understand better than you think, sir. The tool Orsini used was hardly clean.'

'You poor child,' said Cavour, 'I had forgotten——'

'It was for Italy,' said Jenny. '*Per l'Italia*; I've heard Madame di Castiglione use the same words. And I can't help thinking of a little boy who lost an arm in the Rue Le Peletier. He was a little Neapolitan acrobat—in a pink suit—laughing and harming nobody. I saw him again at Orsini's trial and we wanted to help him. He was taken from hospital by a man claiming to be his uncle and we lost all trace of him. A little boy lost in Paris, crippled for life. Can you put his fate into the scales, and weigh it against the fate of Italy?'

The hypnotic scene, the rushing clouds, the swollen river, vanished as a prosaic *vettura* carried the silent prime minister and Jenny to the Palazzo Cavour. Between the shutters of a corner room fingers of lamplight pointed across the narrow street.

'The lamps are lit in your study, sir,' said Jenny. 'I often look at that light and think of you, when we drive home at night.'

Cavour roused himself from his reverie.

'Do you indeed? That's kind of you! I hope you'll always think of me kindly, signorina—as a man who tries to do his duty according to his lights.'

He helped Jenny down, and led her into the warm cluttered vestibule of the old mansion, where a maid came running to take her sodden cloak. Cavour's confidential valet, who had been waiting for his master, drew him at once into the far corner of the hall.

'What, all three of them? When? *Corpo di Bacco,* he

wasn't intended to arrive until tomorrow!' was what Jenny heard, and then the voices were lowered to a whisper. She pulled her blue gauze flounces into place, longing for a mirror, and suddenly felt tired to death. From far away she heard Count Cavour speak her name.

'My dear,' he said pleasantly, 'I find my niece has not returned yet from her evening engagements. But an old friend of yours has arrived unexpectedly, who will be very glad indeed to see you. I shall only ask you to be very discreet about anyone else you may meet here to-night.'

'It's not a party, sir?' said Jenny, shrinking back.

'No, it isn't a party.' The valet, waiting in the shadows, led the way up the main staircase. A corridor led away from the reception rooms Jenny knew so well into an unfamiliar passage, which turned with the angle of the walls of the old house, and ended in a red baize door. The valet unlocked it, and ushered Jenny in to the private apartments of Cavour.

They were in an inner lobby, heavy with oil-paintings of battle scenes, where a many-coloured lamp hung from the dark ceiling, and a murmur of voices could be heard. Cavour gave a few low-toned directions to the valet and then opened a door quietly. He entered the room ahead of Jenny and there was a movement of men rising to their feet. Beyond Cavour's shoulder Jenny saw the tawny head of Steven Blake.

'Good evening, gentlemen. This is an unexpected pleasure.'

There was a blue haze of cigar smoke in the little room, and a salver with decanters stood on a console table. The man nearest the door, holding a half-empty glass, put it quickly back on the tray and held out his hand to Cavour.

'*Eccellenza!* I am happy to be here. A day earlier than

105

we agreed, but after last night's wonderful reception by the National Society in Genoa I was impatient to reach Turin. Signor La Farina approved entirely of my haste——'

Cavour stopped him with uplifted hand. 'You know you are welcome here, signore,' he said. 'I presume you reached Turin with Mr. Blake's assistance?'

The man smiled. He was of medium height, with blue sailor's eyes, and was dressed in the rough frieze of a sailor's go-ashores. A chestnut beard and thick hair of the same colour, tinged with grey, gave his square face something of a lion's look.

'Signor Blake was most efficient, Excellency.' He smiled at Steven, but Steven was looking only at Jenny, standing shyly in the open door behind Cavour. The prime minister, following his eyes, drew the girl forward.

'This young lady,' he said, 'is a friend of my niece, Madame di Alfieri, and an old acquaintance of Mr. Blake. I propose we leave the young people to entertain each other while we begin our conversation in my study. Will you step this way?'

The man with the sailor's eyes gave Jenny a keen look and a smile; both he and his companion bowed to her politely before passing through the inner door Cavour held open. He closed it after them and kept his hand on the latch.

'The facts, quickly!' he said to Steve.

'The reception he got last night was tremendous,' Steven said. 'He was cheered to the echo when he came in and when he addressed the Society, and Mercantini began to compose some sort of battle-hymn in his honour. I think the whole thing went to his head a bit— in any event he wanted to start for Turin right away. La Farina said no at first. Then we realised the danger of keeping him in a small hotel in Genoa. By noon today so many people knew he had arrived, there might have been a demonstration in the streets.'

'Go on,' said Cavour.

'Well, sir, I arranged for them to travel on the 5.30 up, due here at 9.40, so we could get him to the station after dark. I had a private carriage attached to the brake van, and I thought I'd better come up with them myself in case of trouble at Alessandria. There wasn't any. I don't think any of the train crew recognised him.'

'Excellent,' said Cavour. 'He'll have to stay here tonight, of course, and La Farina too, but Rinaldo will take care of that. Well!' he sighed. 'I'm in for it now; he'll talk till two o'clock tomorrow morning, and I expected to have twenty-four hours in hand before we started. It can't be helped. I don't wonder at his impatience; he's waited nearly ten years for this.' Cavour shrugged. 'And so have we, God knows ... and so have we!'

'Jenny!'

They were alone in the little room, and Steven had taken two strides from his place behind the desk to Jenny in her blue dress, with her bare shoulders and tumbled curls and her brown eyes shining.

'Jenny—darling—you came to me again——'

She was in his arms, where she had longed to be in the unforgettable last hours of her childhood, and the lips Steven kissed were a woman's lips, burning towards the fulfilment of that early love.

'Little Jenny ... little sweetheart ... my God, I thought this would never happen!'

'You wanted it to happen?'

'Ever since that day at Plombières, when you were like a rose——' He began kissing her neck and naked shoulders, forcing her backwards by sheer weight and height. She bent like a reed before him, with her body moulded and clinging to his own, and in her ears there echoed the roar of the torrent and the wind in the California pines of long ago.

'Steven, please, you're hurting me.'

He muttered something with his mouth on hers, and let her go, but keeping one arm around her made her sit down beside him on a little red rep sofa near the fire. Jenny turned towards his shoulder, hiding her eyes. Very far away at the back of her mind there was a thought, the memory of a taunt which she rejected; the reason for a recent flight, which she wanted only to forget.

'Jenny, look up, and tell me that you're happy now.'

'Are you?'

'My God, yes!' She wanted him to say 'I love you', to give her the right to say that she loved him, but instead he began to kiss her desperately, and between kisses to repeat the words 'happy' and 'happy now', until (lying back on the sofa cushions, with his dark red hair brushing her white shoulder) she thought she heard him say 'happy at Bardonnechia', and raised her head to whisper,

'Oh yes, Steven, yes, I would be very happy at Bardonnechia.'

As soon as she said the words she could see the log cabin, snow-covered between its two sentinel pines, the bedroom with the turkey-red covers and the living-room window which framed the Aiguille de Scolette, and understood that this was the image of home and love which she had carried in her heart for weeks past. She waited smiling, with closed eyes, for his kiss.

It did not come. Instead, she heard the words, as if wrenched from him:

'But God knows when I'll ever get back there.'

Jenny opened her eyes. The vision of the cabin faded, and she was in the anteroom to Count Cavour's study, where every inch of the red flock wallpaper was covered with the portraits of European celebrities respectfully offered to the prime minister of Sardinia. A bronze bust of King Victor Emmanuel II stood on the mantelpiece.

'Haven't you *been* there, working on the Tunnel, all this while?'

'I've been in Genoa since the fifteenth of November, dear.'

'Supervising the drilling machinery—the Sommeiller rock drill, isn't it? To be delivered at Bardonnechia next June?'

'You're a clever girl to remember.' Steve's clasp on Jenny relaxed. He sat back in his own corner of the sofa.

'Yes; I went down to discuss the machinery and stayed to work on another job which took priority even of the Tunnel. Then tonight, just as you heard me tell Cavour, I was obliged to come back on the express to Turin.'

Jenny cried in sudden fear:

'Steve, who was that man whom Cavour shook by the hand and welcomed?'

'You didn't recognise him, then. At Plombières you said you knew Cavour from the newspaper pictures. I thought that somewhere or other you might have seen a sketch of General Garibaldi.'

'Garibaldi here!'

'Cavour sent for him a week ago.'

'I thought he looked like a seafaring man.'

'He was a sailor in his youth, you know, and again after the Roman Republic fell. He's been most things in his life, Jenny, even a candlemaker on Staten Island not so very long ago. He was telling me about it in the train.'

'I thought General Garibaldi lived at Nice.'

'He was born at Nice. His mother, Rosa Raimondi, brought up his children there after his wife died. He's been living on a little island called Caprera, just north of Sardinia, until now.'

'So Italy's greatest champion—greatest hero—is in the next room now with Count Cavour,' said Jenny slowly. 'Now I understand what Cavour meant tonight—about the sacrifices that must be made for Italy.'

'What do you mean?'

'Because Garibaldi could raise an army tomorrow from the veterans of the War of Independence and the men who fought the French with him in Rome. He could inspire them all to lay down their lives for Cavour's dream of Italy——'

She stopped, her eyes sombre, and Steve said eagerly:

'But, Jenny love, you don't have to worry. If war comes, you'll be safe in Paris or Switzerland. There's no need to be afraid.'

'I'm not afraid. I'm only worried about you.'

'Sweetheart!'

'No, wait, don't kiss me yet. Aren't you nearly as deep in it as you can be? You were in Genoa to meet Garibaldi yesterday. What is this National Society he talked about?'

'A—a sort of dining club,' Steve was inspired to say. 'They gave him a big dinner last night in Genoa. The man with him, La Farina, is the secretary.'

'It's more than a dining club, isn't it?'

'You could call it a charitable society, I suppose. Jenny, don't look like that! It's not like the Carbonari, or even like Young Italy; it's intended to help the refugees from other states, that's all.'

'But you're a member, Steve?'

'Yes, I'm a member. But only to be useful to Count Cavour, not from any particular conviction.' Steven got up from the sofa and leaned against the desk. Once again, he admired what he thought of as Jenny's 'smartness'. She had been 'smart' enough to see at once the significance of Cavour's summons to Garibaldi and she had made a good guess at the importance of the National Society. But she knew nothing—how could she?—about the work he had been doing and had still to do. There was the extension of the freight sheds and the installation of new turntables in the terminal at Genoa. There was the expansion of the marshalling yards at Alessandria, a key town in Piedmont as the junction from which troop trains could be switched north-west to Turin or north-east to Novara on the way into Austrian-held Lombardy. Steven Blake had been working on these war preparations with four or five of the best engineers in the Kingdom of Sardinia: it was in such work, not in the cloak and sword dramatics of the National Society nor the personal charm of Giuseppe Garibaldi, that he had found romance and fascination.

Jenny had risen too. He took her hands in his and tried to draw her to his arms.

'Steve, up at Bardonnechia you said working on the Tunnel was the most worthwhile job you could imagine for any man. Why have you given it up?'

'But I haven't given it up, darling! I'm working for Sardinian Railroads and I have to go where I'm sent! Just now work is suspended on the Tunnel, they can't get ahead without the drills, especially at this time of year, so I'm more useful at Genoa for the present, that's all. Jenny, don't let's talk any more about what we can't help or alter. Why don't we leave Italy to the patriots and talk about ourselves?'

The face she lifted to his coaxing was still troubled, but she was smiling, yielding, when a light knock fell on the door.

'Yes, who is it?' said Steve, raising his voice.

'Rinaldo, sir. May I come in?' The valet, given permission, entered with a small tray in one hand and a pair of lady's shoes in the other.

'Forgive me, signorina,' he said, 'my master ordered hot wine for you—to be sure, that didn't take long—but the shoes, that was another matter, Rosa was certain the Marchesà's would be too small. These are Rosa's own Sunday slippers, signorina; she is happy to lend them, and humbly hopes that they will fit.'

'How kind of Rosa,' said Jenny. 'Tell her the shoes will be sent back tomorrow.'

'May I pour some wine for you, signorina? You might like to drink it while it's hot.'

She drank the spicy wine obediently, thankful for the heat it sent through all her body, while Rinaldo deftly made up the fire and took away the salver with the decanter and glasses used by the earlier guests.

'Who's Rosa?' asked Steven when they were alone.

'Madame di Alfieri's maid.'

'Why should she be lending you her Sunday slippers?'

'Because Count Cavour thinks of everything,' said Jenny. 'He knew without my telling him that my own shoes must be soaking——'

Beneath her skirts she kicked off the bronze slippers, stained with the frost and mire of the road, and bent down to put on the black leather shoes with the square toes and silver buckles which represented the height of fashion to a pretty Piedmontese girl.

'Jenny, where did you come from? Isn't there a reception going on downstairs?' Steve had not noticed the torn flounces; he had only seen Jenny dressed for the evening, desirable and sweet.

'There isn't any party downstairs,' she said. 'Madame di Alfieri and her husband have gone out, I don't know where. I was at the Villa Gloria for part of the evening. I met Count Cavour on the bridge as I was walking back to town.'

'*Walking* back?'

'Yes.'

'Have you been taken to that house often?'

'I went there of my own free will. But I've no intentions of ever going back.'

'Kate struck a bargain with me at Bardonnechia. She promised to keep you away from the Queen of Hearts if I got her the entrée to the Palazzo Cavour. The lying devil!'

'Are you calling my mother a liar, Steve?'

'Jenny, listen——'

'Because I hope you're right. I hope it was a lie she told me about you tonight?'

'What did she tell you?'

'That she gave you money when you left Rough and Ready. A lot of money, and you gave her full value for every cent. Steven, is it true?'

'Was that all she said?'

'Wasn't it enough? I thought you were able to go East because you struck pay dirt.'

'Kate told you that, not me. It wasn't true.'

'But Steven, why should you take money from my mother? You had your wages, what did she have to give you money for?'

'I can't answer that, Jenny. It was a private arrangement. Part of something that was over and done with, years ago, when you were just a kid. Please forget it, darling. Please.'

He was Steven, he was the boy she had adored, the man in whose arms, just half an hour ago, her own desire had kindled for the first time, yet Jenny backed away from him, her hands stiff in protest, as with every clumsy word he seemed to confirm the vile suspicion, which could only have crossed her mind in the polluted atmosphere of the Villa Gloria, that he had been her mother's lover.

'Steven, if it was something you did for payment—up at the mine, or helping her with her law business, anything, just tell me what it was and then we can forget about it, never mention it again——'

'I can't tell you, Jenny. It's not my secret to tell. Jenny, for God's sake——'

'Hush,' she said, as a light step was heard in the little hall, 'Madame di Alfieri has come back.' Over his protest she pulled open the door.

It was not the Marchesà who stood outside, with her hand raised to knock. It was a girl of Jenny's own age, wearing a green cloak over a crinoline of the same colour, and carrying a little green velvet muff trimmed with ermine tails. The light of the many-coloured lamp shook rays of ruby, emerald and amber over her very fair hair, and her skin of a glowing translucence which could only be compared to gold.

'You must be Jenny,' said the girl, offering her hand with a smile. 'I'm George's sister, Claire Lascaris! We took your mother home from the Villa and came on here to fetch you.'

'Jenny,' said Steve hoarsely, 'don't go away yet! Don't leave me without giving me time to explain——'

Claire Lascaris tightened her fingers around Jenny's unresisting hand. 'Please!' she said, with lazy authority, 'it will be so much easier if you come with us.'

Seven

ROYAL WEDDING

JENNY had a chill, and was obliged to spend one day in
bed, and the next sitting up in her bedroom, wrapped in
a dressing-gown and shawls. Sometimes, when she was
alone, she risked the draughts which crept in at the
ancient window-frames to watch the tenement across the
street, where some preparations were being made for the
Natale, but for the most part she spent the two days of
enforced seclusion in trying to come to terms with Jenny
Cameron.

Claire Lascaris had been quite right in supposing it
would be easier for Jenny to return to the Hotel de
l'Europe with her brother and herself. In the presence of
George Lascaris and his sister, it was possible for both
the Camerons to pretend that nothing unusual had
happened that evening, and that Jenny had merely left
the Villa Gloria to go on to a previous engagement at
the Palazzo Cavour. Even when the smiling couple had
bowed and curtsied themselves out, Kate had no com-
plaints to make to Jenny. She expressed her feelings by
scolding Isabella, and making the sleepy chambermaid
prepare a very hot bath for the signorina, as well as putting a warming-pan of hot charcoal in her bed.

Kate, in fact, had had a bad fright, and for more than
one reason regretted the revelation she had made to
Jenny. In her own way she was fond of her daughter, and
was not sorry that Jenny's indisposition gave her an

excuse to discontinue her visits to the court of the Queen of Hearts. She had lost large sums of money at the Villa Gloria since the beginning of December.

Jenny drank her mother's herbal teas, based on the potions of some Mexican *curandero*, and dozed, and lay or sat in the firelight despising Kate, despising Steven, loathing herself. I let him hug and kiss me like a servant-girl, she thought; I let him fondle me as he once petted her. Only I didn't pay him for his services. Oh, Steven! And Jenny buried her aching head in the pillow, re-solved to have it out with her mother as soon as she was well.

But on the third day, when the feverish chill was over, and Jenny, fully dressed, was finishing a late breakfast in the panelled living-room, Claire Lascaris was announced, and once again the charming younger girl acted as a lightning-conductor in the stormy climate of the mother and the daughter. She was so pleased to see Jenny quite well again, and ready, she hoped, for fun and Christmas parties. She was so unconscious of any undercurrents beneath the smooth surface of all their lives, so prettily respectful to Mrs. Cameron, that Kate found herself agreeing to go to the Palazzo Cavour on Christmas Eve, and see the children's Crib, and listen to the music of the mountaineers from the Val d'Aosta who came down to play their pipes in the streets of Turin at Christmas time. Jenny hesitated, but when Kate was absent from the room for a moment Claire Lascaris touched her hand and said with a sidelong smile:

'You must come, Jenny! There won't be any awkward encounters! Signor Orario went off to Genoa this morn-ing.'

'Why do you call Steven Blake "Mr Timetable"?' asked Jenny, more coldly than she intended.

'I've always thought of him as Signor Orario since I sat

next to him at dinner one night last year, and literally *all* his conversation was the 8.15 up from Genoa, change at Novara for Milan, Brescia and Venice, or the down train from Turin to Cuneo, change to the diligence for Sospello and Nice. Such a worthy young man,' said Claire with the air of a dowager, 'but a terrible bore about Sardinian Railroads!'

'He takes his work very seriously.' It was impossible to be angry with Claire, any more than with one of the canaries singing in the opposite balconies. The simile came to Jenny's mind because her new friend's hair was very like a canary's plumage—soft and golden, flecked with darker gold and palest brown like the song-bird's wing. By daylight her skin was as golden as it had seemed under the lamp in Cavour's apartment. Her eyes were the same extraordinary grey-green as George's eyes, and her profile was very like her brother's, with a straight Greek nose and a firm chin. She took her bonnet off, like a child, and held it in her lap while she talked to Jenny. Mrs. Cameron, amused, remarked later that she had done the same thing, uninvited, on each of the two visits she had paid with her brother 'to enquire' for Jenny while the girl was confined to her room.

She was obviously very anxious to be friends with Jenny. The use of her Christian name, startling at first (at Miss Lippincott's Academy the senior students had been required to address each other as Miss This or Miss That) had appealed to the American girl after the formal months of 'mademoiselle' and 'signorina', and Claire's almost childish gaiety was the right counterbalance to the scenes of tension which had gone before. Jenny was romping with Claire and the little Alfieri girls when next she saw Count Cavour, and he included her with the others in a pleasant avuncular greeting. She almost expected him to ask her to search his pockets for sugar-plums, as his little great-nieces were enthusiastically doing. It was hard to believe that they had talked of United Italy on the Bridge of the Po, or that inside this pleasant, slightly shabby, family house there was a locked apartment where a red anteroom, filled with the images of the great, led to the study where Cavour and Garibaldi met.

There was gaiety in Turin that Christmas week, and not only for the children. It was the season of the 'Ball of the *Tote*', when every *tota*, or young girl, in Piedmont society had her one chance of the year to attend a dance, and even to invite the young men present to be her partners for the evening. Claire refused to attend unless Jenny came too, and Jenny in a white lace crinoline walked through a number of the old-fashioned square dances without fatigue, and even, in the small hours of the morning, waltzed round the ballroom in the careful arms of George Lascaris. It was the first time since the Fourth of July dance at Poverty Flat that she had danced with a young man, and with her hand on the epaulette of George's Bersaglieri dress coat she thought a little wryly of her old dream of Paris as a place of perpetual moonlight, violins and handsome officers. It was oddly satisfying to see Kate, resplendent in garnet velvet, definitely relegated to sit with the dowagers.

On New Year's day Cavour's long patience was rewarded. One year, less fourteen days, from the night Orsini's bombs exploded in the Rue Le Peletier, five months from his talk with Cavour at Plombières, Napoleon III showed his hand and made his first move on behalf of the independence of Italy. When the Diplomatic Corps assembled at the Tuileries to offer him their New Year greetings, the French Emperor administered a public snub to the Austrian Ambassador.

'I regret,' Napoleon III said gently to Baron von

Hübner, 'that our relations with your government are not so good as formerly. I wish you to tell the Emperor that my personal feelings towards him have not changed.'

'But what was so terrible about that?' asked Kate Cameron in honest bewilderment, after she and Jenny had come home from a soirée at Madame di Alfieri's on the evening of January 2. They had seen Count Cavour for just a moment as he entered to the sound of hand-clapping, radiant, arm-in-arm with his niece's father-in-law. They had heard the voices of all their Turin friends, an octave higher than usual, proclaiming that *now* the day of liberation was not far off, *now* the Risorgimento could truly be said to have begun!

'That's what they call the language of diplomacy, mother. Statesmen say their relations have deteriorated when they really mean they'll go to war.'

'Yes, I gathered that from all the shouting tonight, thank you for nothing,' retorted Kate. They often talked to each other now in this bluff manner, and Jenny had dropped the conventional 'mamma' for 'mother' and even 'Kate'. There was a wary peace between them, like the vigilance of two cats compelled to share the same fireside.

'If it comes to fighting, let's get out of here. I've seen a stampede at the diggings and that was war enough for me,' said Kate, taking up her bedroom candle. Her yawn showed that she did not believe a remark so civil and so simple as the French Emperor's could possibly end in war with Austria. The Turin government did believe it. King Victor Emmanuel II was working on a speech, to be edited by Napoleon III, proclaiming Sardinia's willingness to answer 'the cry of pain' which arose from so many parts of oppressed Italy. Count Cavour launched a new Italian Loan, which was over-subscribed by sixty per cent in the next two days. Kate Cameron put ten thousand dollars into the Italian Loan in Jenny's name, and dropped the certificate into the girl's lap as a New Year present.

The British Government, too, believed in the likelihood of war. In London there rose a cry not of pain but of rage at the duplicity of the French Emperor. Only a few weeks earlier he had been telling Lord Clarendon how anxious he was to get the French garrison out of Rome, and extricate himself from any commitments in the Italian peninsula. Even after the snub to the Austrian Ambassador, which set the chanceries of all Europe buzzing, he was still blandly telling Lord Clarendon, the Foreign Secretary, that he was not committed in any way to King Victor Emmanuel II, and would not support him in any rash act against Austria. It was no wonder that British newspapers were clamouring for the recall of Lord Cowley, the Ambassador to Paris, as being unable to cope with the Emperor's 'megalomania, calculated duplicity, vanity and violence'.

There was no democratic government in France, where the Emperor ruled by sleight of hand, but there were men who had at least the name of Minister. None of these inferior beings had been taken into their imperial master's confidence in regard to Austria, and accustomed as they were to his love of mystification and suspense, few of them supposed that he meant to do more than keep the other Powers in a state of fretful speculation about his plans. But Marshal Vaillant, the Minister of War, knew better. During that month of January 1859, he was ordered to move Renault's division from Algiers to Toulon, Bourbaki's division into the Dauphiné (quartered in Grenoble and Briançon) and alert two divisions stationed at Lyons to stand by for a possible transfer to Marseilles. Culoz was named as a supply base for troops entering Italy over the Mont Cenis pass.

All this was done quietly, and hardly chronicled in the French press. The first of the Emperor's plans to be revealed struck an unexpected note of romance.

'Giannina *mia*, two little girls I know would like us to spend the afternoon with them,' said Claire Lascaris, arriving at the Hotel de l'Europe one windy day.

'Louise and Adèle? They're insatiable,' laughed Jenny as she went to fetch her cloak. Madame di Alfieri's children were always begging 'the big girls' to play with them, and Jenny found the return to nursery jokes and gaiety a welcome escape from adult problems. Claire seemed to enjoy it too, much more than she enjoyed appearing in the salons. Beautiful as she was, the younger men were not attracted to her, and she gave them little encouragement. But Claire was devoted to her brother George, and he to her; when he arrived from palace duty she would kiss him and hang on his arm, and listen eagerly to whatever news he brought.

'No, it isn't Giuseppina's babies,' she told Jenny. 'It's the royal princesses. Clotilde and her young sister—you haven't met them yet?'

'Not I!'

'Princess Clotilde has heard about you. She sent me a note this morning saying she wanted to tell me some tremendous news, and asking me to bring you with me if you were free.'

'That's a royal command,' smiled Jenny, leading the way downstairs.

'I did lessons with her, two winters ago. (Giuseppina lent me the carriage, darling; in you get.) She's not as old as we are, though. She can't be much more than fifteen, and backward for her age. But then she doesn't have much fun, poor dear.'

The children of King Victor Emmanuel II were almost completely out of touch with their father and his people.

Since the Queen of Sardinia faded out of life in 1855, the three boys lived with their tutors at Moncalieri, two miles outside Turin, and Princess Clotilde, with her younger sister Pia, lived with an elderly governess in a wing of the Royal Palace at Turin. *Il Re Galant'uomo* preferred the children he had had by his mistress, a noisy, vigorous creature, the daughter of one of his sentries, now known as the Contessa di Millefiori.

Clotilde of Savoy was a lymphatic girl whose only beauty was her graceful figure. Her round pasty face, with the heavy underlip which betrayed her mother's Hapsburg blood, was flushed with excitement as she greeted Claire and Jenny, an excitement hardly justified by the dull collection of pressed Alpine flowers which she began to show them. Very soon, however, Princess Pia complained of indigestion, and Madame di Villemarina took her off to her own room; whereupon the elder princess clapped her chilblained hands and drew the visitors to a corner sofa.

'Now we can really talk!' she exulted. 'Pia has promised to keep the old cat out of the way as long as she can—and Clara dear, I have such news for you!'

'Oh, what is it, princess?'

Smugly: 'Papa has had an offer for my hand.'

'Good heavens!' Claire caught herself up quickly. 'I mean—you are so very young! Pray who is the ... discriminating gentleman?'

Simpering: 'It's the French Emperor's cousin, Prince Jérôme Napoleon.'

'Prince Napoleon Bonaparte? He must be years and years older than you are!'

'He's thirty-six. Just the right age, Papa thinks. And everybody says he's very nice.'

'Who's everybody?'

'Well—Papa and Count Cavour. It seems the prince has

122

been in love with me for a long time. The Emperor told Cavour so at Plombières.'

'Have you met the prince, Madame?' Jenny enquired. Clotilde turned to her eagerly.

'*No*, and that's why I wanted so much to meet *you*. Of course you met His Imperial Highness when you lived in Paris? You found him amiable, courteous—kind?'

The plain little face was pathetic in its need for reassurance. Jenny said how sorry she was that she had never had the honour——

'But someone told me that your mamma—that Signora Cameron—had the entrée at the Palais Royal, and knew my *futuro*, and all his circle of friends?'

'That may very well be, Madame, but I didn't go into society when we lived in Paris. I had—an accident, and couldn't go about at all.'

'Oh——' with a disappointed look. 'Well, I shall have to wait until the prince arrives in Turin, shan't I?'

'Will that be soon?' asked Claire.

'He intends to leave Paris in a few days. And once he's here, we can begin to plan the wedding.'

'I hope you will be very happy,' Jenny said. 'Your Highness is called to a great position in France.'

'I'll be the second lady in the land, next to the Empress Eugénie. And when Papa and the French have defeated the Austrians, I shall be the Queen of Central Italy. There will be a new kingdom, with a capital at Bologna, and that's where my husband and I will reign.'

'Giannina *mia*, let's stop at a print-shop and see if we can find a picture of the future "King of Central Italy",' said Claire, as the Alfieri carriage took them back across the Piazza Castello.

'There's a good one in the Via Roma, near the church.'

'San Carlo? I know the shop you mean. Jenny, you

must have heard *some* of the talk about the prince in Paris!'

'All I ever heard of him was his nickname, Plon-Plon, and that he was supposed to have behaved badly in the Crimean War.'

'Didn't you know that Madame Rachel was his mistress, Rachel the great tragedienne? I remember the sensation when he came to visit her at Nice when she was dying. How do you suppose *la piccola Clotilda* will compare with *la granda Rachel*?'

'Clotilde is no tragedienne,' said Jenny, 'but this marriage may be a tragedy—for her.'

'Oh, nonsense, darling, she's longing to be violated by some brute like Prince Plon-Plon! Besides which, she's ambitious, like all the House of Savoy; this is more than she ever hoped for, to be a Queen.'

The carriage drew up at the print-shop. The owner came forward bowing in his long alpaca overall; by an odd coincidence, he had just received a whole consignment of pictures of French notables and was about to arrange them in the window. The Emperor was there, and his bastard half-brother the Duc de Morny, with the same clay-cold face and waxed moustachios; and among the soldiers, between MacMahon and Pélissier, was Prince Jérôme Napoleon, in uniform.

'Do you think he looks like the illustrious dead?' whispered Claire with a giggle. Prince Plon-Plon did somewhat resemble Napoleon I, chiefly in the beginnings of a pot-belly and a hand thrust into the breast of his coat. But the large face beneath the cocked hat was stupid, and he had a double chin.

'He looks exactly like the Corsican basso profundo who sang at the Nice opera last season,' Claire commented. 'I wonder if they showed this picture to the future "Queen"?'

Prince Plon-Plon arrived in Turin on Sunday, January 16, and drove from the Genoa station to the Royal Palace through wildly cheering crowds, waving the French Tricolore and the colours of Savoy.

'God knows how the king got General La Marmora to receive him,' George Lascaris reported to Jenny and her mother, during an afternoon call at the Hotel de l'Europe. 'I heard the general muttering under his breath when the train pulled in, "*Assassino! Ruffiano!*" —that was the least of it! He hasn't forgotten Plon-Plon in the Crimea, deserting to the rear with the baggage wagons. Luckily our hero brought General Niel in his suite. La Marmora always got on with Niel, so the State dinner should pass off well enough, and tomorrow we leave on a tour of arsenals and military depots.'

'That's a funny kind of courtship,' commented Kate. 'How much time is he going to devote to the little princess?'

'Dear lady, he hasn't come courting the Princess Clotilde. He's after the Crown of Central Italy, promised to him at Plombières in exchange for men and guns from France, and Cavour can't wait to get the treaty of alliance down on paper!'

It was concluded two days later, Prince Jérôme Napoleon signing as proxy for his cousin the Emperor, and the father of the bride signing in person. It stated that, in the event of war with Austria, France would put two hundred thousand men in the field and Sardinia half that number, the Emperor Napoleon III to lead both armies as Supreme Commander. Then, only two weeks after his arrival in Piedmont, the surly, worn-out roué was married with great pomp to the fifteen-year-old princess; and in her person Cavour paid the first instalment of the bargain struck at Plombières.

Prince and Princess Napoleon were on their way to

Paris, and the bridal wreaths and banners were still displayed in the streets of Turin, when the news that a further price for French military aid would eventually fall due began to spread through the city. When Austria was defeated, Sardinia—in exchange for Lombardy and Venetia—would have to cede part of her own territory to France. The Duchy of Savoy, the cradle both of the royal House and of the Kingdom, and the county and city of Nice, ruled by Savoy for centuries, were the lands which after the victory would become forfeit to the French Emperor.

Jenny had never seen Claire Lascaris so moved and distressed as by the news of the intended cession of Nice to France.

'How dare they do it!' she said passionately. 'If Nice becomes French so will the two Free Cities, Mentone and Roccabruna—Napoleon has had his agents there for years. And if all the Ligurian shore becomes French the Principality of Monaco may lose its independence, and then what will happen to Cap Martin? The Emperor has always wanted to own it. George has had more than one offer from Paris to buy the Casa Lumone and the olive groves. We knew where the offers came from and rejected them of course, but quite soon we may be dispossessed by force. It really is too bad!'

'Well!' said Kate Cameron, who was walking with the two girls in the Public Gardens, 'that's the first time I've ever heard *you* talking politics, Claire.'

Claire Lascaris did not smile. 'I'm thinking of our poor fishermen, drafted into the French Army, and our countryfolk having to pay the Emperor's taxes,' she said, 'and all to satisfy Count Cavour's ambitions! I'm glad I shan't be staying much longer in his house.'

'Are you really going away so soon?' said Jenny, startled.

'George must return to garrison duty at Monaco next week, and wants me to go south with him. But you're coming soon to the Casa Lumone, aren't you, Giannina?' coaxed Claire. 'And you, too, of course, signora! We want you for a long visit. You'll adore the Riviera in early spring, it's so warm, and the flowers are lovely. Promise me to come and enjoy the last of our peace and quietness, before we are annexed to France.'

'George suggested I should rent a house in Monaco,' said Kate carelessly. 'We'll have to see how things turn out. Have you any news of Princess Napoleon, Claire?'

'Just a line from Genoa. She had a great ovation there, poor dear!'

Within twenty-four hours it was known in Turin that the royal bride had had no ovation at all in the streets of Paris. Driving white-faced and stunned in an open carriage to her new home at the Palais Royal, Plon-Plon's wife saw the Emperor's agents trying in vain to make the crowds applaud. She heard one workman shout, and then another, till the cry was repeated right up to the palace gates:

'Don't cheer the kid, friends! We know what she's brought along with her! It's war—war—war!'

George and Claire Lascaris had been gone from Turin for nearly a fortnight before Mrs. Cameron was ready to leave the city. There had to be ceremonious leave-takings, even at the Villa Gloria; there had to be a complete overhaul of last summer's dresses for the warmer climate of the Riviera. As usual the heavy leather trunks were sent ahead to the hotel recommended in Nice where they were to go by steamer from Genoa, and on February 10 Jenny and her mother prepared to board the crack train of the day, leaving Turin at 10 a.m., no change at Alessandria, due at Genoa at 2.10.

There might be political differences between the Italian states, but one thing all Italians had developed in less than twenty years was a lust for railway travel. To take a trip, however short, by train; to eat and drink all the way, to be seen off at one station and welcomed at the other by a swarm of emotional relatives, seemed to satisfy some deep need in the Italian soul. Thanks to Cavour's development of the railway network, the means of satisfaction were more available in Piedmont than elsewhere, and the Genoa station was crowded with people, laughing and crying, embracing and arguing, when the Camerons drove up.

'What a row!' said Kate to one of the friends who had come to bid them goodbye. 'It was a lot quieter when we arrived here last fall, wasn't it, Jenny?'

'Yes, mother.' Jenny remembered the bright October day when they came down from Susa, and the exhilaration of her mood. She crushed the memory down, as she had learned to crush all thoughts of Steven Blake, and smiled, and chattered to the people who brought them parting bouquets and boxes of the famous Turin chocolates. They were all, she saw, from the new business aristocracy of the town.

'It is the idea of war,' said a plump textile manufacturer, fingering his gold watch-chain. 'Since the Austrians sent another army corps into Lombardy, there will be more troop movements on this side of the Ticino. Those young recruits, now, are heroes already to their families.'

'They will delay your departure, *cara signora*.' For the train was shunting inside the station as two extra coaches were added to accommodate the young men in rough new blue uniforms, handling their packs and rifles clumsily. At last a station official invited Kate and Jenny to take their places in the closed saloon, which was separated from the open coaches on either side by an iron platform. The windows of the saloon were not made to open, and Kate stood on the platform, holding a rail, and waving with her free hand, as the express pulled slowly away. She was wearing a close-fitting travelling dress, and a little bonnet with a red ostrich feather. As the train moved it blew across her lips which, even without rouge, were still as red as the ostrich plume.

'Isn't it terribly hot in here?' said Kate when they were clear of the city, and running through the plain of Piedmont where the irrigation channels had overflowed under the February rains.

'It must be that lamp in the roof. I wish we had a man here to lift it down.' They were the only passengers in the saloon.

'It looks as if you have to do it from outside.' The oil pot in the roof had been lit in the semi-darkness of the Turin station, and while the train was in motion could not be extinguished. The wick was smoking. Black smuts dropped greasily on the red velvet seats and curtains of the saloon, and on the faces and clothing of the two women. The passengers in the crowded open coaches were soon black with smoke from the coke-fired engine. Jenny could hear their cheerful singing above the rattle of the train.

At Alessandria there was a long delay. Kate tried repeatedly to attract the guard's attention, and have the oil-pot removed from the roof of the saloon, but the train crew and the porters were concerned with the complicated new system of marshalling yards, which had meant some alteration to the rails. While Kate and Jenny opened their lunch baskets and ate cold chicken and fruit, the points were adjusted by hand several times before the down express was signalled clear. Once on the single line the train picked up speed. The signpost boards, which at night were replaced by signal lamps, began to flash past quickly, and the express went through Novi without stopping.

'What was that station, did you see?' asked Kate a little later.

'It was Busalla. We're due in Genoa in three-quarters of an hour.'

'We're climbing, aren't we?'

'We're in the mountains now, the Apennines. They run down to the sea, or very nearly.'

'I'm looking forward to the sea. Don't we go through a tunnel first?'

'Yes, the Giovi pass.' Giovi had been the prototype for the Mont Cenis Tunnel, to which, with the first spring days, the great army of men would be returning...

'D'you think we should be going as fast as this?' said Kate uneasily. The engineer had in fact increased speed considerably, and the whistle blew one long blast as he approached the north portal of Giovi. Sparks flew past the windows as the train roared into the tunnel. The only light in the saloon came from these sparks, and from the guttering oil-pot on the roof. The coach began to rock from side to side. The train was hurtling downhill and the whistle blew again and again for the guard's brakes to operate. The signal was not obeyed, and as the train leaped from the south portal there was a fearful screech as the engineer applied his own brakes and tried to halt the Genoa express. It was too late. The engine left the rails and fell upon its side. The coach behind it followed. The saloon, which came next, gave a sickening lurch and ran up the embankment. The two next coaches capsized between the bank and the track, while still inside the tunnel the rear brake-van and the two extra coaches filled with soldiers telescoped into splintered wood, broken bodies and spilt blood.

Jenny picked herself up from the floor of the saloon. She was stunned and bruised, but she could stand, even with the floorboards at their crazy angle. There was no glass in any of the windows. For a moment she thought Kate had been flung clear of the train. Then she saw the red ˙ostrich feather, and the body pinned beneath smashed woodwork, hideously writhing, struggling to be free.

'*Mother!*' The girl shrieked when she saw her mother's face. Kate had been struck by the oil-pot falling from the roof, and there was a little flame, nibbling at the edge of her skirt, where the naked light had licked up a splash of oil. Jenny muffled it with her own pelisse; beating it out with gloved hands and screaming, thinking of the flames in other coaches, and the conflagration to follow if the firebox of the engine burst. Then a ladder reared up against the coach, and two strong, capable Italian farmworkers crawled through the empty window frames, released the jammed door of the saloon and helped Jenny down the iron steps to safety.

They brought Kate Cameron out on the ladder, and laid her, among other wounded, in the field at the top of the embankment. She had lost what consciousness she had ever regained, and the wound in her scalp was bleeding profusely. Jenny sat beside her in the damp grass, with no idea of what to do but put a clean handkerchief against the gash and hold it there. Among the many injured not one was able to do more to help his neighbour than weep, and call for help to the Mother of God.

The men working in the fields, the first of the rescuers, were quickly followed by the peasant women of the neighbourhood. They came running, with wooden pails of water, and their own precious linen sheets to tear for bandages. The young soldiers in the telescoped coaches were beyond the need of help. Their bodies, horribly mutilated, were laid beside the track, and the south portal of the Giovi Tunnel looked like the gateway to a battlefield.

'You're not too badly hurt, signorina? You could look after my little boy, maybe?' A man with the appearance of a superior artisan was speaking to Jenny. 'We're among the lucky ones, him and I. And I could give a hand with the injured if you'd be good enough to look after the kid.'

'Certainly, leave him here. But oh! can you tell me what to do to help my mother?'

'Why, not much, signorina,' said the man after a quick look. 'It's a ragged cut, but not a deep one, and you've checked the flow of blood quite nicely. My view is, she'll come round before long, and I've seen a good few wounded in my time. I was in Rome with Garibaldi,' he added proudly.

'Papa, don't go away,' wept the little boy. He was bruised and filthy, but otherwise unhurt.

'You stay with the nice lady, son. It won't be for long,' the Garibaldian said to Jenny, 'the relief train should be here any minute now.'

'There's a relief train coming?'

'Bless you, yes. The man in the signal box kept his head, thank God, and sent a message by electric telegraph to Genoa as soon as we went off the rails. They say the engineer won't live, though, nor the fireman. I'll be off.'

When the man had gone Jenny pulled up her skirt and tore a long strip off her white cambric petticoat to make a bandage for her mother's head. The bleeding had stopped, and Jenny dared to let Kate lie for a moment in the grass, while she stripped off her own short jacket and rolled it into a pillow for the bandaged head. Kate was beginning to stir and mutter, and the little

Italian boy watched her with terrified eyes. Jenny then noticed for the first time that the chain of Kate's morocco jewel case was wound painfully round her wrist, the case itself hidden by her spreading skirts. Jenny unwound the gold chain gently and fastened the jewel case to her own arm. It felt surprisingly light.

There was a great deal of coming and going down by the line, from which the injured were being carried away so that baggage could be salvaged from the capsized coaches. Jenny felt herself isolated, a useless foreign woman, until just over an hour after the crash the relief train, belching black smoke, came panting up the single line from Genoa. Then, like everyone else who was able to stand, she stood up, crying with thankfulness and ignoring the ache of a bruised side and the return of the old grinding pain in her left leg. She stumbled a few steps down the embankment and then stopped. The engineer who came off the footplate of the relief train, rubbing his hands with cotton waste, was Steven Blake.

She saw him turn and speak to his fireman, and then the crowd from the derailed express was screaming round the rescuers. Four Italian doctors, nearly as excited and voluble as those they had come to succour, and six calm Sisters of Mercy came out of the first coach; a gang of railwaymen and labourers from the second. Steven called two men to his side and began to examine the wrecked engine.

Once Jenny would have run to him, confident that her troubles would take first place. Now she stopped, with one hand pressed to her side, the memory of their last meeting a barrier between them, until the thought of her mother's need drove her down towards the wreck.

Steve was making notes in a carpenter's notebook, quite impervious to all the noise and interruption, with his red head higher than the curly or glossy black heads bobbing at his shoulder. His face was blackened with coal smoke and tense with the furious pace he had driven from Genoa. Jenny noticed, as she went up to the engine, that he was wearing, as at Bardonnechia, a thick flannel shirt without a tie.

'Steven, please——'

'For God's sake, Jenny! Were you on the train?'

'On our way to Nice. And mother's hurt. She hurt her head——'

'I'll get a doctor in a minute. Oh Jenny, you need me to look after you!'

His eyes swept over her, bare head, slim body shivering without either jacket or pelisse, and in fear and longing Jenny began to cry.

'Signore!'—'Momento, signore!' 'Signore, per favore!' They were calling him from every side and Steve said rapidly:

'Where were you going to, in Genoa?—All right, I'll try to see you there tonight. Doctor, I'm going to need one of your nurses. Now Jenny, where's your mother? Is she unconscious?'

Kate Cameron had regained consciousness, and using the little Italian boy's shoulder as a crutch had even managed to pull herself into a sitting position. The bandage on her head had been dislodged, and there was a trickle of fresh blood on her right cheek.

'Oh, mother, you must lie down!' cried Jenny, and the Sister of Mercy bent quickly over the injured woman. But Kate was looking beyond them at Steve's concerned and grimy face.

'Is that Steven Blake?' she asked thickly. 'Then get away from me! I don't want you to touch me, you black-mailing dog!'

PART TWO

ENCHANTER'S COUNTRY

Eight

UNDER THE DOG'S HEAD

IT was six o'clock before the first contingent of the Giovi victims could be loaded into the relief train, which was then backed up by its own engine along the single line to Genoa. Kate Cameron was able to travel sitting up, and with her head on Jenny's shoulder she appeared to sleep during the hour-long run to the city.

'The signora has been very fortunate—*very*,' said the Genoese doctor whom the hotel manager brought to Jenny later in the evening. 'A direct blow on the temple might easily have been fatal. The shallow cut is sure to heal by the first intention.'

'Will there be a scar?'

'Nothing that a careful arrangement of the hair won't hide. I should have liked to reassure the signora about that, but unfortunately I don't speak English.'

'Oh, but she speaks Italian fairly well, and French much better.'

'I assure you, signorina, I addressed the lady in both languages, and failed to make her understand a single word.'

'Let me go to her, please.' They were in the corridor outside the bedroom door.

'No, not now. The chambermaid is sitting beside her, and she is resting quietly. The signora is suffering from a slight concussion, and there may well be some loss of memory, or even some wandering of the mind. Sleep is the great healer in such cases, and I shall send in a composing draught in case it is required.'

'Oughtn't she to have a nurse?'

'I'll try to get a Sister of Mercy to come in tomorrow morning. Every nun in Genoa will be needed in the hospital tonight, after this hideous disaster.'

The sedative in a green bottle, and some pleasant-smelling salve prescribed for Jenny's bruised side, were delivered promptly, and Jenny sent the chambermaid away. She took her clothes off and sponged her aching body with tepid water, applying the salve to the bruises and also to her hands, which had begun to smart. As she tied a loose wrapper above her nightdress she heard her mother moving restlessly in the big fourposter, and hoarsely murmuring her name.

'So hot, Jenny! I'm so hot!'

'It *is* hot, dear, I'm going to try to get the windows open.'

After a struggle she succeeded in opening both windows, and the evening noises of the great seaport leaped into the room. Jenny arranged the bed-curtains so that Kate was not lying in a draught. She knew nothing about nursing, but common sense suggested the danger of a chill, for Kate's silk nightdress was already wet with sweat. Jenny got a fresh garment from the bureau and slipped it over the bandaged head.

She had never lived in any physical intimacy with her mother. This was the first time, except for the night in the post-house on the top of the Mont Cenis pass, that they had shared a bedroom since Jenny came to Europe, and she had seldom even seen her mother in any undergarment more revealing than a petticoat and dressing-sacque. Now as she gently turned and lifted Kate, Jenny realised how beautiful her mother's body still was, the olive skin firm over breasts and stomach, and the long shapely legs as slender as a dancer's. She looked critically at her own reflection in the cheval glass.

At ten o'clock she felt the first stirrings of appetite and sent for bouillon and toast. Soon after the tray was removed another tap came to the door; this time it was the hall porter, with a letter he had been 'asked to deliver to the signorina personally, by a gentleman from Sardinian Railroads'.

For an instant Jenny believed the note must say that Steve was waiting in the hall. As she opened the envelope with her thumb she pictured herself dressing, going downstairs, talking to him alone in one of the parlours . . . She unfolded the sheet.

> 'Giovi South Cabin,
> February 10, 1859.
> 7.35 p.m.

'Dearest Jenny,

'I had hoped to see you in Genoa tonight, but I have been ordered by telegraph to proceed to Busalla by the post road and from there by the 11 p.m. freight train to Turin. Count Cavour intends to open a Commission of Enquiry into today's disaster as soon as possible, and my evidence will be required.

'I wish with all my heart that I were free to come to you and help you, if I could, while Kate is ill. I hope she'll make a quick recovery and I think she will.

'If we had another chance to talk together, as we did at the Palazzo Cavour, I sometimes think I might give different, or fuller, answers to the questions you asked me then. But then again I think it would be better if you found out those answers for yourself—because only then I believe you will really trust me. I will come to you whenever you feel that way, if you will send me a word care of our head office in Turin.

139

'I am writing on my knee, by lantern light, and must get this off now with other messages for Genoa. In haste, Steven.'

The letter, badly written and clumsily expressed, lay on Jenny's lap, was taken up, was re-read more than once as the noise of the waterfront grew less and the hours moved on to midnight. Then she heard her mother cry out again, and went quickly to the bedside.

'Steven!' said Kate. 'Do you want to be my death?' She raised herself on her elbow, and looked wildly round the room.

'Steven, *chico mio, niño di mi alma,* for the sake of the old days, I implore you——'

'Mother, you're dreaming. Mother, you must lie down.'

'All right, Steven, you win; but remember, keep your hands off Jenny.'

Kate laid her head on Jenny's shoulder, so wearily, that the girl wept as she settled her on the pillow and held the composing draught to her lips. But when Kate slept again, and Jenny realised that her wandering mind had gone straight to Steven, she wrung her hands in a fury of jealousy, and what she felt for the woman in the great bed was a destructive blend of love and hate.

A fortnight passed before Mrs. Cameron was ready to go on to Nice. The head wound healed as quickly as the Genoese doctor had predicted, but her face was very much discoloured as a result of the blow and the fall, and she refused to let herself be seen in public until she was presentable. She declined even to be moved to another hotel, although the noise of the waterfront gave her constant headaches which, the nun who nursed her through the first week declared, were bound to delay her recovery. Jenny realised that Sister Maria Annunziata was taking the danger of a possible concussion far more seriously than Dr. Bottini, although Kate had no perceptible lapses of memory and was able to talk to the nun in fluent if incorrect Italian.

The nursing Sister taught Jenny to bandage her mother's head, and also how to prepare and roll bandages and slings of various descriptions. She was glad of the instruction. The hours spent sitting on the railroad embankment at Giovi, helpless to give any but the crudest first aid to her mother, while watching scores of human creatures fainting and bleeding for lack of help, had made an impression on her second only to her ordeal at the hands of Orsini and the summons to appear at his trial. She had felt her uselessness and lack of purpose in the world. As the world was constituted there seemed to be very little an unmarried girl could usefully do, except to go out as a governess or train as a nurse, but only five years earlier Florence Nightingale had shown how a nurse's training could be made to serve humanity. Secretly, Jenny resolved to write to Pastor Fliedner, the teacher of Miss Nightingale, and find out if a vacancy existed for herself in the Deaconesses' Hospital at Kaiserswerth. She meant to do this as soon as they again had a fixed address.

As she recovered, Kate Cameron spoke more and more often of spending some time at Monaco, at least until the Riviera season ended after Easter. Until then, Jenny felt obliged to stay with her mother; it was not possible to leave the capricious wilful creature to spend her days in the casino at Monaco as soon as she recovered from the train wreck. Mrs. Cameron firmly believed that within two months the long quarrel between Austria and Sardinia might well be settled at a conference table without recourse to arms. This was the end towards which the British Government was now determinedly working, with some lukewarm support from Russia and Prussia.

These diplomatic exchanges, in which Napoleon III played his usual enigmatic part, were reported on the second page of the Genoese papers; the front page, for several days, was given up to the Giovi disaster, and the evidence given by *'illustrissimo signore Blake'* that the wreck was due to excessive speed plus the failure of the rear brakes to operate, and also to the deterioration of the permanent way under the continuous pressure of high speed traffic. Columns of the illustrious gentleman's recommendations followed, which Jenny skipped. Steve had not written to her again.

Other people wrote to enquire about them. Madame di Alfieri wrote, and George Lascaris, and Claire sent messages assuring them that they would find peace and quiet at Cap Martin. She urged them to travel by road direct to Mentone, but Dr. Bottini objected, on his patient's behalf, to the jolting coach and the rough post-house at Savona. So, on March 3, Kate and Jenny embarked on the short sea journey by steamer from Genoa to Nice.

They reached their destination at sunset, when the mountains enfolding Nice were grape-bloomed with twilight, and the harbour was lit up like a theatre set. There was a pillared church in the background, and round the quays tall houses, painted in shades ranging from terra-cotta to maroon, led the eye upwards to the old Castello on the hill. As the Camerons drove to the Hotel Victoria a chain of lamps flowered along the Promenade des Anglais, and the music of a string band came from the direction of the Corso.

'Not much sign of the Risorgimento here,' said Kate, 'it's as lively as the Champs Elysées.'

'And so warm!' said Jenny. The March evening was so

still that the palm trees in the gardens of the Victoria seemed to be sculptured in bronze, and there was a delicious scent of mimosa. There were jars of roses in their handsome suite, whose windows opened on the Mediterranean, and two bouquets in circles of white lace paper were waiting on a console table with a letter propped between them.

'From George Lascaris,' said Kate, reading it eagerly. 'The flowers are to welcome us to the Riviera.'

'Is George in Nice?'

'No, of course not, he's on duty in Monaco. He's going to send a carriage to take us over there the day after tomorrow.'

'So soon? I thought we were going to stay here until next week, and see the Carnival and the battle of flowers. And you know what Dr. Bottini said about jolting along on these bad roads.'

'Don't treat me like an old lady, please,' said Kate irritably. 'It's only twelve miles from Nice to Monaco.'

'But Claire is expecting us to go to Cap Martin.'

'Maybe so, but I'm in no hurry to go off to a house at the back of nowhere just to please Miss Claire Lascaris. I like her about as well as you liked poor Nini di Castiglione. Besides, George has found a house at Monaco he thinks might suit me.'

'I see.' Jenny's silence said volumes: said casino, roulette, trente-et-quarante; said ruin. It provoked Kate Cameron into saying:

'You don't have to stay at Monaco if you don't want to. Go spend a few weeks with your dear little Claire in the country, and see how you like that for a change!'

Jenny stood motionless. The proposal to separate, over which she had spent sleepless hours in Genoa, had come so smoothly that she knew Kate had prepared it in advance. She said, 'I think we should both be the better for a change.'

'You do, do you?'

'Mother,' said Jenny, 'don't you think it's time to stop pretending? We don't get on well. We never have. Maybe if we had been together while I was growing up it would have been different, but we weren't, and it's too late now. I know I've been a great disappointment to you since I came to Paris, and I'm sorry about that, but I can't stand much more of this sort of life——'

'*This sort of life!* You've been dressed like a princess, and taken about and showed off, and entertained, and you make it sound as if you'd been in prison! You should have been married and off my hands months ago. If you had only held your tongue at Orsini's trial, instead of criticising the Emperor in public, we would never have been taken off the palace list——'

'If we were ever on it,' Jenny said. 'Oh, mother, please don't cry!' But Kate wept, and slapped her daughter's hands away, and called Jenny ungrateful and unfeeling, until Jenny—administering sal volatile, smelling salts, brandy and water, and various other remedies demanded by the hysterical woman—began to wish Fifine were with them still. Fifine had been the personal maid of several actresses, and knew how to deal with hysteria.

But at least there was no return of the shattering headache, and next morning Kate Cameron was docile and willing to be pleased with the sunshine of Nice and the gaiety of the Promenade des Anglais. They went out for a stroll in the forenoon, to see the new hotels, white as wedding-cakes, and the flower-shops displaying the new carnations which, it was predicted, would make a fortune for the flower-growers of Nice. They walked along the continuation of the Promenade, the Quai du Midi, where the English visitors were fewer, as far as the Place des Ponchettes. Girls with flashing Italian good looks were filling their jugs at the fountain, many of them wearing the white frilled *caïreu* on their glossy black braids. They were laughing and looking over their shoulders at the young fishermen coming up from the harbour where the morning catch was sold, and one lovely creature, with coral ear-rings swinging, was taking a red rose from the hand of a tall fisher lad wearing the red stocking cap called a *scouffia,* with the tassel dangling over his left shoulder. The background to the charming picture they made was the blue Mediterranean, with the slope of Mont Boron rising above the sea.

'They're handsome creatures,' Kate Cameron sighed. 'That girl reminds me of myself when I was young in Mexico.'

'At Monterey?'

'Monterey belonged to Mexico then, of course. My sister Ramona always wore a red rose on Sundays. I preferred beads.'

'Had you many brothers and sisters?' Jenny ventured. To hear her mother say 'when I was young' had surprised her. 'When I was your age' was as far as Kate had ever gone in marking the generations.

'There were nine of us scrambling about in a little adobe house with bars on the windows instead of glass, and one real lace mantilla among five sisters. We all took turns to wear it at the fandango, after we turned fifteen.'

'But you were the prettiest?'

'So your father said.'

'How old were you when Dad came to Monterey?'

'Oh—I forget. Younger than you are now. Seventeen, I think. He came to trade in hides, you know. They called hides California bank-notes in those days, before they found the gold.'

She slipped her hand through Jenny's arm in an unusually demonstrative gesture. 'I don't know why this place should make me think of Monterey. It must be the sea, because Nice is a city, and Monterey—well, it was the Governor's seat, and the capital of Alta California, but it was only a little town, with white houses and green lawns all round the Presidio.'

'It must have been a pretty place.'

'It was warm there, too,' said Kate. 'The girls didn't wear petticoats and crinolines like we do now. Our dresses were straight with short sleeves and we never dreamed of wearing bonnets and corsets. We were so free, Jenny. Free to run and play beside the sea. It was so sheltered at Monterey, between Cape Pinos and the Año Nuevo.'

'Did you ever go swimming there?'

'Some of the Indian girls did, not many. We Mexicans liked dancing better than anything. We used to dance in the plaza at Monterey, when the Yankee sailors came.'

Kate looked about her smiling, as if some enchantment of memory lingered on the bright Ligurian shore. 'I see carriages for hire, beyond the fountain. Shall we go for a drive, and see more of the sights of Nice?'

Jenny, thankful for the gracious mood, agreed at once, and the driver, told to drive anywhere and everywhere, set off to the Corso, where a Sardinian Army band was playing. The rule of Victor Emmanuel II still lay on the city which had been Italian for five hundred years, but any stranger could see that the French Emperor had chosen the psychological moment to exact *Nizza la Superba* as the price of his support in war. The proud seaport, founded by the ancient Greeks, had reached a new apex of prosperity as the sunshine of the Riviera winters attracted more and more English and Russian visitors. The new flower industry, added to the traditional production of soap and oil, was in a fair way to equal the revenue that shipping could bring to the harbour. Baskets of lilies and roses, ready for despatch by road to Toulon, lined the pavements of the Corso; the growers were already planning for the time when the French would bring the railway into Nice.

'*Ecco!*' said the driver. He had headed straight into a press of traffic on the way down to the harbour. Carts and carriages were jammed together with some of their wheels and even their shafts interlocked, while round them surged a mass of people, shouting and cheering.

'What in the world is happening?' cried Kate.

The driver, standing up to get a better view, called back across his shoulder: 'It is the son of Garibaldi, ladies! The young Menotti, on a visit to his father's house!'

Jenny stood up then, and over Kate's protest jumped up on the opposite seat, steadying herself with a hand on the driver's shoulder. At the other end of the quay the tall houses faced a shallow beach where rowing-boats were berthed and nets mended, not far from the portico of the church.

'You see *that* house, three stories high, signorina?' The driver pointed with his whip. 'There Giuseppe Garibaldi was born. There his mother lived and reared his orphan children. Here comes the boy now. *Brava*, Menotti, *brava! Benevenuto!*'

The crowd parted enough for Jenny to see an attractive, dark-haired young man standing on the doorstep of the corner house. He sketched a few awkward salutes, blushing, while a storm of hand-clapping broke out.

'Menotti parted with his father there,' said the driver, 'when the hero went into exile with a price on his head. *Viva Garibaldi!* Down with the Austrian tyrant!'

The crowd on the quays of Nice took up the shout: '*Viva Garibaldi! Viva il Risorgimento!*'

*

Nice was still cheering, still effervescent, when the Camerons left for Monaco in the afternoon of the following day. News had come that Garibaldi had left his lonely farm at Caprera and travelled to Turin, where he had been received in audience by King Victor Emmanuel II. This visit, which so far as the world knew was the hero's first return to the mainland since the fall of the Roman Republic, proved to be public and decisive. Garibaldi was charged by the King to organise a brigade of irregular soldiers, to be known as the Cacciatori delle Alpe, or Hunters of the Alps, from the many refugees whom the National Society had helped to flee from other Italian states into Piedmont. At the same time, the Sardinian Government recalled to the colours all men of the classes from 1828 to 1832. From Nice, volunteers and reservists entrained for Genoa together.

While Nice seethed, Monaco was calm. The little Principality had survived its own upheaval ten years earlier, when—due partly to the revolutionary fever of 1848 and partly to the folly of her reigning Prince, Florestan—the towns of Roccabruna and Mentone had declared themselves Free Cities, and cast off the rule of the Grimaldi. Since then Monaco had been impoverished. Only now a thin trickle of money had begun flowing into the Principality from the new casino, but this had not altered the medieval quality of the old town on the Rock. The traveller stepped back three hundred years when his vehicle slowly climbed the Rampe, passing through the three gates, and entered the Piazza d'Armi where the Prince's palace stood under the great crag called the Dog's Head. Only the flag of Sardinia, flying over the barracks where King Victor Emmanuel's troops were housed, was a reminder that the year was 1859, and that the Risorgimento was a living creed in the land on the farther side of the Dog's Head.

The town on the Rock was not only a medieval town, it had about it an indefinable quality of secrecy. Yet it was not without its open spaces. The piazza was large enough to hold, on the north side, a palace built in several styles of architecture, and with the arms of the Grimaldi above the great doors—red diamonds on a white ground, like a gigantic playing-card. These doors, in the reign of Charles III, remained obstinately closed, as if in protest at the presence of the Sardinian garrison. The Hotel de Russie, the gambling rooms, the barracks itself, were all in the immediate neighbourhood of the palace. There was another space further south, where the Church of St. Nicholas, in the form of a Latin cross, faced the town hall, and a larger one at the top of the Rampe which held the Convent of the Visitation. But the sense of spaciousness was artificial. The secrecy of Monaco was in the three narrow streets which linked the palace square to the church and the convent. There in tall old houses, with sacred images above the doors and windows commemorating some ancient delivery from plague, a thousand Monégasques lived in tiny rooms, dimly lit and pungent with humanity, as their forefathers had lived huddled together for safety in days when the Saracens ravaged the Mediterranean shores.

The house which Major Lascaris had found for Mrs. Cameron was not in this crowded centre of the Rock. It stood with two or three others on a lower level than the piazza, and was reached by a shallow flight of steps leading from the Promenade de Sainte Barbe on the west side of the square. A narrow path, passing in front of the houses to return on the upper level to the church, was dignified by the name of the Ruelle Sainte Barbe.

'It's very small,' said Jenny doubtfully, surveying the outside of the house. It was of plaster, painted a weather-beaten terra-cotta, and the window-shutters, one downstairs and one up, were blue.

'It may be larger than it looks,' said George Lascaris, who had brought them there. 'That side door in the wall leads to the kitchen premises, I believe.'

'And that wooden railing looks extremely dangerous,' said Jenny. The Ruelle Sainte Barbe was almost too narrow for three persons all together, and beneath it there was a sheer drop of two hundred feet to the boulders and waves of a narrow gully. To the right and left of this spot the cliff was wooded and covered with greenery; here all that Jenny could see when she looked over was a solitary cistus shrub, already covered with white flowers. George gave the rail an experimental shake. 'It seems quite firm,' he said.

'My daughter is full of prudence, as usual,' said Kate. 'Come on, let's see what the house is like inside.' The blue front door was opened, so quickly as to suggest that someone had been listening on the other side, by a comely middle-aged woman wearing a plain white apron over a black dress.

'This is Margarita Griva,' said George. 'She will look after the house if you decide to take it.' He stood aside to let the ladies enter, and tactfully remained outside while they looked over the premises. This was not likely to take long. There was a little parlour on the ground level, quite well furnished, and with a charcoal brazier which the servant had lighted although the afternoon was warm. Up an extremely steep stair there was a big bed-room with a dressing-alcove, and a small room behind it containing nothing but a bed and a wash-stand, with a view over a plot of scrub lemon trees.

'Just as well you're going to stay with Claire,' said Kate Cameron lightly. 'This wouldn't be much of a room for you.'

'No, it wouldn't.'

'But the view from the front is magnificent,' said Kate, leading the way back to it. The bedroom, hung with *toile de jouy* in a rosy pattern of birds and flowers, was filled with the light of the westering sun. The sea was very calm, and the headland called the Capo d'Aglio seemed very close. Far away a blue finger stretched at the horizon was the point of San Giono Capo Ferrato. Kate walked to the window and looked down at Major Lascaris leaning on the rail. 'I don't see why I shouldn't be quite comfortable here for the next few weeks,' she said defiantly. 'After all, nobody could want to stay longer than one night at that wretched hotel.'

Jenny acknowledged the deficiencies of the Hotel de Russie. 'But what is there to do in Monaco?' she asked reasonably. 'You can't spend *all* your time in the casino.'

'I'll go for drives, sit in the sun, take you and Claire to Nice for an evening at the theatre—listen, Jenny, I don't have to account for my actions to you, do I?'

'I'm not sure,' said Jenny and Kate retorted, 'Well, I am! I'm going to have a look at the kitchen and a talk with that woman now.'

'Just a minute. Who owns this house, and why is it for rent?'

'I'm sure I don't know why, but the Princess Dowager owns it. She spends most of her time on her French estates since her husband died, and a man called Bosio acts as her agent. He has an office somewhere near the town hall.'

'Well, mother, please don't be too hasty. It's such a lonely place——'

'With a doctor and his family right next door?'

'Where is the maid going to sleep?'

In the kitchen, where a fire of logs was laid between two tiled ovens, well equipped with copper pans, Margarita Griva volubly explained that she expected to go home every evening to her family in the Rue Basse.

'But if the signora requires your attendance, where could you spend the night?' Jenny interrupted the flow of words.

'In the little room upstairs, if the signora wishes.'

'No, that room must be kept for me,' said Jenny with decision. 'The signora has been ill, and may need me beside her. What's in here?'

Margarita Griva admitted sulkily that there was a bed in the back room off the kitchen, with its entrance in the side yard, and Jenny, with a word of thanks, rejoined her mother in the parlour. Kate was looking through a cupboard containing table silver and glass-ware.

'Mother,' said Jenny urgently. 'I really don't think you should stay here alone. I don't like that woman, and I'm sure the house is damp. You've never lived in a little cramped place like this—at least, not for years and years——'

'Oh, do stop whining, Jenny,' said Kate impatiently. 'I'm not going to *buy* the place, you know!'

...'But if you enjoy the Riviera, as I know you will,' said George Lascaris, leading the way back to the Piazza d'Armi, 'you might consider building a villa here one of these days. The Council passed a tax exemption law for residents last February, and the Princess Dowager is convinced that people will want to live in the neighbourhood of the new casino, where the ground is selling at twenty centimes a square metre.'

'I thought this was the new casino.'

'The rooms on the Rock? They're only an extension of the Villa Bellevue down there in La Condamine. The Sea Bathing Company is going to build something really grand on the Plateau des Spélugues, on the far side of the harbour. The boy, Prince Albert, laid the foundation stone last May.'

'"Spélugues" is a queer name for a casino.'

'Oh, they're going to name it for Prince Charles. Either Charleville or Monte Carlo.'

'It's too far away,' said Kate, as they all surveyed the hillside covered with mimosa and almond blossom lying beneath the frown of the Dog's Head. 'They'll have to bring the railroad in before a site like that pays off.' She turned with alacrity to the entrance to the gambling rooms which had to some extent replaced the Villa Bellevue, opened little more than two years earlier, and already a resounding failure.

'May I present two of my brother officers?' said George, as two young men lounging by the door of the rooms came up and saluted the ladies. 'Captain Roncalli, Captain Bosetti. With your permission, I've invited them to dine with us tonight. Not at the Hotel de Russie, don't be alarmed! We know a little tavern called the *Rouge et Blanc,* owned by a widow and her son, who will serve you the finest *loup de Méditerranée* you've ever tasted, grilled over fennel sticks, and with a *vin du pays——*'

'Major Lascaris is a gourmet,' said Captain Roncalli. 'I suggest a glass of champagne before we dine. And the casino, such as it is, deserves a visit.'

Before Jenny could suggest going first to the hotel, where their dressing-bags were still unpacked, a man in evening dress emerged from the little casino and bowed obsequiously to George.

'My dear Major—honoured sir—I trust we are about to enjoy your patronage! Your servant, ladies. *Par ici, madame la marquise, s'il vous plaît.*' This was to Kate, who took it as her due. She was not aware that Pierre-Auguste Daval, the third nominee to hold the gambling concession of the Sea Bathing Company in its three years of existence, promoted every lady who entered the

153

Monaco casino to be at least a countess. Kate, sweeping past him in emerald taffeta, was obviously entitled to be called *marquise*.

There was nobody in the first of the two gaming-rooms. A bored croupier and a *chef de partie*, leaning against the roulette table, became alert at the sight of new arrivals, but George led his friends into the back room, where a dozen dingy 'countesses' and as many blue jowled men were following the *tableau* at trent-et-quarante. The game was played with six packs of cards on a marked table. Kate took a chair at once and sat down at the green baize, quite at home in that sinister company.

The two Sardinian captains, after a glance at Major Lascaris, took the places opposite, and Jenny bent over her mother to whisper, 'Please don't play too long!'

'Don't you want to play yourself, Jenny?' asked George.

'Jenny's too Scotch, she's afraid she'll lose her money,' said Kate without looking up from the cards. An attendant in a grimy livery arrived with champagne, which Monsieur Daval insisted was at the expense of the house, and she set a full glass at her elbow, carelessly, as if she were back in the salon at the Villa Gloria.

Jenny had seen gambling on the *petits chevaux* at Luxeuil, and had rather enjoyed watching the model horses moving round the flag, and the miniature jockeys wearing the different colours. Trente-et-quarante, where everything turned on the number of pips on the cards dealt and the colour of the first card turned up, was boring to watch, and a move to the roulette table, which Kate and the two officers made after half an hour, was no improvement. Daval brought her champagne, and Jenny sipped from her second glass, watching the *tourneur* give his expert flick to the brass crosshead, and the race of the ivory ball round the edge of the wheel. In the badly lighted, stuffy room there was something hypnotic in the croupier's chant, from *'Faites vos jeux, messieurs, mesdames,'* to *'Les jeux sont faits! Rien ne va plus.'* The women in the terrible finery who had followed Kate from the back room clawed frantically at their winnings as the croupier's rake pushed the plaques towards them.

'Shall we sit down in the reading-room, Jenny?'

'George, I didn't know there was a reading-room.'

'It's supposed to be a great attraction for the foreign guests.'

There was, in fact, a dusty anteroom, furnished with a few rattan chairs and tables, a dog-eared collection of the *Illustrated London News,* and an almost complete file of the *Times* for March 1857. Jenny settled her moiré skirts with a great sigh, and George replenished her champagne glass.

'My mother's winning, isn't she?'

'She's having a good run at roulette. You saw what happened at trente-et-quarante? She simply didn't have enough patience to wait for the *grand coup.*'

'I couldn't quite follow it,' said Jenny, 'but I hope she'll soon make up her mind to stop. And George, I do beg you, don't encourage her to sit for hours at a time at the tables. Please promise me, or else I shall worry all the time at Cap Martin.'

He laughed at her. 'You're very careful of your mother, Jenny. Sometimes when I listen to you I wonder which one is the mother and which the daughter, eh? But you mustn't worry while you're staying in our house. Claire is looking forward so much to your visit. In fact the only thing that's going to vex her about the new arrangement will be that she wasn't here to greet you and take you straight home with her tonight. But I've sent a message to the Casa Lumone, and Mario will be here to fetch you in the mule-cart tomorrow morning.'

'Mario's your butler, or your steward—which?'

'Mario looks after everything. He was my orderly in the Crimea.'

Jenny nodded. The third glass of champagne had gone to her head a little. She felt relaxed and at ease. George Lascaris, astride one of the rattan chairs, was smiling as he watched her.

'Jenny! George! You should have been there to see!' Kate burst in upon them, radiant, her hands full of plaques, Captain Bosetti behind her with more plaques in his handkerchief. 'I changed my last bet, at the last minute, from *en plein* to *transversale pleine,* and look what happened! I'm going to quit now while I'm ahead of the game!'

'How splendid, mamma, now we can go to dinner.' Jenny said thankfully, and looked her gratitude as Captain Roncalli came up with her mother's cloak. Kate was in her element. In the dishevelled emerald taffeta, with the black hair she usually wore with a high comb, Spanish fashion, dressed low to hide the Giovi scar, she looked no older than the Sardinian officers. Her brilliant eyes were flashing on them both.

'Just at the last moment I pushed my counter off *en plein*——'

'Bosetti,' George Lascaris said, 'see about getting cash for Mrs. Cameron's winnings, and follow us down to the *Rouge et Blanc*. We two will go ahead and order the *loup de mer.*'

Kate hardly noticed their departure. She was arranging her plaques, in piles of ten, on the ramshackle table which held the magazines.

'Aren't we going right into the town?' asked Jenny, as George Lascaris made for the west side of the palace piazza.

'There's no hurry.' He looked down at her, with something more proprietary in his tone than she had yet heard there. 'Bosetti will take a very long time to change the plaques, because it's like drawing eye-teeth to get cash out of Daval at present. The casino is running short of money—and the bank's reserves on the roulette table are only five thousand francs.'

'You don't mean my mother has actually *broken* the bank?'

'Not quite,' he said, 'but the Princess Dowager had better start looking for a new concessionaire.'

'What has she to do with it?'

'The old Princess? The casino—the Sea Bathing Company—was her idea. A way to raise money for the Grimaldi.'

The palace was all in darkness, although two Monégasque carabiniers were posted at the great doors, beneath the shield like a gigantic playing-card. The piazza was not dark, for the stars were very bright, and the lines of the Dog's Head plain to be seen. The thickest shadows lay under the trees of the little Promenade de Sainte Barbe, bounded only by a low wall above the cliff and the sheer drop to the Mediterranean. And here the secrets of the Rock of Monaco were revealed in a girl's laugh, a muttered word, a breath that ended in a kiss.

George Lascaris put his arm round Jenny, and drew her into the shadow of a pine. She let him hold her close, not turning to him, not responding in any way except by the slow, mounting thrill within her own body as she stared into the darkness above the sea. She was aware of the young lovers all around them: her own youth was hungry for a man's embrace.

'George, what is this thing crouched in front of us, like a lion?' she murmured, as her eyes grew accustomed to the dark.

157

'It's an old French cannon, *carina*, the Sun King gave sixteen of them to some Grimaldi long ago. There!' He took off his képi—he was in undress uniform—and hung it on the muzzle of the antique gun.

His blond hair gleamed in the starlight as he bent his head, and Jenny closed her eyes as she lifted her face for his first kiss. She wanted to be loved and desired, to feel as if Steven were with her again, and as she put her arms round George's neck she felt him gasp with pleasure, and the sudden tautening as he pulled her hard against his body. He was not as tall as Steven, and his shoulders were less broad: there was a slimness and a suppleness in George Lascaris quite unlike Steven's solid strength. He kissed her in a new way, subtle and exploring, and Jenny felt her body responding and melting, until in a hot confusion she buried her face on his shoulder.

The Italian did not allow her one moment for retreat, but moved very gently until he held Jenny's weight on one arm and could turn her face towards him with his free hand.

'*Giannina carissima*, can I believe—dare I hope you will one day make me the happiest of men?'

He let his words fall into the warm silence and waited patiently. At last Jenny whispered, 'Kiss me!'

'You give me your lips, *adorata Giannina*, will you give me your promise to be my wife some day?'

Smiling with closed eyes: 'You ask too much tonight.'

'But you won't blame me tomorrow, for seeking these enchanted moments alone with you? You will allow me to pay my addresses to you more formally at the Casa Lumone? To consider myself as your accepted suitor?'

'I won't blame anybody but myself.'

Nine

CIRCE

CAP MARTIN could be seen from high up on the Corniche road, and Mario pointed it out with his whip to Jenny as the mule-cart jolted on its way. It was a beautiful headland, densely wooded with Aleppo pine and olive, and as they came near the crossroads the breeze brought a scent of rosemary from the *maquis* growing almost to the edge of the limestone crags.

The crossroads had once been a station on the great Roman road, the Via Julia. It was still marked by the ruins of a Roman tomb, with a diamond pattern in the brickwork like the Grimaldi playing-card, all that was left of the ancient colony of Lumone from which the Lascaris house derived its name. Round the crossroads were clustered a few *cabanons*, home of the peasants, with a tavern, a smithy and a woodcutter's sawmill. The Roman road ran along the high land and down to the point of Cap Martin, from where it wound its way to Mentone by the shore of the beautiful bay which the Romans called the Bay of Peace.

'These are the signorina's olive groves,' said Mario when the crossroads lay behind them. 'March is the last month for the harvest. The country folk are a lazy lot, but we have a full score of them working for us now.'

He turned the mules, as he spoke, into a short avenue half hidden by red roses climbing over the gate posts, and Claire Lascaris came running out to meet them.

'Jenny! Darling! I'm so glad to see you! Welcome to the Casa Lumone! Did that horrible cart of Mario's shake you to death? He insisted on taking it because of the luggage, but after this *I'm* going to drive you everywhere. Down to Mentone and up to Castellare! I'll show you all my favourite places.'

She was delighted to see Jenny, certain that her home would please, and Jenny was enchanted with what she saw. The Casa Lumone stood on the rising ground above the point of Cap Martin, and from a gravel sweep before the door of the gardens were laid out in terraces as far as the jagged, samphire-covered rocks below. The house, built in the previous century, bore no resemblance to the new Italian villas now appearing all the way from Genoa to Nice, each with its terra-cotta turret and swags of coloured plaster flowers. The Casa Lumone was entirely French in the harmony of its proportions. The walls were painted white, the shutters lemon yellow, and a balcony which ran across the front was draped with yellow roses.

The gravel sweep before the loggia, to which the balcony served as a roof, was contained by a low stone wall over which pink geraniums fell in a cascade continued down the terraces, while wistaria climbed round eucalyptus and caruba and even round the palms which bore great spikes of white bloom. Down one broad path a procession of mimosa trees marched to a little beach with a jetty slightly east of the cape, and all over the gardens a carpet of white narcissus was spangled with the last of the wild cyclamen and clumps of dwarf blue iris.

'I'm so glad you like it. Now let me take you to your room and after luncheon we'll explore the garden properly.'

The Casa Lumone was not large, and the rooms were very clean, bare, and open to sea air and sun. The dining-room, somewhat darkened by the loggia, contained little but a polished refectory table, already set for two, some chairs with plaited willow seats and a sideboard. There was no vestibule; the dining-room was entered by the front door, and from it a staircase led to a big white room overlooking the sea, with a white fur rug in front of the hearth, and a grey marble floor. This was obviously the focus of the house and Claire's own domain, containing tapestries she had embroidered, crayon sketches, a lute, a lady's writing-desk and pottery jars of flowers everywhere. One entire wall was covered with books in the leather bindings of the eighteenth century, their gilt lettering tarnished by the salt air.

There were four bedrooms on this floor of the Casa Lumone, two at the back with windows on the olive grove. Claire's own bedroom was next to the big white living-room, and she ushered Jenny into a guest-room where the walls were also painted white. The long french windows stood open to the sea.

'We can have breakfast on the balcony,' said Claire, stepping out. 'It'll soon be warm enough for that.'

'It's gloriously warm already,' Jenny said. She laid her dusty travelling cloak on a chair in the guest-room, and followed Claire. 'What a heavenly view!'

'We can see a long way into Italy,' Claire looked to the east. 'First Capo Mortola, and then Bordighera—after dark you can see the harbour lights, quite clear. And on the west, the Rock of Monaco and the Testa di Cane.'

'There's no snow on the mountains here,' said Jenny. Claire laughed. 'It's springtime, Jenny! There was snow on the Berceau when I came back from Turin; it was very cold and bright. One early morning I even saw Corsica, for the first time in my whole life.'

'What did it look like?'

'Like a bouquet of violets—Bonaparte violets.' She

laughed again at Jenny's look of aversion, and slipped her hand through the other girl's arm.

'But don't let's talk about the boring Bonapartes. Let's talk about you, Giannina. What have you been doing to yourself? You've lost all your lovely colour! Have you been cooped up indoors, looking after your mother? How is she now?'

'She seems to be quite well again.'

'And is she being good?'

'Please, Claire!'

'There, darling, I didn't mean to tease you. I only want you to spend all day out of doors with me, and sleep well at night, and grow pretty again at Cap Martin.'

She smiled, and if Jenny had thought Claire Lascaris lovely and strange in the winter rooms at Turin, she thought her more beautiful still on the fabled Ligurian shore, with the breeze stirring her gold hair and the sun's warmth printed on her skin.

Still smiling, but quite deliberately, Claire took Jenny in her arms and kissed her on the mouth.

She had often kissed Jenny's cheek, but never her lips, and now she was quick to sense the other girl's withdrawal. She whispered into Jenny's ear: 'That's what George would like to do!'

'Ah!' said Jenny with dancing eyes.

'You mean George *has*? Last night? And wasn't it wonderful?' She kissed Jenny again.

'Was that for George or for yourself?'

'For myself, darling.'

That was the beginning of the halcyon time, when the days passed without being counted, and every day was a happy day for Jenny. There was, first, the waking to the light on the white wall as the sun climbed over the rim of the Mediterranean, and the sitting up on her pillow to look out across the sea which in early March wore its winter colour, a deep indigo, and later changed to a milky, translucent blue which melted into cloud on the horizon. There was the sound of swallows chirping as Jenny dressed, for the halcyon birds came back from Africa early that year and a pair built their nest in a water-spout above her window. Then, after the breakfast of fruit and coffee with Claire on the balcony, there was the interest and absorption of the long day in the gardens.

All things considered, the household at the Casa Lumone was a very small one. It was ruled by Mario, George's former soldier-servant, a tall grizzled Torinese perpetually scornful of the happy-go-lucky Ligurian country folk. He could turn his own hand to anything, from waiting at table to shoeing the mules, and it was he who fetched the supplies of food and wine from Mentone, the nearest town. The maids, Bianca and Isotta, went in awe of him, and so did the unidentified boys who skulked around the kitchen premises, ready to do odd jobs and work under Claire in the gardens.

Although Claire, in Turin, had been concerned for the future of the peasants and fishermen if the Riviera became French, she had little to do with them at the Casa Lumone. She never went into the groves where the olive harvest was in progress, although all day long the sound of men beating the trees was heard, and the rattle as the black drupes fell to the ground. Women and children filled great baskets with the berries, coming from the crossroads hamlet and the *cabanons* on the way to Mentone, and even from the mountain village of Roccabruna. It was Mario who paid their wages at the end of each day.

Claire's main task at this time was stripping the orange

and lemon trees of the blossom which was collected by carts from the Rimmel perfume distillery in the Condamine at Monaco. Rose petals were also needed, and lavender would follow. While Claire and the boys worked to fill their hampers, Jenny weeded the flower beds nearest the house, beaten at her task every day as the cornucopia of spring brimmed over in the gardens of Lumone. The white narcissus faded before Jenny was tired of parting the sweet-scented blooms to find the tiny arums with brown hooded spathes which the peasants called Cappucini, and which lingered on all winter in that sheltered spot. In place of the narcissus a tide of freesias broke over the gardens. Mauve heads of echium rose above the agave cactus, which shook out buds of living coral, smooth as the ear-rings which Claire sometimes wore. The sun grew hot, and Isotta, who had clever fingers, made Jenny a dress such as the country girls wore, a white linen bodice and a red and white striped skirt with a deep bias-cut hem of the same colours. Sometimes at noon she wore a straw *capellina* with black velvet bows, bought in the market at Mentone, but she preferred the country kerchief of white bordered with red, tied closely over her dark hair. After a few days of the Cap Martin sunshine Jenny was far more deeply tanned than Claire.

'Good heavens, you're as brown as a Mexican!' cried Mrs. Cameron, when she paid a state visit to the Casa Lumone. 'You might be the double of my sister Ramona.'

'But doesn't she look well!' said Claire. Kate grudgingly agreed. She looked tired herself, and the rouge on her cheek-bones was obvious. She insisted, however, that she was enjoying herself at Monaco. Some pleasant English people had arrived at the Hotel de Russie, and the Princess Dowager was expected at the palace for Easter.

'And the Ruelle Sainte Barbe? You're sure you don't want me there?' asked Jenny, alone with her mother in her white bedroom.

'No, of course not. Stay here and enjoy yourself. It certainly seems to suit you, though God knows why, if all you get to eat is eggs and oranges.'

'S-sh! You know it's very difficult to get good meat, or even milk, down at Mentone. It has to be brought in from across the mountains. Besides, I enjoy eating eggs and fruit, and fresh salads from the kitchen garden. And *pasta*, mother! Don't you think Bianca makes wonderful pasta?'

'You'll get fat.' Privately, Kate was impressed by the Jenny of Cap Martin, more definitely a personality, much more a woman. She made an effort to be pleasant. 'I don't want you living off anyone as poor as Claire seems to be. I'm going to open a bank account for you down at Mentone, and then you can buy her anything she needs for the house or for herself. I'm told there's a clever banker called Palmero at Mentone, he'll show you how to write a cheque.'

'I might embarrass Claire by giving her a present.'

'Try her and see.'

Claire, it soon appeared, wanted nanny goats to provide milk and cheese for the Casa Lumone. The scene, when Jenny's gift arrived, held all the pastoral grace of antiquity, as the two white goats were turned loose under an arbour of grape vines and Claire offered them handfuls of sweet hay. 'If I could only paint your portrait, or take a sun-picture of you now!' said Jenny as Claire stood with a hand on each goat's neck and a dozen rabbits lolloping round her feet. All animals came to Claire instinctively. After sunset, when she walked slowly down the gardens with a basin of scraps, nearly a dozen cats slid out to meet her—cats who slept in the barn and stables and by day lay supine in the *maquis,* waiting for twilight and hunting. Except for Claire's favourite, a big black fellow with a battle-scarred head, the cats of Casa Lumone were half-wild. They were perfectly in tune with their protectress, whose grey-green eyes sometimes narrowed as her hair gave off sparks of electricity in the twilit time which Jenny called 'the cats' hour'.

George Lascaris visited the Casa Lumone on alternate mornings, and once, at least, he came at night and by sea. A favouring wind allowed him to come by boat from the harbour of Monaco to the little anchorage, where a cross-grained old fisherman named Rocco lived in a cabin on the shore, and to Jenny's surprise and pleasure she found breakfast spread in the loggia next morning, and George laughing over the coffee-cups at her amazement. He was in civilian clothes that day and by no means so impressive in a baggy coat, and trousers much too tight at the ankles, as in his regimentals. When he rode across from Monaco he was invariably in uniform, mounted on a sure-footed beast quite equal to the rough track, which might some day become a road, between the Lumone crossroads and the Plateau des Spélugues where an army of workmen was raising the new casino.

Major Lascaris was the most correct of suitors. Sometimes Jenny felt she must have dreamed that gust of passion which had so nearly swept her off her feet under the trees of the Promenade de Sainte Barbe. Sometimes he kissed her, when their garden stroll brought them into the shelter of a caruba tree whose glossy dark green leaves were as thick as a roof over their heads, and Jenny always responded to his kisses: they stilled, for a time, the hunger first aroused on a winter night in the Palazzo Cavour. But more often George was content with playing with her fingers, and asking if she would have rubies or diamonds for her engagement ring, or calling her his *bellissima bambola,* his *Giannina tant' adorata con la vocett' angelica,* and all the other tender names for which the Italian tongue was made.

George and Jenny were never alone for long before Claire came to join them, treading so softly on the pine needles which carpeted every path that they seldom heard her approach. Then they walked up and down the mimosa alley three abreast, George with one arm round Claire's waist and one round Jenny, talking until Mario came to call them to lunch before George rode back to Monaco. The talk seldom turned on public affairs. Even Major Lascaris seemed to have yielded to the tranced peace of the warm south, for he seldom expressed impatience at being so far removed from Turin and the passions of the Risorgimento. Monaco was in communication with Turin, and Cavour, it was known, had been to Paris, to urge the vacillating Emperor along the path of war. He had found Napoleon III inclined to accept Lord Malmesbury's proposal for a disarmament conference, and in despair had vainly urged Prince 'Plon-Plon', as King Victor Emmanuel's son-in-law, to use his influence on the Sardinian side. Since the beginning of April Cavour was back in Turin, working against time, now enlisting Lombards out of the Austrian dominions into the Sardinian Army, doing everything he could to goad the Austrians into a preventive war. All this seemed incredibly remote from Cap Martin, where the only difference between one day and another was the change from blue to green, and green to silver, on the shifting surface of the sea.

After George rode back to barracks, as the April days grew very hot, Claire and Jenny bathed in a tank filled by the winter rains. Mario had constructed it out of the foundations of an old watch-tower as a reservoir for irrigating the gardens in the arid summer months. The olive harvest was over, and no one came near the girls, who were free to wear only their camisoles and short white petticoats as they lay in the sun on the tank's broad coping, covered with the fleshy leaves and pink flowers of mesembryanthemum. The frogs kept up a steady croaking, and under the eucalyptus trees the air was sweet with terebinth, lentisk and thyme. Presently Claire would stand up and hold out her hands to Jenny. There was space in the tank to swim only a few strokes, but Claire was fearless about plunging, and soon Jenny was confident enough to jump hand in hand with her into the soft dark water. There was a shock and a chill, and then they rose up from the green depths with Claire's hands at Jenny's waist, her face suddenly like a drowned face, and her hair streaming gold as Jenny's spread black across the surface of the water.

Sometimes they carried a rug down to the rocks, and lay in the sun in a sheltered spot, where Claire would amuse Jenny with old legends of the place while the waves broke over the point in showers of flying foam. She would tell of the Gift of Paradise, which Eve carried out of Eden to plant as the first lemon tree of Mentone, and of the Cabro d'Oro, the Golden Goat who guards the buried treasure of Provence. She spoke of the Grimaldi pirates, who had grown rich and bought Roccabruna and Peglione and other lands and castles of the Lascaris, and with especial disdain of the modern Grimaldi, whose folly had only been redeemed by Princess Caroline, 'a French businessman's daughter'—said Claire with a curl of the lip—who had founded the Sea Bathing Company and the casino. Then, as the sun sank behind the Dog's Head, she told of Hercules, the 'solitary man' from whom Monaco took its name, and said Hercules was walking across the sky now, driving the red horses of the sunset. Jenny, watching her caught between foam and sky, thought of Claire as a very young enchantress, singing the same song the Sirens sang.

Jenny was less at ease with her friend after darkness fell, when they sat in the white room above the sea. Some of the tapestries were seen, on closer examination, to reveal strange scenes in the past of the Làscari; some of the heraldic banners Claire had sewn threw heavy shadows across the firelight and the flowers. They showed the arms of the noble families allied with Claire's by marriage: Grimaldi, Vento, Vintimillia, Benso di Cavour. She saw Jenny looking closely at the last one evening and smiled.

'Shall I embroider a coat of arms for you, Giannina, when you marry George?'

'I don't believe I have one, dear.'

'But Cameron is a Scottish name, you said. Is it a tribe, or a clan, or whatever they call it in Scotland?'

'My father said it was a clan. But he wasn't a noble-man! His father was a farm boy in a county called Inverness before he emigrated to the United States.'

'And your mother's father?'

'His name was Villaverde. She was one of nine brothers and sisters, that's all I know.'

'Lucky Giannina!'

'Lucky, why?'

'To have no roots—no ancestors—no ties with the past ... no heritage of ancient sins...'

'You understand, Claire,' said Jenny, 'such things don't matter where I come from. Nobody bothered about ancestors in the High Sierra; all they cared about was gold.'

'I know that, Jenny.... George is a fortunate man.'

'You think so?'

'To make a new beginning with a girl like you. New

blood instead of old stained shields. The Làscari have always suffered from too much—in-breeding.'

She rose and blew out the candles, keeping a lighted taper in her hand. The windows of the white room were uncurtained, and through them Jenny could see the waxing moon.

'Ours is such a terrible history, Giannina. Think of the Lascaris Emperors of Nicea and their bloody feuds with the Crusaders and the Comneni. Think of John Lascaris, a child of ten, becoming Emperor six hundred years ago, and having his eyes put out at twelve and driven from the East by Michael Palaeologus. Think of the murders and incest, the rape and torture and kidnappings, by which the Làscari fought to keep their foothold on a new shore——'

'I don't understand you.' Jenny drew back, the taper was shaking grease over the white rug. 'You say yours is a terrible history, and yet you keep the past alive in this room—the tortures, and the blindings and the deaths. You're proud of the old Lascaris strongholds and hate to think the Grimaldi took them all from you. Do you regret the past? Are you sorry you're not the Principessa Clara, living in a mountain castle with a hundred soldiers to protect you, instead of Mario and the little garden boys?'

'A mountain castle!' Claire mocked gently. 'I'll take you up to Castellare tomorrow morning, and show you what state the Lascaris used to keep.'

The next day was Palm Sunday, and for the first time Claire proposed going to church. There was a Church of England chaplain in Mentone, ministering to the many consumptives who found the climate beneficial, but Jenny did not insist on going to his service. She accompanied Claire to the Catholic chapel of St. Roch at the entrance to Mentone, which was crowded with the lively townsfolk, now solemn in their Sunday clothes.

They had driven into town in Claire's own little mule-cart, which had a gay fringed canopy of yellow and white, and left it at the Hotel des Quatre Nations. There the stable boys put side-saddles on the two white mules, and the girls set gaily off up the paved donkey track leading to Castellare. The way led through the Valle di Mentone, the most sheltered of all the valleys near the sea, where drifts of violet and anemone lay beneath blossoming orchards of apple, peach and plum, and nearer Castellare there were olive groves, and rows of artichokes growing beneath well cultivated vines. The village stood high above the fertile valley, heaving itself up like an animal of stone, a lion couchant guarding the mountains from the sea pirates, and the villagers keeping their feast day in the piazza were as grim-faced and with-drawn as their home.

This was the last stronghold of the Lascaris on the Ligurian shore. Claire tied up the mules beneath an olive tree and led the way along the narrow street to a small stone building next to a wineshop. It was different only from the other houses of Castellare in the possession of a clumsy turret with a dome, and a hall, with the door standing open, stacked with barrels of the last year's wine.

'*Ecco il palazzo Lascaris!*' said Claire in her mocking tone. 'The hall used to be the guardroom, when my ancestors kept their men-at-arms. Now it belongs to the *albergo*. See that fresco, peeling off the roof? It was by Carleone, who painted the walls and ceilings in our *palazzo* at Nice.'

'Where George lives sometimes?'

'Where George would like to live always.'

'But there are people living here still!'

'The upper floors are let out in rooms.' Windows were opening above, and behind the inevitable canary cages a few suspicious faces looked down on the two girls. A stone staircase, once trodden by the mailed Lascaris lords, showed how those humble homes were reached.

'So the glory passes,' said Claire flippantly. 'I suppose we're better off at the Casa Lumone.' She linked her arm in Jenny's and drew her away past the church to the ancient walls, where beneath pleached lime trees a plume of fresh water dripped into a stone trough. There was a wide view across the valley.

'What a very odd-looking place!' said Jenny, shading her eyes with her hand. She was looking at a strange spire on the slope of a distant hill.

'Gingerbread Gothic!' said Claire. 'Another Grimaldi nonsense, of course! Honore V built that church to show the goodness of his heart, after he taxed the Mentonese nearly out of existence. I wonder they didn't burn it down.'

She looked affectionately at the Castellare church by which they stood, and its white walls, like her white dress, drew to them all the sunshine of the mountains. Claire, *clarté*; Lumone, *lumière, luminosité*: all the words of light seemed to glow in her that day.

'I'm thirsty, Jenny,' she said like a child.

There was no drinking vessel near the spring. With a laugh Claire took Jenny's wrist and held her cupped hand beneath the water.

'I drink to our life at Cap Martin, my darling. The three of us—together, always.'

Into Jenny's wet palm Claire's teeth sank in a passionate kiss.

The wind was blowing up again as they drove home, a *tramontana*, coming across the Maritime Alps with a threat of rain, and all evening the shutters creaked and the fires smoked in the Casa Lumone. Both girls were unusually quiet and oppressed. Jenny made an excuse to go to bed early; her heart indeed was so heavy that she fell asleep as soon as her head touched the pillow, to waken before the dawn was in the sky.

The wind had dropped. She opened her shutters quietly, and wrapping a shawl round her bare shoulders propped herself on her pillows to watch for the dawn. It was near the time of the full moon, but the clouds were hanging low over the Mediterranean, and the only lights to be seen were the lanterns of the fishing boats far out at sea. From time to time Jenny could see a smaller flash, close to the surface of the sea. She knew that some fisherman was using the forbidden *speïou*, with its six twinkling slits of mirror glass, to lure the fish to his iron spear. The effect, from the Casa Lumone, was of fireflies dancing on the water.

There was another light, not at sea, which caught Jenny's eyes, and which moved a short distance, this way and that, as if someone who held it were pacing up and down. It seemed to come from Rocco's cabin. Only the hour—which her watch showed to be nearly five o'clock —made Jenny take special notice of that light, for the fishermen of the shore were accustomed to move up and down the Roman road until midnight, visiting a popular cabaret near the ancient portico of Cap Martin. But this light now appeared to be stationary, and on the ground.

She could hardly have known when she realised that Claire was awake. There was not the faintest sound from the bedroom next door, and yet Jenny felt a movement, and strained her ears in vain for a step on the stairs. But the stairs were of heavy oak and never creaked, the front door bolts were kept well oiled by Mario, and Jenny in her nightdress had to slip out on her balcony to catch the sound of a light foot on the gravel, and see the gleam of Claire's fair hair as she went towards the garden.

There was a dress of dark blue cotton, ready for the morning, lying across the chair by Jenny's bed. She pulled on dress and shoes with a fast-beating heart, quickly, wild to be after Claire, to know what tryst was to be kept among the flowers of Lumone. She remembered that George had once come from Monaco by sea.

From the level of the gravel sweep she could no longer see the lantern near old Rocco's landing-stage. Only the flashes of light from the *speïous* still flickered, but now closer inshore, as if the boats were turning homeward before dawn.

She had no sense of spying upon Claire. Rather she had a sense of liberation, of having broken out of the enchantment of life at the Casa Lumone. Perhaps that process had begun earlier in the day, beside the spring at Castellare; now she meant to meet the test of reality. She went quietly down the path from the first terrace to the second and saw a pair of green cat's eyes staring at her from beneath the leaves of a giant aloe. She heard footsteps coming up the mimosa alley, soft on the pine needles, and George's voice, thrilling and deep, as she had listened to it beside the French cannon on the Promenade de Sainte Barbe.

It would have been easy and almost natural to go forward and confront them with a happy greeting, a simple explanation of her presence there. But Jenny shrank back into the shelter of the great caruba tree, and watched intently as the brother and sister came to the top of the mimosa walk. Her eyes were accustomed to the darkness now and she saw the gleam of George's epaulettes as he pushed the heavy boat-cloak off his shoulders. He took his sister into a close embrace and bent his head to hers. While that long kiss lasted the blood seemed to leave Jenny's heart; she dug her nails into the palms of her hands and pressed closer than ever to the caruba trunk. At last she saw the bell of gold hair shake free as Claire's head moved against her brother's breast, and Jenny heard her say in a voice which held the shadow of laughter:

'*Tesoro mio,* have you made up your mind between them yet?'

Ten

LES JEUX SONT FAITS

1

SOME time later, as the first cirrus clouds of a windy dawn were appearing in the sky above Bordighera, Jenny found herself on the stretch of turf among the crags where old Rocco had his hut. A small boat with its sail furled was moored to the jetty, and upon a couple of sacks in the bottom of the boat lay a Monégasque fisherman, sound asleep.

She must have tripped and fallen between the time she left the shadow of the caruba tree and crossed the rocks of Cap Martin, because the palms of both hands were scraped and powdered with limestone dust. They were just beginning to sting and ache as she knocked at the door of the fisherman's cottage.

'Signorina!'

'I beg your pardon for disturbing you so early. I— could I have some water for my hands, Rocco—please?'

The man was fully dressed, even to his heavy boots and scarlet *scouffia*, and the bed in the hut's one room was tidily made up. A black pot of water, slung from a tripod, was bubbling over a charcoal brazier. Jenny took in these details as Rocco held his door wide open to let her enter.

'What have you been up to, signorina?' he said in his gruff way. 'You shouldn't go clambering about the rocks alone. Put your hands in that bucket of cold water and soak them; I was just going to prepare my coffee.'

'You keep early hours, signor Rocco.'

'Not as early as some.' The coffee, already ground and ready for the boiling water, added its agreeable smell to the odours of fish, stale air and tobacco which filled the hut. It was scantily furnished. Above the bed there was a crucifix and a fresh sprig of palm; above the rough shelf which held an assortment of tin mugs and plates there was a creased chromolithograph of a man, carrying a fainting woman, striding knee-deep through a swamp in just such a wind-streaked dawn as was now gilding the little window of old Rocco's cabin.

'Garibaldi and Anita,' said the fisherman briefly, following Jenny's eyes. 'Drink some coffee, signorina, and let me put a measure of cognac in it. You're chilled to the bone.'

'You're very kind, Rocco.' Jenny sipped the fiery drink gratefully. 'But—wasn't this meant for the man who brought Major Lascaris from La Condamine?'

'You've seen the major then? Where? At the Casa?'

'In the garden, with the Principessa Claire.'

'*Principessa!*' growled the fisherman. 'Yes, the Làscari have a right to their title, I suppose... Don't concern yourself about the Monégasque, signorina; drink your coffee and get warm.' He eyed the blue cotton dress, which was wet with dew.

'Signorina,' Rocco said abruptly, setting down his tin mug as he spoke. 'I was going to see to my lobster pots when you knocked. Won't you stay here where it's warm until the sun is up? You can drop the bar across the door, but no fisherman on all this coast would ever disturb you.'

Uncertainly: 'I ought to go back to the Casa now.'

'*Wait a while!*' Rocco busied himself with putting charcoal into the brazier. The red glow of the replenished fire was on his face when he said, 'Signorina, you must go away from the Casa Lumone. It is not a good place for a girl like you.'

'What do you mean?'

'The *contadini* know it as well as I do, but they will never have the courage to speak out. They are the Prince —the major's tenants, and they find employment in the olive groves; besides, they nearly all owe money to that Mario. But I, Rocco, am not a *contadino*. I am a free fisherman, and also I was once a soldier.' He looked reverently at the gaudy picture above the shelf. 'Ten years ago I was in Rome with Garibaldi. And so *I* have the courage to tell you to leave the Capo Martino now. You have a mother, I know, young lady; go back to her. And leave those two before they ruin you.'

'*Ecco la signorina!*'

Mario was the first to see Jenny coming back through the gardens. He had just carried the breakfast tray into the loggia, where George and Claire stood hesitating beside the table.

Claire ran across the gravel sweep in a flurry of red and white striped skirts. 'Giannina *cara*, what a fright you gave me! Where have you been?'

'Did you miss me?' Jenny asked lightly. 'Good morning, George. You're more alert than your boatman; he's sound asleep down at the jetty.'

'Have you been down at Rocco's?'—sharply.

'Claire looked for you in your room,' said George, kissing Jenny's hand. 'She was quite alarmed when she found it empty.'

'I went out for an early stroll along the road to Mentone, and Rocco gave me coffee. Please start breakfast, both of you. I must make myself tidy before I sit down with you.'

In the white bedroom Jenny took time over her sponge bath and, wearing a crinoline for the first time in weeks, put on a dull pink dress with a black silk jacket and bonnet. Her appearance, so attired, made both the Lascaris rise to their feet.

'Jenny darling, why are you dressed like that?' said Claire. 'George has a whole day's leave from barracks. He wants to drive you up to Roccabruna and see the castle and the chapel of La Pausa; you'll be much more comfortable in country clothes.'

'Thank you, George,' smiled Jenny. 'But I saw one Lascaris stronghold yesterday, and enjoyed it very much——'

'I told him we went up to Castellare.'

'——And I really think it's time I paid a visit to my mother. If Mario and his mules are free, may I borrow them this morning to drive over to Monaco?'

The *tramontana* of the night before must have brought heavy rain to Monaco, for the shallow steps leading down to the Ruelle Sainte Barbe were plastered with wet leaves, and there was a mud puddle in front of the little house with the blue shutters. Jenny picked her steps with care. She heard noisy singing in the kitchen yard.

'Good morning, Margarita, is the signora at home?' asked Jenny coldly, when the servant, with a song on her lips, at last deigned to answer her knock.

'*Madre di Dio!* It's the young lady! What a surprise! Come in, my dear, your mother is down at La Condamine this morning,' (here a knowing wink) 'but she'll be back for luncheon and her beauty sleep, of course. Was she expecting you?'

'Then we can have luncheon together,' said Jenny, stepping inside the parlour. 'I hope that won't upset your kitchen arrangements, Margarita.'

'There isn't enough food for two, dear.'

'I am not Dear, I am Miss Cameron,' said Jenny distinctly. 'And there are shops, I believe, not very far from here.'

'Your mother won't be wanting much today,' said the woman, not quelled by Jenny's manner. 'Not after yesterday's outing to Nice with her friend the major.'

'That will do, Margarita.' The kitchen door banged. Jenny went upstairs. The small back room was precisely as she had seen it last, and the big room with the wonderful view of the sea was hot and stuffy. A fly was buzzing angrily against the closed window. The bed had been made, but Kate Cameron's silk nightdress still hung on the bedrail, and her toilet articles were strewn on a dressing-table covered with a faint film of powder. The air was heavy with Kate's especial perfume, called *Green Fruit,* made up for her in Paris from her own Mexican formula.

Jenny flung the window open, took off her bonnet and jacket, and went down to the kitchen. 'The signora's room is not at all tidy,' she said, 'you had better see to it before she comes home.'

'I've only just got here, signorina.'

'You don't sleep in the house?'

'It's never been required of me. Which am I to do first, the bedroom or the shopping?'

'The room, of course.'

Jenny sat in the parlour, trying to read the Nice paper, which existed principally to chronicle the doings of the English colony, until the clattering overhead had ended and Margarita went grumbling off to market. Then she gave up the pretence of reading and in a silence broken only by the tick-tock of a clock in a glass case and the sound of the waves on the boulders far below struggled to assess all that had been brought home to her within twenty-four hours. She could still feel Claire's mouth and Claire's tongue in the palm of her wet hand, hear Claire's mocking question to her brother; what was she presently to hear when her mother came back from the casino in the Condamine? I ought to have my own story ready, she thought wearily, and remembered the two months' grace she had given herself before writing to the nurses' training school at Kaiserswerth. I had better write to Pastor Fliedner now.

There were no writing materials in the parlour, but there was an escritoire in one corner, gimcrack like everything else in the furnished house. Jenny found ink and pens, a blotter, sealing-wax; hunted through the shelves in vain for writing paper. She tried the large drawer under the desk top. It was locked, but the lock had been tampered with, and so clumsily repaired that at Jenny's strong pull it broke again, and the drawer, after sticking obstinately, came out with a run. At the front, on a pile of papers, lay a lady's pistol.

Jenny's hand flew to her mouth. She recognised the weapon, short-barrelled, ivory-handled: it was one which Kate Cameron had always carried in the pocket of her skirt during the wild days before and after the staking of the claim which became the Catalina mine. Jenny had never been allowed to touch it. Her careless, cheerful, boozing Dad had been adamant about keeping children away from firearms, and even now she moved the pistol in the drawer gingerly, as if it might explode of its own accord. The papers which it weighted were I.O.U.s signed in the past few weeks by various officers of the Sardinian Army.

'She must have had a wonderful run of luck to be lending money right and left,' said Jenny aloud. 'Or did all this come out of capital?' She pushed the drawer back in place, impatiently, and once again it stuck. Jenny's questing hand found that the obstacle was a piece of leather—the fold of a man's tobacco pouch.

She knew it was her father's as soon as she touched it. She had seen Big Jim fill his pipe from it a thousand times, and she sat turning it over in her hands, not grieving for him any more, but only wishing he were with her now. Then she opened it. There was nothing inside but a single sheet of paper and a faded press-cutting.

The paper was headed in Kate's angular handwriting, 'Gift repaid by Steven Blake'. It was a list of payments, beginning in January 1854 with the sum of one hundred dollars forwarded in a money order from Chicago, and continuing with payments from Chicago, Bristol and Turin which added up to one thousand dollars. The last instalment had been received at the Hotel Meurice, Paris, on September 11, 1857, and against it Kate had noted 'Forwarded from Saratoga. Repayment now made in full.'

The cutting was from a Sacramento newspaper of October 1853, and was headed:

Rough Justice at Rough and Ready
DASTARDLY ATTEMPT TO IMPLICATE
JIM CAMERON'S WIDOW.

There was a cellaret on a side table in the parlour, on which a glass decanter of brandy stood, half full, with other spirits and half a dozen glasses. Jenny poured herself a dram of brandy and drank it at a gulp. It dispelled the dizzy faintness which had overtaken her and gave her the wits to turn the key in the parlour door before she sat down to read further. Then she began on the flowery prose in which a Californian editor had chronicled her father's murder.

For the first time, she learned that the killer had not

taken part in the fatal card game at Rough and Ready. Diego Valdez had not even been in the saloon when the dispute began, but had entered 'with Mrs. Cameron, from the back premises', taking advantage of the uproar to shoot and kill James Cameron from the rear of the saloon. Arrested, he had declared that he deliberately fired wide, while the fatal shot had actually been fired by Mrs. Katharine Cameron, standing beside but a little behind himself.

'This disgraceful imputation,' said the report, 'was hotly resented by the miners present. Valdez was severely manhandled before being arraigned before a miners' court, constituted and presided over by Mr. Dermot Callaghan. The court found him guilty, and a summary execution followed.' The editor, with a genial warning that the administration of justice in the High Sierra should be left to the law enforcement officers, the Sheriffs and the courts of the State of California, concluded with an expression of sympathy for Mrs. Cameron, who was 'understood to be prostrated by grief and shock'.

When Jenny had read the report for the third time, she found herself half-lying, half-kneeling on the parlour floor, with her crinoline like a great crushed foxglove around her, and the yellowing paper crumpled in her hands. The first coherent thought that came to her was that the man Valdez had been lying to save his own skin. He had tried to 'implicate' Jim Cameron's wife, as the newspaper said, and of course he had been proved a liar as soon as the miners' court was constituted... Or had he? Jenny read the report again, despairingly, without finding one word of proof, one shred of evidence, which proved Diego Valdez Guilty.

And what was Valdez doing in the 'back premises' with Mrs. Cameron? The only back rooms in the rear of the saloon were the living quarters of the Cameron family, to which only a few old friends were ever admitted; and Valdez had been a newcomer to the camp. The kitchen, not too conveniently, was reached through a door behind the bar, and if Valdez had come through that door shooting, he would have found himself within a yard of Steven Blake. Of Steven, who had not had time to draw before Jim Cameron was shot down.

A fit of shivering overtook Jenny. She was afraid to think why these two papers, the report and the list, had been preserved together. Valdez had fired a gun and Valdez had been lynched, accusing her mother of attempted murder, and Steven Blake had at about the same time received one thousand dollars and left the State. She was even more afraid to admit that there was any connection. All that stood to Steven's credit was that he regarded the thousand dollars, however come by, as a loan—which slowly and regularly he had discharged in full.

Steven, you blackmailing dog! Chico mio, niño di mi alma, for the sake of old times ... That was after Giovi. Kate's mind was wandering when she said that.

Dastardly Attempt to Implicate Jim Cameron's Widow. ... When she heard Margarita come back and start slamming pots and pans about in the kitchen, Jenny scrambled to her feet, and put everything back as she had found it in the drawer. Once again, as on the night she fled from the Villa Gloria, she made up her mind to challenge her mother about Steven Blake, and cut her way out of the net of intrigue in which they had all been caught too long. But it could not be done with the chattering servant in the house, or at any time while they could be interrupted; Mario might even come to drive her back to Cap Martin, although she had deliberately left the time of her return open. Jenny went upstairs to wash her hands and curl her hair round her fingers, and take a fresh grip of her self-command for the hours ahead.

The clock in the glass case ticked away the minutes, the surf at the foot of the gully boomed unceasingly, and from the kitchen came the smell of an inferior leg of mutton, over-cooked and stuck over-full of slivers of garlic. It was nearly half past two before Kate Cameron returned from the Condamine, in a creaking fly which deposited her at the top of the stair to the Ruelle Sainte Barbe.

'Well, what are you doing here?' was her greeting to Jenny. 'Tired of life at the Casa Lumone?'

'I thought I'd come and spend the day with you, mother.'

'You might have let me know first, Jenny. I've an engagement with my English friends, the Andertons. But not till six o'clock, that is.'

'You said they were so charming.' She hardly knew how to handle the situation. Kate was looking worse than Jenny had ever seen her, worn out and yet excited; but her black obsidian eyes lit up her face when, over the luncheon table, she answered Jenny's questions about her visit to Nice.

'Who *told* you I had gone to Nice? Margarita? That woman talks too much.'

'She's much too familiar, and not a very good servant, I should think.'

'Oh, she's not so bad. Pull down the blind, Jenny, the sun is shining straight into my eyes.'

'You've got a headache!'

'If you want to know, I have; the Corniche road is really a disgrace. But Nice was very lively yesterday, and George was so anxious to show me his ancestral home——'

'But he only rents a couple of rooms there now.'

'It's still his ancestral home, isn't it? Beautiful place. The Lascaris coat of arms above the door, and frescoes by Caramba, I mean Carleone, on the walls and ceilings. And the family chapel, Jenny, where George's ancestors were baptised and married for nearly five hundred years ... George has held on to that, of course.'

'Claire has been telling me about it.'

'Mind!' said Mrs. Cameron, drinking wine thirstily, 'I don't say it's in a pleasant part of town. Nothing like the Promenade des Anglais, just a dirty old street, very narrow, and swarming with poor people. But it *is* the Palazzo Lascaris, it *does* mean something in Nice, and as George was saying, if a person of taste cared to spend enough money, it could be made magnificent.'

The topic kept Kate interested until they rose from table at four o'clock, when she announced her intention of taking a quarter of a grain of chloral and sleeping until half past five.

'You'll find some way to amuse yourself, Jenny, won't you? There are some fashion papers in the parlour. Or you could go out for a walk. I often walk alone in Monaco.'

'I might do that, then.'

When Margarita had finished in the kitchen and left to see to her own household, Jenny put her mother's long cloak round her shoulders and slipped out. The sun which had plagued Kate had not dried up all the puddles on the Ruelle Sainte Barbe, and when Jenny looked over the wooden rail into the gully where the cistus bush grew alone, she saw the cliff-face wet and glistening in the westering sun. Nevertheless she continued on that wet and narrow path, the short cut which so successfully avoided the piazza and the narrow teeming streets under the Dog's Head to reach the official buildings of Monaco. She knew, of course, that the quickest means of communication with Turin was through the Sardinian Army headquarters, but to use that was obviously impossible. She would have to use the civilian telegraph line which went, by messenger, through Nice. And Jenny knew that she would never rest until she sent her message. She had it pat in her head, and wrote it down without an erasure as soon as the telegraph clerk gave her pen and paper.

'To Steven Blake, Sardinian Railroads, Torino:

'I know one of the answers please forgive me stop I would like to know the rest.

'From Jenny Cameron, Ruelle Saint Barbe, Monaco.'

The gaming rooms on the Rock of Monaco had changed somewhat, and for the better, since Jenny's first visit early in March, though it was probably too late to save Monsieur Daval's position as concessionaire, which had been ruined in the sordid Villa Bellevue down in La Condamine. The Bellevue casino had depended entirely on gamblers from Nice, travelling daily over the Corniche road in a coach accommodating twelve, or who were willing to risk the trip in an unseaworthy craft called the *Palmaria*, whose voyages to Monaco depended entirely on her captain's sobriety. Now, on the Rock, the Hotel de Russie was providing meals as well as rooms, and some English visitors of the better class had begun to migrate from further along the coast. They were hardy enough to patronise the Sea Bathing Establishment, which was very little more than a fenced-off corner of the harbour, and they spent the evening in the gambling rooms. Kate's new friends, the Andertons, were well-scrubbed, well-dressed and prosperous. They, and a few more like them, were a leaven of prosperity in the mass of dingy *comtesses* and *marquises* who by seven o'clock crowded the roulette table, coaxing counters from the foreigners 'for luck', and keeping an eager eye on Monsieur Daval's service of free champagne.

Kate had eaten nothing since her very late luncheon. Margarita, she said vaguely, usually had supper ready later on; sometimes she had a guest to share it, sometimes not. She made Jenny pour her a tumbler of brandy and water before they went out, without considering whether brandy and a dose of chloral would mix well, and she was drinking champagne liberally now. In the rooms, after introducing her daughter to the Andertons, she paid little attention to Jenny. The feverish glitter in her eyes, and the eagerness with which she settled down to roulette, showed that Mrs. Cameron was at grips with the serious business of the night.

She had, of course, a system; and equally of course, that system did not work. Jenny, sitting opposite, saw pile after pile of her mother's *plaques* shovelled away by the croupier's rake. Two hard spots of colour began to burn in Kate Cameron's cheeks, and several times, with uncontrollable nervousness, she jumped to her feet to place her counters on the far side of the table. Jenny herself had the traditional beginner's luck. Jovial Mr. Anderton, delighted to have a pretty girl sitting beside him, bought a few *plaques* to start her off, and by dint of flinging these upon the green baize indiscriminately and caring not at all where they fell, Jenny soon found a large pile of counters in front of her. She was not elated. The heat and the lamps made her yawn, and there was something intolerably boring in the flick of the little ball round the revolving wheel, and the croupier's monotonous chant: '*Faites vos jeux, mesdames, messieurs ... Les jeux sont faits! Rien ne va plus.*'

At about half past nine there was a movement among the Sardinian officers grouped near the door, and George Lascaris came in. Jenny saw him at once, and noticed that he had been back to barracks, for the uniform of his night visit to Cap Martin had been exchanged for full regimentals, and he was wearing his dress sword and white gloves. He looked handsome and determined, what Italians called *prepotente*, as he pushed his way through the little crowd and came up to kiss Jenny's hand. '*Giannina cara!*' he said, and then, across the table, 'Signora, may I have the favour of a word with you?'

'In a moment, George.'

'*Les jeux sont faits!*' intoned the croupier. '*Rien ne va plus.*'

The wheel spun, the ball fell into the slot, the croupier pushed the *plaques* across the table to the winners. Kate rose reluctantly.

'Yes, George, what is it?'

'Will you come into the reading-room? You too, Jenny?'

The empty reading-room, to which a vase of flowers and a few copies of *L'Illustration* had been added, smelled execrably of stale cigar smoke. George began at once: 'Jenny, Mario and the mules are waiting. May I have the pleasure of escorting you back to Cap Martin?'

'It's rather late, isn't it, for a five-mile drive? I thought I might stay at the Ruelle Sainte Barbe tonight.'

Kate said, with affected indifference, 'I don't know if the room has been made ready. But Margarita must arrange something; it *is* too late for a drive across the Corniche—even in your care, George.'

'It's bright moonlight, and Mario knows the way blindfold. Come, Jenny! What am I to say to poor little Claire? She's been crying her eyes out since you left us so abruptly this morning.'

'What! Were you at Cap Martin today?' cried Kate.

'We had breakfast together this morning, mother.'

'You never told me that. What a sly little cat you are!'

'May we go to your house, Kate? There's something I want to say to you—and not in the casino, please.'

'It must be something very serious!' But Kate allowed him to fetch their cloaks, and change Jenny's winnings, and then to escort them across the piazza in the clear moonlight, that made a shining path across the sea.

'Go into the parlour, please.' Kate went straight upstairs, and George with the confidence of familiarity applied a vesta match to the oil lamp in the moonlit parlour. Margarita appeared from the kitchen premises. *'Ecco il signor maggiore!'* she said in her familiar way. 'Does she want me to serve supper now?'

'Wait until we ring for it,' said George. He was standing on the rug before the fireless hearth with his back to the clock in the glass case, much more the master of the house in the Ruelle Sainte Barbe than Claire's gentle authority allowed at the Casa Lumone. He swung round on Jenny as the servant closed the door.

'Giannina, I've been in hell all day!' he said dramatically. 'Why did you leave us, why won't you come back to Claire with me? Have we offended you in any way? Have you forgotten that wonderful night here in Monaco, when you first allowed me to tell you of my hopes?'

'When you told me of your hopes for the first and last time,' said Jenny. 'Does your presence here tonight mean that you have made up your mind between the two of us—my mother and me?'

George Lascaris started. For a moment he honestly failed to understand her. Then the recollection of Claire's words in the hour before the dawn, and all that had come after, broke over him in a wave of heat and anger.

'You were listening!'

'Who was listening?' Kate swept in, trailing the scent

of *Green Fruit*, with her heavy eyelids powdered and her lip-rouge fresh. '*I'm* ready to listen now, George. Do you want a drink?'

'No, never mind that.' He set his teeth hard upon his temper. 'I am here for a purpose, my dear Kate. To ask formally for the hand of your daughter in marriage. She has allowed me to hope that she will not be indifferent to my suit.'

'You and Jenny? *Jenny?* No!'

Jenny covered her eyes with her hands. Instinct told her that repetition of her name meant only one thing: 'Jenny—and not me!' She could not bear her mother's stricken face.

'Dear lady, it is six months since I first met your lovely and accomplished daughter. You must have been aware how deeply I admired her, how anxious I was for her to know my sister better, how happy I was when you brought her to the Riviera——'

'How happy you've been, night after night, in this house, with me.'

'Mother!'

'Giannina, for God's sake, don't wilfully misunderstand her——'

'You think I don't know what I'm saying?' cried Kate Cameron. 'You think I'm trying to make you believe George was my lover?'

'I'm sure he never was,' said Jenny flatly, 'I'm also sure he took, and you gave willingly, every possible favour—except the last.'

Major Lascaris caught at Kate's uplifted arm. 'Don't be a damned fool!' he said. The real man, brutal and cold, came out from beneath the prepared speeches, and then Kate Cameron, as if his touch had set her on fire, flung herself sobbing into his arms.

'*Giorgio! Giorgio mio!* Weren't we happy here, you

and I alone with the night and the sea? And weren't we happy yesterday, when you took me to Nice and showed me the old *palazzo* which means so much to you? Do you remember how you kissed me when I said the place needed a fortune to restore it, but it could be done?'

'Perhaps he was thinking of my fortune, and not yours?' suggested Jenny.

'Tell her *that's* not true,' gasped Kate.

'Giannina, your mother quite misunderstands me. I wanted her to visit the home of my ancestors, certainly, so that she might see how it could be made a fit home for her daughter. The title of Principessa di Làscari can surely be put into the balance of any marriage settlement in Europe!'

'You expect me to give Jenny money, so that she can marry *you*?'

George smiled. 'I don't know how Americans arrange these things. But I know the fortune, which you seem to be doing your best to dissipate, was made by the late James Cameron, and Jenny, it must follow, is her father's heiress.'

'You fool, I was never married to her father!' shrieked Kate Cameron, and collapsed sobbing on the couch.

'The signora is better now, Margarita. You may take the water-jug away.'

These were the first words which made sense to Kate as she came back to an awareness of water on her forehead and the breast of her gown. She was half sitting and half lying on the sofa, with her head twisted round on the horsehair pillow, and Jenny was kneeling on the floor beside her with a glass of water in her hand. Kate sat up stiffly, pressing her hands to her head.

'Are you really better, mother? Well enough to talk?'

'My head aches.'

193

'I'm sorry.' Jenny got up and took a chair. Her face was in deep shadow, her young body erect: Kate could not see the immense effort she made to keep her shoulders squared.

'Where's George?'

'I asked him to leave us, and I imagine he was glad to go. Mother, was that the truth you told us, or a lie? Was I really—born out of wedlock?'

'Yes, Jenny.'

'Oh-h!' Over that gasp Kate Cameron spoke rapidly. 'I told you I was only seventeen when your father came to Monterey. I ran off with him to get away from my family —it was my only chance; and Jim promised to marry me when we got to Yerba Buena. Then you were born, and after a while we moved to Sacramento.'

'But you were never married?'

'Jim had a wife and child already, back in Boston.'

'Oh my God!' It was the image of Dad that was crumbling now: foolish, drinking, genial Dad, who had never been anyone's enemy except his own. Jenny sat stunned, and the slow tears began to run down her cheeks. She heard the clink of a glass stopper as Kate poured a measure from the decanter of brandy. Presently the woman said defiantly:

'I'm not sorry I blurted it out to George Lascaris, except for your sake. Do you think he'll tell anybody?'

'He'll tell his sister, certainly. Don't you realise that George loves his sister far better than either you or me?'

'Have you any idea what you're saying, Jenny?'

'I'm saying George Lascaris loves his sister dearly. Is there any harm in that?'

'I can't make up my mind if you're too innocent to live, or else——'

'Or else a sly little cat.'

'You were sly enough to keep it a secret from me that

194

George was making love to you. Oh, Jenny, why did you encourage him—the last man I shall ever care for, taken away from me!'

'Oh, for heaven's sake, mother! A man of his age, in love with a woman of yours!'

'My age!' repeated Kate. 'Why, how old do you think I am?'

'We never kept your birthday, did we?'

'I was almost nineteen when you were born. I'll be thirty-nine at the end of August, Jenny.' She sprang up, with her black hair slipping out of its pins, and caught Jenny roughly by the shoulders. 'Wait until *you're* thirty-nine, and see if *your* feelings are dried up and dead! See if *you* don't find out what it is to be driven and tormented, with your whole body on fire for the body of the man you love! And if he cheats you and starves you, leaving you gasping for the thrill that never comes, then you'll understand how George Lascaris treated me! George! George! I know what happened now! Jenny, it was you who came between us. You took George away from me!'

'Stop screaming, you madwoman,' gasped Jenny, struggling with her. '*You* came between me and Steven Blake.'

It was out now, the buried anger, and Kate fell away from her, staring.

'Are you still thinking about him? I thought I'd put an end to that nonsense six years ago, when I packed you off to the nuns in San Francisco——'

'You sent me to the convent, just because of Steve?'

'You were as hot as hell for him, and don't deny it. I kept my eye on the pair of you, the night of that dance at Poverty Flat, and I saw plenty. I didn't want a shotgun wedding on my hands——'

'Is that why you made those horrible insinuations about Steven, in front of that woman at the Villa

Gloria? When you said he'd given you full value for your money, and implied that he had been your lover?'

'That kid?'

'But you like the young ones, don't you, mother? George Lascaris is only twenty-eight. How old was Diego Valdez?'

Triumph and rage flooded in together as Jenny saw her mother's features shrivel. 'I read the report of the trial today,' she said, 'but it didn't give his age. Just—an account of what he said.'

Kate sprang to the drawer of the writing table; the broken lock gave way.

'You little thief.'

'*I* didn't force it,' said Jenny. 'That woman in the kitchen must have used a chisel. She probably can't read English, but I'm sure she understood the I.O.U.s.'

Kate's hand reached inside the drawer and came out holding the ivory-handled pistol.

'Put that gun down,' said Jenny, and fear gave such authority to her voice that Kate indeed laid the weapon on the table with the blunt barrel pointing straight at the girl. *Can I reach it before she does if I jump for it? And why didn't I find out this morning if it's loaded?*

'Is that the gun you killed my father with?' She hadn't meant to say the words, but they came out in one final burst of venom, one determination to be free.

'You—read—the report,' said Kate with chattering teeth. 'Valdez lied.'

'That's what the court said,' Jenny agreed, with her eyes on the gun. 'What did Steven say? What did he see?'

'He saw nothing—nothing, I swear!'

'But you gave him money to make sure. Why give Steven a thousand dollars if you were truly innocent? The court believed you, but he didn't. He knew you had a gun in your hand, and shot to kill!'

'I had to save the mine, Jenny! The Catalina! Callaghan had a mortgage on it already, and in another year Jim would have drunk or gambled all the rest away!'

'So you killed the man who took you out of Monterey, just to save a miserable hole in the ground and the gold they could get out of it. You killed him, do you hear me? Admit it! Say you did!'

'I did,' said Kate Cameron in a dead voice. 'Oh God. Yes, I did.'

She snatched up the weapon she had kept so long, and as Jenny lunged she heard the click of the safety catch and knew the gun was loaded. She seized Kate's right wrist, and threw her against the writing-desk, hearing Margarita's scream from a great distance, and the crash of glass and crockery. Then the gun went off, close to her ear, and a bullet hit the plaster cornice.

'Drop that gun!'

Kate sank her teeth in Jenny's hand. She wrenched herself clear, flung the pistol on the floor and tore the front door open. They heard her call out 'Giorgio!' and 'George, come back!' Then, as Jenny and the servant rushed to the door, Kate Cameron seemed to reel and slip on the wet path. She lost her balance, struggled vainly to regain it, and went through the guard-rail as if it had been made of matchwood. They heard her body strike the cliff twice before it met the sea.

II

The flowering cistus sprang from a cleft in the rock face. Its blossoms, gold in the afternoon sunshine, were blanched in the moonlight, its narrow stem silvered like the barrel of a gun. It seemed to Jenny that she hung to the shrub by one hand, screaming, until the roots gave way and the rocks below rushed up to meet her as she fell.

Then the faces came round her in a great circle, advancing, retreating, whispering, but all staring, so that she turned away from them and scratched her cheek on the hard gold bullion of an officer's epaulette. She was being supported on the shoulder of George Lascaris, who knelt beside her on the ground.

'How is the poor child now?' said a voice from a great distance, and George, equally far away, said humbly, 'Still unconscious, I fear, Your Serene Highness.'

'I'm not surprised,' said the strange lady's voice. 'Come now, good people, be off home. You can do nothing for anybody here, and as for you, signori, I'm sure your urgent military duties require you to return to barracks.'

Jenny opened her eyes. She was lying on the kitchen floor in the Ruelle Sainte Barbe, where Margarita Griva was snivelling in a corner, and the supper was still simmering on the fire. Three Sardinian Army officers, their white dress trousers stained with green, were saluting as they withdrew before the pointing cane of a stately lady with white hair.

'No possible chance? No, I thought not,' said the lady, to someone in the shadow of the kitchen yard. 'You understand, Daniele, no more lives are to be risked tonight. Try again at sunrise—and then send to the palace at once.'

The meaning of the words came through to Jenny. She sat up, clutching at George's belt, begging him to find her mother, not to let her die——

'There, my dear,' said the strange lady, helping Jenny to her feet, 'you're better now. You'll be brave and calm, and come home with me, and no one shall disturb you until tomorrow.'

'Who are you, please?'

'Madame is the Princess Caroline—the Dowager Princess of Monaco,' said George Lascaris, at attention. Jenny dropped an unsteady curtsey.

'Never mind your manners,' said the princess. 'Margarita, you very foolish woman, can't you find a cloak for your young lady? Major Lascaris, we shall dispense with your escort. This is one occasion when we do *not* require Sardinian protection.'

The Dowager Princess must have brought her own escort from the palace, for at the head of the shallow steps men in the white uniform of the Monégasque carabiniers fell in behind the two women. A crowd had gathered in the Piazza d'Armi. Jenny heard a man shout '*La voilà!*', and the princess said in the same language to someone who approached her from the shadows, 'Nonsense! Perfectly safe until tomorrow morning!' Then the doors beneath the monstrous playing-card were swinging open, and sentries presented arms as the Dowager Princess led Jenny Cameron into the palace of the Grimaldi.

The Piazza d'Armi was full of moonlight. The interior courtyard was almost in darkness, for the buildings threw a shadow on all but the centre of the patterned cobbles. In the wing opposite the entrance a light shone behind the *grisaille* in the private chapel of St. John the Baptist, and shapes of angels seemed to float in the warm air. Lamps were set at intervals on the double white marble staircase which led, on the west side of the courtyard, to a gallery painted with frescoes depicting the labours of Hercules. Along this gallery the princess conducted Jenny to her own apartments.

'I always have a fire in this room,' she said casually, as they entered a pretty boudoir. 'Come close to the hearth and get warm. That's better! Now sit down and let me see your hands.'

Jenny held them out, obediently. To the abrasions of

the morning dried blood had been added where she had clutched the splintering wood of the guard-rail. She looked down with shame at her muddied dress, and saw her bodice gaping open underneath the cloak.

'Margarita must have—cut my staylaces—Madame.'

'I'm glad to hear she'd sense enough for that,' said the old lady, touching a bell. 'You must let my maid attend to those hands at once, and give you a wrapper to wear instead of that ridiculous crinoline. Whalebone and hoops are *no* use in an emergency, and very tiring after it's all over.'

But at the words 'all over' Jenny pushed the princess's kind hand away and sprang up, gasping that it couldn't be all over, her mother must be alive down on those terrible rocks still, with nobody doing anything to help her, nobody!

'My poor child, everybody did their best. The Sardinians tried to go down the cliff with rope ladders, and they had to turn back. Some of our fishermen put off from the cove below the palace, and they found nothing —nothing as yet, that is. There's a bad groundswell to-night, and I've forbidden them to go out again before morning. Now, will you go with Marie, and let her give you some sal volatile, and afterwards come and tell me how this very sad affair came about?'

While Jenny was absent from the room Princess Caroline received an official of the palace, who gave her a version of the tragedy in the Ruelle Sainte Barbe which made her frown and tap her foot impatiently.

'One thing is perfectly clear,' she said to the official as he bowed himself out, 'there ought to be a stone wall at that place and not a flimsy railing. I've told the Council so a hundred times. Why is nothing done properly in Monaco unless I see to it myself?'

'Come in, my dear,' she said in a gentler tone, as Jenny

appeared hesitantly in the other doorway. The maid had put her into a white silk wrapper, and brushed her dark hair into a simple knot. Her hands had been washed clean of blood.

'So your name is Jenny Cameron,' said the princess, motioning her to a chair. 'Until now, I fully believed your poor mother was a Spanish lady.'

'She was born in Mexico, Madame. Spanish is—was— her mother tongue.' She hesitated. 'Did you—know her?'

'She was pointed out to me when I came back from France. After that I used often to see her out walking, or driving with her English friends... You were a guest at the Casa Lumone, it appears. Did you know your mother had been losing very heavily at the casino?'

Jenny raised her heavy eyes. 'Is that why Your Highness came so quickly to our help tonight?'

'I hope I should hurry at once to any house in the Principality where such a fearful accident had taken place,' said Princess Caroline severely. '...It is true that I feel a certain responsibility for what goes on at the casino.'

'You need feel no responsibility for my mother, Madame. It was I who taunted her and drove her wild and desperate——'

'What! You think her death was *not* an accident?'

'I don't know what to think!' cried Jenny, and the tears came.

'So you quarrelled with your mother,' said the princess, when the first frantic sobbing had subsided. 'You will be sorry to remember that.'

'I'm sorry now.'

'Yes. And I could give you a sleeping draught to make you forget your grief and your repentance, and give you oblivion for a few hours. Then at four o'clock in the morning you would waken with every devil in hell wait-

ing to torture you with the thought that years hence you
will remember this night, and the quarrel, and your
mother's death, as acutely as your tears show me you feel
it now. How old are you, Jenny?'

'Nineteen, Madame.'

'At nineteen we believe remorse will last a lifetime.
But no one is required to live a lifetime in a single night.
All you have to do at present is live through this one
night, and it can't be done by sedatives that blur reality.
Come, child! Face the truth with me and tell me everything. Remember, not a word of what you tell me will
ever go beyond these four walls.'

The old woman had so far won the girl's confidence
that after a pause Jenny began to talk, haltingly at first
and then more freely, until the pent-up anxiety of her
eighteen months in Europe was released at last. She
began at Sacramento, the saloon and the faro games, and
the red-headed boy who swept out the bar in the
mornings. She described the camp at Rough and Ready,
and told what she knew of her father's death, but without revealing what had been his true relation to her
mother. That fact was so monstrous in all its impli-
cations that Jenny had not yet fully apprehended it.
There was no sound in the boudoir but the crackle of
the fire, and once the twelve strokes of midnight from a
gilt French clock. The bombs of Orsini, the reunion with
Steve at Plombières, the court of the Queen of Hearts—
all was told without comment from the old princess.
Only her gold-rimmed spectacles flashed now and then as
she looked at Jenny over the top of the glasses, until at
last the flash of the gold and the flicker of the fire began
to spin together in Jenny's head and she saw nothing but
a wheel of sparks. Then she felt something soft and warm
wrapped around her, and heard through engulfing darkness a gentle whisper: 'I think you must find your

American friend again and show him how much you care for him.'

When she awoke the curtains had been drawn, the sun was shining, and the Dowager Princess of Monaco was sitting at a table spread with a lace cloth, with a coffee service placed in front of her. She turned with a half-smile as Jenny moved.

'Awake? That's right,' she said. 'And now the first night is over, Jenny; you won't have to live through those hours again. Drink your coffee, child; I think Marie must have woken you when she brought it in.'

'Have you been here all night, Madame?' said Jenny shyly.

'Yes. I could hardly leave you alone, and there is always work to do.' She glanced at a desk piled high with documents.

'How can I ever thank you for your goodness to me?'

'By going on as bravely as you have begun ... They tell me your friend from the Casa Lumone was here an hour ago.'

'Major Lascaris?'

'No, the Principessa Clara. H'm, I forgot, of course they're much too grand to use their title. She brought your dressing-bag and something dark to wear. Not black, but it will do.'

'Is Claire here now?'

'She proposed to wait at the Hotel de Russie and take you home with her. I sent a message advising her to go home alone. Really,' said the princess, 'I don't think you can return to the Casa Lumone after what has happened. We must find some other place for you to spend the next few days. Have you no American friends on the Riviera?'

'I don't know *anybody* on the Riviera, except Signor Palmero, the banker at Mentone.'

'Francisco Palmero—I'll send to him at once!' exclaimed Princess Caroline. 'The very man to help you, as soon as you are free.'

'As soon as I am *free*, Princess?'

The old lady put her hands on Jenny's shoulders. 'Now you must be very brave, my dear,' she said. 'Your mother's body has been recovered. They say that besides the—the effects of the fall, it bears marks of a struggle. And Margarita Griva talked a great deal of nonsense to the police last night. If I had not insisted on taking you into my own care, they might have held you on a charge of attempted murder.'

The parlour of the little house in the Ruelle Sainte Barbe had been restored to some sort of order, and two men seated at the table with pens and paper before them gave it almost an official look. George Lascaris was standing by the window, in a soldier's 'at ease' position, and the carabiniers who escorted Jenny from the palace had joined two others who were with Margarita Griva in the kitchen. Jenny came in with a frightened look around the room. What she had feared to see was not there.

'Miss Cameron? I am Dr. Verrano,' said the better-dressed of the two men, with a slight bow. 'I live in the house next door. I happen to be a member of the Prince's Council; this gentleman is one of the Council clerks. Now, Princess Caroline sent me a letter early this morning asking me to make a preliminary investigation into last night's sad ocurrence. You understand that as a physician I have to issue a certificate of death, and on this certificate depends whether or not the case should be presented to the examining magistrate of the Principality.'

'I understand, sir,' said Jenny with dry lips. '... The Dowager Princess told me that my mother—mother's body had been recovered.'

'At six o'clock this morning, mademoiselle.'

'Where—where is she?'

'The body is at present in a room at the Hotel de Ville. We did not require you to identify it,' said the doctor gently, 'because Major Lascaris and Monsieur Daval made themselves responsible for the identification, and here are two rings which we took off the deceased lady's hand.'

He lifted a white handkerchief spread on the table, and gave Jenny the rings she knew so well. One was the diamond band Jim Cameron gave Kate when he first struck gold; the other, her false wedding-ring.

'Was your mother wearing any other jewellery last night?'

'She must have—no, now I come to think of it, only these rings. And, if you please, I would like them to be sold, and the money given to the fishermen who went to look for her.'

'To Daniele and his crew? Both rings, mademoiselle?'

'Yes.'

'The wedding-ring is generally kept by the family,' said the clerk, speaking for the first time.

'I don't want it.'

'The fishermen will be grateful,' said Dr. Verrano. 'I'll look after the matter. And now, mademoiselle, we come to the matter of the death certificate. I must tell you,' he went on over Jenny's silence, 'that last night, when the carabiniers arrived on the scene, a very serious statement was made to them. By the woman Margarita Griva, employed by your mother as a daily servant. She deposed, although not under oath, that you and your mother had quarrelled violently over the attentions of Major Lascaris, while he was here with you. That the quarrel continued, and that just before her fall you and she struggled bodily with each other on the path outside.'

'Not on the path,' said Jenny.

'But you agree there was a struggle?'

'In this room. Yes.'

'Now before he identified the corpse this morning, Major Lascaris made a statement to the police. You understand that as an officer of the army of the Protecting Power this gentleman is not subject to Monégasque jurisdiction, and came forward of his own free will. Will you repeat, sir, before mademoiselle, the testimony you gave to us?'

Jenny looked up at George. His face, haughty and cold, revealed nothing; she was certain that, like herself, he was weighing his words with care.

'I was present, as the woman Griva says, when Mrs. Cameron, who had been losing heavily at play, objected strongly to my request for her daughter's hand in marriage. I left the house with the intention of returning to the casino. I then felt some anxiety on Miss Cameron's behalf and started walking back across the piazza, where I was joined by Captain Bosetti. At the top of the steps we heard Mrs. Cameron calling my name.'

'*She* was at the top of the steps?'

'No, we were.'

'She was calling "Major Lascaris"?'

'She was calling "George, come back!"'

'Where was Miss Cameron at this time?'

'We couldn't see her from the steps. We saw Mrs. Cameron slip in the mud and fall. We were able to restrain Miss Cameron, who had rushed to the rail, and might easily have fallen, too.'

Dr. Verrano leaned back in his chair and pulled at his moustache.

'Thank you, major. It seems very clear that Mrs. Cameron rushed out of the house in a state of great agitation, and that she was quite alone on the path when she fell.' He raised the cloth again and took out the ivory-handled pistol.

'This weapon was found on the floor of this room after the tragedy. Was it produced in your presence, Major Lascaris?'

'No, sir.'

'Mademoiselle, you have admitted that you had a struggle with your mother in this room, and Margarita Griva testifies that she saw the two of you fighting for possession of this pistol. Is it your property?'

'It belonged to my mother. She kept it in the drawer of that desk, loaded. I was trying to take it away from her——'

'Is that how she got the marks of finger-nails I discovered on her left cheek?'

'Possibly. Would you ask the woman to describe our positions when she came in?'

Margarita was brought to the parlour, sobbing, and Dr. Verrano put the question to her.

'The poor signora—had her back to the desk. The daughter—was facing her and holding the gun——'

'The signorina was holding the gun?'

'Yes.'

Jenny said: 'My mother had her back to the desk and held the gun in her hand when it went off. You'll find the bullet somewhere in the cornice, near the door.'

The clerk, with an exclamation, jumped on a chair and groped in the dusty plaster above the picture rail.

'Here it is, sir.' There was silence while the doctor examined the bullet and the weapon. He looked at George, a long considering look which made the young man turn away his head. He looked thoughtfully at Jenny in her dark dress, and motioned to the carabinier to take Margarita out.

'Miss Cameron, this pistol was your mother's, it was

produced by your mother, and it was fired by your mother. In your opinion, was her intention to maim or destroy you, or to destroy herself?'

Jenny struck her hand on the table with a force that shocked them all. 'Before God!' she said, 'and if I were on oath. I couldn't tell you! She was beside herself—she was hysterical! She had been drinking, she had taken chloral, she had absolutely no idea of what she was doing!'

'Mrs. Cameron suffered from the effects of a head injury and concussion, after the Giovi train wreck,' George Lascaris said.

'Ah! Who was the attending physician at that time?'

'Dr. Bottini, of Genoa,' said Jenny.

'I know his reputation, which is excellent,' said Dr. Verrano. 'More than can be said for Margarita Griva... Well, Miss Cameron, there is no need to prolong this painful scene. The facts seem clear enough, and since none of the principals are natives of Monaco, I see no point in bringing the matter before the *juge d'instruction*. I am quite prepared to sign a certificate of Accidental Death and release the body.'

'The proper arrangements will be made at once,' said George Lascaris quickly.

'Thank you. Your testimony was of the first importance, major,' said the doctor, watching while his clerk began to fill in the official form. 'The fact that the deceased called to you, desired to speak to you, makes it reasonably clear that she had no suicidal intent. Which of course' (he signed his name with a flourish) 'will greatly simplify arrangements for the funeral.'

Jenny was destined never to know the complications of Kate Cameron's funeral. She was protected, through the next two days, by two persons who hardly knew her, but who between them wielded considerable power along the

Ligurian shore. Princess Caroline, whose letter to Dr. Verrano had greatly influenced that good man's judgement, made herself responsible for the necessary arrangements in Monaco. Signor Palmero, the banker of Mentone, was the man who made sure that Kate Cameron received a Christian burial.

It was a topic which rent the English colony in Mentone for many months to come. That colony, in winter, numbered at least three hundred souls, with reinforcements continually arriving from rain-sodden England, and in the reading-room, at the local branch of Mudie's Circulating Library, on the botanising rambles up the Gorbio valley, and along the shore where work had begun on the new Promenade du Midi, the English ladies and gentlemen bitterly debated their chaplain's attitude. Had dear Mr. Morgan been justified in refusing to read the Church of England service over the body of a lapsed Catholic? Was Mr. Wood, an invalid visitor who had offered to conduct the funeral service, really a clerk in Holy Orders? Was it true that 'the daughter, poor girl', had paid a large sum of money for her mother's grave in the Mentone cemetery?

Only Signor Francesco Palmero knew the answers to all those questions. The banker's influence, much more than money, had secured a burial place for Kate Cameron in a corner of the graveyard which for a few years past had been reserved for Protestant foreigners. The Church had not been easy to persuade. The dead woman, according to her daughter, had at least been baptised a Catholic, and according to the rumours current from Nice to Vintimillia, she was one of the already notorious 'casino suicides'. But Signor Palmero had prevailed, and in the end the only serious opposition he met was Jenny's. She had flatly refused to allow her mother to be buried, as was the local custom, in a torchlight procession in the dead of night.

The banker had compromised by fixing the ceremony for an hour in the morning when the fishermen would be occupied with their nets and boats down on the beach, and their wives preparing the noon meal. Few were free to come, out of mere curiosity, to stare at the little procession on its way past the Cathedral of San Michele. Only the dwellers in the tall dark houses on the staircase, called in the local speech *è rampé*, came to their doors and windows to make the sign of the Cross as the coffin passed.

E rampé was a hard road for Jenny to walk, for each stair, set with a mosaic of cobbles, was at once too wide and too shallow for the length of a woman's stride. She made each step a prayer for forgiveness: for whatever sins and errors had stained her mother's life; for the impatience and dislike she had so often felt for the dead woman, and for those last taunts, never to be forgotten, which had driven Kate Cameron beyond the bounds of reason. She hardly realised that behind Signor Palmero, who walked close on her heels, George Lascaris was following in his black civilian clothes and silk hat, and that he had on his arm someone whose gold hair and sidelong grey-green glance Jenny had only glimpsed through the long black veil. And yet, as they entered the graveyard, she was still in Lascaris territory. The stones which formed the wall beneath which Kate would lie had been part, in days gone by, of the old castle where the Làscari Counts of Vintimillia had held the coast against the Saracens.

The gravediggers had completed their work and withdrawn to an upper level of the cemetery among the ornate Italian marble tombstones. Mr. Wood was waiting alone beside the empty grave. As a visitor to Mentone he had of course no surplice; nothing but his clerical collar and the book in his hand revealed his office, and his own wasted form and hectic flush were warnings that soon a grave would open for him too.

It was a miserable corner in the angle of the ancient wall. A stunted palm tree, growing alone, stood in a pile of withered leaves and flowers. Low headstones marked the grave of a young Danish officer, a Swedish nobleman, an English squire's daughter who had preceded Kate Cameron to this last resting place in Italian soil.

Mr. Wood repeated a passage from the Gospel of St. John. Jenny, who had never been present at a funeral, did not know that the invalid clergyman was drawing on his memory, and that the promise of the house of many mansions was not included in the rubric. She let the comforting words flow over her, while her eyes wandered from the dark walls and the coffin at her feet over the beautiful prospect of the enchanted shore. She did not look at Claire, standing veiled at a little distance, but it was Claire who had taught her to love those places, know those names: Capo Mortola, the Berceau, Capo Martino, and the Dog's Head under which the last drama of Kate Cameron's life had been played out. Beyond the red-tiled roofs of Mentone, beyond the ancient Bastion, the Mediterranean stretched calm under the April sun. The ochre-coloured lateen sails of a few *tartanes*, running before a light west wind for Genoa, were the only colours visible in that great expanse of blue.

'And again in the book of the prophecy of Joel,' said the sick clergyman, 'The Almighty promises to restore unto us the years that the locust hath eaten.

'"I will pour out my spirits upon all flesh, and your sons and your daughters shall prophesy, your old men shall dream dreams, your young men shall see visions...

'"And I will show wonders in the heavens and in the earth, blood and fire, and pillars of smoke.

' "The sun shall be turned into darkness, and the moon into blood, before the great and the terrible day of the Lord come." '

Jenny saw the locust years redeemed, and the soul restored of a girl who, by such a sea as this, had run barefoot on the beach at Monterey.

Mr. Wood opened his Prayer Book, and read aloud of the Resurrection and the Life.

PART THREE

FOR ITALY: GARIBALDI

Eleven

THE MOUNTAIN ROAD

'JENNY dear,' said Claire Lascaris, 'won't you please come and talk to George? He's absolutely miserable. You hardly spoke a word to him at luncheon and he doesn't think you should go back to Monaco today!'

Jenny sighed. They were in her little bedroom in the Casa Lumone. The swallows were chirping in the waterspout, the surf crashing on the rocks of Cap Martin. All was as it had been for six happy weeks, but now Jenny's possessions were packed into one leather portmanteau and a bag, and the cupboards and dressing-table had been stripped.

'Where is he?' she said. 'I'm ready now.'

Major Lascaris was in the white living-room, looking out at the sea. He turned at once when the girls came in and led Jenny to a low, broad sofa which stood in the window. His manner was attentive and gentle, as it had been since, at the foot of *è rampé*, he had taken her hand from the guardian hand of Signor Palmero.

'Claire tells me you're planning to go to Monaco. Do you think it's quite wise to hurry back there today?'

'Yes, if you'll kindly send me over in the cart, with Mario.'

George looked at his watch. 'Two o'clock—siesta time. I'll drive you to Monaco myself, if you insist.'

'I don't think *that* would be quite wise, George, all things considered.'

Claire sat down by Jenny and took the girl's cold hand in hers. 'Darling,' she said, 'is this because of what Signor Palmero said after the funeral, about going through the inventory with the house agent?'

'Partly.'

'Because you can see Bosio about that any time in the next week,' said George. 'Your—the rent at the Ruelle Sainte Barbe was paid up to the thirtieth of April. Today's only the twenty-first.'

'And surely you don't want to *stay* in that house now?' said Claire. Jenny looked from the sister to the brother. The two fair heads, the two striking Greek profiles, the two soft voices—the two Lascaris were twining themselves round her life again. She said,

'There's no reason why I shouldn't stay at the Hotel de Russie. Those pleasant English people are living there, and I shouldn't come to any harm. Besides, I want to go through my mother's papers and valuables in peace.'

'Councillor Verrano put seals on both the doors.'

'These can be removed if I say so.' Jenny looked directly at George. 'By the way, there are quite a few I.O.U.s among her papers, signed by your brother officers. Please tell Captain Bosetti and the others that these will be destroyed. I don't mean to collect their so-called debts of honour.'

George said, 'You blame me, don't you, for Kate's high play at the casino?'

'I did ask you, when I left her in Monaco, to keep her away from the tables as much as possible. I admit I could do nothing to stop her myself, but you might have had more influence than me. After all, she was in love with you.'

'You can't possibly believe my attentions to your mother were ever meant to be taken seriously?'

216

'I don't want to discuss it,' said Jenny. 'It's all over now.'

Claire made a quick sign to her brother, meaning 'be quiet!' She put her arm around Jenny's neck and said coaxingly, '*Carissima*, it *is* all over now. Your poor mother was a very sick woman; that horrible concussion must have been far worse than any of us knew. But really, you mustn't dwell on the past. By and by, you'll understand how happy you and George and I can all be here together.'

'But Claire, you wouldn't want to see a bar sinister among the Lascaris shields? I can't even bring you the name of Clan Cameron any more; and George, I don't know how the law stands on an illegitimate child's inheritance, but I'm sure it won't be in my power to restore the Palazzo Lascaris!'

He went white with temper at that, and began to damn the Palazzo Lascaris and everything in it, when Claire held up her hand for silence.

'I hear wheels,' she said. 'We have a visitor.'

'Who the devil would come pestering us at a time like this?'

From the window they saw a livery stable horse, an old-fashioned mule-cart heavily splashed with mud, and a tall man with red hair, who got stiffly down from the driver's seat and looped the reins over his arm.

'It's Steven Blake,' said Jenny quietly. She turned her face away.

'Mr. Timetable!' said Claire. 'What brings *him* here? Mario won't let him in if you don't want to see him.'

'I do want to see him.'

Mario appeared on the gravel sweep in his shirt and trousers, wearing the injured air of a man whose siesta has been interrupted in the first half-hour. Claire went to the landing and gave a quiet order. Jenny heard Steven coming upstairs, almost inaudibly, heard his subdued greeting and the words 'Where is she?' Then he was in the room, bending over her where she still sat on the sofa, incapable of moving.

'Jenny love, Jenny pet, I'm so sorry for you! I heard the news in Mentone—I came on here as fast as I could travel.'

'I'm so glad you did,' she said faintly, clinging to his hand.

'Major Lascaris!' said Steven, straightening up. 'I apologise for this untimely interruption. The fact is, I couldn't wait to offer my condolences to Jenny. We're old friends, you know.'

'Have you had luncheon?' was all Major Lascaris found to say.

'I had a bite at the Quatre Nations in Mentone.'

'A glass of port?'

'Thank you.' Steven looked at Jenny. 'It was a terrible accident, I hear.'

'All the fault of those fools in Monaco, who don't even trouble to mend their fences,' said George.

He looked meaningly at Jenny and shook his head to discourage Steven from dwelling on the tragedy. 'What brings you to the Riviera, Mr. Blake? One always thinks of you at Alessandria junction, switching trains from one track to another.'

'Does one? As a matter of fact I was at Cuneo, when my plans were changed. I took the diligence over the Col di Tenda, slept last night at Sospello and left for Mentone in a rented mule-cart at half-past six this morning.'

Behind Steven's back Jenny saw Claire's smiling mouth shape the words 'Signor Orario—Mr. Timetable!' George Lascaris said:

'I didn't know the mountain road was in any shape for

wheeled traffic between Sospello and Monti.'

'That's what they told me at Sospello,' Steven agreed. 'But I hired a couple of mules and came on down.'

'And what's going forward at Cuneo?'

'Garibaldi and General Cialdini are there with the Cacciatori delle Alpe.'

'Oh, the irregulars, of course! Presumably they'll be disbanded now.'

'Why?'

'Why? Because the French Emperor has given in to the British diplomats. He agreed to a peace congress as the only means of solving the Italian Question.'

'When?' said Jenny.

'When was it decided? Jenny dear, I'm sorry; it was on the eighteenth, the day your mother died,' said George.

'Are you quoting from the Nice newspaper, or your despatches from Turin?' said Steven with a smile.

'The despatches, of course'—stiffly. 'All the garrison's information comes direct from Turin.'

'Then the garrison can't interpret it correctly, major. Don't you know by this time that when Louis Napoleon says one thing, he means another? Don't you realise that he hasn't recalled a single unit of the four Army Corps he has waiting at Lyons and Marseilles to move into Italy? And hasn't it struck you that whatever lies he may have told the British, the Austrians are pretty near the breaking-point? Count Cavour has goaded them so far, they're just about ready to toss him an ultimatum, and when that happens, he'll start the shooting war.'

'What it is to have the ear of the prime minister!' said George. Jenny raised her head. She had hardly dared to speak since Steven entered. She was listening to him, to his hard, realistic assessment of a situation clouded for so long by the boasting of the Turin patriots and the sweet idleness of the Ligurian country folk.

'Would it inconvenience you if I had a word alone with Jenny?' Steven set down his empty glass. 'I was sent for to Monaco on urgent business, and I've got to think about getting back to Cuneo.'

'Pray consider our house as your own,' said Claire sweetly. 'George, shall we withdraw?'

'Don't trouble,' said Steven. 'Jenny looks as if she could do with some fresh air.'

Jenny stood up. 'I was planning to go over to Monaco myself this afternoon,' she said, 'to wind up matters at the Ruelle Sainte Barbe. Since you have to go to the Principality, Steven, perhaps you'd drive me there?'

'Of course I will.'

'I really don't think we can let you go off quite like this,' protested Claire. 'You're our guest, Jenny, we do feel some responsibility for you——!'

'You can call it tit for tat, Miss Lascaris,' said Steven easily. 'Remember the night you got Jenny to go away with you and leave me standing? I reckon this is my turn! Maybe Jenny is ready now to trust herself to me.'

Along the Roman road a thick hedge of pittisporum had been planted to protect the Casa Lumone from the *tramontana*. The exotic lemony smell of the flowers filled the warm afternoon as Steven drove away with Jenny by his side.

'Well!' he said when they were among the olive groves, 'thank God I took the short cut from Sospello to Mentone. I only wish I could have got here earlier.'

'For the funeral. Oh Steven!'

'Signor Palmero told me about it.'

'You've seen him? Are people gossiping about us then, down in Mentone?'

'No, of course not.' He had no intention of telling her that the stablemen had been sniggering about Major

Lascaris and his American mistresses, the mother and the daughter. When he stabled the mules hired at Sospello at the Hotel des Quatre Nations he had offered to break their filthy jaws for them. He said, 'I can't drive and talk about it, dear. Do you really want to go on to Monaco?'

'Pull up at the crossroads,' Jenny said.

They were very nearly at the Roman tomb. The heart-breaking curve of the Bay of Peace, far below the high place of ancient Lumone, stretched blue between the Roman's burial place and the grave where Kate Cameron lay.

'I only wanted to go to Monaco to wait for you,' said Jenny simply. 'Oh Steve, thank God you came so fast!'

'How long after you sent the telegram was it?'

'I don't know. About five or six hours, I suppose. I was ashamed to telegraph again.... You can drive straight into the olive grove through the gate behind the smithy.'

In the olive wood all was silence. The ancient trees, symbol of wisdom throughout the Mediterranean world, spread their silver-green leaves thickly above the turf. The bougainvillea which flung its purple flowers over all the outbuildings of the Casa Lumone was not permitted to stray among the olives, but some of the tree-trunks were wreathed with vines where pale tea-roses bloomed. Steven tethered the horse and helped Jenny down.

'Take your bonnet off,' he said. 'I hate to see you tied up in that black veil.'

When her head was bare he ran his fingers through the hair at the nape of her neck, shaking the dark curls free. Then he kissed her until the colour came back to her pale face.

'That's better,' he said. 'Now tell me why you sent for me.'

'Because I know the answers to all my questions now.'

'All of them?'

'Before she died, my mother told me she shot and killed my father.'

Steven seized Jenny in his arms, crushing her face against his coat.

'She *did*, Jenny? She confessed to it?'

'You knew she shot him——'

'I wasn't sure. She always denied it——'

'She gave you money to say you didn't know.'

'I repaid it all,' said Steven Blake. 'I had my back to the room when it happened, Jenny. I was setting up the bottles on the ledge behind the bar, and I saw Kate and Valdez in the mirror, coming into the saloon. Next off, Valdez was shooting, and the mirror was starred, and that's why I only thought I saw Kate take the gun out of her skirt, and fire.'

'But now you know she did fire?'

'If you tell me she said so. Ah, Jenny love——'

'No, don't pet me. Tell me when she offered you the money.'

'Late that same night. I couldn't sleep. I was trying to make up my mind what to do. Because Valdez *had* accused her, you see. So she came to me down by the draw, with a lot of sweet talk——'

' "*Chico mio, niño di mi alma,* for old times' sake"— that sort of talk?'

'She *was* good to my father, back in the old days,' said Steven stubbornly.

'So you took her money, and you let Diego Valdez hang.'

'Valdez was a no-good *hombre,* Jenny. Nobody cared much what became of him.'

'Oh God!' said Jenny, with her hands over her eyes. 'Was human life so cheap in the High Sierra? Was justice such a wretched farce? There *are* ways of finding out how a man was shot, you know! When my mother

222

fired that same gun last Monday night——'

'Kate fired at *you*!'

'I don't know. I don't suppose I'll ever know, if she meant to kill me or herself. But we fought like two dance-hall girls in Sacramento, scratching and biting, and the gun went off, perhaps of itself, I can't tell. Next day I showed the Councillor where the bullet lodged in the wall. It's a long story, we needn't go into it all now—but in the last two days, I thought why couldn't the miners' court have—have found the bullet that really killed my father? And then said whose gun it had been fired from? Wouldn't that have been possible, Steve?'

'I guess it would,' he said slowly, 'if we'd had a regular Sheriff, and a doctor anywhere nearer than Sacramento. But Callaghan was president of the court, such as it was; and it was all in Callaghan's interest to get the trial over and make his bid to buy the mine from Kate. He held a first mortgage on the Catalina, anyway.'

'I see,' said Jenny slowly. 'Callaghan, of course. Oh Steven, what a fool I've been!'

'Not nearly as big a fool as me.'

'I should have listened to you that night in Turin, and not rushed away——'

'With that damned girl,' said Steve. 'What are you doing back in their house now?'

'I told you—I was going to Monaco, to wait for you.'

'You knew I would come?'

'Yes.' It was the softest breath of a word, and Steve took her in his arms again, whispering in triumph and desire:

'It was all over Turin that you were going to marry Lascaris.'

'I wouldn't marry George Lascaris if he were the last man on earth!'

'You're going to marry me.'

'Yes.'

'You'll come back to Turin with me tonight and marry me as soon as we get there?'

'You know I will.'

'Jenny, we must be crazy! We can't—I can't take you over to Sospello in a rig like that. It's too rough a road for any woman, it's too long. We've got to plan some way that's easier for you. Couldn't you stay with your friends down in Mentone for a day or two? Could they send you on by coach to Genoa, where you'd be looked after? In Turin you could go to Madame di Alfieri——'

'Steven,' said Jenny, 'aren't you forgetting something?'

'What?'

'I'm not a package consigned to Sardinian Railroads.'

'Sweetheart, of course you're not——'

'I can't go on,' said Jenny desperately. 'Even for you, my darling, I just can't go on being sent from one person's care to another! First I was a victim of Orsini, injured and to be pitied. Then I was lame and a drag on my mother, and after that a doll to be dressed up and shown off. And do you realise that in the past week total *strangers* have been looking after me—Princess Caroline and the Palmeros? Do you think I want to stay with Madame di Alfieri, and go through the whole story of my mother at Monaco——'

'That's enough,' said Steven. 'Stop it, Jenny. We'll see this through together, war or no war. I only wish I had a home to offer you instead of a hotel room in Turin, but that won't last for ever——'

'Do you think *I've* so much to offer?' she said. 'I'm the bastard daughter of a gambler and a——'

Once again Steve pressed her face into his coat. He felt her sobbing and was glad of it. She was whispering something about the money, as if he cared a damn about the money! Callaghan had boasted far and wide that he got the Catalina cheap from Big Jim Cameron's widow. Two hundred thousand dollars bought it, after the mortgage was cleared; and now Dermot Callaghan was a big man on Wall Street, and Steve was prepared to bet that Kate Cameron had dropped most of her gains between the casinos and the Saratoga race track. Jenny was whimpering something about a name.

'So many papers—to sign about the funeral—and every time I wrote "Jane Ann Cameron" I thought, now here's another lie! If I'm anybody, I'm Jenny Villaverde——'

'Jenny Blake.'

She looked up at that and smiled, a child's smile through tears, and Steven kissed her wet face, saying soberly:

'Now let's go right back to the house and tell those two what you've decided.'

They walked along the track through the olive wood, with Steven leading the horse and cart. He tethered the horse again near the tank where Claire had bathed with Jenny, leaving the reins long enough to let the animal crop the grass, and they entered the Casa Lumone by the back door. The kitchen premises were deserted, and a warm silence lay over dining-room and loggia.

'It's still siesta time,' said Jenny, instinctively lowering her voice to suit the hush. 'They're all in their rooms and probably asleep. Let's go up to the living-room, and you can wait there while I speak to Claire.'

They went on tiptoe up the silent stair, and Jenny pushed open the door of the white room.

She stopped frozen and aghast at what she saw. George Lascaris lay in his sister's arms on the wide couch. His blond head was on her bare breast. The rest was a confusion of limbs like a fresco by Carleone in a crumbling palace, a picture of incest woven into an ancient tapestry, a confession of inherited corruption beneath the Lascaris shields...

Then Claire raised her head from the cushions, and with her smile of a young enchantress, the Circe smile, she held out her hand to Jenny in a dreadful invitation, a reminder of how happy they were all to be, together.

The next two hours passed in a blur for Jenny. She remembered Steve's voice saying: 'Get your things,' she remembered Steve lashing the livery horse past Rocco's hut, and the old man coming out to stare and then to wave his red *scouffia* with what sounded like a yell of 'Good luck!' She remembered sitting in a back parlour in the Hotel des Quatre Nations, where too many Englishmen had smoked too many pipes, while a waiter experienced in the ways of English ladies brought her a pot of stewed tea. Finally, and more clearly, she was aware of Steven coming in and saying he had seen Signor Palmero, and the banker had promised to look after everything and would write to her at Turin.

'He isn't coming here himself?'

'I said I thought you'd rather not. He's a good fellow—he didn't insist on it. But he says this envelope is important, darling, better put it in your bag.'

The livery horse had been led out of the hired cart and the Sospello mules backed in. When Jenny came out of the hotel the stable-boys were watching, and there was an unusually large gathering at the town fountain under the plane trees. She kept her eyes on Steven, as he lifted her from the cobbles to the passenger's seat.

'Up you go, Mrs. Blake!' he said with a grin. 'Now we're off to the war!'

The mules clattered up the Strada San Michele, swung right, and started up the Careï valley.

'Fifteen miles to Sospello,' said Jenny, reading a signpost. 'Do you think this team can possibly get us there tonight?'

'I'm not going to ask them to, after the day they've had. It's a good six hours' drive to Sospello, and there's no carriage road at all for twelve miles after Monti. That's where I thought we might stop for the night. There's a nice little inn at Monti, I noticed it on the way down.'

'You mean it's just a three-mile drive? That isn't very far.'

'I know, but it means we do the bad stretch in daylight tomorrow. If we leave at six we'll be in Sospello around noon, and have two hours in hand before the diligence comes up from Nice.'

'And when does the coach arrive at Cuneo?'

'Four o'clock on Saturday morning.'

'Tomorrow is Good Friday, Steve. Do you think the coach will run?'

'I checked that on the way down.'

Mr. and Mrs. Timetable, off to the war. Jenny felt steadied and calmed by the banal conversation. She wanted to put more than three miles between herself and the enchanted coast, but already she saw that on their short drive up the winding road they had left the sea behind them. The red roofs of Mentone, as she had looked down at them from the graveyard only that morning, were hidden by the terraced slopes of olive groves and vineyards. Ahead, partly hidden by low-lying clouds, towered the limestone peaks of Mont St. Agnes and the Berceau.

'I don't know the weather signs in these parts, Jenny. What d'you think of the clouds? Do they mean rain?'

'Sometimes they pass over very quickly. Let's hope these will, for our sakes!'

She gave him what was meant to be a confident smile,

and Steven's heart smote him. If they ran into one of Italy's torrential mountain rainstorms tomorrow, she would be soaked to the skin; if she had any walking to do on the worst stretch, between Castillon and Sospello, it might start up the mischief in her foot again. Any other girl, not as game as Jenny, would have insisted on taking the coast road to Genoa. He figured she wanted to get as far as possible from those two damned Greek perverts; but Steven knew, better than Jenny, that there was a more urgent reason to take the mountain road. He was thankful to see the church of Monti, with its odd elongated spire, and the whitewashed *albergo*, with a leafy grapevine growing over hooped canes to make an arbour before the door. He was glad to greet the plump landlady in her black velvet bodice and striped skirt, who took Jenny indoors at once and upstairs. Steve drove off to the barn.

The landlady apologised for the smallness of the room. It was the only guest-room, she explained; they were too near Mentone to have many overnight visitors, but it was clean. The bed itself was enormous. There was hardly room for any other furniture except a table holding a basin and a ewer of water. Alone, Jenny edged round it and opened the window wide.

As they approached Monti, her eyes had been fixed on the mountains, and she had scarcely glanced at the Careï valley. Now it was spread before her; she saw the peasant cabins among the vineyards and a blue glimpse of the sea. Across the river bed, almost touching the hanging clouds, were the roofs of Castellare. Jenny recognised the Lascaris stronghold immediately. Although the dome of the little palazzo was outside her line of vision, she could see the tower and the red roof of the old church and even the lime trees in the little square by the curtain wall where she had stood with Claire. She realised for the first time that Monti was the village they had seen across the valley, and that the church opposite the *albergo* was the church Claire had called 'Honoré V's gingerbread Gothic!' and dismissed, with the subtle amusement she kept for anything that was Grimaldi. In a flash of vivid recollection Jenny remembered the water pouring from the spring at Castellare, and Claire drinking from her hand, and the feel of the small teeth in her wet palms. With a shiver of revulsion she hung her jacket and bonnet on a hook behind the door and hurried downstairs to Steve.

He was sitting at a table beneath the vine with a glass in his hand and his long legs stretched out in front of him, and the relaxed, unconcerned attitude was more reassuring to Jenny than the loverlike impatience an Italian would have shown. She had seen him lounging like that a hundred times outside the horse barns at Poverty Flat, but at the Flat he would have called 'Hey, Jenny!' whereas now he sprang to his feet with a look which made her heart move in her breast, and seated her opposite to himself.

'This is *grappa*,' he said, indicating his glass. 'Too strong for you, I guess, but here's a bottle of white wine from their own vineyard. Try some, darling, it's good and cold. They must have had it in the well.'

The wine was chilled enough to mist the glass. It was the palest gold in colour, with an elusive flavour: a mountain wine. Steve touched Jenny's wineglass with the heavy tumbler which held the *grappa*.

'To us!' he said, and Jenny drained her wine with her dark eyes on that familiar, long-loved face, now so happy in her nearness and her trust.

'To you and me!' she said, and Steven filled her glass again.

'I don't know what they're going to give us for supper,

probably veal,' he said, 'but I bet it won't be ready for an hour yet.'

'There's no hurry,' said Jenny, and promptly on her words the clock of Monti church chimed six with sharp raucous strokes which sounded oddly in the quiet hamlet. The inn and the church were the focus of Monti. A spring leaping into a horse-trough just below the church was the main supply of water for man and beast; a dusty space between two lime trees near the inn was where the peasants met on Sundays to talk and play *petanque*. On the hills above, *gli monti,* the olive woods rose in terraces covered with wild flowers.

'Jenny,' said Steven, taking her hand. 'I reckon you don't want to talk about what we saw this afternoon. But we can't start out with another misunderstanding, everything's got to be fair and square between us from now on in.'

Faintly: 'What is it you want to know?'

'Just this: you had no idea, of course, that they were——' he paused to find words that would be neither coy nor brutal.

Jenny said: 'That they were lovers.'

'Yes.'

'I knew she was very, very fond of him. But you see, Steve, I began to be afraid that she was getting far too fond of—me.'

'Ah!' he said, beginning to see light.

'And then one night, one early morning rather, I saw them together in the garden, and that's why I went to Monaco. It may have been the wrong thing to do, that I'll never know. But I felt I couldn't spend another night at the Casa Lumone.'

'I blame the girl,' said Steven, after a pause. 'Left to himself, Lascaris isn't a bad fellow. After all, he was quite straight about wanting to marry you.'

'It was she who kept saying how happy we would *all three* be together. I didn't understand what she meant, of course. I do now.'

'All right, Jenny, it's over. You'll never have to see either of them again. Forget it.'

'Aren't we collecting rather a lot of things to forget?'

'Ah, but think of all the wonderful things we'll have to remember!'

Under Steven's eyes Jenny felt herself blushing, she knew her hand was hot and trembling in his clasp.

'People are watching!' was all she found to say.

There were not many people in Monti, but the priest from the 'gingerbread' church had emerged from his presbytery, breviary in hand, a carter with a load of timber had stopped for drink at the inn, a maid was laying a table for supper, very slowly, and all three, with two barefoot children, were passionately interested in the Americans. Jenny was further discountenanced by the stare of the two inn cats, apparently cut out of black velvet like the landlady's bodice.

'Let's walk a bit,' said Steven, rising. 'The carriage road goes about half a mile beyond Monti, so the footing isn't bad.' They came out hand in hand from the shadow of the arbour, and the cats and children scattered to the back yard of the inn. The warm April twilight turned the dusty road to violet. Jenny walked with Steven between olives and wild flowers, into a fold of the ancient land where crab-apples blossomed, and the scent of wet grass rose from the river bottom. Down the gorge of the Ora a cascade ran to the Careï.

'Listen to the waterfall!' she said, delighted.

'Jenny, there's only one more thing I want to ask you, but it's important. You know I love you, my own darling girl? And you're sure you love me for the future, not the past?'

'I love you for always, Steven.'

They stood embraced in the green land beneath the limestone mountains, in the Italy of an April dream. But Steven dragged his mouth from Jenny's to beg her again:

'You're sure you're not running away from bad memories back to good memories? I mean the old days in the High Sierra and the dance at Poverty Flat?'

'How funny you should say that!' said Jenny innocently. 'I was just thinking, as we came along, how wonderful it would be if we could put the clock back to that time, and have it be the night of the dance again, and you swimming the North Fork——'

'And bringing you the blue satin slippers,' Steve buried his face in Jenny's hair with a sound that was half a sigh and half a groan. 'Darling, we can't go back. Not by that road. There isn't any North Fork on the way to Turin. And I want a woman in my arms when we get there, not the cute little girl who used to ride stage with me from Poker Gulch to Rough and Ready.'

'I'm in your arms now, my darling!'

Steven released her with a kiss. 'I know,' he said. 'But I reckon it doesn't happen to many men to run away with a girl on her mother's funeral day, with a Palais Royal performance for the matinée ... I'm going to sleep in the barn tonight, my sweetheart. It won't be the first time, and if this war goes the way I think it will, it probably won't be the last.'

Twelve

THE HUNTERS OF THE ALPS

It was nearly six o'clock on Saturday morning, April 23, when the coach from Nice and Sospello rumbled slowly into the railhead town of Cuneo in Piedmont. The journey over the Col di Tenda had not been easy. On several sections, while daylight lasted, the passengers were invited to get out and walk, and shortly before midnight one of the leaders cast a shoe. There was an interval of clumsy farriery by the driver and the guard, while the anxious passengers sat in darkness by the roadside. Jenny was wrapped in a shepherd's cloak of thick grey cloth which Steven bought for her in Sospello, but in spite of that she got back inside the diligence chilled to the bone.

'We're two hours late, but at least they'll be up and doing at the inn,' said Steven, as the housetops of Cuneo came into view. 'We'll get hot coffee soon.'

'If the kettle's boiling,' said Jenny out of her knowledge of Italian inns. 'When does the first train leave for Turin?'

'There's an up freighter at 7.45, but you don't want to get on that, do you?'

'You mean we could?'

'Sure we could, but you'd be more comfortable on the *rapido* at 9. In any event I've got to go to the station first; there may be orders for me from Turin.'

'I'll come with you.'

'Not too tired?'

'Of course not.'

He kissed her as he lifted her down from the diligence. He didn't care who saw it, she'd been so dead game, and he was so proud of her! At the little *albergo*, dignified since the line came to Cuneo by the name of Railway Hotel, they handed the bags to a yawning boy and ordered breakfast. Then Steve hurried Jenny across a dusty little square to the silent station.

'There's a light in the telegraph office.' Steven pushed open the door. Inside the hot little room an elderly man and a boy, sitting beside the telegraph instruments, looked up eagerly.

'Signore! Turin sent you a message half an hour ago!'

'The coach was late. You mean the office was open at half-past five?'

'We're on a twenty-four hour day since Wednesday, signore. Federico and I came on at four o'clock. Rico! The telegram for Signor Blake.'

The boy had the flimsy paper in his hand. Steve read it aloud.

'To Steven Blake at Cuneo from Sardinian Railroads, Turin. Message begins: Put yourself immediate disposition Cacciatori delle Alpe for completion their transport to Turin today. Message ends.'

'Well, that's that,' said Steve. He opened a door which led to the station platform and motioned Jenny out. There was nothing to be seen but the single line of tracks, gleaming in the early sunshine beyond the station roof, and a pile of packing cases ready for the freighter. The freight train itself was drawn up at the platform, a string of roofless cattle cars behind an obsolescent engine with a wood-burning furnace.

'We shan't be going to Turin this morning, Steve?' said Jenny.

'And probably not this afternoon. You see, darling, that message means that three thousand men, all Garibaldi's volunteers, have got to be moved north before midnight. I'll have to ride out to their camp, two miles the other side of town, and see the General, and hear what his orders were, and then get the movement going. I worked out a complete entrainment plan with General Cialdini a few days ago, but now I've got to find out what rolling stock is on hand here, and what can be sent down from Turin.'

'Signore!' The elderly telegraph clerk shouted through the open door. 'Signor Blake, have a look at the message coming through!'

Cuneo was on the Bonelli telegraph system, and received despatches by plain lettering. The lines in Roman capitals, one-eighth of an inch high, were immediately legible, and Steve and Jenny, looking over the clerk's shoulder, read together:

'To all Stationmasters. Message begins: Austrian envoys Baron von Kellersberg and Count Ceschi di Santa Croce arrived at Novara station at zero five hours this morning en route for Turin stop Sardinian Railroads are on a war footing from zero six hours today stop Signed Camillo Cavour. Message ends.'

The operator tore off the completed message and looked at Steven. 'I'll have to rouse the stationmaster, sir!' he said. 'He must see this immediately.'

'Tell him I'll meet him here in twenty minutes,' said Steven. 'Tell him both the freight train and the *rapido* are requisitioned for the use of troops ... Quick, Jenny dear, there's not much time to spare.'

'Steven, what does it mean?' begged Jenny, as they turned back to the *albergo*.

'First off, it means Cavour has won his diplomatic battle. If two Austrian envoys are on their way to Turin you can bet a dollar they've come with an ultimatum from Vienna, and no Austrian ultimatum will ever be accepted in Turin. So we're at war. The next thing is, civilian traffic will be restricted, which doesn't affect me much. What does is that I need far more rolling stock than the two locomotives and the cars already here at Cuneo if I'm to get Garibaldi's boys up to Turin tonight, and that means I'll have to move troops up and trains down along a single track. I don't know if the local despatcher is up to it, but we can try.'

'What can I do to help you?' Jenny said.

'Be a darling and hurry them up with the coffee.'

A slatternly maid was actually putting coffee and fresh bread on the breakfast table. Steven shouted for shaving water, sent the yawning boy flying to put a saddle on a horse, gulped down his coffee, ran upstairs to shave and change into his last clean shirt, and came down ready for the day before a quarter of an hour was up. 'I'm going to ride straight out to the camp when I've seen the station-master,' he told Jenny. 'Try to get some sleep this morning, darling. If I'm not back by noon go ahead and have something to eat without me.'

The *albergo* at Cuneo, unlike the little inn at Monti, had more than one guest bedroom, but the room to which Jenny was shown was dirty and depressing, with grease-stained pillows on the bed and dingy sheets. With a good imitation of Steven's brisk executive manner she made the servant bring fresh linen and take away her camisole and cambric petticoats to be washed and ironed by noon. Then Jenny in her nightdress lay down with the shepherd's cloak for a cover instead of the grimy quilt. Her last thought before she fell asleep was that her leg must be completely better. She had felt no pain in that night walk over the mountain road.

She was awakened by the tramp of marching men. It was after noon, and the maid had been and gone, for a neat pile of Jenny's undergarments lay on the dresser, smelling of fresh air and a hot iron. She could see the woman down in the street, standing at the gate with the yard boy and other inn servants, all staring at the marchers. What they saw was the advance guard of the Risorgimento, the first battalion of the 1st Regiment of the Hunters of the Alps, at the beginning of their road to glory.

The three thousand volunteers who formed the Cacciatori delle Alpe had been divided into three regiments, each consisting of two battalions of five hundred men. The commander of the 1st Regiment, whom Jenny hidden by a window curtain now saw at the head of his men, was Enrico Cosenz, one of the great defenders of the Venetian Republic. The commander of the 2nd, no less famous, was Medici, who with Garibaldi had worn the red shirt on the pampas, during the campaign in Uruguay. These two veteran soldiers, with Nicolo Ardoino leading the 3rd Regiment, had begun to drill the Cacciatori into a disciplined although unarmed fighting force. The men in the ranks were for the most part very young. It was no exaggeration to call them the flower of Italy, for they came from the best families of Lombardy and Venetia—boys gently reared, well educated and brought up in the faith of the Risorgimento to avenge everything their friends had suffered at Austrian hands during and since the War of Independence. They came marching into Cuneo wearing civilian clothes, all the shabbier for several weeks spent under canvas, with their few possessions in wallets or handkerchief bundles, and the sun bright on their faces. The townsfolk of Cuneo cheered them and flung spring flowers in their path, and as the boys marched to the waiting trains they sang 'Garibaldi's Hymn':

> *'The tombs are uncovered, the dead come from far,*
> *The ghosts of our martyrs are rising to war.'*

It was the song Mercantini had begun to compose on the December night when Garibaldi returned to Genoa, before Steven Blake brought him in secret to the Palazzo Cavour.

There was a brief pause after the first battalion passed. Then the cheering began again, louder than before, and mixed with shouts of '*Garibaldi! Viva Garibaldi!*' The general himself was riding into town.

Jenny saw the 'seafaring man' of Cavour's study, now dressed in the uniform of a general of the Sardinian Army, riding with the long stirrup and the slouch he had acquired long ago on the pampas of Uruguay. The liberator of Montevideo, the exile of Caprera, had come into his own again, was back on the soil of Italy, and as he came into the little town his face was as bright as if he returned a conqueror to Rome. On his right hand rode a gigantic grizzled figure with the bearing of a British cavalryman, dressed in an old frock-coat of London cut. On his left, with a western lope not so unlike the general's, rode Steven Blake.

So we're at war. With a catch at her heart Jenny remembered Steven's words when the telegram came through. It was the first time she had ever heard him say *we* instead of *they*, identify himself completely with the Italian cause. And now he was riding with Garibaldi, and the girl he loved was stirred, in spite of herself, by the tossing of the horses' heads and the music of the fife and drum.

As the second battalion of the Cacciatori passed Jenny

was dressing quickly. Her hair was out of curl, and she arranged it in a net which she hoped would give her a sober, matronly appearance if by any chance she had to meet the stationmaster of Cuneo before they left for Turin. She was not prepared for what Steven had to tell her when he ran upstairs and rapped at her bedroom door.

'Jenny, General Garibaldi is here and wants to meet you. Are you ready to come down?'

'Meet *me*? Oh, but Steven, I can't possibly appear!'

'Why not? You look wonderful!'

'It's not how I look, it's ... what will he think of me, travelling alone with you?'

'Sweetheart, it's not Miss Lippincott you're going to see! I've told Garibaldi we're on our way to Turin to be married, and he insisted on meeting you. Please, Jenny! I want to show them both how proud I am of my girl.'

'Both? But who's the other man? Not General Cialdini?'

'It's an Englishman called Peard, a volunteer, who rode in with us. We're all going to have luncheon together, you can't hide up here in your room.'

It cost an effort, but Jenny went into the dining-room calmly, more appealing than she knew in her black dress, and was met with very low bows from General Garibaldi and Mr. Peard.

'Gentlemen, this is my fiancée, Miss Jenny Cameron,' said Steven, leading her forward, and Garibaldi, in his warm-hearted way, took both her hands and kissed them.

'Now we can truly congratulate our good friend Signor Blake,' he said, 'and wish every happiness to him and his lovely bride!'

'Thank you, sir,' said Jenny, blushing. Garibaldi looked kindly at her mourning clothes.

'You have been in sad trouble, I know,' he said sympathetically. 'May God bless you, child, and bring you and your husband safe to better times!'

Jenny's eyes filled with tears. It was the first blessing ever given to Steven and herself, the first invocation of God's power over their future lives, and she found herself quite unable to say more. But there was wine on the table; she was given a glass, and when her health was drunk with Steven's she could laugh again, with her hand in the hand of the man she loved.

'We must apologise, signorina,' said Garibaldi gallantly, 'for delaying your journey to your marriage for military reasons. But not for long; your fiancé has done wonders with the authorities and guarantees to get the last of our men out of Cuneo by seven o'clock tonight.'

'Four hours earlier then I could have hoped, this morning,' Steven said.

'In such haste?' said Jenny, understanding. 'Has there been another message from the capital?'

'Yes, Jenny,' said Steve, and Garibaldi explained gravely that Cavour had received the Austrian envoys and at once made public the Austrian Emperor's ultimatum: Sardinia was to suspend all armed preparations within three days. If any new enlistments or troop movements continued after that time, the Emperor Franz Josef would treat these as an act of hostility.

'And the mere fact that you're entraining for Turin shows what answer Count Cavour means to give,' said Jenny. 'But, general, your soldiers look so very young!'

'Not so young as the lads I enlisted in '48. We took boys of fourteen in the First Italian Legion when Ugo Bassi and I began recruiting in Bologna, and sixteen was considered a fair age for the defenders of Rome. My older boy, Menotti, is nineteen.'

'I saw your son in Nice six weeks ago,' said Jenny. 'Standing on the doorstep of your birthplace, sir, with a crowd all round the harbour shouting itself hoarse at the name of Garibaldi.'

'You did? You've come from Nice? My own beloved city; Peard, we must find some way to persuade the King that *Nizza la Superba* must remain Italian.'

The blue sailor's eyes smiled at Jenny. Garibaldi was susceptible to women; if his heart was in his wife's grave, said his enemies, his body was often in the bed of women Anita would have scorned. There were scandalous rumours about the servant girl in his lonely farm at Caprera, about a crazy poetess who followed him from town to town, and many more. It was the eye of a connoisseur which appraised Jenny's shadowed eyes and lovely sensuous mouth.

'Shall we sit down, general?' suggested Steven. 'I think they're bringing in the *antipasta* now.'

The maids, with sidelong looks at Garibaldi, brought in the hors d'œuvres, with bread and raw Chianti in wicker-covered flasks, and the general unbuckled his sword with a sigh of relief.

'I'm not accustomed to my new harness yet,' he said whimsically. 'The Red Shirt and my old *puncio* suit me better when I go to war. However, I'm forbidden to wear the Red Shirt for fear of offending the French Emperor, on whom I'm told the fate of Italy depends; and if I fight for Victor Emmanuel, I suppose I ought to wear his uniform. You admire my sword, signorina? I call it the sword of London. When I returned to Europe five years ago, as captain of the *Commonwealth*, I was met at the London Docks by a deputation of Newcastle miners. They had come all the way to London to present me with this sword of honour, purchased by the working men of the North country. Each man paid one penny towards it, representing—so the address ran—"a heart which beats true to European freedom". You can imagine how I value it.'

'Wonderful fellows those Newcastle miners,' said Mr. Peard, when Garibaldi courteously turned to Steven with a question about the entrainment of the 2nd Regiment at three o'clock. The gigantic Englishman had been a silent but friendly presence, eating hugely of the *lasagne* when it came to table and quaffing great tumblers of Chianti. He was not fat but heavily muscled, and his grizzled hair suggested that he was nearer fifty than forty, decidedly a veteran volunteer to be found among the young Hunters of the Alps.

'Are you a Northcountryman, Mr. Peard?' asked Jenny.

'I? Bless your heart, no; I hail from Cornwall. Live there, too, when I'm on the Western circuit. I'm a barrister-at-law. *And* an officer in the Duke of Cornwall's Rangers, so you see I keep up my old ties with the Duchy.'

'Are the Rangers a yeomanry regiment, sir?' It was the most obvious luncheon-table gambit, and Peard's eyes twinkled at Jenny.

'You're thinking it's a far cry from the Duke of Cornwall's Own to the Cacciatori delle Alpe,' he said. 'Well, so it is, but the Cacciatori will be fighting for a free Italy, and that's more fun than guarding the coast of Cornwall against an imaginary invasion by our friend Louis Napoleon. And then I made the journey, so to speak, by Naples. I've seen Bourbon tyranny doing its beastly work there, Miss Cameron, just as Mr. Gladstone saw it, and other public men in England who've done what they could to rescue those poor devils of Neapolitan refugees. I tell you, the prisons of Naples cry out to high heaven——'

Jenny listened. She had heard it all before, with the names of other Italian cities substituted for or added to

Naples. In Orsini's case it had been Mantua, and Orsini must have reasoned, at the start, much like this genial English fanatic. Garibaldi, sitting at the head of the table talking quietly to Steve, was much the calmest apostle of the Risorgimento she had ever known. He was only fifty-one, but the sea-faring wrinkles round his eyes and the grey-streaked chestnut hair and beard gave him a leonine air of sagacity; his voice was slow and warm. He might make mild fun of wearing King Victor Emmanuel's uniform, but the Piedmontese dark blue suited him very well with its green bands and silver filigree work at cuffs and collar. But that it did not extinguish the spirit of the Red Shirt was proved when the republican struck the table with his hand and cried,

'But when are they going to give us uniforms, Mr. Blake? When do we get rifles and bayonets, not to mention artillery? Do you know that my fifty Genoese sharpshooters are carrying their own arms, and my scouts are mounted on their own horses? Will the king give us ambulances and field kitchens, or are we to tie up our own wounds and live on the country?'

'I think your liaison officer, General Cialdini, is the one to tell you that,' said Steven. 'I can provide you with rolling stock, but not muzzle-loaders; and if you'll excuse me, I think you credit me with far more influence in Turin than I have.'

'You got us the trains today, and I'm grateful for that. But have you any idea where the Cacciatori will be sent after they reach Turin?'

'Into barracks, I hope, sir,' said Steven dryly. 'I'm not anxious to route you anywhere else tonight.' Under cover of Garibaldi's laugh he turned to Jenny. 'The general has been good enough to offer us places on the last troop train, due to leave at seven. It won't be saloon class travel; can you face it?'

'Of course,' said Jenny, and Garibaldi smiled.

'She is like my Anita,' he said, 'who dared anything, from the day she ran away from her home and joined her life to mine, until the day she rode out of the gates of Rome with me on the last journey of all. You remind me of Anita, signorina. There is something in your eyes and hair, and most of all in your smile, that brings her back to me. Did you ever see her portrait?'

'Never a real portrait,' said Jenny hesitatingly, 'but in an old fisherman's cabin on the Riviera I saw a coloured print, a lithograph, where she was—you were carrying her——'

'I was carrying her to the place where she died,' said Garibaldi. 'And I thank you for your delicacy, signorina. I know the thing you mean, it was taken from a painting, and I am told it hangs in many a humble home in Italy ... I ought to be—I *am*—grateful for such remembrance. But the day that one kind friend sent me a copy, when I was a workman on Staten Island, thousands of miles from her Italian grave ... that day the old wounds opened, and I wept.'

The three around the table waited silently.

'That picture with its cheap crude colours tells the truth,' he said. 'I carried my wife in my arms from the boat—it seemed for miles—through the fever marshes of Commachio, with the signs of death upon her, and the Austrians ravening at our backs. She was expecting a child. She was safe in Nizza with my mother, and our little boys and girl, but safety meant nothing to Anita. She came to me in Rome, she fled with me, she died. Anita gave her life for Italy ... and for me.'

'And you are willing to give your life for Italy, again,' said Jenny. Steven gave her one look of surprise, and lowered his eyes.

'If Italy requires it, yes,' the general said. He rose.

'Now, Peard, we must get back to camp. I shall see you at the station, signorina; I too am going to the city on the last train. It arrives at eight, Mr. Blake?'

'I can't answer for delays today, but around eight, yes.'

'And tomorrow is Easter Sunday,' said Garibaldi, buckling on his sword. 'It will be a great day for Turin. Our Lord's Resurrection is bringing with it, at last, the resurrection of Italy!'

It was a great day for Turin, but as the sunlit hours of Easter Sunday passed it never became a day of jubilation. Cavour had goaded the Austrians into the delivery of an ultimatum, and that was much; but his decision to let the full three days' grace pass before he gave his answer imposed a heavy strain on the collective nerves of the Torinesi. Every man and woman was aware that somewhere in the city the two Austrian envoys were held virtually incommunicado, waiting to take back to their Imperial master the message that meant war.

At such a time all thoughts turned to the other Emperor, Napoleon III. For all his advances and withdrawals, all his secret pacts and pledges, not one French soldier had as yet arrived in the dominions of the Sardinian king. It was known that since early April four French divisions had been stationed at Lyons, exclusive of Bourbaki's division in the Dauphiné, but the great barrier of the Cottian Alps lay between these divisions and Turin. On this same Easter Sunday Canrobert's III Corps had been ordered to start the move from France into Savoy, and Marshal Niel's IV Corps would follow, but the Alpine passes were clogged with snow, and the handling of artillery was bound to be slow and difficult. Also on Easter Sunday—and this news somewhat improved morale in Turin—Napoleon III ordered the Paris regiments to entrain at the Gare de Lyon, to join

Forey and Ladmirault's divisions of I Corps, already based on Marseilles and Toulon for embarkation to Genoa. On paper, the French Army of Italy would consist of four Corps, I and II Corps entering Piedmont by sea and III and IV by the Alpine passes; but thanks to the lessons learned in the Crimean War the French Army now moved with heavy transport echelons for reserve ammunition and supplies. It was impossible that a force of one hundred and fifty thousand men, so burdened, could join its Sardinian allies in less than seven days.

Meanwhile the Austrians had seven full Corps, more than two hundred thousand men, in Lombardy and Venetia alone, before any reinforcements arrived across the Brenner Pass from the Austrian Empire. Any or all of these seven Corps could be moved by rail to the frontier of Piedmont which ran along the river Ticino, or if necessary on foot across the flat terrain presented by the Plain of Lombardy. If the Austrians left the shelter of their four great fortresses at Mantua, Verona, Peschiera and Legnano—known as the Quadrilateral—it was estimated that on Day 3 they could cross the Ticino and occupy Novara; on Day 4, Vercelli; and on Day 5 stand before Turin on the line of the Dora Baltea river.

Against this tremendous threat King Victor Emmanuel II would have to muster the entire Sardinian Army, fifty thousand strong, with fewer than one hundred and fifty heavy guns, to defend not only his capital but the key fortresses of Alessandria and Casale.

The problems of strategy and logistics confronting Victor Emmanuel II and Cavour were thus so simple that every child in Turin could understand them, and many older citizens began to think of the tragic ending of the War of Independence. Then Field-Marshal Radetzky had inflicted a crushing defeat on the Italians at

Novara. The only consolation was that Radetzky had since died, his successor as commander-in-chief, Count Gyulai, being a far less brilliant soldier. The Austrian governor of Lombardy-Venetia was the Archduke Maximilian, who had been trained exclusively for the Navy.

In this mixed mood of hope and fear, the inhabitants of Turin strolled out on the afternoon of Easter Sunday to see the Hunters of the Alps in their barracks, and if possible to catch a glimpse of Garibaldi. The general had not allowed the young volunteers to enter the city, but they could be seen and admired in the barracks yard. The Bersaglieri would always be the crack corps of Turin, but the Cacciatori were volunteers and patriots, and they looked their best in the Piedmontese uniforms issued during the morning hours. The Garibaldini had never been based on Turin in the War of Independence, but there were many citizens who remembered the defenders of Rome, looking like stage brigands in their flowing green capes and tall Calabrian hats with ostrich plumes. They were impressed by the new generation in plain army blue.

Jenny and Steve walked in that direction after their talk with the minister of the Vaudois church which Jenny had attended during her first visit to Turin. They heard the young troops in the barracks yard singing, and the singing swell as the Torinesi picked up the words of 'Garibaldi's Hymn'.

'Jenny, why won't you marry me tomorrow?' urged Steven, not for the first time that afternoon.

'Because I—absolutely—refuse to be married in black.'

'And do you seriously think you can find a dressmaker to make you a wedding dress in thirty-six hours?'

'Madame Suzette will do it,' said Jenny confidently. 'I mean to be at her salon at nine o'clock tomorrow morning. And I'm sure she can produce something fit to wear by Tuesday afternoon at three.'

'The preacher seemed to think three o'clock was pretty late in the day.'

'Oh Steve, he thinks the whole thing is quite irregular. All that fuss about registering the marriage! Does he think American Consuls grow on trees?'

Steven looked down at her with love. He had been 'in love' with Jenny Cameron since their meeting at Plombières, but in the past few days the love which had been as much protective as passionate had grown into something stronger, something which derived from Jenny's new-found strength. Steven Blake had not a large vocabulary of tenderness or admiration; 'dead game' were the words which occurred to him most often as he remembered how well Jenny had stood up to that rough trip across the mountains, and the next night's journey in a troop train to Turin. There hadn't been one word of weariness or complaint, not even when he left her at a wretched hotel called La Pergola, next door to his own in the Piazza Carlo Felice. It occurred to him that his room there, which he had kept for months as a pied-à-terre for his visits to the city, would have to be thoroughly cleaned up, and a lot of old maps and papers and unmended underclothes thrown out, before he brought his bride home to it. Meanwhile the Pergola, which seemed to cater exclusively for unemployed ballet girls, was of course no place for Jenny Cameron. He had naively supposed that she would want to go back to the Hotel de l'Europe, the best hotel in town, but she had jibbed at that, he couldn't imagine why.

... On Tuesday afternoon, at three o'clock, she came to him in the little Protestant church, wearing a simple dress of white Turin silk, which the French dressmaker had been able to alter for Jenny from a cancelled order (there were many such in a city threatened by invasion) and a bonnet with a white rose beneath the brim. She had Steve's white roses in her hands, and Jenny Cameron carried her head as high as if she were sailing up the aisle in a great New York church with twelve tittering bridesmaids behind her dressed in *mousseline de soie*. But in spite of her pride, and Steven's pride in her, it was a sad little wedding in the empty church, with the minister's wife and servant for the necessary witnesses. The minister read the service in French, which Steven scarcely understood, and over his words they could hear the shunting of trains being routed up to Susa to wait for the French troops. The servant girl, who had a sweetheart in the garrison at Casale, wept steadily throughout the service. For, the three days of grace having expired, the Austrian ultimatum had been officially rejected that morning and the envoys were on their way back to Vienna. The Kingdom of Sardinia, and by the January treaty of alliance, France, were now at war with Austria.

The bride and groom, who had come so far from Rough and Ready to this day, did not make a lengthy wedding journey. They hired a *vettura*, and drove through the square where the Duke of Savoy pranced on his bronze horse (and where they were later to eat their wedding dinner in one of the best restaurants in Turin) to that other, greater square which held the Royal Palace and the Palazzo Madama. It was black with people, crowding together from the Via Po to the Via Roma, hanging on the grille-work of the palace, climbing on the recently erected memorial to the heroes of the Crimean War. The cheering rose and fell in waves as King Victor Emmanuel II rode out of the palace courtyard, accompanied by all his Savoyard generals. *Il Re Galant'uomo*'s square face was red that day, and his beard and moustache seemed to be bristling with energy. His flush was an odd contrast to the weary pallor of Cavour, when the statesman emerged on the balcony of the Palazzo Madama to address the crowd.

Cavour had a practised rather than a powerful voice. It came to the two Americans, in their cab on the edge of the square, in a series of finely-uttered phrases, broken only by the sighs or cheering of the crowd.

'My fellow-countrymen, the die is cast. Today we have held the last meeting of the Parliament of Piedmont. The next time your elected representatives meet in a legislative assembly, it will be as the Parliament of a United Italy...

'Savoy and Piedmont—and Sardinia—the mainland and the island, are not alone in the great struggle which will free our beloved Italy from the Austrian yoke. We have an ally. A great ally. One who has not forgotten the aid we gave him in the Crimea. Nor the cry of pain from the lips of a patriot—perhaps a misguided patriot—from Orsini, in the shadow of the guillotine...

'The Emperor Napoleon stands ready and pledged to help us. Three days ago, when the Austrian ultimatum reached us in Turin, he told our envoys in Paris that he and his gallant troops, by the side of our Army, would liberate Italy from the Alps to the Adriatic. I can tell you more than that. The Emperor Napoleon has gone even further in his pledges of loyalty to us. At Plombières last July he gave me his sworn word to make no peace until the Austrian Emperor, in his palace at Vienna, should sign an instrument of unconditional surrender. *Vive l'Empereur Napoleon! Evviva l'Italia liberata!* We march together to the resurrection of our Italy ... united, glorious ... and free.'

... As the *vetturino* picked his way through the crowd to the Via Roma, Steven Blake kissed his bride. 'Well, darling,' he said, turning the new gold ring on her finger, 'as a wedding trip I guess that hardly measured up to seeing Niagara Falls. But it'll be something to tell our grandchildren, that we heard Cavour declare war on Austria the day you and I were married.'

In the nacreous daybreak Jenny awoke in Steven's narrow bed. On the table beside her, next to a stub of candle in an enamel stick, lay Steven's silver watch. It was too dark to read the time. She could hear rain against the window pane.

She moved her cramped body gently in her husband's arms. For Steve's arms were round her, she soon discovered: the right beneath her bare shoulders, the left flung across her thighs. There was no escaping from him, if she had wanted to escape. Her husband held her in a loose embrace, which if he chose could immediately become a vice.

Steven was sound asleep. She saw his face closer than she had ever seen it before. What could a smiling face, even coming closer for a kiss, reveal compared to this harsh mask of oblivion laid beside her on the pillow? Steve's dark red hair was damp with sweat. Jenny saw with curiosity that the stubble beginning to show on his chin was darker than his hair, the same colour as his lashes, tobacco brown. With his eyes closed, without that dark familiar gaze, it was a stranger's face she studied. Steven sighed. His bare chest, white-skinned beneath the strong tanned neck, rose and fell in the same rhythm as Jenny's breathing. Softly, at last, she felt her wrenched body begin to harmonise with his. With a tentative finger she traced the smooth outline of his shoulder and upper arm. He opened his eyes, and knew her, and was Steve.

'Oh Jenny! Here with me at last! My darling wife!'

A heavy knock fell on the door, and the porter's hoarse voice said,

'Six o'clock, signore! Signor Blake! You're wanted immediately at the Genoa station!'

Thirteen

LIVING IN A POEM

THE emergency which called Steven to the station was
the abdication of the Grand Duke of Tuscany, a
timorous old gentleman who saw in Cavour's rejection of
the Austrian ultimatum a threat to his own peace. His
departure from Florence left the way clear for Prince
'Plon-Plon', who with General Uhrich and V Corps of
the French Army was waiting for transportation at
Marseilles. Steven Blake and the key personnel of Sardinian Railroads began to revise the entire plan for the
disembarkation of I and II Corps at Genoa.

Facing the immediate problem of moving five thousand troops a day as soon as III and IV Corps came
through the Alpine passes (so clogged with snowdrifts
that the Sardinian *carabinieri* were called out to clear a
way for the advance guard on Mont Cenis and Mont
Genèvre), Steven was at his desk in the Genoa station
from six in the morning until six at night. Jenny had to
received her bridal callers alone. They were all gentlemen, for Madame di Alfieri had gone to Leri with her
children, and the wives of the rich industrialists had fled
by steamer across Lake Maggiore into neutral Switzerland. But Count Cavour called, smiling his public smile,
and carrying a bouquet of roses and mimosa, which
brought the scent of Cap Martin to the musty parlour of
the Hotel Felice. General Garibaldi came, with his son
Menotti as his aide-de-camp, and various directors of

Sardinian Railroads also came to honour the bride of 'Cavour's American'. One day, Steve hurried back from the station with Peter Easton, the young surveyor from Bardonnechia, who had been drafted to work in Genoa during the emergency, and Peter gaily declared that he had expected to hear of their marriage from the moment Steven had returned from Plombières. He had recently become engaged himself, and showed Jenny an attractive photograph of Miss Julia Mansfield, who had promised to marry him at midsummer.

The evenings, of course, belonged to Steve and Jenny, and in spite of the continual rain a cab was called at eight o'clock every night to take the bride and groom to dine in the square of the Bronze Horse or at a famous restaurant near the Palazzo Carignano. Jenny wore her wedding dress and carried a small bouquet, and Steven was immensely proud of the impression she made on the few people still cool enough to dine out in a city threatened by invasion. He watched her glowing among the candlelight and flowers, and savoured the thought of the coming hour of joy. He was a headlong and passionate lover, and in the shabby bedroom at the Hotel Felice he overpowered her so completely that Jenny, in all succeeding awakenings as on the first, was left with a deep sense of her own failure; a rueful wonder that so much poetry had been written about an act so different from her innocent imagining.

Sometimes she wished that Steven had been less chivalrous at Monti, herself less paralysed by that vile scene at the Casa Lumone. She might have yielded to him more naturally and easily that night, in the first spontaneous uprush of emotion, than after the interruption at Cuneo. For Jenny saw that her young husband was changing since his transactions with the Hunters of the Alps. He was completely immersed in the war now, and hardly spoke of the Mont Cenis Tunnel, except during Peter Easton's visit. His whole interest in Bardonnechia was the speed at which the French troops could march over the Mont Cenis and entrain at Susa for Turin and the switch to Alessandria. As for the immediate past, he seemed literally to have blotted it from his memory. In his confession to Jenny, he had purged himself of guilt for his silence when Jim Cameron died, and would have died himself sooner than mention Kate Cameron's name. All that was over. Jenny and he had been kept apart; now they were together, and life for Steven held nothing better than Jenny's kisses, and a job to do, and the war for Italy to win.

Meantime, General Gyulai was reluctant to leave the protection of the Quadrilateral. Four days—each of vital importance to the Sardinian Army—passed before he fumbled his Whitecoats across the Plain of Lombardy to the Piedmont frontier on the Ticino. Certainly the weather was against him, and the torrential rainfall made every inhabitant of Turin newly conscious of the rivers of Italy. The Po, flowing from Monte Viso to its Adriatic delta, had risen fifteen feet above its usual level. So had the tributaries of the Po, flowing south from the Alpine lakes. The Mincio, flooded from Lake Garda to the Po, had to be crossed by the Austrians as they emerged from the Quadrilateral. The Adda, from Lake Lecco, the Olona from Lake Lugano, the Ticino itself flowing from Lake Maggiore, were all swollen by the spring rains. Even the Sesia and the Dora Baltea might under flood conditions offer some protection to Turin, and in addition to the rivers there were the canals constructed during Cavour's ministry. The Marzano, the Cavour and the Villoresi canals irrigated the vast rice-fields of the Plain of Piedmont, and between the River Ticino and the town of Magenta the Naviglio Grande, thirty feet wide and thirty feet below the earth's surface, was in itself a formidable barrier. Across this land of waters, only a few road bridges and the slender span of the railway stood; it was not until the fifth day, May 1, that the Austrians crossed the frontier and occupied the unfortified town of Novara.

On that same day, the first contingent of the French force to cross the Alps arrived in Turin, and the people —feeling that their city was saved—turned out to cheer them as they marched through the streets to the Milan station. Although the line into Lombardy was now cut at Novara, an entire French division was to be moved up to King Victor Emmanuel's headquarters, and the sight of the hard-bitten professional soldiers of France delighted and at the same time awed the Torinesi. There were rumours that the French Emperor's men were not as well organised as they appeared to be; that an entire commissariat department had been stranded at Briançon, and that troops accustomed to rations of bread and bacon had taken unkindly to Italian polenta, but this did not alter the glorious fact that by their mere arrival the French had scared General Gyulai back across the river and into the natural quadrilateral called the Lomellina. On the Riviera, Nice, the town whose future depended on the issue of the war, opened her gates to the French cavalry: Cuirassiers, Lancers, Hussars and Chasseurs à Cheval, as they made for the Corniche road. In Monaco, the casino was closed for the duration of the war, and Prince Charles III gave permission for the French to pass through his territory on their way to Genoa. Finally, after the first skirmishes between the Allies and the Austrians had begun, Napoleon III himself appeared upon the scene. He too disembarked at Genoa, after a night journey by rail through France, where in every town and village his subjects turned out with torchlight and brass bands to hail the triumphal progress of Louis Napoleon Bonaparte, the Saviour of Society.

'Jenny!' said Steve, coming back early to the hotel one afternoon in May, 'I've just been at the Madama palace. Count Cavour sent for me at three o'clock.'

'Darling, I'm so glad to see you home so soon!' It wasn't much of a home, this hotel room which now that the rainstorms were over had become hot and stuffy, and Jenny had been looking out of the window rather listlessly at the treetops in the square gardens. Now she sat down happily on the hard leather sofa with Steve's arm around her, prepared to hear all the news of the day. 'What did the great man have to say?'

'The great man has another job for me. He told me to talk it over with you before I took it on, but he wants me to do it; I can see that.'

'A railroad job?'

'Well, that's just it, I don't know how much railroading will be involved. The thing is, Garibaldi wants me to join him in the north.'

'Join the *Cacciatori*?'

'Not as an enlisted man, darling, don't be silly! "Technical adviser" would be the title, I suppose. You see, Garibaldi is the best guerilla fighter in the world, but he learned his trade on the pampas, and it's only begun to dawn on him that the railroad is a powerful weapon of war. Now he's afraid the Austrians will use the Camerlata track to move troops against him if he gets to Como.'

'But where *is* he, Steve?'

'You know the Cacciatori marched north to Lake Maggiore a few days ago? Garibaldi means to use Arona as his base for the invasion of Alpine Lombardy, striking

257

through the mountain towns of Bergamo and Brescia. That way, his force would become the left wing of the Allied armies, and French V Corps, in Tuscany, would be the right.'

'Yes, I understand all that, but where do you come in?'

'Garibaldi thinks I can queer the Austrian pitch at Camerlata, if it's necessary, and help him use the rail to Brescia, if he gets that far.'

'By "queering the pitch" you mean destroying the track, don't you?'

'Yes.'

'Isn't that dangerous?'

'Merely destructive.' Steven got up, stretched his long arms and lit a cigarette. 'That's what I told Cavour. I said, "You've been working for years to give this country a modern railroad system, and now you've got it the whole thing has to be blown up." He said of course the Austrians would start destroying the whole track eastwards, as soon as they were challenged by Garibaldi.'

Jenny looked at him sorrowfully. She might have told Steve that great political journeys begun in optimism at Plombières ofter ended in destruction on an unimportant line from Milan to Lake Como; but she saw he had much more to say.

'*Rebuilding* a railroad, now that's a decent job. I wouldn't mind doing that, and there must be plenty of labour in Alpine Lombardy. Every man and woman there would give their lives to see the Austrians defeated.'

'You want to go then? Leaving me here?'

'No, darling, that's just it; that's why Cavour wanted me to discuss it with you. You see, we're American citizens. There's no need for me to skulk around behind the Cacciatori: the Austrians can't refuse me a safe conduct through their lines if I'm escorting an American lady who wants to cross the lake to Switzerland.'

Jenny began to smile. 'You mean I'm in this too? I can travel along with you, up to Arona?'

'Cavour thought you might really want to go on to Locarno.'

'What made him think such a ridiculous thing? Leave you, and go off with the refugees to Switzerland, when no one has ever been in the slightest danger in Turin?'

'He said, "I know Mrs. Blake has no sympathy with the aims of the Risorgimento. I haven't forgotten a talk we had one night on the Bridge of the Po, and she may welcome a chance to live in a neutral country until the campaign is over."'

'It hasn't really started yet,' said Jenny. 'How can he tell how long it's going to last? And why should we be parted again, Steve, just to suit Cavour and Italy?'

'Jenny, for God's sake, I only want to do what's best for you!'

'But you want to go to Garibaldi, don't you?' she asked, and read the answer in his eyes. 'Then take me with you! Steven, don't send me to Locarno! Don't leave me here in Turin! Let me go up to Arona along with you!'

'If it was any other girl in the world, I would say no——'

'But you didn't marry any other girl in the world, you married me.'

Four nights later, Jenny was sheltering from the rain in a peasant's hut in the woods on the Lombardy side of the Ticino, and the Austrian safe-conduct in Steven's pocket was so much waste paper.

Garibaldi was not at Arona, and never had been. The seasoned *guerillero* had kept his plan a secret from all but one of his officers and also from the Supreme Command. Drawing off the Austrians by a feint towards the town of Arona, he crossed the river several miles lower down and, now far in front of the whole line of the Allied armies, had liberated the hill town of Varese.

'He caught the Whitecoats asleep in their beds at Sesto Calende,' exulted the peasant, who said his name was Benedetto, 'and they say the whole countryside has risen in support of the Hunters of the Alps. Eleven years, sir and lady, we have waited for this day! Eleven years of the Austrian police, the Austrian tax collectors, the Austrian troopers riding over our fields and robbing us of hens and cattle! Had your honours but seen Captain Simonetta leading the Cacciatori across the river in the moonlight——'

'*How* does he say he led them?' Jenny whispered, for the north Lombard dialect was difficult to follow.

'Took them across in barges, as far as I can make out,' said Steve. 'Where the devil did Simonetta *get* the barges for three thousand men? Somebody must have planned that movement down to the last detail. And yet they say in Turin that Garibaldi's not an organiser!'

'Would your honours wish to sleep now?' asked Benedetto, struggling with a yawn. 'The lady must be weary after the river crossing, so I'll lie down in the stable and you shall have the hut. There's no one else here to disturb you, for my son went off to follow Garibaldi, and the Whitecoats have left the district and gone off to Varese. They won't catch Garibaldi, though! Good-night.'

'Let's leave the door ajar, Steve, it's so close in here,' said Jenny when the man had shuffled out.

'I don't think the mosquitoes will annoy us this far north.' Steven propped open the door, and came back to his chair beside the dying fire. With the candle blown out, Jenny could see the Ticino's high rapid flow beyond the poplars, and see the white foam on the pebble bank up which Steve had helped her when Benedetto rowed them across the river two hours before.

'Jenny, what in the world am I going to do with you?'

'What would you do if you were alone?'

'Find Garibaldi, of course.'

'Then that's what we'll both do.'

'It's madness, darling. I might be taking you into the middle of a pitched battle, and neither Garibaldi nor an Austrian safe-conduct could save you then.'

'You can't leave me here with Benedetto, can you? And I refuse to go back across that horrible river. That was our Rubicon, and we crossed it when we came over into Lombardy.'

'I could take you up to Arona; after all, that's where we were supposed to be going. Damn Garibaldi; why couldn't he have carried out Cavour's directives?'

'Because Count Cavour isn't a soldier, I suppose.'

'Now, Jenny, you're begging the question! It's the damnedest thing, the way you always stand up for Garibaldi! You've never shown much enthusiasm for United Italy.'

'Cavour couldn't make me believe in it, but Garibaldi can. He makes the Risorgimento sound like poetry.'

'You've never liked Cavour, just because you saw him first at Plombières with the Emperor.' Steven's eyes were closing. He laid his red head against the high back of the peasant's chair, and soon Jenny saw that he was asleep. She sat without moving, acknowledging the truth in his flash of perception. The long animosity to Napoleon III, kindled when Jenny felt herself to be a victim not so much of Orsini as of the Emperor's *coup de théâtre* at Orsini's trial, had indeed kept her from admiring the statecraft of Cavour. She had not gone far enough in self-observation to realise that her admiration for Garibaldi was born precisely at the time when the image of her natural father had been destroyed.

As the fresh scent of the poplars filled the hut, and lulled Jenny in her turn to sleep, her last waking thoughts were of thankfulness to be out of Turin. She had been too much alone there, with too much time to brood on her father and mother (and speculate painfully on the rejected child in Boston, her own half-brother or half-sister) and on George and Claire Lascaris and their guilty love. She had been forced to exchange letters with Signor Palmero, acknowledging the draft on a Turin bank for the balance of her account, which he had given her by Steven, and the safe arrival of the portmanteau he had personally forwarded from the Casa Lumone. She had written to Nice about the trunks full of Paris dresses left in storage there, and—though as yet, of course, without an answer—to the New York bank which had handled Kate Cameron's affairs. She, unlike Steven, had not been able to walk away from the past and to all appearances forget it; the past was there to remind her of Kate and Claire in every street and half the *palazzi* of Turin. The new clothes she had bought, the money in her purse, the certificate of a ten thousand dollar investment in the Italian Loan, were all due to Kate Cameron's capricious generosity. Her daughter paid her the tribute of remorseful memories.

But even tired and hungry, even by a peasant's fireside on the perimeter of a combat area, Jenny felt herself freer and happier than in her bridal room at the Hotel Felice. Happier still she was in the bright morning, when the rain had ceased, and Steve came back with Benedetto from a neighbouring farm where they had transacted the purchase of two horses to take Steve and Jenny to Varese. They made off by the shores of Lake Comabbio, into a landscape like a canvas of the Italian Primitives, with the

262

high Alps towering in the background, a hill town in the middle distance, and in the foreground lake waters which reflected skies of burning blue.

It was well that Benedetto saw them some miles on their way, and passed them on to a woodcutter's guidance through the forests beyond Comabbio, for the tracks north to Lake Varese were narrow and confusing, and it was not until noon that out of the silent country-side there burst a crowd of distraught countryfolk to give the Americans the first news of the battle. To them the name of Garibaldi was a password. They crowded round the horses, shouting the story of his triumphs and his men.

'Signori, they came up the hill to Varese in the rain, singing their marching song and shouting "*Italia! Noi siamo l'Italia!*" And they found the brave Varesini with their arms open to embrace them, their mouths eager to kiss them, and the green, white and red flag flying from every house and belfry, to welcome the liberators. So, our Garibaldi rested two days, and when the Austrian, Urban, came with three thousand men of the Rupprecht Brigade——'

'And heavy guns.'

'And cavalry.'

'——the Cacciatori delle Alpe fell upon them with the bayonet——'

'Through the mulberry trees.'

'And through the corn.'

'The Whitecoats ran, the victory was for Italy. *Viva Garibaldi! Viva Varese liberata!*'

'But more Whitecoats came,' said a one-eyed man on the outskirts of the crowd. 'Came by the railway from Milan.'

'And Urban bombarded the empty houses of Varese. Austrian dog! The Varesini paid for their freedom with their homes.'

'The *empty* houses!' Steven Blake caught at the word. 'Where are the townsfolk now?'

'They took refuge on the mountainside, signore. At the pilgrim's shrine of Santa Maria del Monte.'

'But General Garibaldi isn't with them?'

'*Corpo di Bacco,* no, signore! He drove the Austrians out of Como on the twenty-seventh of May, and he has gone back to Como. He is in Como now.'

'How far are we from Como here?'

'Ten miles as the crow flies, signore. Fifteen by our mountain paths and the pass of Santo Fermo.'

'Can you do it, Jenny?'

'Of course I can.'

'We'd better eat something first.'

They were given bread and cheese, and rough red wine at a farm where the woman of the place refused to accept payment. Her menfolk, the father and two sons, had all left to follow Garibaldi, carrying rifles concealed in the thatch for years. The Cacciatori had cleaned out her larder and barnyard; poor boys, wonderful boys. They had no commissariat, no sutler's wagons, the only food they carried was in the huge patch pockets the General had made them sew on their Piedmontese uniforms. Still, the lads were welcome to it, *è per l'Italia*; and she took no money from the friends of Garibaldi.

They rode again, with here a boy and there a handsome girl, and once a priest in a dusty soutane to rise out of the vines and the underbrush and point out the next stage of the way. The Austrians held the railhead at Camerlata; it would be rash to go anywhere near that town, though it was little more than two miles from Lake Como. They must go through the pass, where Garibaldi had dislodged the Hungarians the day before to capture Como town, and then down a road with many steep descents, the lady must take care. The lady laughed joy-fully. The intoxication of the day acted like wine on Jenny. Sometimes she rode hand in hand with Steve; sometimes when he was riding ahead she heard him singing tuneless snatches of old songs, most of them ribald, she remembered from the Sacramento days. To both young hearts had come the foolish assurance that this was war at its best and noblest; where the just cause armed only with the bayonet triumphed over the tyrant with the heavy guns. This was the Risorgimento at its best and bravest, with Garibaldi riding ahead and the young men of Lombardy hurrying from farms and villages to join the Hunters of the Alps; and this adventure, to Jenny and Steve, meant their own liberation from all the sad recollections of the past.

They halted for half an hour before beginning the descent to Como. It was fully eighteen months since Jenny had been on horseback, and the style of their journey was quite different from the canters in Central Park under the eye of the discreet riding-master who gave lessons at Miss Lippincott's Academy. She was beginning to feel stiff, and had a stitch in her side. Steve found the European saddle uncomfortable, and both horses were burdened by the saddle-bags which held changes of boots and clothing. After a rest they started down the pass of Santo Fermo, glimpsing at every zig-zag bend in the road the Lake of Como far below, with figures in army blue moving in the Piazza d'Armi, and lights beginning to twinkle in the hilltop village of Brunate. A new moon hung in the twilit sky above the mountains. There was nothing to reveal that a battle had been fought with bayonets in that defile, for rain had washed away the stains of blood, and the Cacciatori had taken their wounded into Como. Jenny did not know that here and there among the brushwood lay the body of a Hungarian soldier, already stained by the changes of mortality; she laughed with pleasure when a cloud of fireflies rose from the sweet-scented bushes and settled on her dress and hair. The fireflies sparkled on Steven's shoulders and in the horses' manes. In a shimmer of living diamonds they rode into Como.

General Garibaldi had established his headquarters in a house in the centre of the town, a short walk from the lake and near the cathedral and the Piazza d'Armi. So half a dozen joyful people told them, and a merry matron, wearing the Italian colours in her hair, offered to guide Jenny and the horses to the Hotel Corona, while Steven reported at once to Garibaldi. The Corona was on the outskirts of the town near the Milan Gate; it was clean and quiet. Como was in time of peace an isolated place, linked with the world only by the lake steamers which twice daily plied to Colico and back, and by the coach which met the trains at Camerlata. Many of the inhabitants went abroad as travelling pedlars, selling the stucco images made in the town. Those who remained were amazed to find themselves in the forward post of the Allied line, with the Hunters of the Alps inside the gates, and not far away a raging Austrian general with eleven thousand men waiting to avenge themselves on Garibaldi.

Jenny had changed from the crumpled and mud-splashed black garment of her journey into a plain white cotton dress when Steven arrived from headquarters with Peard, the gigantic Englishman, as his guide, and a smaller, more dapper, moustachioed man walking between them.

'Jenny, you look lovely,' he said gratefully, accepting the glass of *grappa* she at once poured for him, and lighting a cigarette. 'Garibaldi thinks you're a heroine to have come along with me.'

'But he must have been delighted to see *you*?'

'I told him I should have been sent north a week ahead of him, if the line to Milan was really to be put out of action. Now Urban is here with three brigades—Rupprecht, Augustin and Schaffgotsche; and the last two certainly came up by rail. They could only have been prevented if the line had been blown before they left Milan.'

'Which nobody thought of doing?'

'Which nobody did. Not that the General cares much about that. He's very proud of containing the enemy up here in front of Como. He doesn't seem to realise that Urban might think it more useful to take his eleven thousand Austrians right back to Milan and throw them into the big battle with the Allies, which won't be fought up here.'

'How do you come to know so much about strategy, darling?'

'Because I'm a railroadman, that's why; and I don't think any general, on either side, has a notion of how to *use* the railroads. Oh, to transport troops, yes; they can do that, but once they've got the boys to the scene they leave 'em to lam into one another just as they did in olden days. I told Cavour if he wanted to be certain of containing General Urban he ought to destroy the rolling stock at Camerlata. He said he'd order Simonetta and the scouts out to reconnoitre.'

'Not you?'

'He pointed out that I'm a neutral and a non-combatant, and mustn't take part in any military action. What about that fellow Peard? He walked to the Corona with me, he and Nino Bixio. He's an Englishman, a neutral, isn't he? Bixio says he fought like a wild-cat when they were clearing the pass of Santo Fermo. A man old enough to be my father, how do you suppose that makes me feel?'

Steven had been buttoning on a clean shirt as he
spoke. They were to dine with Garibaldi, he said, and
some of his staff officers. Oh, and the general wondered if
Jenny would help Dr. Bertani in the emergency hospital
tomorrow. There weren't many casualties after Santo
Fermo, but as Garibaldi had no ambulance service every
woman who could nurse was needed. Did Jenny mind?

She said she was glad, and meant it; as she walked on
Steven's arm to Garibaldi's headquarters, Jenny felt an
inward satisfaction that her old idea of expiation and
fulfilment in joining Pastor Fliedner's nurses in Germany
would be realised on the shores of Lake Como.

Garibaldi welcomed her to Como with a paternal kiss.
In the hour of his triumph, his outwitting by sheer
virtuosity of the better-armed but slower-moving Urban,
he was all things to all men. A father to Jenny, a colleague
to Steven Blake, a boy with his boy soldiers, a chieftain
among his veterans, he moved from the big refectory
where the leading citizens of Como took wine with the
Cacciatori to the room where his closest comrades sat
around him.

'We must have our bride with us,' he said. 'Come,
signora, sit at my right hand; unless you are too timid to
be among rough soldiers like ourselves, and prefer the
company of the mayor's wife and her friends?'

'I'm glad to be with the rough soldiers, general.' Jenny
was excited by the excitement in the air. Garibaldi took
a flower from a vase on the table and handed it to her.

'You shall wear our colours, signora,' he said. 'Green
leaves, red roses, white dress—the three colours Lombardy wears again—and drink to the King and Cialdini,
the victors of Palestro.'

'Has there been a victory in the south, too, general?'

There had been a battle (half a dozen voices explained, as the wine went round and platters of food were brought) on the line of the railroad at a place called Palestro, between Novara and Alessandria. There the Sardinians, led by Victor Emmanuel II and General Cialdini, his first liaison officer with the Garibaldini, had defeated the Austrians on the night of May 29/30— 'without any support from the French', was frequently emphasised. It was a more important action than the first real battle of the war, at Montebello on May 20, and valuable to Sardinian morale, but it was far from a decisive action. Garibaldi's officers considered that the titular Supreme Commander, Napoleon III, must take such action soon.

After placing her by his side with the honours due to a bride, Garibaldi spoke little to Jenny. The conversation was strictly military, except when John Peard took part in it. Peard, whom the mountain folk had begun to call 'Garibaldi's Englishman', felt a huge personal exultation over the death of the King of Naples—'King Bomba' as he had been called since the slaughter of Messina in 1848, when he bombarded his rebellious subjects into docility.

'Yes, the tyrants are disappearing one by one,' agreed Garibaldi. 'King Bomba's son will ascend the throne, but for how long? I could take Naples with a thousand men like those quartered in Como town tonight!'

'Here's to it, chief!' cried Nino Bixio, the fiery, dapper captain who had walked with Steve and Peard to the hotel. He was the most violent of all the Garibaldini, the most ruthlessly demanding of his men, and he had fought like a demon with Garibaldi in the defence of Rome. 'Here's to the meeting of every man round this table, on the day Naples falls to the forces of liberty!'

Jenny saw Steven touch his lips to his glass, and set it down with a moody look. She smiled at him across the table and his face cleared. She was aware of her beauty alluring him and unfolding like the petals of the red rose at her breast.

'We must see Venice free before we march on Naples,' Garibaldi said. 'Yours was a good toast, Nino *amico*, but unchivalrous! It excluded Mrs. Blake, whom we can hardly ask to march with us against the Bourbons.'

'Signora,' cried the excitable Bixio, 'we drink to you as the representative of all our wives and sweethearts!'

'Have you written yet to *your* wife, Nino *mio*?'

'General, I wrote to tell her of our victory at Como. I said, "Our men cast themselves down the pass of Santo Fermo like a torrent. Now I am living in a poem."'

From all the ardent Italians at that supper table, there was an instant, emotional response to Bixio's vivid words. Garibaldi's blue eyes glowed. He raised his glass.

'Let us drink to the memory of *my* wife, who is not here to share our victory,' he said quietly. 'To Anita!'

'Anita.' That toast, which few of the men present had heard Garibaldi propose before, was drunk standing. When they were seated, the general smiled at Jenny and said to Captain Medici:

'Don't you think Mrs. Blake looks very like Anita?'

Medici exchanged a glance with Bixio. They both recalled Anita Garibaldi as they had last seen her, with her hair cropped like a man's and wearing a trooper's jacket, gaunt-faced and swollen with her six months' pregnancy, as she rode out of Rome with her husband. Neither could remember the bright beauty of eighteen who had fled with Garibaldi from her friends and family.

'The eyes are very like,' said Medici tactfully.

'I was at San Marino,' said a grey-haired man at the foot of the table. 'I remember Anita standing beside you, general, when you made your speech to the people who had given us refuge. "I offer you nothing but blood, suffering and exile," you said, "for bargain with the foreigner, that I never will!"'

'"I offer you nothing but battles, suffering, pain and tears,"' corrected Captain Medici.

'That was at Rome,' said Bixio. 'My God, man, every word of what was said that last day is graven on my memory. "I am going out of Rome," the general said. "Whoever wishes to continue the war against the stranger, let him follow me. I promise neither pay nor provisions, I promise only bread and water; I have nothing to offer you but blood, hunger, tears and sweat. Once we are past the gates of Rome, a step to the rear is a step to death."'

Garibaldi shaded his eyes with his hand. 'And it was so,' he said. 'Four thousand men left Rome with me; before long, with the Austrians in close pursuit, I bade them scatter. We had a brief respite in the Republic of San Marino—the only state in Italy with the courage to open its frontier to us. But we were only two hundred when we left San Marino, and very soon we were fewer still. We were at sea on the second of August, chased by an Austrian squadron in bright moonlight; the moon was fatal to us that night. Then we were only three when we waded through the surf on the Bosco Eliseo: Leggiero and me, and Anita; and already I thought I saw the death look in her face. She died the next day in my arms, at the farm of the Guiccioli, and we were two—two out of the defenders of Rome, surviving; and dear Leggiero died later of his wounds. Then I was all alone, with nothing left me but the sword of Rome, and nothing before me but a life in exile.'

'But you returned, my general!'

Steven and Jenny walked back to their quarters in the warm June night. One or two of the taverns near the little harbour were still lighted, and the sound of singing could be heard. The Hunters of the Alps were living in their poem: their songs now were not of war, but of love, and the linked cadences of the guitars sang to *amore* and *cuore* as plaintively as the waters of Lake Como lapped against the shore. Jenny's white dress was a pale blur in the darkness. Her body was pliant to Steven's arm. The wine they had drunk, the vivid imagery of all the Garibaldini said, the delicious sense of danger not far off but held at bay, had conspired to liberate the spirits of them both. That night, for the first time, Jenny knew ecstasy in her husband's arms, spent the force of her body as recklessly as he spent his, moaned her pleasure against his mouth. They had no longer any care for what the future brought: the poetry of the Risorgimento rose like a tide around them, and swept them together to the final harmony of love.

Next morning, Steven returned alone to headquarters, to discuss with Captain Simonetta the possibility of destroying the Austrian locomotives at Camerlata. At almost the same hour, the Allied Commander-in-Chief, Napoleon III, took the field in person. He attacked the Austrians at Magenta, on the railroad between Turin and Novara, and within sight of the Duomo at Milan. The French fought all day along the line of the railroad and the Naviglio Grande, taking five thousand Austrian prisoners-of-war. Their own losses at the end of the day were seven hundred killed and three thousand two hundred wounded. A Te Deum was sung at Notre Dame and in every church in France, and on June 8 Napoleon III entered Milan in triumph.

Fourteen

THE EMPEROR BY MOONLIGHT

THE Emperor of the French lay sleeping. He dreamed he was back in Milan, riding a white charger along the Corso with King Victor Emmanuel II riding by his side. A squadron of his Cent-Gardes rode behind him with their silver breast-plates gleaming, and ahead the Bishop of Milan stood waiting with his canons to greet the victorious sovereigns on the steps of the cathedral. All along the Corso the Milanese were shouting *'Viva Napoleone! Viva il Liberatore!'* The cheering rose through the windless morning to the blue Italian sky.

There were girls on the silk and velvet-hung balconies —girls with red lips and burning eyes, who were throwing flowers at the Emperor of the French. A rose brushed his wrist, and he raised his gloved hand in salute. It was taken firmly by another hand, and a voice above his head said 'Sire! Your orders were to call you if anything came in from I Corps!' The dream vanished: Napoleon III was lying on a camp bed at Montechiaro, and the triumphal entry to Milan was already two weeks in the past.

'What time is it?' he said, and raised himself upon his elbow.

'Just past two o'clock, Sire,' the equerry replied.

'You may read the message.'

'It is signed by General Baraguay d'Hilliers, Sire. It reads, "Advanced units under my command made contact with the enemy at half past midnight." '

Louis Napoleon grunted. 'Send my valet to me.' When the young equerry had gone he got out of bed yawning, an ungainly man of fifty-one, too old and too flabby for these night alarms, or for the task which might lie before him in the next few hours. When the valet had shaved him and corseted him into his uniform he was seized by a violent fit of shivering.

'Sire, may I call Dr. Conneau?' the servant said, alarmed by the clay-cold face and trembling lips of his master.

'Yes, ask him to come in.' Conneau was an old comrade, they had been in prison together; he had no objection to being seen by Conneau in an hour of weakness.

'You don't feel the onset of a chill, I hope?' said Dr. Conneau, entering quietly.

'I feel that three hours' sleep is not enough for any man!'

'Bring coffee for His Majesty,' Conneau told the servant. '—They shouldn't have aroused you, Louis. But Baraguay——'

'Baraguay seems to have bumped into the Austrians.' The Emperor lit the first cigarette of the day, and noticed with pleasure that his hand had stopped shaking. He gave satisfactory replies to Conneau's questions about headache and fever. The doctor, he knew was taking the right precautions. The French Army had been ravaged by malaria and dysentery since it began plunging through the flooded rice-fields and mulberry groves of the Plain of Piedmont; it would have been foolhardy to suppose that the Emperor was necessarily exempt from infection. The coffee was brought, and Napoleon drank it thirstily. He felt better with Conneau there. What he needed was someone to lean on, someone to tell him he was doing the right thing if he accepted a pitched battle now rather than sit down to a long siege of the fortresses of the Quadrilateral. His nerves jumped again: he remembered the pitched battle at Magenta.

Within twenty minutes he was in the saddle and riding towards Castiglione, the little town previously selected as forward headquarters if the retreating Austrians stood to fight along the line of the Mincio. It was eighteen miles south-east of Brescia, which had been in Allied hands for ten days, and only five from the railway which the Austrians had attempted to destroy. It was also a town whose name had powerful associations for Louis Napoleon Bonaparte.

These memories were not romantic. The Emperor had long since put out of his mind the vain and lovely Contessa di Castiglione, called the Queen of Hearts, who still, in her haunted villa on the slopes above Turin, sulked and hoped for the return of her imperial lover. He thought instead of his uncle, the great Napoleon, who had defeated the Austrians at Castiglione, Lodi, Arcola, and staged his own triumphal entry into Milan. Those were the battles, and this the Bonaparte mystique, which had sent Napoleon the Less stumbling across Lombardy at the head of one hundred and forty thousand men. Here, if anywhere in Europe, he expected history to repeat itself.

The Emperor checked his horse at three o'clock and the General Staff and the Household jingled to a standstill around and behind him.

'Sire?' A galloper pressed forward, ready to carry a message or a written order, and the Emperor sighed.

'How far are we from Castiglione?'

'Less than two miles, Sire.'

'Bring me a map and a lantern, if you please.'

The moon, which had just entered its last quarter,

shed a grey light on the vineyards and the rising hills south of Lake Garda. Somewhere in that misty pallor, beyond his own great army, lay the Austrians, almost one hundred and thirty thousand strong. They had a new Commander-in-Chief, for General Gyulai had been removed after his defeat at Magenta, and the Emperor Franz Josef had taken the supreme command himself. It was possible that Franz Josef, too, was suffering from an attack of nerves.

The large-scale ordnance map was brought, in its leather case. The equerry who handed it to his Imperial master asked if he should hold the lantern, and was dismissed. There was no real need for a light. The Emperor had studied the terrain on paper until he knew it by heart; all he wanted was an excuse to halt, to ask himself once more if he was right to join battle with Franz Josef now.

After his day of glory in Milan, the Austrians had seemed to crumble before the Allied advance. Pavia, Cremona, Brescia were liberated, the Rivers Adda, Oglio and Chiese crossed. But if the Allies avoided an immediate battle, and chased the enemy across the Mincio, they would find themselves entrapped under the great guns of Peschiera, Verona, Legnano and Mantua—the Quadrilateral—and Napoleon III had had more than enough of setting siege to fortresses. Only four years earlier, in the Crimean War, all the French corps commanders now ready to go into action had spent months on the capture of Sevastopol, weeks on the reduction of a minor Baltic fortress, Bomarsund; and in the end Sveaborg, covering Helsingfors, had proved to be impregnable.

Napoleon III heard the slight movements and subdued voices of his staff. He wondered, as he had been wondering ever since Magenta, what they thought of their Emperor now. The troops had cheered him on the field the day after the battle, and he had created Marshal MacMahon Duke of Magenta; but he knew, and MacMahon knew too, that between them they had nearly lost that engagement, and in fact had won it only by default. He remembered, far more clearly than the triumphal entry to Milan, the hours he spent on horseback at the bridge of Buffalora, smoking endless cigarettes, watching the carnage of Magenta and somehow powerless to prevent or end it.

He had set out to liberate Italy from purely selfish motives. As the liberator, he would obtain Nice and Savoy, have a vassal state in Central Italy, and a sphere of influence through the whole peninsula. He saw already that two of these aims would never be fulfilled, and for his defeat he had to thank two men: Cavour and Garibaldi.

Cavour, as supple and astute as Louis Napoleon Bonaparte, had never meant a Kingdom of Central Italy to be created. All the States which had revolted since the war began—Tuscany, Parma, Modena, the Romagna—were declaring their allegiance to the Kingdom of Sardinia, and were ready to acknowledge Victor Emmanuel as their King. Garibaldi had gone through Alpine Lombardy like a flame, rallying in one month no fewer than twelve thousand young men to his cause, which was the cause of a totally united, completely independent Italy. Napoleon III, as Supreme Commander, had disposed of Garibaldi by ordering the Cacciatori delle Alpe and their rabble of followers into the snows of the Valtellina on the pretext of guarding the Stelvio pass. But in all the hill towns, in all the liberated cities of Northern Italy, the legend of Garibaldi was vividly, movingly alive.

'I have nothing to offer you but blood, labour, hunger

and tears'—that was Garibaldi's promise, repeated in different words in every town and village he passed through. *Fame, sete, marcie forzate, battaglie e morte*— how came such a sombre rallying-cry to stir the souls of men? How could such an offer compare with *La Gloire*, the prize which through seven years of force and fraud the Emperor Napoleon III had dangled before the nose of France?

The sound of a rider coming west along the road was heard, and the Prince de la Moskowa, as senior among the eleven aides-de-camp following the Emperor, moved forward to intercept the messenger.

'A despatch from the Marshal-Duke of Magenta, Sire.'

The Emperor's brain had taken to moving so sluggishly that he had to pause to identify MacMahon by his brand-new title. He allowed the Prince de la Moskowa to hold the lantern, and with fumbling fingers opened the despatch.

The commander of II Corps announced that his vedettes had seen Austrian pickets stationed on the hills round Cavriana. They were reported to belong to General Stadion's command.

'The Austrians seem eager to be up and doing,' said Napoleon III. 'I don't think we need to wait to hear from Niel and Canrobert. Order the Garde Impériale forward to Castiglione.'

That was all, but with these words the French were committed to the battle. Napoleon III heard the crackle of orders break out at his back, and the thud of hoofbeats down the road to Brescia. Very soon this silent hollow where they now stood would be choked with caissons and limbers, ambulance wagons, loads of food and forage for man and beast, and all along the Allied line, extending for fifteen miles southward of Lake Garda, the drums would start beating the call to arms.

There was no hope for it, he had to fight. Since his quasi-victory at Magenta, Europe had begun to rise against him. His old enemy, Lord Palmerston, had returned to power in England, and Prussia was massing troops at Cologne and Coblenz. The Empress Eugénie had written frantically to say she doubted whether Pelissier's little French Army of the Rhine could ever withstand an invasion, if Prussia chose to strike while the Emperor was away in Lombardy. Clearly he could no longer risk involvement in a war of attrition. This must be the decisive day.

The French must win as they had won under General Bonaparte, and die like men for Louis Napoleon. But the Emperor, grey-faced in the grey moonlight, knew the truth. He was no military genius, nor even an efficient commander: he was a hollow man, a man of straw. The first bugles sounded, miles away, as he urged his horse forward. The moon went down, the dark Star of Louis Napoleon began to pale, and slowly the sun rose on the field of Solferino.

Fifteen

MONSIEUR DUNANT

At ten o'clock on that Friday morning, June 24, the
Garde Impériale—or what was left of it after the
slaughter of Magenta—marched out of the little town of
Castiglione to take up a position at the foot of Monte
Medole, somewhat to the rear of General Forey's Voltigeurs. Their departure eased, for the time being, the
traffic on the two roads leading into Castiglione, the
highway from Brescia up which caissons and ambulances
were being brought to the front, and the less important
road from Lonato, where among the commissariat
wagons and carts a few peasant tumbrils and even some
private carriages were to be seen. One of the latter, a
light vehicle intended for pleasure trips along the shores
of Lake Garda, was being driven at speed by Jenny
Blake.

The sun was burning down from a sky of the deepest
blue and the little carriage had no canopy. Driving a
frightened horse through the army traffic, with the sound
of cannon fire already deafening, was a different matter
from driving Claire's petted white mules, in the gay
white and yellow cart, along the old Roman road to
Mentone, and Jenny's arms ached with the strain. Her
feet were braced on the floor-board and her Italian straw
hat had slipped to the back of her head. From time to
time she glanced anxiously at her companion, a French
lady considerably older than herself, whose closed eyes

and set mouth revealed that she was suffering.

'Madame Douay,' Jenny said at last, 'we're only about a mile from Castiglione, if the last signpost was right.'

'So near?' The Frenchwoman sat up and tried to smile. 'Dear Mrs. Blake, how can I ever thank you for all you've done?'

'By remembering the promise you made before we left Lonato!'

'To help other wounded men if I can't find my husband'—obediently. Then, in a cry of pent-up feeling, 'But I *shall* find Charles! He must be there! My father would never have sent the messenger if he hadn't been brought safely up to Castiglione.'

'Of course he's there,' soothed Jenny. 'But madame—they've been fighting since six o'clock this morning! There must be hundreds of wounded men back in the town now. You may not be able to find General Douay at once. Even General Le Breton may have been ordered elsewhere. We must both try to be useful everywhere—or else we should have stayed in the hotel at Lonato, where at least we weren't getting in the way.'

'How calmly you can speak, and think, in this hell of noise!'

'I don't feel calm,' said Jenny, shaking. 'I never heard cannon in my life before.'

'Not even when you rode with Garibaldi?'

'General Garibaldi had no artillery. And in the ten days we were with the Cacciatori they were only in action once, at Seriate.'

'But you actually nursed the wounded men?'

'I helped Dr. Bertani with the bandaging. A nursing Sister in Genoa showed me how.'

'You have seen—soldiers—die?'

'One,' said Jenny with set teeth.

'I have never seen death,' said Madame Charles Douay.

'Oh God! I'm so frightened—of what we're going to see!'

'You were brave enough to come to Italy with your husband. Brave enough to follow him to the battlefield!'

'I swore I would,' said the general's wife. 'After Charles came safely back from the Crimea. He led the 2nd Voltigeurs at the Malakoff—he was wounded there. I told him if France ever went to war again, he would have to take me too!'

'I understand,' said Jenny. A wheel passed over some obstacle in the road, and the vehicle lurched dangerously. A man driving army mules pulled out of the way, and swore.

'What will your own husband say, when he comes back to Lonato tonight, and finds you gone?'

'God knows. But he was sent for to Sardinian Headquarters, and since the Sardinians are in the battle too——' She left the sentence unfinished. In her heart Jenny was sure that Steven was somewhere in the enormous line of battle which Napoleon III had launched across the foothills guarding the River Mincio.

'You were at Lonato when our brigade arrived. Had you been there long?'

'Only a few days. Steven started working up and down the track from Lonato after Garibaldi was sent up to the Valtellina.'

'I heard General Garibaldi's farewell speech in Brescia. It was very moving.'

I offer you nothing but blood and tears and sweat. Jenny had heard Garibaldi's magnificent challenge in every market place from Como through Bergamo to Brescia; she knew that it made women weep, and men lay down their tools to follow the Hunters of the Alps. 'He knows what to promise Italy,' she said. 'It was all— with his love—he gave his own Anita.'

'Oh!' said Madame Douay faintly, 'do you think we shall ever be able to enter Castiglione?'

The traffic round the town was almost at a standstill. They had reached the junction with the Brescia road, blocked by an overturned gun-carriage, and the provost-marshals were struggling to restore movement in all directions. The noise of the guns reverberated through the blazing morning.

'You're not going to faint *now*,' said Jenny sharply. 'There's brandy in that leather bag beneath the seat.'

'*Mesdames!*' said a soft voice at her side. '*Je vous en prie, mesdames!*'

Jenny looked away from her passenger's white face to the driver of a cabriolet of which the near wheels were very nearly locking with their own. He was a man of about thirty, wearing a white linen suit now stained with sweat and dust. Whatever good looks he might have had were effectively disguised by a heavy beard.

'You're all right,' said Jenny. 'There's enough room for your cab to pass.'

'Madame,' said the man politely, 'I have no fear of that, for I see you're an excellent whip, but I ventured to address you ... to ask if you can direct me to Imperial Headquarters.'

'I am so sorry,' Jenny said. 'I have really no idea. This lady and I are going to the hospital, and I don't even know where that is! We shall all have to ask directions in the town—if we can ever get there.'

'I admit my mission is personal,' said the man. 'But it is rather urgent. I've come a long way for an interview with the French Emperor!'

'On behalf of a newspaper, sir?' said Jenny. She had had her own picture sketched at the trial of Orsini, and again—for the *Illustrated London News*—when the Garibaldini entered Brescia; she understood a little of

284

the pertinacity of the war correspondents.

'My card, madame.' As the army mules reared and plunged around them, the gentleman in white produced his card-case as calmly as if he were in a drawing-room and handed a slip of pasteboard, at arm's length, to Jenny. She read:

Monsieur Henry Dunant,
Director of the Mons-Gemila Mills, Algiers.

'How do you do,' said Jenny. 'I'm Mrs. Steven Blake.' She had to shout her name across the yelling of the army drivers. 'Watch out! We can go forward now!' She seized her chance and slid the little carriage through an opening in the traffic. Behind her she heard Monsieur Dunant shouting a polite reply, of which she only caught the last word—'hospital'.

The operation launched by the two Emperors was of the simplest nature known to military textbooks. The Emperor of Austria turned his back on the Mincio—and his fortresses—and drew up his men in two armies on the heights facing the French. Among those heights there were several little towns, including Pozzolengo, Solferino and Guidizzolo; as the day wore on Solferino emerged as the key to the whole gigantic action.

The Emperor of the French was therefore required to storm the heights and drive the Austrians from their positions. He had to send his men across a plain which at first sight seemed a more favourable terrain than Magenta, without the canals and sodden rice-fields, but presenting its own problems in the way of ditches, broad stone walls and festoons of vine and mulberry which all too often held the red-trousered Frenchmen trapped under the fire of the Whitecoats on the slopes above. It was not that the Austrian fire was particularly accurate, or the French unwilling to advance. They went forward with their usual *élan*, but they were in poor condition; fever and dysentery had weakened many of them, and they had nothing to eat or drink but coffee before the battle. The Austrians, who had had no bread ration for three days, had a double ration of liquor: the effect on both sides was much the same. If the French faltered, in the first few hours of that day of carnage, it was because every corps commander sensed that the conductor directing this orchestra of death had an uncertain hand on the baton. The Emperor made a classic opening, sending in the infantry with cavalry support. He began the day, however, with forebodings about the morale of the Sardinians on his left wing, where King Victor Emmanuel II and General Fanti were opposing the best of the Austrian commanders, Benedek. Napoleon III fumbled his first approaches through the centre and the right. By noon two hundred and seventy thousand men, forty thousand horses and seven hundred guns were in action along a front which swayed backwards and forwards for fully fifteen miles, here including the village of Medole, there engulfing the hill shrine called the Madonna del' Pieve, where the Austrian Emperor watched the beginning of the battle.

The French generals, confused at first, successfully retrieved the fumblings of their Emperor. They pushed their brigades forward, one after the other, until the Austrian centre broke, and Canrobert's and Niel's corps smashed clear through Wimpffen's First Army. But their success was due, in the last analysis, to the fighting spirit of their sick and hungry men. Pure rage finally possessed the Frenchmen; pure rage was responsively kindled in the Austrians. When Napoleon III rode out from Castiglione to establish forward headquarters at Cavriana, from where Franz Josef had withdrawn to Volta, he saw the corpses of men who had flung away their conventional weapons—the broken bayonet, the rifle with the empty cartridge belt—to stone one another, to disembowel with the knife, to bite and suffocate. He saw horses possessed by the same rage as their dead masters, flying riderless across the field and smiting each other down with iron-shod hooves. He saw the turbaned Turcos of his own African contingent, the Croats from Franz Josef's eastern domains—the most ruthlessly cruel of the two armies—strangling each other with their bare hands. The Saviour of Society wept, and his awe-struck entourage heard his pious whisper: 'Poor creatures! Poor creatures! War is a horrible thing!'

Finally God wearied of the spectacle. At half-past four in the afternoon a tremendous storm broke over the field of Solferino: thunder and lightning raged, and torrential rain drowned wounded men who were feebly clawing their way out of the blood and slime where the guns had passed. Into this storm Napoleon III ordered his last reserves. The bearskins of the Imperial Guard moved up the slope, as once at Waterloo, the Tricolore was planted on the hill of Solferino. By six, the Austrians were in full retreat across the Mincio. There was no question of winning by default this time. Napoleon III was justified in the telegram he at once dictated to the Empress Eugénie—'Grande bataille, grande victoire'.

It was so great a victory that more than forty thousand men lay killed or wounded on the field. In the wet darkness of the night that followed, many thousands more, groping their way back to bases which had shifted with the fluctuations of the fight, were smitten with the chills and fevers which in the space of the next three months were to claim their lives too. The field hospitals, distinguished only by black flags and the coloured pennants of the different nations, had been bombarded; many army doctors had been killed. Priests, led by the Abbé Laine, Napoleon III's own chaplain, administered the last rites until darkness fell. Medical aid, in all but a few parts of the field, was not forthcoming till the morning.

At Castiglione, as Jenny had predicted, several hundred wounded had been received during the early stages of the battle. It had also been predictable that no trace of General Douay, nor even of his father-in-law General Le Breton, would be found in the demented town, but Madame Douay kept her promise nobly and, with Jenny, offered her services at once in the little hospital. The gentleman in the white suit, who had accosted them on the road, reached the hospital almost as soon as they did.

'Have you had any experience of nursing, Mrs. Blake?' he asked in his soft yet authoritative voice when he saw Jenny tie an apron taken from the kitchen over her black dress, and roll her sleeves up to the elbow.

'Practically none. I worked for two days with Dr. Bertani in the hospital at Como, but that was very different from this.' There was fear and disgust in her voice.

'How, different?'

'It was a cool, clean place beside a lake ... and the people brought clean sheets ... and lemon drinks and fans ... and the boys were so brave, and made light of their wounds; and there was no—gunfire.'

'We're going to hear the guns for some time yet, I fear,' said Monsieur Dunant, 'and these men are too badly wounded to be brave. Do you think you could get together a party of Italian women to collect clean linen, and tear it up to give us a good supply of bandages? They'll do anything to help, you know, but they need someone to tell them what to do.'

'But—aren't there bandages in those huge bales?'

'Only charpie. The Ambulance Service has brought in caisson loads of charpie, as if the French had been shredding lint for years to prepare for this; but unfortunately they neglected to bring bandages. I called at their headquarters on the way here.'

'Are you a doctor, sir?'

'No, but in Algeria I learned something about first aid, and my father was the head of an orphanage in Switzerland, where I was born. I think I know a little about organisation,' said Monsieur Dunant modestly, 'and organisation alone is going to get us through the next few days. Forgive a personal question, madame—where is your husband?'

'Oh God!' cried Jenny, 'how I wish I knew!'

'Is he a Frenchman? In the Army?'

'He's an American. Count Cavour called him a neutral and a non-combatant.'

'But he has a battle of his own to fight, like me.'

'He's a railroad engineer. He had to go to Desenzano two days ago. But I left a letter telling him I was coming here.'

'He'll follow you.' Henri Dunant was not a frivolous man, but a twinkle came into his eyes as he studied the lovely flushed face of the slender girl in the big apron. 'Now will you talk to these good women about the linen? And straw—we shall need several hundred bales of straw before tomorrow.'

"The strongest will be needed at the wash-tubs." Jenny remembered having read somewhere that Florence Nightingale, with these words, had snubbed some gushing aspirant to selection for Crimean service; they came true for herself long before the day of Solferino ended. If she washed no linen, she stood for an hour at the pump in the hospital yard, filling tubs and buckets for the Italian women; she carried bundles of foul and blood-stained clothing to the laundry; she tugged and pulled at the inert and helpless men to be laid down on clean straw in the hospital corridors. All the time she was despairingly aware that this was only the beginning of it; that while one thousand wounded men had been received in Castiglione before the ambulances stopped their search in the storm, there would be twice, perhaps four times, as many to come in later. To care for them were two Italian doctors, medieval in their long black robes, a few nuns, a crowd of inexperienced and emotional volunteers, and Monsieur Henri Dunant.

The Swiss was calm through all the horrors of that night. Jenny only saw his self-control shaken once, when a severely wounded Frenchman, complaining that one of the enemy, a Croat, was being examined by the doctor before himself, drew a knife from his belt and buried it in the Croat's thigh. Yet it was not Dunant, but an ignorant Italian peasant woman, who calmed the ensuing uproar with some very simple words. 'All are brothers!' she said reproachfully to the Frenchman, and the cursing comrades of the injured Croat. *Sono tutti fratelli!*

'All men are brothers,' repeated Dunant. 'Little children, love one another!' He drew his hand across his tired eyes. 'There is our watchword, Mrs. Blake. "Tutti fratelli!" We should write it upon every hospital room in Castiglione.'

'And in the palaces of Paris and Vienna,' Jenny said. She was deathly tired, terrified of the days ahead, but confident that Steven, if he had not been caught in the battle, would soon come to her. And come he did before midnight, riding into town with a Sardinian convoy bringing food and wine for the wounded, and lifting Jenny off her feet into his thankful embrace.

'Were you worried when you found your wife had left Lonato, Mr. Blake?' asked Dunant, beaming. There was no hope of privacy in the hospital; half a dozen people were in what had been the senior doctor's room.

'I was worried some, but not surprised. Jenny gets into every row that's going,' said her husband cheerfully. 'Where's Madame Douay?'

'She's lying down, tired out. She really was a Trojan today, though, Steve. And she's heart-broken about her husband.'

'She needn't be, I found him for her,' Steven announced. 'Both he and her father are in the emergency ward at the police barracks. Some fool driver started off with them down the Brescia road and had to turn back, fortunately.'

'Oh, Steven, what a piece of luck! Right here in the same town all the time! I'll go to her at once, I'm sure she's not asleep.'

'No, I'll look after Madame Douay and take her to the general,' said Dunant, rising. 'You must look after your own husband, Mrs. Blake. And tomorrow will be another day, you know ... How long can you stay with us, monsieur?'

'Tomorrow is another day for me too,' said Steve. 'I'll have to get men working double shifts between Lonato halt and Brescia. You're going to have a big problem when you start evacuating wounded.'

'You're a man after my own heart, Mr. Blake.' They measured each other up, and it struck Jenny that here were two who would make their own decisions in a crisis. She had not heard Monsieur Dunant, in all the confusion of the day, pay any special attention to the town councillors and police of Castiglione, or to any officers of the French Army except the doctors. The wounded and their attendants had been his sole concern.

'Will you really have to go away tomorrow, Steve?' she whispered as she led him out of the hospital, where an uneasy silence of exhaustion had been established, towards the yard where she had pumped water earlier in the day.

'I must, darling. There's sure to be some army transport going to Brescia. I'll be at the station, off and on; you send me a telegram every morning through Headquarters to let me know how you are and what's going on here, and when you're ready to move I'll come and get you.'

'You aren't angry with me for coming here?'

'Not angry, darling. I expected you to do something like this, ever since our time with Garibaldi.'

'Why Garibaldi?' The moon was extinguished by the weeping darkness, but Steven could just see Jenny's face by the light from the hospital buildings beyond the poplars; it was pale and lined with fatigue.

'Because he got you, Jenny; just like he got me and everyone who ever met him. He made you believe in the fight for Italy and want to fight yourself, in your own way—didn't he?'

He saw her shake her head. 'I don't think ... it was exactly that. It was ... when those awful guns were firing, all day long, I kept thinking they were the echoes of—that noise in a Paris street long ago, the noise of Orsini's bombs magnified a hundred thousand times... And I was there at the beginning, Steve. I wanted to be there at the end—if it ever ends.'

'It's got to end sometime,' Steven muttered.

'And then I thought of mother,' Jenny said with a catch in her dry voice. 'I've never stopped thinking that her life might have been saved, and she might have become—quite a different person—if I hadn't driven her so hard and fought with her that night. I can't do anything for her now: I never could. But if I can do something instead to help those poor fellows ... do you think it might make up for—everything?'

'Ah, little Jenny!' He gathered her to his heart and felt her relax with a sigh in the familiar shelter of his arms. 'Have you been brooding—worrying on about Kate, all this time when I thought you were happy with me?'

'I have been happy, Steven dear. Too happy.' She took his kisses, her mouth opening beneath his like a flower. 'But isn't it wrong to be happy in a world like this?'

'No, it isn't wrong.' She was at the last extreme of exhaustion, he realised that. He asked her if she had a room, or any place where they could sleep. Madame Douay by now had certainly gone to her husband.

'There are three other women in the room we were going to share. But there's clean straw in the barn, about a ton of it.'

'We've got to get some rest before morning, dear.'

'I know.' She led him to the smaller barn where the straw was. The horses from Lonato and Dunant's animal had been stabled, with the two vehicles, in the other. Steven spread his jacket on the clean yellow straw.

'Those Sardinians I rode down with had news of George Lascaris,' he said through the complete darkness which now enclosed them. 'He was in the thick of it at San Martino this afternoon.'

'Was he, Steve?'

'They told me he'd been fighting like a hero. But the Bersaglieri took a terrible hammering from Benedek. Lascaris was severely wounded, about four o'clock.'

She stiffened in his arms. 'Where is he, Steve?'

'Most of the Sardinians were to be taken in to Desenzano. But the San Martino action was so fluid that if

Lascaris was with the Piedmont Battalion he might be brought in here.'

Jenny stretched herself on the improvised bed, and sighed.

'There will be thousands of them, brought in here to-morrow. Steven, I'm frightened.'

'Then come back with me to Brescia!'

'No, I've got to stay and see it through.' He said no more, but caressed her, feeling the swell of her breasts beneath the thin cotton bodice, and the smooth skin of her bared shoulder. Jenny whispered,

'Do you remember, that night at Monti, you said there would be lots of chances to sleep in hay before the war was over?'

'But at Monti you were inside the *albergo*, and I was outside in the barn——'

'M'm?'

'Now we're together.'

He was gone in the morning, a full hour before the ambulances delivered the first load of wounded men. Many of the sufferers were delirious; they had lain all night on the drenched battlefield, succoured only by the peasants who crept out at last from the cellars and shelters where they had hidden while the battle raged. Such bandages as had been put on were soaked with blood and pus, and clotted hard into the uniforms and body hair of the wounded: to cut and soak them off was a major operation. There was no time to lose over it, for once the army surgeons started work the ambulances delivered new convoys of wounded every quarter of an hour. Then the amputations started, the chloroform ran short, and men were carried screaming to the operating tables.

Henri Dunant deferred only to the army surgeons. His

self-appointed task was the visitation of the wounded and the local arrangements for their nursing, and in this he won the surprised admiration of the mayor and councillors. They would have been useless and submerged without the Swiss gentleman, who appeared on the morning after the battle in a fresh white suit, and walked through the distracted streets of Castiglione like the embodiment of cleanliness and calm. Jenny followed his example by wearing a clean white blouse over her black skirt. She walked by his side carrying a notebook and a little portable writing set which he lent her, with the ink in a leather-covered jar, and kept a record on some system of Dunant's own of the admissions to all the emergency hospitals opening in the town. Castiglione was a little place, but it was still the largest in the whole stricken district, and therefore by far the largest receiving area. In the next three days, the period of time required for burying the dead found on the field of Solferino, six thousand casualties were admitted to Castiglione.

Jenny saw broken bodies laid on the straw where Steven had embraced her in the dark. The hospital barns were filled with wounded; the hospital and the police barracks, even the churches, could take in no more. Straw was laid down in the streets, the squares, the courtyards; in the sunshine which followed the storm the whole of Castiglione became a vast out-door hospital. The women went among the wounded with jars of water and fans to brush away the flies. They gave what help they could to friend and foe alike, for so 'the gentleman in white' decreed. *'Le monsieur blanc dit "tutti fratelli"*——' so, in a confusion of languages, the wounded Frenchmen began to say.

But one man, however dedicated, could not stem the tide of death and disease which rose after Solferino.

Dunant did everything one man could do: he sent his cabriolet, with an Italian driver, into Brescia to be filled at his own expense with oranges, lemons, cigars and tobacco for the men: he co-opted newspapermen and other foreigners (some of whom arrived out of mere curiosity) to the care committees he was beginning to organise in all the cities of Lombardy. The rail repairs were being carried out in twenty-four-hour shifts, and Milan, Cremona, Bergamo and Brescia were waiting impatiently to receive the wounded who could only be evacuated by ambulance and ox-cart until the trains went through. But still the cry went up for nurses, and for nurses who could turn their hands to anything. Jenny, flinching and shrinking, washed filthy bodies, listened to the vilest oaths of the Paris gutters, had broken fingernails driven into her own palm as delirious men clutched her hands in their last agonies, wrote into her thick notebook the last messages to loved ones left at home. She learned to conquer her nausea and swallow down her tears. She learned, as never before, to pray, for the great church of Castiglione, the Chiesa Maggiore, where five hundred men lay in the nave and a hundred more on straw spread round the door, became a new Gethsemane where every hour of vigil was in itself a prayer.

It was not until three days after the battle that George Lascaris was carried in. He had been taken up, with three of his Bersaglieri, by peasant folk, who had no means of transport but did their ignorant best for the men until an ambulance came by. It was too late for the major—the army surgeon shook his head—the man had lost too much blood, and that shattered leg should have been taken off at least two days ago. Now gangrene had set in, d'you see, madame; he wouldn't last very long now.

'Would you call Monsieur Dunant, please, signora?' said Jenny to one of the Italian women standing by. They had helped Jenny to cut away the rags of George's blouse and wash the upper part of his body. The lower, bandaged and tightly wrapped in an army blanket, gave off the foul sweet smell of the gangrenous flesh.

'What's the matter, Jenny?' Henri Dunant was by her side, and all formalities of address had been dropped in the inferno of Castiglione.

'The surgeon says this man is dying. He is—a friend of mine. I want to stay beside him; he may still regain consciousness, and know me, and I think you ought to bring a priest.'

'I'll get the old Franciscan padre; he's a gentle, plain-spoken fellow,' said the Swiss. 'But Jenny, I'm going to need you soon. Will you join me in the market square as soon as you can?'

'I will.' She took her place by George Lascaris's pallet and mechanically began to fan the flies away from his head. A man on the next pallet was feverish and coughing, and the man beyond was calling for his mother. The tainted afternoon hung heavy over the Chiesa Maggiore.

About half an hour after they laid him down, the grey-green eyes of George Lascaris opened, and he recognised the pale girl sitting by his side.

'Jenny?'

'Yes, George.' She shifted slightly, so that he could see and hear her better; she thought his eyes were very dim.

'Is Claire here?'

'No.'

'Where—is this?'

'A sort of hospital, in Castiglione. You were at a farm——'

'I know.' He frowned with the effort at recollection. 'Where are—my men?'

'All safe, and going to do well.'

'But—not—me?'

'Oh George!' Jenny swallowed the rising sob, and went on resolutely. 'The sergeant says you were a hero in the battle. You saved your company from being cut to pieces——'

'Where?'

'At San Martino.' He turned his head away, as if all that was past and done. Then: 'Would you put your arms around me, Jenny?'

She laid down the fan, and slipped one arm beneath George's shoulders, raising his head until against her own cheek lay the cheek growing cold beneath the rough blond stubble. His breathing had changed to a quick harsh rattle in his chest.

'You married Blake?'

'Yes.'

'And you're happy?'

'Very—very happy. But oh, George, to see you so, and all the others—all the wretchedness!' Through her tears, Jenny saw the gardens of the Casa Lumone, and this man, with the sister too dearly loved, walking tall and straight in his Bersaglieri uniform down the mimosa alley to the sea. Was Claire walking alone there now, with only her cats for company, watching and waiting for news of the last Lascaris prince?

'Have you forgiven us, Jenny?'

'Oh, George, I forgive you freely!'

'I think I loved you.' She had to strain to catch the words. 'Or I could have loved you—but I don't know which. What Kate said...' His voice tailed off, and the Italian woman, coming to kneel on the other side, whispered to Jenny.

'He is going fast!'

'Is the priest here?' Jenny whispered back.

'He is coming in at the door with *il signore blanco*.'

'Jenny,' said George drowsily. 'Will you kiss me now?' She laid her lips on his. There was no disloyalty to Steven in that kiss, that mutual plea for pardon and farewell.

'Tell Claire,' said George Lascaris, and his head fell sideways. Jenny held the dead weight on her breast until the priest came, to speed the departed soul along its way to Heaven.

Sixteen

THE BETRAYAL

'*Cara mia Clara, Giorgio è morte per l'Italia.*' Jenny had written that sentence half a dozen times without being able to complete the letter. How could she tell that sister, waiting by the southern sea, that the brother who had survived Novara and the Tchernaya had died miserably of a neglected wound and fever in the charnel house of the Chiesa Maggiore? How to describe that burial, in a mass grave with a hundred others, in the teeming graveyard of Castiglione?

Jenny laid her heavy head upon her hand. It was three o'clock on Tuesday, four days after the battle, and Henri Dunant, for the first time, had gone out of town on some private errand of his own. It was hardly true to say that they were lost without him, for help was coming in from Brescia now, and the emergency organisation which Dunant had constructed was strong enough to work by itself for a night and a day. But sitting in his own small office in the hospital, Jenny found herself listening anxiously for the sounds of his return.

He drove in just as she completed the letter to Claire, in sentences which to her own eyes seemed cold, and sealed it up. *Le monsieur blanc* was less immaculate than usual, for his white linen suit showed signs of a long drive in extreme heat, but he was as composed as ever when he shook Jenny's hand, and asked to see the lists of supplies received and distributed, the letters from outlying care committees, and all the work done in his temporary absence.

'Did you see Steve in Brescia?' Jenny could no longer keep back the question.

'I haven't been to Brescia.'

'Oh? I thought you——'

'I've been at Cavriana, at Imperial Headquarters. I was hoping for an audience of the Emperor of the French.'

'You *were!*' said Jenny. 'Oh, I remember now. You were on your way to Headquarters when we first met, last Friday morning.'

'I came on here instead.' Dunant seemed disposed to say more, and Jenny waited while he fidgeted with the papers on the desk. At last she prompted:

'Well, did you see him?'

'Not the Emperor, no. He sent a message by an aide-de-camp, but was too busy to see me personally. I had a long talk with the Duke of Magenta, though, at six o'clock this morning.'

'The Duke of——?'

'Marshal MacMahon. I knew him when he was commander-in-chief of the Army of Africa.'

'Did you go to Cavriana to talk about our wounded, Henri?'

'No.' And then silence. 'Well, I'd like to tell you about my disappointment; I know you'll keep it to yourself. The fact is, I've written a book about the French Emperor.'

'About Louis Napoleon!'

'It's called *The Empire of Charlemagne*. Comparing Napoleon III to Charlemagne, you understand. The greatest monarchy of modern times, compared with the greatest ruler of the early Middle Ages, the man who led Europe from darkness into light——'

'Wait a minute,' said Jenny. Her headache had grown worse; she felt she had not heard correctly what Dunant said. 'You mean that *Louis Napoleon* is leading Europe out of darkness?'

'I think he's a great man. And so I wanted his permission to dedicate my book to him. I'd written several letters but got no reply, so I decided to follow him into Italy and make a personal appeal. That's why, when I felt the situation was a little easier here, I took a few hours off and went to Cavriana.'

'But he wouldn't see you, he sent a message by an aide-de-camp. What did he say about the book?'

'He refused to allow me to dedicate it to him. He said that under the present political circumstances he would prefer that the book didn't appear at all, but if I insisted on publishing, the title should be changed to *The Roman Empire*.'

'No comparison of himself to Charlemagne. I'm glad he had that much sense.' Jenny was too angry to laugh, although Dunant's expression was doleful enough to be funny. Her strained nerves snapped in a quick flash of temper. 'Good God, has that wretched man deluded the whole of Europe? The great Emperor, the new Charlemagne! Oh Henri, how could you toady to him? You of all men—after what you've done, and seen, and suffered, right here in the past few days? Don't you realise that all those men are dead or maimed because of Louis Napoleon's terrible ambition?'

'I don't agree at all,' Dunant said coldly. 'It takes two sides to make a war.'

'But only one side starts it. Oh, it's no good,' sighed Jenny. 'I'm not clever enough to argue it out with you. I only know I hate that Emperor and what he does to those who believe in him... Did you hear anything really important at Headquarters?'

'I'm quite aware a book is only important to its author,' said Dunant stiffly. 'As to the Emperor, we must agree to differ, Mrs. Blake. I regard him as the only legitimate successor of the Roman Empire—the Caesar of our days.'

'Oh, for heaven's sake!' said Jenny. She was sharply disappointed in Dunant. She had begun to think of him as a man of vision, and had listened eagerly to his plans for an international relief organisation to function in peace and war. He thought of calling it the Red Cross.

'I did hear one piece of news from Marshal Mac-Mahon,' Dunant said placatingly. 'Another thing I must ask you to regard as private.'

'Certainly.'

'The Emperor is not very pleased with his Sardinian friends. He always felt Victor Emmanuel didn't give him enough support at Magenta, and since Solferino, where the Sardinians did much better, he has been very head-strong. He wants to take his Piedmontese and lay siege to the fortress of Peschiera.'

'He should recall Garibaldi first,' said Jenny. Then, understanding, 'You mean the Emperor doesn't want to go right in to the Quadrilateral?'

'Not to please Victor Emmanuel. He thinks the King and Cavour have acted behind his back in annexing territories he meant to be ruled by his cousin, Princess Clotilde's husband. He may feel, under these circumstances, that he's done enough for them.'

'He's bound to them by a treaty of alliance,' said Jenny. 'Not that that would matter to the new Charlemagne! You said just now it takes two to make a war. How many does it take to make a peace?'

The answer to that question was revealed exactly two weeks later, when Castiglione had been cleared of all the wounded men fit to travel as far as Brescia by carriage or ambulance cart. Brescia now became the great staging-post for the evacuation of the wounded by rail to Milan, and the men passed into the care of doctors, nursing nuns and townspeople more than eager to take over the burden from the veteran helpers of Castiglione.

The French were the heroes of the hour in Brescia, where Italian patriotism had been flaming high since the city's liberation by Garibaldi. Brescia had suffered atrociously at Austrian hands after the War of Independence. The flogging of women and the torturing of men had been indiscriminately ordered by General Haynau, 'the Hyena of Brescia', and every family in the town rejoiced whole-heartedly in the freedom given to Lombardy. Woman came in from the sub-alpine regions to help nurse the wounded, and the whole population followed to the Campo Santo the coffins of the French who died while in the city.

Jenny and Steven were together again, in one of the series of hotel rooms in which all their short married life had been spent. It was a happy home, for to the new joy of their physical harmony Jenny added a more peaceful spirit, as if some of her inner troubles had been burned away in the crucible of Castiglione. She rested for a whole day and night after reaching Brescia, drowsing away the warm hours in bed, where sometimes she was alone and sometimes Steven lay beside her, weary after love.

He was still working at top pitch on the railway repairs. The track between Milan and Turin was in surprisingly good shape, for the Austrian sappers had failed to blow up a viaduct and another key bridge near Magenta, but the stretch between Milan and Brescia had been seriously damaged. July came in, even more brassily hot than June, before the first convoys of wounded could be transported to Milan. Already, little detachments of convalescent men had started tramping down the white roads to Turin, but the sick were to be received at Milan, travelling in contingents of one thousand every night. In the great heat, daytime travel was too hard for them; as it was, the trains had to be stopped at several intermediate stations during the four-hour journey for the wounded to be given cool drinks and have their dressings changed. Long sheds had been hastily constructed to hold mattresses and charpie, and Lombard boys, too young to join Garibaldi, held torches to light the nurses while the bandages were changed.

'Jenny,' said Steven, coming in late in the evening of the ninth of July, 'I'm going on a special job tonight. Going back to the footplate for a few hours, what d'you say to that?'

'You haven't driven since Giovi, have you? What are you going to do, take a hospital train down to Milan yourself?'

'I've got to take Cavour to see the King.'

'Cavour's American,' she teased him gently. 'May I come to the station and see you start?'

'At two in the morning? Nobody's supposed to know about this trip, though I don't see how they can very well keep it a secret. Anyway, you'll be in bed and sound asleep when we pull out... Kiss me, Jenny love. I wish I could stay with you tonight. I'm just so goddamned tired.'

'Poor Steve! You must really take a few hours off when you come back. Tomorrow evening, will it be?'

'Hope so.'

Jenny slept later than usual on the following morning. Their hotel was very near the station, and the room was not a quiet one, but the sense of being alone, with no

Steven to get off to work, helped her to have her sleep out and she woke refreshed. She was not expected on hospital duty until the afternoon.

The great heat continued through the morning hours. Jenny went out of doors, and sat beneath the trees in the piazza, where Garibaldi had addressed the Brescians before leaving for the Stelvio pass. She wondered if the Hunters of the Alps would be brought back now, to fill the gaps in the ranks made at Solferino.

A thought hovering for some days past on the rim of Jenny's consciousness warned her that it might be time for her to begin thinking of her own body and its claims. She had been far too busy in the desperate week after the battle to calculate times and seasons, but in the relative tranquillity of Brescia it began to seem to her that a child might be born of those enchanted nights at Como when she had first known the intensity of love. It was a dizzying thought, so full of hope and joy that Jenny wished for a dozen symptoms of approaching motherhood to declare themselves at once. It was far too soon to be quite certain by the calendar. 'I'll wait until next month and then tell Steve,' she thought. 'Surely the future will be clearer then.'

What the future might hold began to be foreshadowed after noon, when a rumour began to spread in Brescia that the King had sent for his prime minister because the French were about to make a separate peace with Austria. The only confirmation of this was that Cavour had certainly been seen at the railroad station, and that a few days earlier General Fleury had driven under a flag of truce to the fortress of Verona. These two facts, added together, were not necessarily ominous, but as night fell Jenny began to long for Steve's return. Another day passed, and the special train did not come back. On that day, the eleventh of July, it became known throughout

Lombardy that Napoleon III had driven to Villafranca to meet the Emperor Franz Josef.

It was very early on the twelfth, little more than forty-eight hours after Steven's departure, that a messenger from the station was sent to ask Jenny to come at once to her husband's office there. The special train had returned, she saw its single saloon carriage behind the locomotive at the down platform, but in the dawn twilight there was nobody on duty but the telegraph clerks. She ran upstairs and tapped at the door of Steve's office. He opened it at once, unshaven and haggard: she saw the prime minister of Sardinia collapsed in the one armchair.

'Steven, what has happened?'

'Count Cavour was taken ill on the train,' said Steve. 'He doesn't want anyone to know. What should we do for him?'

'Where's his secretary?'

'He travelled down alone.'

'We ought to get a doctor, Steve.'

'Can't you do anything?'

Jenny approached the sick man doubtfully. He had removed his spectacles, and without them his face looked round and pitiful, like a sick child's. There was a bluish shadow round his mouth, and his breathing was shallow. She took from her reticule the little flask of brandy which she now always carried for an emergency, and mixed a small measure of the spirit with water.

'Would you try to drink this, Count Cavour?'

He let her hold the glass to his lips, and swallowed some of the contents; a little colour came back to his pallid face. 'Ah, my little friend of the Po Bridge!' he said, and tried to smile. 'Stefano ought not to have disturbed your rest.'

'He looked terrible when we came in to Brescia,' said Steven in an undertone. 'I didn't know what to do.'

'Will you come to our room and rest?' said Jenny to the Italian. 'I'm sure you ought to lie down, for a few hours at least.'

'I must go on!' Cavour said, rousing himself. 'Although I don't know why, or where, or what we can do now that all is lost——'

'All!' Jenny exclaimed. 'You mean the French——'

'I mean Louis Napoleon has betrayed us,' said Cavour, and his face became alarmingly suffused with blood. 'Your husband knows, they all know up at Desenzano; today Italy and France will know, and then the world, that all our sacrifices have been in vain. The Emperor betrayed the terms of our alliance. He signed an agreement with Franz Josef at Villafranca, without our King's knowledge or consent. The Austrians give up Lombardy but keep Venetia; the revolted states go back to their old tyrants; the Pope is to preside over a new Italian confederation, and I am no longer prime minister of Sardinia.'

'Was *that* in the treaty signed at Villafranca?' Jenny cried.

'My ministry? No, no, but I placed my resignation in the King's hands as soon as we received a copy of the terms. In his hands! God forgive me, I think I almost struck the King; I know they had to hold me back. That dog, Louis Napoleon, that upstart bastard who swore to me at Plombières never to cease the fight until Franz Josef signed his unconditional surrender! And now—with Solferino won, he turns back *now*! After thousands of men have died in vain he deserts Italy! He leaves us to return to Paris, and Venice must still bear the yoke of Austria!'

'But Lombardy is free, sir; remember that,' said Steven Blake.

'It's not enough, it never was,' Cavour said drearily. 'Villafranca has put our clock back again to 1848.'

'Italy still has Garibaldi,' Steven said.

Seventeen

THE RAILHEAD

THEY were to go up to Susa in the royal train. That was
Jenny's first thought when she woke to find herself again
in Turin, a few days after the Emperors had signed the
Peace of Villafranca.

It was a privilege obtained as a last favour from
Cavour, who was remaining in the kingdom only until
Napoleon III had left Italian soil. The ex-prime minister
was forced to attend the ceremonies of the Emperor's
farewell, and after that he meant to go to Switzerland for
the long rest decreed by his medical advisers.

'Louis Napoleon has broken his heart,' said Steven
Blake. Steve had been silent and uncommunicative after
Cavour left Brescia; he cleared his temporary office there
and took Jenny back to Turin on the fourteenth of July,
for a long consultation with the directors of Sardinian
Railroads. All he would say about it was that he had
been highly praised for his work in what was now called
'the emergency', and would have his salary considerably
increased on returning to Bardonnechia.

Jenny tried to draw him out about the Tunnel, but
Steven refused to be drawn. He smoked more than usual,
made passionate demands on Jenny, and on the morning
of the fifteenth drove a locomotive up to Susa and back to
examine the condition of the permanent way. Napoleon
III, who had entered Italy by Genoa, was leaving by the
railhead at Susa and the Mont Cenis pass. Already,

whole regiments of his soldiers were climbing up the Alte Valle di Susa, going home—without thousands of their comrades—by the road of their arrival at the end of April. They were still cheered by the people in the towns and hailed as liberators; for the Emperor there was a real danger of assassination.

By 5 p.m. on the fifteenth, when he arrived in Turin from Milan, the Torinesi had hung out as many pictures of Orsini as the print shops could sell. 'Patriot, hero, martyr!' the old legends ran, and underneath the handsome face was scrawled a new slogan: Napoleon the Traitor. *Napoleone Traditore*. Down the Via Roma, with Orsini's face ever before him, the French Emperor drove with the King to the Palazzo Reale for the empty mockery of a state banquet. The people cheered the King and reviled the Emperor. *Evviva Vittorio Emmanuele! Napoleone Traditore!*

Jenny heard the same shouts as she waited at the station for the cortège to appear next day. They had advanced the Emperor's departure time as a security precaution, but the Torinesi were up and doing, ready to boo him out of their town and country.

'The train seems safe enough,' said Steven, coming up to her. 'I've had them check every coupling and every single wheel. Now, if no one takes a pot-shot at the Emperor as we go along, we should get rid of him in less than a couple of hours.'

Napoleon III appeared on the station platform. A military band struck up *'Partant pour la Syrie'*, a guard of honour presented arms, and Count Cavour, well in the background raised his hat to Jenny. He looked ill but quite composed at this moment of the destruction of his dream.

There were only three saloon carriages attached to the royal train. Steven and Jenny had places in the last, with minor court officials and equerries of the King; no one spoke much as the train pulled out of Turin and started westward to the line of the Cottian Alps. Most of the men, sharing Steve's fear of an assassin in the fields, kept glancing out of the windows; Steven, Jenny knew, was listening to the sound of the wheels. There appeared to be no threat of danger either in or outside the train.

She tried to tell herself that this was the last journey; that in the months ahead, when the coming of a child was certain, she would stay quietly in the mountains, making the little cabin between the pine trees into a real home. Steven would build his Tunnel, and win new laurels, and there would be peace in Italy. She tried to forget what she had heard him say to Count Cavour: *but Italy still has Garibaldi.*

There was nothing to be learned from Steven's face. He sat opposite her with his arms folded, ready to smile when Jenny smiled, as formal as any of the Italian officials in his black frock coat and tall silk hat. Jenny too was in black silk and wore a crinoline. 'We're different from the tramps we were at Como,' was her thought. 'We almost look like parents now!'

The green fields gave way to rising uplands, the snow peaks of Mont Cenis and Mont Genèvre came nearer. They were almost into Susa; there was a settling of uniforms and accoutrements, and a young lady, the wife of one of the officials, proved her gentility by having a belated attack of train faintness. The train pulled in to the little station with its arched portico, hastily scrubbed and beflagged for the Emperor's departure. The imperial berline and other carriages were waiting in the road outside.

The only spectators, out of the thousands of Italians who had cheered the Emperor, were those who had travelled in the royal train. Susa had seen too many

Frenchmen in the past three months to turn out for another, especially when the main street was lined with *carabinieri,* prepared to the last to foil an attempted assassination. Jenny pushed forward to the front to see the ceremonious farewells. She had not seen the Emperor so close since Plombières; she noted without pity that there were marks of suffering on his face.

When the berline drove off with its outriders there was an awkward silence among those left behind. Cavour put his hat on and pulled it down over his eyes. Then the King, with his boisterous laugh, clapped his former prime minister on the back. 'Cheer up, man, and don't look so glum,' he said, and spat copiously on the platform. 'Thank God he's gone!'

'Where are *they* going now?' asked Jenny curiously.

'Into the town,' said Steve. 'The *sindaco* and the local bigwigs are giving the King a breakfast. He'll enjoy that, he likes a country *festa,* and he's in no hurry to get back to Turin. The train won't start back until noon.'

'Then what shall we do? When does the coach leave for Bardonnechia? I think Peter Easton might have come down to meet us.'

'I reckon he's busy at the Tunnel,' Steven said. 'Let's walk along to the Albergo Cottio and have a decent breakfast for ourselves.'

It was delightful to walk in the cool morning, fresher here than in Turin, across a bridge over the brawling river called the Dora Riparia, into the garden of the little inn. The imperial convoy was out of sight already. Susa, that ancient place, had absorbed and digested the visit of Napoleon III, as it had long ago digested Augustus Caesar and Frederick Barbarossa, of whom there was nothing left in the quiet valley but a crumbling triumphal arch and a rusty sword.

'You like Peter Easton, don't you, dear?' said Steven

when the food was brought.

'Yes, I do.'

'And that girl of his, Miss Julia, looks like the right sort, doesn't she?'

'Very much so.'

'And we could all be good friends, and have a fine life on the mountain, couldn't we?'

'I'm sure we could. Oh Steven, what's the matter?'

'You make me feel such an infernal brute,' he said, and all the trouble Jenny had sensed in him for days past was in his dark eyes now. 'I ought never to have dragged you all the way up here. I knew Cavour wanted me to be on the train, but I ought to have come alone and left you in Turin. Because I can't go up to Bardonnechia, dear—not yet.'

'But it's your job!' she said.

'Not while the other job's not done.'

'Steven, the war is over, the peace is signed, the French are going home——'

'And Garibaldi is coming down from the Stelvio, ready to fight again.'

She had known it all along, refused to believe it, saw truth staring at her from his resolute face.

'Listen, Jenny, and let me tell you all I know. The Central States have already refused to take their old rulers back. They're preparing to form a League to fight for their attachment to Piedmont and keep Victor Emmanuel for their king. Now General Fanti, who led the Sardinians at Solferino, has been put in command of another body of volunteers, the Hunters of the Apennines. Garibaldi is willing to be his second in command. Cosenz, Medici, Nino Bixio, they're all going with him to Ravenna.'

'But that has nothing whatever to do with you!'

'Ah!' said Steven. 'If they all said that! Darling, I'm

trying to make you understand. These men are going to fight on for a united Italy, and I want to fight along with them. Because I've come to see that nothing worth while will ever be done in Italy until this whole land is truly free and truly one. So far there's been nothing but destruction and dissension. Everything we built in the past ten years has been pretty well destroyed in the past three months. What do you think I felt when I saw those tracks ripped up in Lombardy and all those trestle bridges blown?'

'What did you think when you saw the dead and wounded after Solferino?'

'Like hell,' he said promptly. 'Like a damned looker-on, a neutral, a non-combatant, a man of twenty-six who wasn't in the fight——'

'Henri Dunant isn't so much older, and he was the real hero of Solferino. If he stops writing books about the Emperor, he may turn out to be the greatest man of this or any war.'

'Do you remember what Garibaldi said that night at Como?' Steve asked. 'He said if he had a thousand men he could take Naples and free the South. He has more than a thousand men already, and Ravenna will only be his starting place. What Louis Napoleon couldn't do, he can; he's the real fighter, and next time he'll have a real chance to win.'

She saw that it was hopeless, that her husband was infected with the rage that possesses men at war, but she tried to use a woman's argument of common sense:

'And do *you* remember what you said to me the day I first saw Bardonnechia, that you were doing a worth-while job at the Tunnel, one of the most important jobs of all? You were building something! Steve! Don't you want to go back to doing constructive work instead of playing wilderness scouts with Garibaldi?'

'It won't be play next time. And when we build again in Italy, it's got to be on a permanent foundation.'

She wanted to scream at him, with the argument of a woman's emotions: 'Look at me! Don't you owe me anything? I'm your wife. I may soon be the mother of your child. Haven't I suffered? Haven't we all suffered enough?' But then he took her hand and smiled, and was Steve, her old playmate, the true love of her life.

'Come to Ravenna with me, Jenny ... please.'

'Ravenna!' she said, struck. 'Isn't that where Anita Garibaldi died?'

'Yes, somewhere in the marshes north of there.'

She saw the cheap lithograph which hung in thousands of Italian homes: the man with chestnut hair and blue sailor's eyes, carrying the body of the dying woman through the dreadful swampland of Comacchio, fugitives both, with a price upon their heads.

'How long have you been thinking about this, Steven?'

'Ever since Como. Remember that first wonderful night at Como? And I suppose the feeling that I ought to fight, that I *must* fight, that I must give up everything and follow Garibaldi, grew stronger every time I heard him speak. Especially that last day before he left us, when every house in Brescia was hung with flags. It was what he said over and over, but somehow that day it was different. "I have nothing to offer you but blood, toil, tears and sweat"—wasn't that it?'

'Yes,' said Jenny, and accepted her destiny. 'Those were the very words.'

The
Fortress

This is the true story of a war the historians have almost forgotten—one in which the hero was the Royal Navy; the unwilling captive, Finland; and the villain of the piece, Imperial Russia.

The Baltic—1854. While the Crimean war was smouldering at the far side of Europe, Britain and Russia were locked in a furious struggle at sea off the coast of Finland with, as prize, the impregnable citadel of Sveaborg—the fortress of the title.

Among those deeply involved were Brand Endicott, a tough young gunner in the Royal Navy, and the Finnish girl he loved, Alexandra Gyllenlöve. As the panorama of mid-19th-century life is majestically unfolded—the social brilliance of St. Petersburg and Paris contrasting with the infamous convict hulks and the lawless London underworld—these two share the excitement of their struggle for freedom at every turn: in prison and on the high seas, in war and in peace.

'It would be quite possible to get into the habit of learning history simply by reading Catherine Gavin's engrossing novels.'
The Bookman

'Her writing cuts across life and death, love and war, debauchery and devotion, with the boldness and not a little of the grasp of a Tolstoy.'
Los Angeles Mirror-News

The
Cactus
and the
Crown

In the late 1860's, when Maximilian von Hapsburg and his beautiful wife Carlota became Emperor and Empress of the turbulent state of Mexico, young Sally Lorimer and her brother, Dr Andrew Lorimer, come to take up an inheritance from their uncle and find themselves destined to play a large part in the fate of Mexico.

In *The Cactus and The Crown* Catherine Gavin exploits, with the success due to her powerful sense of history and her whole perception of human motives, the encounter between 19th-century liberalism and the principle of European monarchy ... The reading of the book means a spontaneous and complete engagement with the richness of the author's imagination.'
The Scotsman